HEIRS *of* FALCON POINT

In the early days of World War II, the Lang family lost everything.

Eighty years later, it's time to take it back.

HEIRS *of* FALCON POINT

TRACI HUNTER ABRAMSON · SIAN ANN BESSEY
PAIGE EDWARDS · A. L. SOWARDS

Covenant Communications, Inc.

Cover image: *Close Up of Thoughtful Brunette Woman* © Alexey Kazantsev / Trevillion Images

Cover design by Natalie Brown

Published by Covenant Communications, Inc.
American Fork, Utah

Printed in Mexico
First Printing: October 2021

10 9 8 7 6 5 4 3 2

ISBN: 978-1-52441-779-6

PRAISE FOR *HEIRS OF FALCON POINT*

"The beginning of [*Heirs of Falcon Point*] is intriguing, and I was engrossed in reading, hoping the three children would find their way back to each other. Then the story switches decades later to the present time. There was a lot going on, with lots of different characters to meet, but I enjoyed the continued story of meeting the Lang family's ancestors. I loved Anna, Cole, and Tess, and their friends, and I was so scared for them at times. There was a lot at stake, more than anyone realized. The riveting story of *Heirs of Falcon Point* ended well and will stay with me for a while. If you enjoy historical fiction, you will especially enjoy this story."

—Readers' Favorite five-star review

"Be sure to take your heart medication when reading *Heirs of Falcon Point* because the suspense and surprises are sure to raise your heart rate. Four award-winning authors have come together to create a multifaceted book: thrillers, mystery, multiple romances, and a settling of scores for ancient crimes—and some really determined villains to boot. For those of us who love historical fiction, this book is particularly satisfying in that it creates historical scenes that are brought forward to the present day to tell the rest of the story. I highly recommend it."

—Jerry Borrowman, author of the 'Til the Boys Come Home World War I and World War II fiction series and other award-winning nonfiction

For Amy Parker,

whose tireless efforts are known by few but valued by so many.
We love and appreciate you.

ACKNOWLEDGMENTS

We have so many people who helped us bring this book to life, but we must begin by thanking Paige Edwards, who came up with the original idea of bringing the four of us together, and Samantha Millburn for letting us run with it. Thanks to the Smithsonian Air and Space Museum for providing the backdrop for the original brainstorming session.

Also, thank you, Samantha, for sharing your amazing editing talents with us. This book is so much better because of you. Our continued appreciation goes to the rest of the Covenant family for supporting us in our creative endeavors. A special thanks to Amy Parker for your tireless efforts in marketing and helping launch this novel into the world.

Thank you to Tyler Sommer and Coco Francois for sharing your medical expertise, often at crazy hours of the day and night. And thanks to Ellie Whitney for your help during the early stages of this manuscript and for sharing your wealth of artistic knowledge.

We also want to thank the CIA Publication Review Board for your assistance and for clearing this manuscript so quickly.

Finally, we want to thank our families for your constant support and our readers for your unfailing encouragement. You are the ones who enable us to continue doing what we love.

AUTHOR CONTRIBUTIONS BY MAIN CHARACTER

A. L. SOWARDS

Karl Lang
Ingrid Lang
Anna Lang
Wilhelm Sauermann

TRACI HUNTER ABRAMSON

Gunnar Sauermann
Cole Bridger
Isabelle Roberts

PAIGE EDWARDS

Anna Cavendish
Beckett Campbell
Petra Sauermann

SIAN ANN BESSEY

Tess Hendriks
Lars Hendriks
Bram Dekker

CHAPTER 1

February 1940

Karl Lang kept his back ramrod straight as his father bid Herr Sauermann farewell from the gravel drive in front of their two-hundred-year-old manor. Part of the posture was upbringing—boys from families like his didn't slouch when seeing visitors off. Part of it was a desire to close the gap in height. Herr Sauermann loomed over all of them like a statue of a Hapsburg war hero.

Herr Sauermann shook Karl's hand. "You look just like your father did when I met him. That blond hair and straight nose. Fine Aryan specimens." The warmth of the compliment lessened the effect of the bitter winter wind slicing through their coats. Herr Sauermann turned to Papa. "Give it some thought, Leopold. You're needed."

"I'm a widower with three children to care for." Papa kept a polite expression, but his blue eyes contained a hardness that Karl wasn't accustomed to seeing from his father, especially not around old family friends.

With a wave of his hand, Herr Sauermann directed his driver to open the door of his black Gräf & Stift automobile. "You've the means to hire help for the children. And your son will soon be in uniform just like you."

The muscles along Papa's jaw hardened. "Karl is only seventeen. He's too young to fight."

"For now." Herr Sauermann slipped into the car. "I'll see you in a few days, Leopold. Be ready."

At a nod from Herr Sauermann, the driver closed the door and walked around to the driver's seat.

Karl held his tongue until the man climbed in and started the engine. "I'm not afraid to be a soldier."

Papa folded his arms. "But for whom will you fight?"

"For Austria. Just like you, in the last war."

Papa watched Herr Sauermann's car pull away. "Austria no longer exists. Do you wish to fight for Herr Hitler, Karl?"

Karl didn't answer immediately. He'd found little to like of the Führer in the newsreels, and he'd picked up on his father's less-than-enthusiastic response to the Anschluss of two years before, but Karl couldn't very well change the course of history. Herr Kaufmann, the literature teacher at his boarding school, was quick to point out the economic benefits of union with Germany. Most people agreed with him, but now Karl wasn't sure. "I just want to be brave like my father."

"Courage isn't always about fighting."

"Herr Sauermann seems to think you should fight again." Karl watched Herr Sauermann's automobile disappear around the stone lions that marked the estate's entrance. "I would think you too old to fight."

"He's not asking me to pick up a rifle again." Papa chuckled. "Too old? Is forty-four so old?"

Karl straightened his back again, trying to stretch the inch of height he had over his father into something more impressive. "No, I don't suppose you're that old or that short. But I imagine they'll give the rifles to strapping recruits like me."

"Well then, my strapping son, run to the top of that hill to make sure Sauermann really leaves. Then meet me in the study and bring your sisters."

"You think he might not really leave?"

Papa shrugged. "I need to know for sure. Plan the first has failed, and I don't expect plan the second to work out either. Which brings us to plan the third."

"What's plan the third?" Papa always had multiple plans, but this was the first Karl had heard about anything related to Herr Sauermann. "And what was plan the first and plan the second?"

"Later, Karl. I'll tell you later." Papa pointed to the hill. "You brought your field glasses, as I asked?"

Karl nodded and ran off. He wore his best suit and dress coat in honor of Herr Sauermann's visit, not his normal choice for taking a shortcut through the damp woods that encircled the manor, but none of the staff would reprimand him if he abused the clothing just a bit. His father certainly wouldn't, not after being the one to send him on this errand.

Thick growths of spruce, pine, and larch surrounded the snowy lawns and gardens of the estate. Karl ran awhile, then trudged the rest of the way over the brambles and uneven roots. The top of the hill cleared just enough to offer a view of the entire estate. Schloss die Punkt Falke stretched out to the north and the west. Falcon Point. The turrets of the limestone manor house peeked above a thick curtain of tree branches, and flashes of light reflected off the surface of the lake to the east. Most of Kristall Lake was still frozen, but parts had thawed over the last week. Karl turned to the village and caught sight of the black automobile making its way down the slope. He pulled the small field glasses from his pocket and verified there was still a passenger in the back seat.

Wilhelm Sauermann had been his father's friend for years, and he'd stayed at Falcon Point time after time. Karl didn't buy the excuse that there was less staff now, so the Lang family wasn't in a position to host. They still had a maid, a gardener, and a cook who doubled as a housekeeper. Welcoming Herr Sauermann into one of the dozens of empty rooms would have been a simple enough affair. Something had changed. Now Herr Sauermann was staying in the village and making what sounded like threats if Papa didn't agree to whatever Herr Sauermann had asked. And Karl had been sent to make sure their guest had really left Falcon Point—it felt a lot like spying.

Karl watched until the car passed the kirche, with its pointed spire, and disappeared between the steep-roofed buildings of the village. The small inn on the settlement's eastern end hadn't anything so grand as one of the rooms at Falcon Point. Would Herr Sauermann resent not being asked to stay?

Karl was at the wrong angle to see the rest of Herr Sauermann's progress, so he trekked back to the manor. Going downhill was far easier than going uphill, but he didn't rush. He avoided the roots that seemed determined to trip him and did his best to ignore the way the cold mud clung to his shoes, making them ever heavier. What was his father planning? And which two plans had already failed? Karl could keep a secret—his father should have confided in him.

When he reached the manor, he left his muddy shoes by the kitchen entrance and grabbed a slice of *gugelhupf* while the cook's back was turned.

"I know what you've taken, young man." Frau Pichler scrubbed out a pot from the early supper they'd shared with Herr Sauermann.

"But you don't mind, do you?"

She chuckled. "No, I remember what an appetite teenage boys can have. But don't track dirt across my kitchen, or Gerta will put green wood in with your coal. She just cleaned the floor." Frau Pichler turned around and nodded when she noticed Karl's stockinged feet.

"Have you seen Ingrid and Anna?" Karl asked.

"I believe I heard Miss Anna making some sort of noise on the piano."

Karl climbed the flight of stairs to the foyer, then took the wide floating staircase to the next level and went through the hall to the music room. Anna's simple tune drifted out to meet him. She played the notes with precision but without feeling. Maybe that would come with time. She was only seven years old, and as Karl walked around the piano to get a view of her wheat-colored curls and furrowed concentration, he held his tongue rather than comment on her unemotional style.

Anna finished her line with a flourish and smiled up at him. "Did you hear that? No mistakes."

"Well done, Anna. Are you finished? Papa wants us in his study."

Anna stood and scurried toward the hall.

"Have you seen Ingrid?" he asked as Anna dashed through the door.

"I'm over here."

Karl followed his sister's voice to a wingback chair turned toward the window. Ingrid sat with her feet pulled up and tucked at her side. A novel lay in her lap.

"You'll strain your eyes reading in the dark."

Ingrid pulled a ribbon into her book to mark her place. "It wasn't dark when I sat down."

Karl turned the chair—with Ingrid still in it—to its proper position. "Papa asked to see us in his study."

"I heard you tell Anna."

"Let's not keep him waiting."

Ingrid ran her finger along the spine of her book. "I can't very well stand up while you're moving the furniture."

"It would have been a lot easier to move if you weren't still sitting in it. And anyway, I'm not moving it now. Come on."

Ingrid took her time putting her book away and heading for the hallway. *Sisters*. Brothers would have been easier. If Ingrid were a boy, Karl could use a little more force, but Papa would scold him if he didn't treat Ingrid like a lady, regardless of how she acted.

Papa was crouched by the hearth when they arrived, coaxing a fire from the day's embers. He stood and pulled the curtains shut against the fading daylight and gestured to a table overflowing with piles of paper. "Ingrid, I need you to burn these. Anna can help, but make sure she doesn't get singed."

"Burn them?" Ingrid's mouth pulled into a frown. "Why?"

Papa put one hand on Ingrid's shoulder and his other on the table. "Just trust me. Don't go too fast, or you'll smother the fire. And don't read them; just destroy them. Only the ones here." He tapped the table again, then pointed to his massive Victorian-era desk. "Those aren't to be touched."

"Yes, Papa." Ingrid picked up a folder and held it. Anna picked up a pile too, but she didn't hesitate. She went right to the hearth and began feeding the fire, one paper at a time.

"Good, Anna. Just like I told you. Not too fast," Papa said.

Anna grinned. Karl would have, too, at her age, had their father granted permission to play with fire.

"Come, Karl. I need your help."

Karl followed Papa from the room. "What papers are those? And why are you burning them?"

His father held a finger to his lips. "Not now."

Karl grunted his irritation, but he obeyed. Curiosity as much as discipline kept him from rebelling.

"You'll need shoes."

"Mine were muddy, so I left them by the kitchen."

"Fine, we'll go that way." But Papa didn't head toward the kitchen. He led Karl upstairs to the manor's top floor, toward the suite where Karl's parents had once slept. Since Mama's death, Papa had slept in one of the other suites—one that was still comfortable but not quite so grand.

They passed through the main room, with its enormous four-poster bed, and went into a dressing chamber off to the side. Papa bent to pick up one end of a trunk. "Grab the other end."

The trunk was about the size of a wine crate, so Karl was surprised by how much it weighed when he lifted his end. "What's inside?"

"Some of your mother's things."

The dressing room still held most of Mama's gowns. At fifteen, Ingrid wasn't quite old enough for them to be reworked to fit her, and some were no longer in fashion. The trunk had to have more than clothing inside, unless the clothing was made of chain mail. "Why is it so heavy if it's full of satin and velvet?"

Papa's eyes flashed with memory, something sweet and sad at the same time. "Not her clothes. Her jewelry."

Karl glanced at the trunk. "She had that much?"

Papa nodded. "And a little more. I asked Gerta to sew a few pieces into all your coats."

"Why?"

"Wait until we're outside. Gerta is trustworthy enough, but it's best she stay ignorant about most of it."

"And Herr and Frau Pichler?

"I've given them the evening off. Frau Pichler might be tinkering in the kitchen still, but I imagine Herr Pichler has gone down to the village."

"You don't trust them?"

Papa shrugged the shoulder that wasn't involved in hefting the trunk. "I prefer to keep as much as I can a secret. Only those who must know the truth should have to bear its burden."

Was truth a burden? "I don't understand."

Papa motioned for them to set the trunk down before descending the stairs. They switched sides, then lifted it again. "I'll explain once we're outside."

Karl held his tongue. The trunk seemed to grow heavier as they made their way down two long flights of stairs, then a shorter set to the kitchen and back entrance, but Karl wouldn't complain about the weight, not after the conversation they'd had when they'd said farewell to Herr Sauermann. If Karl wanted to be treated like a man, he couldn't very well complain that a trunk full of his mother's jewelry was too heavy. But he was relieved when they set the trunk down long enough for him to put on his boots. He followed his father's example and pulled on wool mittens and a coat.

The sun had sunk beyond the western horizon by the time they left the manor, turning the sky a dim gray that matched the shadowed snow.

"Do you remember the gamekeeper's home?" Papa asked.

Karl changed his hold on the trunk. The mittens helped with the cold, but they didn't help with his grip. "No. I remember hearing about it, but I've never seen it."

Papa nodded. "It burned down when you were a baby. Most of it, anyway. I've repaired the root cellar, and we're putting a few things there."

Karl eyed the trunk. "A few rather valuable things."

Papa shuffled past one of the ice-covered hedges marking the boundary of the garden. "They'll be safe until we return."

"Are we leaving?" Karl tried to keep his voice down in case one of the servants was still around, but he couldn't remove the surprise that crept into his words. Falcon Point had been his home his entire life. It had been in the family for generations. They were tied to the land almost as deeply as they were tied to each other.

"That's plan the third."

"And the other plans? What were they?"

Papa was silent for a while, leading Karl up a slope and into the trees. "After the Anschluss, I held out hope that Hitler's bluster would blow over, that we'd still have some autonomy. But I've watched what's happening—here and in Czechoslovakia and in Poland. Herr Hitler is leading us to ruin. If it were only our ruin, I might not feel the need to protest. We can weather economic downturn, and we can even weather a drawn-out war. But I've heard things. He won't just destroy Germany and Austria. He'll ravage all of Europe. He's evil, Karl. I can't support him. I certainly can't work for him and help him with his plans."

"Is that why Herr Sauermann was here? To get you to work for Hitler?"

"Yes."

"Doing what?"

Papa hesitated, then seemed to come to a decision. "Let's switch sides again on the trunk." They paused at a bulbous rock formation that jutted from the hillside, traded places, and continued. "Not a word to anyone. Do you understand, Karl? I'm putting my life in your hands."

Karl swallowed hard. "You can trust me."

Papa pulled them on, up the slope that was gradually growing steeper and steeper. "Codes. That's what I did in the last war. That's what I do most of the time when we go to Vienna."

Karl shook his head. "I thought you worked with the university. You're a professor, aren't you?"

"Yes, but that's mostly a cover." Papa sighed. "I don't want to make better codes for the Reich or try to break the codes of their enemies."

"But Germany is our country now, isn't it? If you're asked and if you refuse, isn't that . . . ?" Karl couldn't say the word, couldn't accuse his father of anything so dishonorable.

"Dangerous? Treasonous?"

Karl nodded.

Papa began lowering their burden. "It's time to switch sides."

Karl set the trunk down with relief. He went to pick up the other side, but Papa held his shoulder. "I can betray my country, or I can betray my conscience. Which would you have me do?"

Karl stared into his father's eyes. They were blue, like Karl's, though it was hard to see the color in the twilight. Maybe Karl wasn't ready to be a man, not if being a man meant facing choices like this. "You have to do what is right, Papa. That's what you've always taught me."

Papa nodded and motioned to the trunk. They marched on with only the crunch of snow and their heavy breaths to accompany them. "What is right is plan the third."

"What were plan the first and plan the second?"

"Plan the first was that we'd all stay at Falcon Point and wait out the conflict. We'd ignore the war and let it ignore us."

"And Herr Sauermann isn't letting that happen?"

"No. Nor will he allow plan the second—me taking up a respectable position at a university. Teaching young people—that wouldn't be wrong, wouldn't weigh on my conscience."

"So what will you do?" Karl's words came out with a puff of cold, opaque breath.

"I'll take my family and leave."

"Where will we go?"

"I have friends. I met Jean-Yves Poncet when I worked in Paris, back when Ingrid was a baby. He's with the Deuxième Bureau. And the defense attaché at the British Consulate in Zurich is an acquaintance. If we get to either of them, I have useful information, and I expect they will help me in exchange."

A chill not related to the weather crept into Karl's chest. "That sounds . . . dangerous. And treasonous."

Papa rested the trunk on a fallen tree. "Are you with me, Karl?"

It might be dangerous, and it might be treasonous, but Karl trusted his father to do the right thing. "Yes, Papa. I'm with you."

Papa walked a few steps forward, then bent and hefted what looked like a trapdoor. Karl rushed to help him, first with a wooden door, then with a pair of metal ones.

"Is this the root cellar?"

Papa nodded and handed Karl a flashlight. Karl switched it on and pointed the beam down narrow wooden stairs.

"I'll go first," Papa said. "Watch the third step. It wiggles."

They hauled the jewelry down and placed it on the floor. A metal door roughly Karl's height dominated the far wall. A keyhole and a padlock protected whatever was inside. Papa took a key from his pocket and pressed it into the keyhole, then twisted the brass tumblers of the padlock into a series of five letters. He removed the padlock and pulled open the door to reveal a small room. Karl turned the flashlight on the contents: trunks of various sizes and three large wooden crates.

"You've been planning this for a while," Karl said.

"Yes. I didn't want to involve you if I didn't have to. It's a burden, what I've told you. But Herr Sauermann's visit means we're out of time. We leave tomorrow."

That was sooner than Karl had expected. "Will we ever come back?"

"I certainly hope so. And if you and I and both your sisters return to reclaim all we've left behind, we'll have the greatest treasure of all."

The greatest treasure of all. Karl scanned the trunks and crates, then focused on his father.

Papa patted a wooden crate. "I'd like to add a few more paintings to the collection. Will you help?"

"Yes. Is that where Anna's favorite painting went?" Karl pointed to the crate.

Papa smiled. "All the most valuable, including Anna's favorite. I think it will snow before morning, so let's get a few more, and then the fresh snow will cover our footprints. I think everything will be safe here—for years, if needed."

They stowed the trunk of jewelry, locked the metal door, and left the cellar, closing it behind them.

"There's something else, Karl."

"Yes?"

"Plan the fourth. If for any reason I can't go with you, I need you to keep your sisters safe. And I need you to take the papers to my contact in Paris or Zurich. I hope it won't come to that."

Karl nodded, accepting the new weight of responsibility that pressed on his shoulders. "But you always have another plan."

"Not always." Papa's voice grew wistful. "I never planned on meeting your mother. It was the best thing that ever happened to me, and it was an accident. Nor did I plan to bury her. Life is full of surprises and hardships, Karl. Plan for what you can, and do your best to get back up when you're knocked over by something unexpected."

CHAPTER 2

KARL SLEPT LATER THAN NORMAL the next morning, and when he finally pushed himself from bed, his muscles protested—sore from hiking to the root cellar with heavy loads multiple times the night before. He grunted as he shuffled across a thick rug to the window. When he pulled the curtains back, Papa's prediction was proved correct. A fresh blanket of white covered everything within view.

He hoped Papa was right about everything else too—that fleeing from the Nazis, fighting against them, even, was the right thing to do. Karl pulled on his clothes. He left his room, intending to find his father to see what needed to be done for their planned departure, but a grumble in his stomach convinced him to find breakfast first.

Ingrid sat in the dining hall, her book open on the table and her empty dishes pushed away. They said their good mornings as Karl went to the sideboard and grabbed a bread roll, slathered it in butter, and added ham and a boiled egg to his plate.

While Karl sat and poured his coffee, Ingrid placed a ribbon in her book. "Did Papa tell you why he wanted his papers burned?"

Karl didn't answer, not directly. "Did he tell you?"

Ingrid frowned. "No. They were his work papers, as far as I could tell."

"I thought he said not to read them."

Ingrid's shoulder moved in a bit of a flourish. "I didn't *read* them. I happened to glance at some of them. Hard not to when feeding a few sheets at a time into the fire. What of you? What did he have you helping with?"

Karl took a bite of ham so he wouldn't have to answer right away. "Does the ham seem better than usual?" Karl pushed back from the table to add a few more pieces to his plate. It was partially to distract Ingrid, but the ham was also a perfect blend of flavorful and tender.

Ingrid lifted an eyebrow at him as he sat. "So you don't want to tell me, is that it?"

"Papa will, when he's ready."

Ingrid rolled her eyes and pushed back her chair in a flurry of frustration. She nearly ran into Papa on his way into the room.

"We're going on a journey, Ingrid." Papa folded his arms across his chest. "We'll leave soon after lunch, so I'd like you to pack a suitcase this morning. Warm clothing and a few of your favorites. We're meeting Frau Davies in Linz."

Karl waited for Ingrid to protest, to say they didn't need a nanny any longer, but she asked a different question.

"How long will we be gone, Papa?"

"I'm not sure. Pack what will fit into a single suitcase and knapsack."

"How many books shall I bring? I wouldn't want to be without something to read."

A smile lit their father's face. "Bring five or so. I'll buy new ones if you run out." He turned to Karl. "I'd like you to help Anna pack. She'll need her most practical clothes. Warm ones. And none of the ones that she's almost outgrown. Perhaps her favorite doll, but no more than a few toys. We need to pack light."

"Where's the painting of the lake?" Panic laced Ingrid's voice. "The one with the swans?"

Karl felt his face heat. He'd helped his father wrap that painting last night, then carried it to the root cellar.

"Don't worry; the painting is safe." Papa drew a red jewelry box from his pocket. "I'd like you to pack this, Ingrid. It's very important that you take good care of it."

"Was it Mother's?"

"Yes. A reminder of your heritage."

Ingrid fingered the box reverently, then opened it to reveal a pair of earrings with tear-drop-shaped diamonds suspended from sapphires. Karl remembered them dangling from his mother's ears at all their fanciest parties.

"These were hers too?" Ingrid touched one earring, then the other.

Papa nodded.

Ingrid's smile was bright enough to rival the chandelier that hung over the table. They all left the dining room, and Ingrid didn't ask any more questions about the paintings, even though several were missing on the way from the dining room to the bedrooms.

Karl headed to Anna's room to help her pack. Her excitement over seeing their former nanny again came out in small skips as she moved along the carpet, carrying her warmest dresses to her suitcase. The emotion doubled when Papa handed her a small, framed picture and asked her to keep it for him. Inside the silver frame was a photograph from two years ago, before their mother's death. The family of five posed on the front lawn, with the elegant lines of the manor as a backdrop. It was springtime in the photo, with the flowerbeds in full bloom. Everyone was smiling.

"Just in case you need help remembering," Papa said.

Anna's happiness turned to something more serious. "How could I ever forget? And we'll be back soon, won't we?"

Papa knelt so he was closer to Anna's height. "I hope we'll return soon. But war is changing everything." He tapped the picture. "We'll never be exactly like that again."

"No. Because Mama is gone now."

"Yes. And you're older. You won't go back to being five, will you?"

Anna shook her head. "Nor will Ingrid be thirteen again or Karl fifteen."

Papa stood and turned to Karl. He handed him a leather-bound book. "I'd like you to keep this. It will help you find the way back, if you ever get lost."

Karl turned the hand-trimmed pages of the New Testament. Papa hadn't spoken much about religion since Mama died, and the silence had been deafening. Karl had wondered if Papa really believed anymore. The gift confirmed his father's faith. "Thank you, Papa."

Papa walked toward the window that overlooked the grounds in front of the manor. His frown seemed as dark as the heavy clouds to the east.

Karl stepped forward for a better view and immediately saw the black Gräf & Stift. "Is that Herr Sauermann? Back already?"

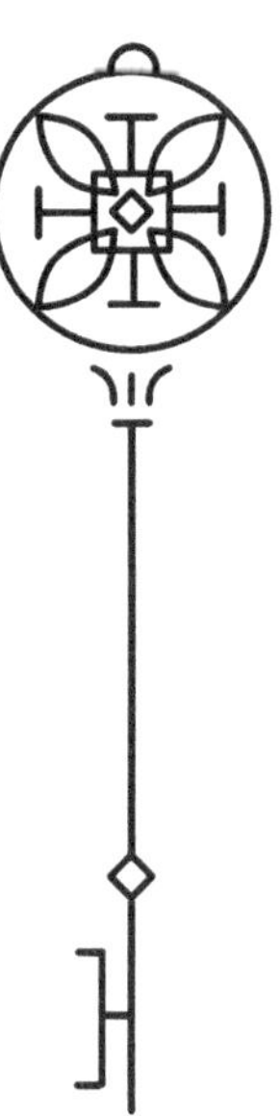

CHAPTER 3

Papa put a hand on Karl's shoulder. "Herr Sauermann is not to know of our upcoming journey. I'll take him to the study. The three of you will have lunch in the kitchen. Load the luggage, Karl, discreetly, and then help Frau Pichler put together some food for the journey."

Karl followed Papa into the hallway. Papa turned back to him. "Plan the third is still our goal. But remember plan the fourth if, somehow, Herr Sauermann forces me to leave with him. You're to go to Linz and meet Frau Davies. I've a dossier in the pocket of my gray coat for my contacts. You remember who they are?"

"If I make it to Paris, I find Jean-Yves Poncet with French Intelligence. If I make it to Zurich, I'm to seek out the defense attaché at the British Consulate."

Papa gave a soft smile. "You've a good memory, Karl. I'll see to Herr Sauermann. Make sure everything is ready, all right?"

Karl nodded. Papa walked down the stairs as Herr Pichler announced a visitor. Karl stepped softly toward the banister and waited until his father led Herr Sauermann into the study. Herr Sauermann wore the uniform of an SS *sturmbannführer* now, suggesting this was an official visit rather than a meeting between old friends. Neither man smiled.

Karl rushed into Ingrid's room first. "Are you packed?"

She sat on her bed, her book open again. "Yes."

"I need your help with the luggage."

Ingrid scowled at her large suitcase. "It's heavy. Can't we ask Herr Pichler to take it for me?"

Karl shook his head. "Papa doesn't want anyone to know we're leaving, especially not Herr Sauermann, who's in the study with him now. I need you to make sure no one sees us."

"I can help." Anna bounced from foot to foot the same way she did when they planned games of hide-and-seek.

Karl hadn't realized she'd followed him. "I'll be glad for your help, little dove. I'll need both of you. Ingrid, go keep watch outside the door to the study. Anna, find out where Frau and Herr Pichler are, Gerta, too, and then run back and tell me."

"Would it be better to pull the car around?" Ingrid asked. The garage was a converted barn some distance from the manor house.

"No, it's supposed to be secret. Herr Sauermann would notice if we pulled it to the front of the house, and the Pichlers would see it in the back."

Ingrid sighed. "I don't suppose it can wait five minutes. I've only got a few pages left in my book."

"You can finish after lunch. Or in the car on our way to the train station."

"You know I'll get carsick if I read while we drive." Despite her complaint, Ingrid dutifully strode down the stairs and took up her assigned position. Anna ran off too.

Karl moved his sisters' suitcases into his room—it was the closest to the stairs, both the main ones and the servants' stairs. He went into his father's room, too, to see if he had a bag ready. Sure enough, a suitcase lay on the window seat. Karl opened it to make sure his father was finished packing. He couldn't very well interrupt the meeting with Herr Sauermann to ask. The neatly folded suits, shirts, socks, and underthings confirmed the job was mostly done. Karl added his father's razor, comb, and toothbrush. Anything else Papa needed could go in a separate bag and be added later. Across the bed lay a gray coat. Karl felt the pockets and pulled out a midsized spiral-bound memorandum book. He didn't read it—that would be a violation of his father's privacy, and Karl was starting to understand what his father meant about knowledge sometimes being a burden. He replaced the notebook and grabbed the suitcase.

Anna found him soon after. "Gerta is cleaning the library. Herr Pichler is working behind the manor, and Frau Pichler is in the kitchen."

That meant Gerta would see them if they left by the front door, Frau Pichler would see them if they left by the kitchen door, and Herr Pichler would see them if they went through the servants' quarters. He could at least take the luggage to the ground floor. "Has Gerta cleaned the turquoise salon yet?"

Anna nodded.

"I'll take the luggage there, then we'll think of something. Stand at the bottom of the stairs and let me know if anything changes."

Karl started with his sisters' suitcases. Ingrid's was especially heavy—probably full of books. He hoped she'd packed some clothes too. He paused at the bottom of the stairs, beside the newel carved to look like a falcon. Ingrid, stationed outside the study, waved him on.

Anna, too, gave the all-clear signal as he approached the ground floor, so he tucked the suitcases into the salon under a table covered with a long dust cloth, then went for the next load. Soon, all four suitcases were lined up next to each other.

Ingrid followed him downstairs to the salon. "Strange, isn't it, that we have to sneak out of our own home?" Her voice was barely a whisper.

Karl nodded. "Anna, go see if Herr Pichler has moved. And fetch the keys to the garage and to the Mercedes."

Anna darted away, then flitted back a few minutes later. "He's still clearing away snow."

"Has he done the front yet? All the way to the garage?"

"Yes."

Good. That meant no one would see Karl's footprints. It also meant they needed to leave through the front door, which would lead them right past the library, where Gerta's humming drifted and echoed.

Ingrid held a hand out and crept into the foyer. "Wait in the salon."

She ran up the stairs before Karl could ask what she was doing. He almost followed, but maybe it was time to trust her. They were, after all, working toward the same goal, even if Ingrid knew only part of their father's plans.

Karl grasped Anna's hand and led her away from the salon doorway. He glanced around at the crystal chandeliers, the gold-painted birds on the crown molding, and the turquoise walls. Most of the room's furniture was covered in white cloths—between their mother's death and the drop in staff that came with the war, they hadn't really used the room in years. Still, he would miss this room, miss this house. Maybe they'd all be back soon. Maybe Hitler would be content with adding Austria, Czechoslovakia, and Poland to the Reich, and that would be the end of it.

"What was that?" Anna asked.

"I didn't hear anything."

"Something crashed but not nearby."

"Something in the study?" Were Papa and Herr Sauermann fighting?

"No. From the other direction."

"The kitchen?"

"No, higher."

Karl wasn't sure Anna's ears could pick out not only the sound of something he hadn't heard but also the direction. Still, he waited until Ingrid came down the stairs in a rush. She didn't stop in the salon but went into the library.

"Gerta, I'm so terribly sorry. I've knocked over one of the plants, and it's made a ghastly mess. Can you help me clean it?"

Karl grinned. Clever. He should have given Ingrid more credit. When Gerta and Ingrid disappeared up the stairs, he turned to Anna. "I'll need you to open the doors for me because I'll have my hands full. You've got to be very quiet about it."

Anna nodded. "Just like when I sneak out of my room to spy on a supper party."

"You've snuck out of your room to spy on supper parties?"

Anna's cheeks turned pink. "Only a few times. It's not fair when everyone else gets to stay up and I have to go to bed."

"Right. Let's go before Gerta and Ingrid get the mess sorted or Frau Pichler calls us for lunch."

Anna led, gently pulling the door open for him, then closing it with barely a sound.

"Well done, little dove. Now open the garage."

Sunlight made the fresh snow sparkle. It was beautiful enough that Karl didn't mind the way the chill bit into his nose. That was another thing he would miss about Falcon Point. The winters were spectacular. They'd ski and build snow forts and curl up in front of the fire when they finished. The other seasons had their charms too, but winter was his favorite.

Anna managed the lock on the garage's side door. Karl unlocked the Mercedes-Benz 230's luggage compartment and slid the suitcases inside. "Come on, let's get the last two."

Anna again handled the front door, making sure none of the hinges squeaked and the door and frame parted without so much as a scrape. Karl grabbed the suitcases, went through the front door and down the stone stairs to the drive, then froze in panic when he heard Frau Pichler's voice.

"Don't you think you ought to wear a coat, young lady, before you wander off to play in the snow?"

Anna stood in the doorway, concealing Karl from view. She held her hand behind her back and waved him on. "I suppose. I wasn't going to be gone for long. Karl wants a snowball fight, but I'm hungry. I'd rather eat first."

"Well, lunch is ready. Fetch your brother and your sister, and we'll have it in the kitchen."

"Yes, Frau Pichler."

Karl didn't hear the rest of the conversation because he was rushing to the garage.

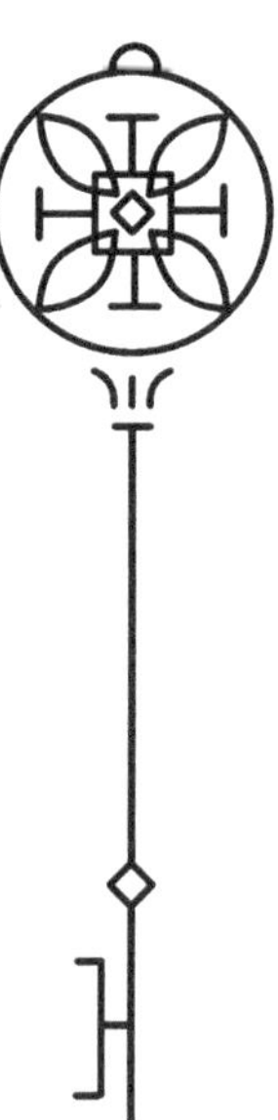

CHAPTER 4

KARL AND HIS SISTERS ATE in the kitchen, sitting at the well-worn table meant for the staff's use. In former times, the house had employed far more than its current three servants, so there was room to spread out, but they all sat close.

When Frau Pichler took a tray up for their father and Herr Sauermann, Ingrid leaned forward from across the table. "I heard them arguing."

"Papa and Herr Sauermann?" Karl paused with his spoon halfway to his lips.

Ingrid nodded.

"Did you hear what they were arguing about?" Karl could count on one hand the number of times he'd heard Papa raise his voice.

"No. It was muffled, but Gerta noticed, too, when we finished cleaning the mess from the plant."

Frau Pichler returned with a frown on her face.

Karl quickly swallowed his soup. "Is everything all right, Frau Pichler?"

She shrugged. "It's nothing, I'm sure. Sometimes politics bring out the worst in people."

"Papa or Herr Sauermann?" Karl wanted to know whose side Frau Pichler was on.

She busied herself gathering up the dishes to be washed. "I'll not say aught against your father, nor against his old friend and current guest."

"Frau Pichler?" Ingrid turned toward the cook. "Could we pack some food? For a picnic?"

"Haven't you got your fill with that soup?"

Ingrid gave the cook her most charming smile. "The soup is delicious, but for supper, we want a picnic."

"A picnic? In the snow? At suppertime, when it's nearly dark?"

"We want to have it in the attic," Anna said.

Karl smiled as his youngest sister joined the conspiracy. Her cherubic cheeks made her pleas far more effective than requests from either of her siblings would be. Even before Frau Pichler said yes, he knew she'd give in. Anna was Frau Pichler's weakness.

Frau Pichler sighed. "I suppose, if you handle the preparation and the cleanup, and if your father doesn't object. He might invite Herr Sauermann to stay for supper." Frau Pichler frowned. "Or maybe not, given what I walked into."

Karl's sisters were brilliant. He'd never noticed that before—perhaps it was a recent development, something new over the last few hours. He helped them clean up, and while the two girls made sandwiches, he slipped from the room.

Karl walked slowly, quietly, up the stairs toward the study. He would collect the lunch tray and use that as an excuse to interrupt the men. He hoped to somehow let Papa know that they'd done as he had asked them, but he was nervous. The men hadn't hid their anger from Frau Pichler. Were they still arguing?

The Lang family was used to political unrest. Karl's earliest memories included radio reports of bombings and assassinations as the Nazis or the Communists tried to sow discord. Austria hadn't been at peace for a long time—not before the Anschluss and not since. Now the unrest had spread into Falcon Point, and it was tearing apart friendships too.

When Karl was midway up the stairs from the foyer to the upper floor, a gunshot echoed through the hallway.

Karl's feet froze to the steps. Gunshots were things that happened on the radio, not in Papa's study. But there was no mistaking what he'd heard. He ran the rest of the way up the staircase.

Herr Sauermann pushed open the door of the study and walked briskly away. He held out a hand to Karl. "You don't want to go inside. There's been a dreadful accident."

Karl brushed past Herr Sauermann and burst into the room.

Papa lay on the floor. A growing stain of dark red marred his chest.

"Papa!" Karl dropped to the floor at his father's side and stared in horror. He grabbed his handkerchief and placed it on the wound, but there was so much blood—more than one little cloth could hold.

Papa's eyes met Karl's. He lifted a shaky hand but soon dropped it. His words were slow and strained. "I think we're on plan the fourth now."

Gerta ran into the room and screamed.

"Call for a doctor!" Karl yelled. While the maid tried to connect to the operator, Karl took off his jacket and used that to sop up the blood. "We'll fix this. We will." But the closest village had no doctor, and the road to Gildenstatt was snowed over. It was doubtful they could get help within the hour. "Did Sauermann do this?"

His father nodded ever so slightly. "Red-white-red."

Karl recognized the slogan from a defiant speech by Austria's last chancellor, Kurt Schuschnigg, only a few weeks before the Anschluss. Red, white, and red were Austria's national colors. Karl knew the next line, and despite the overwhelming shock and sorrow that threatened to strangle him, he managed to get the words out. "Until we're dead."

Papa's lips moved. Was it a gesture of approval? A farewell? Karl never knew because the next moment, his father was gone.

Gerta hung up the phone. "The doctor is coming, but he has a long way to drive, and with all this snow . . ."

Karl inhaled. He couldn't break down, not now. He had to be brave. "It won't matter. He's gone."

Gerta put a hand to her mouth and sobbed.

Wheels crunched snow in the driveway. Surely the doctor wasn't here already. Karl stood to see out the window. A military truck stopped in front of the main entrance, parking behind Sauermann's vehicle, and five uniformed men with Nazi brassards around their arms stepped out. Sauermann walked down the stone stairs to greet them.

Karl looked from the window to his dead father and then back again. "Gerta, can you help us? We have to leave."

Gerta sniffed and nodded.

"Get my sisters to the car. It's all packed. I'll grab the rest of their things. Quietly. Sauermann shot my father—I don't know what he might do to us."

Gerta wiped her face with her apron. "But where will you go?"

"The train station."

"And who will drive?"

Papa had taught Karl the basics of working the Mercedes, but he'd never driven without Papa sitting beside him, and he'd never driven in the snow. "It will have to be Herr Pichler."

Gerta nodded and rushed from the room.

It felt like a desecration to leave Papa lying in his blood like that. Karl bent to close his father's eyes with trembling hands. "I'm sorry, Papa. Sorry that this happened. Sorry that we're leaving you here." Karl swallowed back a lump in his throat. "But you can depend on me. Red-white-red until we're dead."

CHAPTER 5

Karl left the study and took the stairs to the bedrooms two at a time. He washed his father's blood from his hands and hid the stains on his shirt cuffs by pulling on his father's coat. He grabbed Ingrid's knapsack and placed it on one shoulder and put Anna's knapsack on the other. He held his own bag in one hand and ran down the servants' staircase to the basement. He slowed the last few steps and checked the kitchen. It was empty. He hoped that meant his sisters waited in the garage.

He climbed the stairs to the back entrance. Voices drifted from the foyer. Words like *traitor* and *unyielding* and *unfortunate*. Herr Sauermann was the only one who had been close enough to fire a weapon, and Papa had confirmed he was the murderer with a nod, but Karl wasn't an eye witness, not really, and Sauermann was clever. Could he twist it somehow? If they called the local magistrate, would he believe a teenage boy or an SS officer? Karl didn't like his chances. He had to get his sisters and leave.

Herr Pichler met him on the way to the garage. "Gerta said you wanted me to drive you to the train station. It will take a long time in this weather. Are you sure?"

Karl nodded but didn't trust himself to speak.

"What's going on? Gerta seemed upset. And all these soldiers . . ."

"My father's dead."

Herr Pichler's face went pale. "Dead? Do Miss Ingrid and Miss Anna know?"

"No. I'll tell them but not until we're away." Karl's voice cracked. Maybe his obvious grief would help Herr Pichler understand his reasons for waiting. He cleared his throat, trying to ease the sting of emotion. "We have to leave now."

Herr Pichler fell into step beside him until they reached the garage, where Karl's sisters waited.

"We've got the food ready," Ingrid said.

He gave her his bag and took off his sisters' knapsacks. "Good, because it's time to go."

Ingrid put the bags on the back seat of the car. "Why are those soldiers here?"

"They're trouble. That's why we have to go now, without delay." He took Anna's hand and led her to the car.

"Where's Papa?" she asked.

Karl helped her into the car. "We have to leave without him, or we'll miss Frau Davies."

"But we can't leave without Papa." Ingrid bit her lip. "They can't be forcing him into government service right this moment. We've time to say goodbye."

Karl almost told them, but he glanced at Anna's innocent face. He'd have to tell them eventually, but they couldn't delay their start for tears. "Ingrid, please, get in the car."

"I want to say goodbye first." She took a step toward the exit, and Karl grabbed her shoulder. He tried to be gentle, but Ingrid pulled away with fiery resentment. Anger gave her a frown. "What's gotten into you, Karl?"

Karl lowered his voice so Anna and Herr Pichler wouldn't hear. "It's not safe here anymore. Sauermann and his soldiers are dangerous, and we're running out of time."

"So we're to leave Papa to the danger?"

Karl wanted to force Ingrid into the car, but he doubted that would save time because she'd resist. "We've got to get Anna to safety. Before those men prevent us from leaving."

Ingrid glanced at the car and seemed to relent. "All right." She slid into the car, and Karl shut the door for her.

He helped Herr Pichler with the garage door and then sat in the front passenger seat rather than in the back with his sisters. He kept his eyes on the manor house as the car pulled forward. He wasn't sure how much Sauermann knew. Did he suspect Karl had information from his father?

"Does everyone have what they need?" Herr Pichler asked.

"Where's my book?" Ingrid dug through her knapsack.

"Didn't you pack it?" Karl asked.

"It was on my bed, right beside my bag. Of course I meant to take it. I told you I've only a few pages left!"

Herr Pichler pulled to a stop in front of the main entrance.

"We can't stop for it." Karl's words came out sharply.

"It will only take a few minutes." Ingrid reached for the door latch.

"No! Keep driving. It's not safe in there."

Herr Pichler glanced at Karl and began again.

Ingrid folded her arms and fell back into the seat with a huff. "Just because you're the oldest you think you can—" Her words broke off as an armed Nazi soldier left the manor and rushed to their car.

Herr Pichler braked and rolled down the window.

"You don't have permission to leave." The tall man with beady brown eyes didn't aim, but he let the rifle turn toward the girls. "We're conducting an investigation. No one is to enter or leave until we've finished."

"These are only children. They're no threat, and I doubt they can help with your investigation." Herr Pichler's voice shook—with fear, grief, or a combination of the two. "I'm taking them to meet their former nanny. They've a train to catch."

The soldier glanced at the passengers. "I'll have to check with *Sturmbannführer* Sauermann. Come with me."

Herr Pichler turned off the engine and followed the soldier into the manor.

Karl could accuse Sauermann of murder, so the SS officer wouldn't let him leave. Sauermann would detain the girls too because he wouldn't know how much Karl had told them. Karl glanced at the ignition. The key was still inside.

Karl slid across to the driver's seat.

"Karl, what are you doing?" Ingrid's voice was shrill.

"I'm getting us out of here."

"You can't drive!"

"Yes, I can. Papa gave me lessons."

"But in snow, on the mountain?"

Karl started the 230's engine. He put the clutch in, moved the car into first gear, and pressed on the accelerator. The tires spun for several long seconds before gaining traction. Then the car lurched forward. Karl had made it halfway to the lion gates when Anna's cry startled him. A peek in the rearview mirror explained the outcry. Three soldiers were running after them, and another few were climbing into their truck.

"Duck down, just in case they shoot."

"Why would they shoot at us?" Despite her question, Ingrid helped Anna onto the floor and lowered herself flat onto the seat.

Karl had to focus on the car. He couldn't explain what Sauermann had done to Papa, not now. It would have to wait because the Nazis were losing no time in their pursuit. Karl gave the car a little more gas, and it slid a bit as he turned to the right, heading down the mountain.

"What was that?" Ingrid asked.

"I took the turn too fast." It hadn't been all that rapid, but the fresh snow made it slick. He would have to keep the rest of the drive at a more reasonable speed and hope the Nazis did the same.

The road from Falcon Point to the village was a series of steep switchbacks. Karl eased into the next turn, but the truck with Sauermann's men was gaining on them. Its added weight would make it steadier in the snow, so they could drive faster than Karl could. The driver undoubtedly had more experience too.

Which was more of a risk: Nazi bullets or losing control when he went too fast on the snow? No one had shot at him yet. Maybe they didn't need to. Karl was unlikely to pull away from them at his current pace.

Switchback after switchback, Karl crawled down the mountain. His hands ached from holding the steering wheel too firmly, and Ingrid's nervous whimpers whenever he went around a curve didn't help. The truck following him stayed a steady two lengths behind. Ahead, the main road of the village showed tracks of pavement where the snow had melted after another vehicle had made a path. He could go faster there, if he could get to it.

As he reached the last switchback, the truck behind him erased the distance between them. Karl pushed the accelerator down more than he should have, slipped, braked, and lost control. The Mercedes spun, and so did Karl's stomach. Trees and houses and snow blurred as the car made a complete rotation.

Anna screamed, and Ingrid shushed her.

Karl swallowed and pushed the car into neutral. The truck slammed on its brakes, spun, and slid into a ditch, facing up the mountain.

Karl inhaled and exhaled, trying to dispel the fear that had surged when he'd lost control of the car. The Mercedes still moved forward—in the correct direction—unlike their pursuers. But the Nazis weren't giving up. One of them climbed from the truck with a rifle and aimed at the Mercedes.

"Stay down!" Karl shoved the stick back into gear.

He reached a section of road not covered in snow and stomped on the accelerator as the first rifle shot sounded. He hunched low over the steering wheel, moved through the gears, and prayed the moving target would be too hard for Sauermann's men to hit.

The village wasn't large, and the main road would soon curve into another series of switchbacks down the mountain, but there wouldn't be quite as much accumulated snow. He glanced in the mirror. The truck was still off the road despite several soldiers trying to move it back. Karl was running out of good road, but he was also out of reasonable rifle range.

"Ingrid, Anna, sit up and hang on. We've more snowy roads ahead."

CHAPTER 6

THEY DROVE THROUGH A VALLEY, and the road was clear of snow. Karl hadn't seen the truck with Sauermann's henchmen since leaving the village, and there was enough traffic now that he doubted they'd be spotted. Plenty of black Mercedes-Benz 230s drove along the road in both directions.

"Do we have enough petrol to reach Linz?" Ingrid leaned forward from the back of the vehicle.

"I think so. And I know how to refill the tank. We could drive all the way to Zurich." Maybe that was wiser, in case Sauermann guessed their plan and cared enough to pursue them.

Ingrid's voice held a bit of mirth. "I'm not sure I trust your driving for that long of a journey. We're bound to come to more roads with snow. And we're supposed to meet Frau Davies in Linz. Won't it be better to have her help?"

Karl didn't answer right away. He was too old to need a nanny, but he'd be glad to have help with the tasks ahead. He had Papa's papers to deliver, and then there was emigration, a home to find, schools to enroll in, meals to be planned, and clothing to be secured. Frau Davies would be far more competent than he when it came to all those things. If they didn't come, she would wait, or head to Falcon Point, and then she might be in danger. "We'll head to Linz."

"I miss Papa." Anna's voice was soft, but it pierced Karl with sorrow. He missed Papa, too, only his yearning was worse because he knew there would be no reunion in this life. He gripped the steering wheel as rage at Sauermann grew from a snowball to an avalanche. Sauermann had had no right to take their papa from them, no right to drive them from their home, no right to chase them.

"I'll tell you a story, Anna. That will help pass the time," Ingrid said. "So will a sandwich."

"I'll take a sandwich." Karl reached a hand back for it.

"While you're driving?"

Karl grunted. "Yes. The roads are dry, and I'm hungry."

Ingrid sniffed her disapproval, but she handed him a sandwich. He'd have to eat it without a fork and knife, but Frau Davies had told them that was normal in some parts of the world.

"I'm ready for a story." Anna's voice was muffled, probably from food.

"Very well." Ingrid paused dramatically. "Once upon a time, an Austrian princess went on an adventure."

Karl could hear the smile in Ingrid's voice as she recited the familiar story their mother and father had told them so often at bedtime. As the princess and her friends overcame their initial distrust for each other and then cooperated to complete their quest and slay a dragon, it seemed to make Karl's own situation a little less dire. Like the characters in the story, he and his sisters could manage if they worked together. He slowed at a crossroads and took the turn for Linz.

He drove in silence for a while. The light outside grew dim, and then twilight faded into night. He yawned, then did his best to shift around in the seat so he wouldn't fall asleep. Moving wasn't enough; he needed to keep his mind occupied. He caught Ingrid's eye in the mirror. "You tell the story the same way Mama did."

"It seemed to make Anna happy. And take my mind off things, like what on earth happens in the final pages of *Around the World in Eighty Days.*"

"I can tell you what happens. Phileas is certain he's lost the bet, but then—"

"Don't you dare spoil it, Karl. I want to read it for myself."

Karl nodded. He would have grabbed her book for her if he hadn't been in such a hurry. They could probably find a copy at a library or a bookshop when they arrived somewhere safe. "Is Anna asleep?"

"Yes, the little dove."

"Ingrid, there's something I have to tell you. But you mustn't be angry that I didn't tell you sooner."

"As long as it's not the ending to *Around the World in Eighty Day.*"

"No. Nothing so cheerful."

"What is it?" The teasing note in her voice was gone, replaced with dread.

Karl swallowed. "Herr Sauermann shot Papa. He's dead."

"What?" Ingrid's words were strained when she spoke—high-pitched and warbled. "No—he can't be dead!"

"I watched him take his last breath."

Ingrid murmured a few more denials, but mostly, she sobbed for what felt like a long time. Karl adjusted the rearview mirror, and light from a passing car revealed her tears. If it hadn't been for the threat of Sauermann's pursuit, he would have pulled the car over and wept with her. The grief and the anger and the frustration of it all threatened to choke him. The road beneath them slid by in a blur, dark and shiny, and still his sister cried.

"I don't understand." Ingrid had mastered her sobs, but her voice was still uneven. "Papa and Herr Sauermann were friends."

"Sauermann's a Swastika. Papa wasn't. He wasn't willing to work with the Reich, no matter how much they wanted him."

"But wouldn't it have been better to cooperate than be murdered?"

Karl sighed. "A few days ago, I would have said yes. Peace—for a country or for a person—it's worth a lot. But it can come at too high a cost. Papa would have always regretted going against his conscience."

"Things haven't been peaceful for a long time. Between the Reds and the Swastikas . . ." Ingrid trailed off with another sob.

"We haven't had peace and security, but we had our independence, at least for a while. The last thing Papa said to me was 'red-white-red.' Do you know what that means?"

"That he was committed to an independent Austria until the end. But where does that leave us?"

"It means we're children of a man the Nazis consider a traitor. We can't stay, not now. If Sauermann could kill a man he's called a friend for twenty-five years, we aren't safe either, not from him, not from the men he works with." Karl met Ingrid's eyes for a moment in the mirror, then focused on the road. "Papa had a plan, a way to resist the Reich. It's up to me to finish his work."

"How? You're only seventeen. We're all alone now. We've no one to help us."

"We have Frau Davies. And Papa had friends in Zurich and Paris. You know Papa. He had plans. Feel your coat, near the bottom."

"Something's wrong with the lining. It was digging into my skin on the way down the mountain."

"Gerta sewed jewelry into it. Into Anna's too. Probably mine as well, but I grabbed Papa's coat instead. We'll have something to tide us over until we can go back. And Papa hid away some of our treasures where Sauermann will never find them. They'll be waiting for us when we return."

"The painting with the swans . . . and the one of the Hofburg."

"Those and others. Most of Mama's jewelry too. Who knows what else. We just have to slay our dragon and go back to claim our castle."

Ingrid sniffed. "Slaying a dragon? It almost sounds easy compared to stopping Hitler." Then her voice crumpled again. "And neither will bring back Papa."

"No. We'll have to tell Anna, but maybe we should wait until we're somewhere safe. She'll be devastated, and we have to keep our wits. It won't be difficult for Sauermann to guess we've gone to Linz." Herr Pichler and Gerta knew where they'd gone, so Karl had to assume Sauermann would find out too. Karl and his sisters were just children, but if Sauermann hadn't wanted them to leave Falcon Point, he wouldn't want them to leave Linz either. If he marshalled the resources he had as an SS officer and called the station, they might be walking into a dragon's lair. But the alternative—leaving Frau Davies to face the dragon alone—was unacceptable.

Karl parked the Mercedes at Linz Central Station and told his sisters to wait in the car. He walked along the building and peeked into the station house. No sign of the SS. Maybe Sauermann hadn't called ahead. Maybe he'd given up his pursuit.

They would need a cart to help with the luggage, so Karl rented one, then returned to the car. "It's safe," he told his sisters. They climbed out, and Ingrid helped Anna fasten the buttons of her coat.

Karl loaded the luggage onto the cart, then paused as he removed Papa's suitcase from the car. He would bring it, not because he expected his father to return but because he wasn't ready to abandon it.

"Keep an eye out for Frau Davies," he said. If they didn't find her, Karl would manage, but he hoped it wouldn't come to that. Frau Davies was half English, though she'd spent much of her life in Austria, held a Reich passport, and spoke impeccable German. Having British blood could lead to problems if the Nazis found out, but as long as her paperwork was correct and Sauermann didn't show up, the four of them ought to have smooth travels.

"There she is!" Anna broke into a run and darted out of sight.

Panic swelled as Anna disappeared into the crowd. Karl couldn't lose his sisters, but chasing Anna would mean abandoning the luggage. "Go after her," he told Ingrid.

Soon, both sisters had vanished into the building of long windows and modernist concrete. A few minutes later, they reappeared from the throng of waiting passengers with the addition of their former nanny.

"Karl!" Frau Davies hugged him, then held his arms. She used to grab his shoulders when she wanted a good look at him, but he was too tall for that now. "How time has flown. You're every bit the young man now. But where is Herr Lang?" She looked around for their father.

"He . . . he's not coming." Ingrid bit her lip and glanced at Anna.

"We had to leave in a hurry, I'm afraid. Herr Sauermann is no longer a friend. He almost prevented our departure." Karl would have to tell Frau Davies more eventually but hoped that moment hadn't yet come.

"Your father told me ages ago that Herr Sauermann is no longer a friend." Frau Davies held Anna's hand but directed her remarks at Karl.

Karl wished Papa would have told him sooner, but of course Frau Davies knew. If Papa had arranged for her help, he would have also told her who was ally and who was enemy.

Frau Davies continued. "But I was expecting your father and a few items he promised to bring. Did he send anything with you?"

Anna nodded. "He gave me a picture of Falcon Point manor. And Karl a book, and Ingrid a jewelry box."

A frown pulled at the woman's mouth. "Perhaps the book has what we need. He promised passports and visas."

Ingrid dug into her pocket and pulled out two passports. "I've mine and Anna's."

"And I've mine." Karl had packed it into his knapsack.

Frau Davies motioned them toward a portion of the station that wasn't quite so busy. "We'll make do with those, if needed. I have five tickets to Budapest. When we get there, I'll buy tickets to Istanbul, then we'll sail to England. Your Papa thought it best to travel under different names, but I don't imagine the Nazis care over much about children of your ages, regardless of who your father is."

Karl took the New Testament his father had given him from the backpack and flipped through its pages. No passports were hidden inside the cover. The only thing he noticed were five handwritten letters, *F E T R L,* along the inside margin. He squinted but couldn't make sense of it.

"What is it?" Ingrid asked.

Karl showed her. She turned the page and found another set of five letters in the margin of the next page and another set on the page after that. But the letters didn't make words. "Could this be what he meant to send?"

Frau Davies shook her head. "I'm sure it's from your father, and I'm sure he had a very good reason for writing it, but I don't think it's going to help us flee the Reich."

Karl nodded and put the book away. He'd ponder that mystery another time. He pulled his father's luggage from the cart so he and Ingrid could dig through the items. There, folded neatly into a crisp, white dress shirt, were five sets of travel documents. The pictures were of their faces, and they still had the same first names, but the birthdays were off by a few weeks, and everyone, including Frau Davies, had a new last name: Eckerstorfer.

Frau Davies nodded her approval. "If anyone asks, I'm your aunt. Come, let's board. If we miss this next train, we'll have to wait until tomorrow, and I think it's best we leave today."

Karl agreed. So far, the station was unthreatening—Sauermann hadn't shown up, nor did the SS have a larger-than-normal presence—but the sooner they left, the better. They showed their new papers to the correct official and boarded the train. Then they settled into a sleeper. Karl didn't normally go to bed so early, but he was exhausted from all that had happened.

Anna, on the other hand, seemed full of energy. "Can't we wait until the train starts before we try to sleep?"

"Some of us weren't able to nap during the drive to the station." Ingrid cupped Anna's face in her hand and chuckled. "Karl had to drive, and I had to keep him awake."

"But we're starting a journey all the way to . . ." Anna looked around to make sure they were alone and continued only in a whisper. "All the way to England. I'm too excited to sleep now."

Karl knew exactly what to tell her to remedy the undue excitement, but he didn't have the heart. He didn't want to listen to her cry herself to sleep when she learned they were orphans. He'd tell her in Budapest or in Istanbul. "Just until we leave the station, then we'll try to sleep."

Anna nodded her agreement.

Frau Davies pulled out her knitting. Anna stared out the window at the people passing by, Ingrid read a newspaper, and Karl looked at the identity papers from his father—the ones with his picture and the ones with Papa's. How had Papa managed to get five sets of documents that looked so genuine? Karl compared the real ones with the faux ones and couldn't detect any difference. Had he bribed someone? Papa had said he worked with codes, not with forgery. Maybe he had professional connections. He must have been planning their escape for some time.

Anna gasped.

"What is it, little dove?" Karl went to the window and looked over her shoulder.

Anna pointed. "It's Herr Sauermann!"

The train carriage was heated pleasantly, but Karl's blood turned to ice. With Sauermann were five soldiers, all of them speaking with a railway official.

"Will he see us watching?" Ingrid asked.

"Put a hat on, Karl." Frau Davies kept her voice even. "You'll look almost like an adult. See what they're up to. Anna, you'll need to stay away from the window—they'll be looking for children. Ingrid, let me rework your hair so you look a little older."

Karl obeyed Frau Davies. He pulled a fedora from his father's suitcase and hid his blond hair beneath it. Then he watched, using an abandoned newspaper to hide behind should Sauermann or his men start checking the windows.

They did worse.

The railway official gathered some of his coworkers, and they and Sauermann's soldiers split into three teams. One group boarded a different train, an express headed west, and began examining passengers and papers.

Sauermann's group walked toward the train to Budapest.

"They're coming." Karl tried to keep his voice calm, but inside, fear, panic, and anger churned. Sauermann was a murderer, but because he had the right political stance, he was unlikely to be punished.

"What should we do?" Ingrid asked.

The men were searching for two girls, aged seven and fifteen, and a boy of seventeen. If they all split up, perhaps they wouldn't cause suspicion. But Sauermann would recognize each of the children, regardless of where they were, and he was boarding their train. He might even recognize Frau Davies. They couldn't let Sauermann see any of them, especially not together. "I have a plan. Anna, you'll have to hide behind the luggage. Frau Davies will tell you when it's safe to come out. Can you do that? And be perfectly quiet?"

Anna nodded, her normally cheerful face solemn now. Karl hoisted her up to the luggage rack and reorganized the suitcases and coats around her so she couldn't be seen.

"Can you breathe, Anna?"

"Yes."

"You're a brave little dove. Don't worry, soon we'll be able to stop hiding from dragons."

Karl turned to Ingrid. "You'll have to go to the dining car. If Sauermann sees only Frau Davies without any of us, maybe he won't recognize her. And none of the soldiers will recognize you—they didn't see enough of you when we fled. Hide in the lavatory if Sauermann comes into the dining car."

Ingrid nodded. She grabbed her smaller bag and left.

"And you, Karl?" Frau Davies asked.

Karl pulled on his coat and knapsack. "I expect I'll see you soon. If not, I know where you're headed."

Frau Davies stood and blocked the exit. "I have an inkling of what you might be trying, and I don't think it's a good idea."

"Can you think of a better one? Sauermann will recognize me, even if I put on an engineer's uniform."

Frau Davies softened her stance. "They're starting at the front of the car. Get off and double back to where they've already checked."

Karl nodded. He glanced at where Anna was hidden for a moment before leaving the sleeper. He went to the nearest exit and left the train. He stayed near the side of the cars, where the shadows were a little deeper. After passing several of the train carriages, he realized he should have taken Ingrid with him. What if she wasn't able to hide? Or what if Sauermann recognized Frau Davies? If he saw her, he'd know the Lang children were nearby. If Sauermann remembered she was partially British, she'd be in just as much trouble as Karl was, maybe more.

Karl changed his strategy. He walked farther from the train, along the center of the platform. He removed his hat and walked where he wouldn't be hidden by the crowds. When he saw Sauermann, he waited, willing him to look up and notice him.

Eventually, he did. Even from a distance, the satisfaction and malice that swirled on Sauermann's face was apparent. He yelled, though Karl couldn't hear, and pointed. Karl waited until Sauermann himself appeared on the platform.

Then he ran.

CHAPTER 7

Karl had succeeded with the first part of the plan—he'd drawn Sauermann off the train. His sisters and Frau Davies were safe. But the next part of the plan—losing the men and sneaking back onto the train without them noticing—now seemed impossible.

Sauermann and two others followed him, and one of them was fast. Karl gasped for breath as he sprinted along the train. He ran down a set of stairs and kept up the speed, slowing only when he reached a group of detraining passengers. He put his hat back on and tried to steady his racing heart. Maybe Sauermann wouldn't be able to pick him out in the crowd.

The train to Budapest whistled. It would move soon. Plan the first: he'd be quick enough to lose Sauermann's men and climb on board before it started. Plan the second: he'd jump on after it started moving but before it was up to speed, before it left the station. Plan the third: he'd catch up to them, either in Budapest or in Istanbul.

As the crowd dispersed, Karl kept his head down and strode with purpose, like someone in a hurry to board a train. Hopefully, not like someone trying to hide. He stepped onto an empty track, then over the coupling of a waiting train, and then back onto the platform near the train to Budapest. It rolled forward, slowly. He could still catch it if he hurried.

"Hold there." Someone tugged on Karl's elbow.

He turned to face one of the railway officials and tried to act calm. Maybe he was simply to be reprimanded for crossing the tracks. "Can I help you?"

The official huffed. So did the train to Budapest. It was moving faster now. Karl would have to run to catch it, but it was still possible. "I'll need to see your papers."

Karl didn't want to show the man his real papers or the fake ones, but one of Sauermann's thugs joined the official, so he couldn't really refuse. "Just a moment. They're in here."

Karl knelt beside a pillar and sorted through his bag, taking his time. He had the fake papers in his pocket. Showing those would threaten his sisters and Frau Davies with discovery—Sauermann could phone or telegraph the next station and have anyone with that surname detained. But the men would be looking for the Lang name, so he didn't want to show them those papers either.

"Come on, speed it up."

The train to Budapest disappeared from the station. An empty cavern seemed to open up in Karl's chest. He was all alone. If his sisters were safe, it was worth it. He'd catch up to them, eventually. He fastened his bag and stood with his passport. Sauermann already knew Karl's real name, so he would show his real papers. He tried not to focus on the empty track where the train to Budapest had been. But he found it impossible not to stare at a trolley full of luggage that barreled toward the group.

The official and the soldier stood with their back to the oncoming cart—they couldn't see it and were unlikely to hear it over the noise of the station. The official reached for Karl's papers. Karl dropped them a bit too early, so the passport fell to the platform. He bent to retrieve it, then rolled out of the way as the trolley rammed into the men who'd detained him.

"Come on, Karl!"

Ingrid. Why was Ingrid still in the station? She was supposed to be on the train to Budapest, not shoving a cart of luggage into railroad officials.

"What are you doing here?" he asked.

"Come on!" she repeated.

He scrambled away from the tangle of luggage and men and followed her as she ran to another platform.

"You're supposed to be with Frau Davies on your way to safety!"

Ingrid grabbed his arm and pulled him along. "I saw Sauermann chasing you."

"I wanted him to chase me so he'd get off the train before he recognized you."

"Yes, but it looked like he was going to catch you."

Karl couldn't refute that, but he stiffened when he saw where she was leading him. "What are you doing, Ingrid? I can't go in there!"

Ingrid pushed his hat in front of his face. "Not a word." She pulled him into the ladies' room.

Karl couldn't see, but Ingrid tugged him along. Silence greeted them. He hoped that meant the toilets were empty, save for the two of them.

"Lock yourself in a stall and stay here. I'll buy two tickets for the next train heading east and fetch you in time to board." She took his hat and set it on her own head.

"But it's the ladies' room!"

"Exactly. They'll never look for you in here."

"What if Sauermann recognizes you?"

She pointed to the fedora. "I have a disguise."

"Not a very thorough one."

"I know. But it's the best I can come up with. I'll try to avoid him. Trust me, Karl. Stay out of sight. There's another ladies' room closer to the ticket counter, so this one is unlikely to turn busy, especially this time of night. I'll come right back after I've got our tickets." She pushed him toward a stall. "They're less likely to notice me."

Karl wasn't sure about that, but he was out of ideas, so he obeyed his sister.

Karl was normally patient enough to wait when waiting was required, but he found himself checking his watch every few seconds. Part of the anxiety was his location. Hiding in a ladies' room had to be the most shameful thing he'd ever done. What would Papa think? Given the alternative—detainment by Sauermann, a baggage search, discovery of his father's intelligence for foreign nationals, and possible execution—Papa might have let it slide, though the thought did little to ease the embarrassment.

But mortification was only part of the problem. What if Sauermann caught Ingrid? She was young, but that was insufficient protection from someone who had murdered a friend of several decades. Ingrid didn't have anything incriminating with her—other than a forged passport. Karl checked his watch again. She'd been gone only five minutes, and he was going mad.

He could trust his sister. She'd been brilliant when they'd snuck out the suitcases. Ramming the railroad official with the trolley had been bold and clever. All she had to do was buy two train tickets and return. She could manage.

That didn't stop the worry.

He couldn't pace and didn't dare leave the stall lest an unsuspecting woman walk in and scream. Ingrid was right—the room was quiet. Karl reordered his bag and checked his watch again. Seven minutes.

Fifteen—he would give her fifteen minutes. After that, he'd go looking for her.

At twelve minutes, the door squeaked open. Soft footsteps walked the length of the room.

"Karl?" Ingrid's voice carried to him in a whisper.

Karl unlocked and exited the stall.

Ingrid frowned. "They'll be looking for that coat, so take it off. Switch bags with me too."

If they'd still had their suitcases, they could have changed clothing completely, but their luggage was on its way to Budapest.

"Did you get the tickets?" Karl asked.

Ingrid held them up. "Vienna. We can board now. It doesn't continue to Budapest, but we can find something there that does."

"You did well, Ingrid. We should leave before someone comes."

Ingrid nodded. "Let me go first." She peeked out the door, then waved for him to follow.

"Which platform is it?" he asked when he caught up.

"Seven."

They headed that direction. Ingrid gave him back the hat and smoothed her own hair. Both kept their eyes moving. There were three of them now who would recognize Karl for certain, and several others who might, depending on how well they'd seen him while he'd been driving. They couldn't have studied Ingrid while she'd been in the back of the Mercedes, but Sauermann might have given them a description.

Once they boarded the train, they found seats in a second-class car. Ingrid sat by the window, and Karl put the hat back on her head since she was easier for outsiders to see. He took the newspaper she handed him and held it so no one could see his face.

Would Sauermann search the trains again? Karl didn't relax until theirs started to move and slowly, then not quite as slowly, pull from the station.

Karl folded the newspaper and forced the tension from his shoulders. He wanted to talk to Ingrid, but he didn't want the passengers seated around them to hear. Ingrid took the paper from him to occupy herself, and he studied the other passengers. Eventually, the man sitting across from them fell asleep.

"Do you think Anna will be all right?" Ingrid whispered.

"She'll worry about us, but she'll be safe. She was always Frau Davies's favorite."

"That's because you had a ghastly habit of bringing nasty things like snakes and frogs into the house, then misplacing them for her to find again."

Karl let out a part sigh, part chuckle. "They might wait for us in Budapest, but we can't spend much time searching, in case they've gone on ahead."

"What if we can't find them?" Worry lines marred Ingrid's otherwise unblemished face.

"Then we'll take passage on a different ship. Frau Davies lives with her sister in London, remember? We had tea there with Mama and Papa."

"That was four years ago, and I don't recall the address. What if we can't find it?"

Karl thought back on that trip, his only one to England. "We took the tube and got off at Stockwell Station. Then we walked past St. Michael's Church. That's where her sister worshipped—we can ask there. Her flat wasn't far from the church. And she had flowerboxes in the windows."

"What type of flowers?"

"Purple ones."

Ingrid half huffed, half snorted. "That's not very helpful."

"We just have to ask the vicar or the warden. They'll help us."

"And if the worst should happen, and we can't find her?"

"Papa no doubt sent Frau Davies a generous sum to help us get to England, and she has the pension he gave her. Anna might not be able to go on as many ski holidays as before, but she won't starve. And anyway, we will find her." He had to find her. He'd never stop looking.

He eventually fell asleep to the rhythmic motion of the train, waking only when Ingrid elbowed him. He blinked and stretched. The train was just starting to slow on its approach to Vienna's Westbahnhof Station. The two of them gathered their things. They only had their smaller bags; the suitcases were with Frau Davies. She'd have to hire a porter to manage it all.

"Do you have both sets of papers?" he asked his sister.

Ingrid nodded.

"Any food left?"

Ingrid cracked a smile, pulled a ham sandwich from her bag, and handed it to him. "That's the last one though."

"Shall we split it?" Karl gave her half, and they ate while the train pulled into the station and stopped completely. "How are you for money?" He had only what he'd found tucked into his father's wallet. Enough to buy train tickets and food but not enough for passage from Turkey to England.

"A few notes. And the jewelry."

If they didn't catch up to Frau Davies, they might have to sell the jewelry. But there was more hidden at Falcon Point, when they made it back.

A clock chimed half past midnight as they detrained to an enormous, mostly empty concourse. Karl stared at the list of upcoming departures. Nothing left for hours. He didn't want to spend money on a hotel room, but maybe they'd have to.

Ingrid stood next to him. "Do you suppose she plans to take the route through Bucharest and Varna or through Belgrade and Sofia?"

"We'll find her in Budapest. We can ask her then."

Ingrid nodded. "And what should we do now? The first train to Budapest doesn't leave until six in the morning."

"We'll take that one."

"And in the meantime?"

Karl led Ingrid to a bench. "Stand in front of me so no one sees me counting my money."

Ingrid did as directed.

Karl sighed as he finished. "I have enough for the tickets to Budapest. Maybe enough for a modest hotel, but if we don't find Frau Davies soon, I don't have enough to get us to Istanbul." He thought she would wait for them, but maybe not. She'd commented on how grown-up Karl looked. He'd made it clear he wanted to be treated like an adult, so maybe that meant finding his own way.

Ingrid yawned. "We better save our money. We're in Vienna. Something's bound to be open somewhere."

Karl wasn't so sure, but Sauermann might have contacts in Vienna, and staying at the station all night would attract attention. They left and wandered the dark streets in search of something that hadn't already closed. Coffee houses would all be shut, and they were too young to gain entry into a club, but maybe something nearby catered to travelers. Even if they didn't find anything, it was better to be away from the station. "Have you slept at all since we left?"

Ingrid shook her head. "Almost, on the train, but then I kept thinking about Papa. Anna too. She probably cried herself to sleep."

Anna still didn't know of Papa's murder. Frau Davies would suspect, but Karl didn't think she would say anything until she knew the truth.

"Thank you for keeping me awake while I drove." Guilt colored his gratitude. Had Ingrid been able to sleep on their drive to Linz, she might not be so tired now. Or maybe she would be. She was usually up with the sun, so she rarely stayed up late, and it was past midnight already.

She stiffened.

"What?" Karl asked.

"That man behind us. He was on the train."

Karl tried to look casual as he bent to the ground, getting a look at the man while he fiddled with a shoelace. He wore a black suit and carried no luggage. Perhaps he was like them—stranded until morning. But for the next several blocks, the man followed their every turn.

With each step, Karl tried to convince himself that he was overreacting. The man was no doubt doing the same thing they were because that was what people did when stranded at a train station. They walked around and explored rather than waiting hours for the ticket counter to open. The stranger wasn't following them; he merely happened to be traveling the same direction, hoping to find a restaurant or café that was open all night.

Ingrid took Karl's arm. Maybe she was nervous too.

Karl led them down another road, doubling back the way they'd come. The man followed all the way back to the train station. That meant he wasn't an innocent passenger who just happened to be taking their same route.

From the opposite direction, another figure approached them. Shadow obscured the man's face, and Ingrid tightened her grip.

"Karl Lang?"

That voice was familiar. "Herr Kaufmann?"

Karl's teacher smiled. "What on earth are you doing outside the Vienna train station at this time of night all by yourselves?"

Karl looked at Ingrid, not sure how much they should say.

She smiled. "We're waiting for the ticket counter to open. We plan to take an early train."

Herr Kaufmann pulled up a sleeve to glance at his watch. In his periphery, Karl noticed the man who'd been following them walk back into the station. Herr Kaufmann frowned. "You'll have quite a wait."

Karl didn't want to admit that they didn't have the money for a room. Or rather, they didn't have it in cash and weren't eager to find a pawn shop at this time of night so they could exchange the jewelry. He gave a noncommittal grunt.

Herr Kaufmann waved them toward the street. "Why don't you join me? A friend lent me the keys to his apartment. It's not far from here. The last time I spoke to your father, he hinted that you might need assistance should certain circumstances arise. I'm prepared to offer you a safe place to rest for the night."

Of course Papa had arranged other people to help in case of need. He always had more than one plan. Frau Davies was plan the first, and Herr Kaufmann was no doubt plan the second. But what was Herr Kaufmann doing in Vienna?

"Are you waiting for a connecting train too? Traveling for the school holiday?" Karl asked.

"Just arrived. I'll spend the holiday in Vienna, but I had to see about a lost piece of luggage." Herr Kaufmann shook his head in frustration. "Nearly everyone is gone for the night, so I didn't make much progress. I'll try again in the morning."

Herr Kaufmann led them four blocks from the station. They entered a gray apartment building and walked up two flights of stairs to a flat. Herr Kaufmann flipped on the lights to reveal walls with dark wood paneling and red damask. He led them past the front room and gestured to a door on the right. "You two can sleep in the library. I'll find some spare blankets. The water closet is through here." He pointed to another door.

"We need to catch a 6:00 a.m. train," Karl said.

Herr Kaufmann nodded, then went into the room on the left.

Karl followed Ingrid into the library. Ingrid went to the larger sofa, and Karl let her claim it. Exhaustion made even the rug look appealing.

Herr Kaufmann knocked, then entered with a handful of blankets and an alarm clock. What luck to run into his literature teacher, who happened to have a place they could sleep. Herr Kaufmann might occasionally extol the economic virtues of Austria's unification with Germany, but he had proved an ally in their time of need. Maybe things were finally taking a turn for the better.

CHAPTER 8

Karl woke to the sound of a telephone ringing in a distant room. It rang twice. He blinked and winced as he remembered all that had happened the day before. His father's murder, leaving Falcon Point, being separated from Anna—

Anna.

He and Ingrid had a train to catch.

"What time is it?" Ingrid's voice was sleepy. Perhaps the phone had woken her too.

Karl grabbed the alarm clock and pulled it toward him. He squinted in the dim light, then sat up in horror. "It's seven thirty."

Ingrid shot up. "We were supposed to catch the six o'clock train!"

Karl fought panic. He'd set the alarm the night before. Why hadn't it rung? He checked to see if he'd set it incorrectly, but he couldn't figure out why it hadn't gone off. "Did you hear the alarm?"

Ingrid shook her head.

"Nor did I." Had they been so tired that they'd both slept through the ring?

They gathered their things. They didn't have much, just their coats, one hat, and the items from their knapsacks.

Ingrid finished first. "We can eat on the train. I don't remember the times of the other departures, but we'd better get to the station. I'd hate to just miss one because we dawdled."

Karl swung his bag onto his shoulder. They ought to fold their bedding and tidy the room, but they didn't have time for that. Herr Kaufmann would understand.

They rushed into the hall and almost bumped into their host.

"Would you like breakfast?" he asked.

"Thank you, but we overslept. We've got to get to the station at once." Karl glanced at Herr Kaufmann. Freshly shaved, dressed. Why hadn't he woken them? Had he forgotten Karl said they needed to get to the station before six? But that was blaming someone else for Karl's mistake—Papa wouldn't approve. Karl had to take responsibility for his own failure and hope Frau Davies and Anna would wait for them either in Budapest or in Istanbul. "Thank you for letting us stay."

Herr Kaufmann nodded. "I'll walk you back. I need to purchase a newspaper."

Outside, daylight gave the apartment building and the street a different look. Something a little more cheerful, offering hope that this day would be less painful than the last one.

Ingrid was quiet. Maybe she was tired. Maybe she was upset because she thought Karl hadn't set the alarm correctly. Exhaustion, disappointment, grief—she had reason not to smile.

"I'm sorry we overslept," he told her.

She glanced at Herr Kaufmann, then back at Karl. "There'll be other trains." She'd never met his teacher before and probably didn't feel comfortable with him.

When they arrived, they repeated their thanks to Herr Kaufmann and stood in line to buy tickets.

"One for Budapest is leaving in an hour." Ingrid frowned. "But it doesn't look as though it continues on to Istanbul."

"At least we'll be out of the Reich. And we'll want to get off the train there anyway to see if Frau Davies left us a message."

Ingrid nodded. "Do we have enough?"

"Yes. But now that I see the schedule, I wish we would have taken Herr Kaufmann up on his offer of breakfast. I doubt we can afford to buy more than one meal until we pawn the jewelry in your coat." Ingrid had the earrings from Mama too, but they wouldn't sell those.

"I'm surprised Papa didn't pack more cash."

"He probably would have, given a little more time. It might have been on him when he died. I didn't search his body. There could be some hidden in his suitcase."

"Strange, running into your teacher from a school in Gildenstatt here in Vienna."

Karl had called it luck. "It's Fasching season. It's not so strange that he'd travel to Vienna for a holiday."

"Yes, but why did he come to the station with us for a newspaper? Last night, he said he had a lost piece of luggage. Wouldn't he come back to the station for that?"

"Maybe he cares more about the news, so he mentioned that first." Not that newspapers had provided much surprise as of late—after the fighting in Poland had ended last October, journalists had taken to calling the current state of affairs a phony war. The fighting might never pick up. Karl had heard enough to know war was awful, so maybe that was just as well. But if no one fought Hitler, the Lang family would be forever exiled from Falcon Point.

Ingrid gripped his arm and squeezed.

Karl flinched in discomfort—her hold was tight—but when he looked in the direction she pointed, the pain in his arm was overwhelmed by a shock that turned his abdomen to ice.

Herr Kaufmann stood beside Herr Sauermann, and they seemed to have plenty to say to each other.

"They're working together." Ingrid's whisper held horror. "That's why Herr Kaufmann happened to be at the station last night."

Karl had known Herr Kaufmann was sympathetic to the Nazis, but he wasn't ruthless. Surely he wouldn't betray one of his own students . . . would he? Karl looked at the schedule. "When is the next train leaving?" Maybe it didn't matter which direction they went, as long as they got out of Vienna and away from Sauermann and Kaufmann.

"We don't have time to buy tickets." Ingrid pointed the other direction, where men in uniform approached.

A train whistled. "We have to get on that train." Karl had no idea where it was headed, but if they could slip aboard without Sauermann or the others seeing them, they could sort everything out later.

"But we don't have tickets."

"An angry train conductor scares me less than Sauermann. Come on." He pulled her away from the train rather than toward it. They were being watched. They would have to get out of sight and board the train at the last moment.

They rushed away from the platforms. They were ahead of the whistling train now, but it would come their direction. They just had to cross a few tracks to get to it. Karl looked around for anyone who might be working with Sauermann. He patted the pockets of his coat. His fake papers and the New Testament from his father were in one. His father's spiral notebook was in the other, along with his wallet and penknife. Everything else was in his knapsack.

He glanced at Ingrid's feet. She wore sensible boots. That was good, because they might have to sprint.

"Give me your bag in case we have to run." Karl was faster, so he could carry her knapsack for her.

Ingrid slipped it off and handed it to him.

"If someone questions us on the train," Karl said, "we claim we lost our tickets—no, they were stolen. Maybe we even go to the engineer early, before he finds us, and tell him our story then. Or we'll switch carriages en route. Most inspections start in the front of the train, so we'll start in the back and then move forward."

Ingrid glanced around the station with stiff motions. "Only if we can't find a decent hiding place."

Ingrid had always been good at hide-and-seek—inside Falcon Point manor and in the wooded hills that surrounded it. If they were found hiding on the train, they'd probably be kicked off. As long as they got out of Vienna, Karl didn't care much where they ended up, for now. They'd find their way eventually.

"Right, we'll hide," he said. "But if anything happens and we get separated—"

"We won't get separated."

"No." Karl steered Ingrid closer to their target train. The engine had just passed them. "But if something happens, you know what to do?"

Ingrid nodded. "I try to get to Istanbul and catch Frau Davies. Or I head for London. I'll take the tube to the Stockwell Station and ask at the church for Frau Davies or her sister."

Karl took her hand and pulled her along. Ingrid could make it on her own, but she didn't have to. They had each other. And Anna had Frau Davies. They'd all be reunited soon enough.

They approached the far side of the open-ended station. Only a few other passengers walked about. The train passing them picked up speed.

Ingrid glanced behind and gasped. "Look!"

Sauermann followed them, trying to cut them off.

"Run!" Karl pulled Ingrid along for a few steps, then she put on a burst of speed to keep up with him.

Sauermann chased them. "Stop!"

Karl glanced back long enough to see Sauermann withdraw a pistol. Sauermann was capable of shooting them—he'd shot their unarmed father in his own study, and it seemed he fully expected to get away with it. The train station was more public, so he might hold his fire, but none of the strangers in the station would help Karl or Ingrid. They had to get on that train.

They were so close. There—the caboose with a platform. Karl swung Ingrid forward. She caught the rail and pulled herself to safety. The train was gaining speed, but Karl could keep up a while longer. He swung Ingrid's bag to her, then his own. Without the bags, it would be easier to grab the rail, and Sauermann was still too far away to stop him.

Karl reached for the railing. His fingers brushed the metal but couldn't grip it. He stumbled a bit and lost a few feet.

"Come on, Karl!" Ingrid's voice shook with worry.

His lungs and legs ached, but he pushed himself and got close enough to try again.

Then Ingrid screamed.

Karl had been so focused on the caboose in front of him and Sauermann behind him that he hadn't noticed a rail official approaching from the other direction. Each stride brought them closer together.

"Karl!" Ingrid reached for him.

Karl lunged forward. He aimed for the rail, not for Ingrid's hand. She wasn't strong enough to pull him up. His fingers felt the tip of the railing and then they fell away, brushing his sister's hand.

He would have fallen—he'd overbalanced himself too much to avoid it after missing the rail—but the official barreled into him, grabbing him and hauling him from the track.

Ingrid's face was a mass of horror. She bent for a moment, then stood with the bags. She was going to come back for him.

"No, Ingrid! Stay there. Find Anna, and I'll find you both!" Karl yelled as loud as he could, and she stayed on the train. She put a hand over her mouth, and though he was too far away to see tears, he could see the convulsions as she sobbed. Part of him wished she wouldn't obey him, that she'd come back. He didn't want to send her on by herself.

And he didn't want to be left alone.

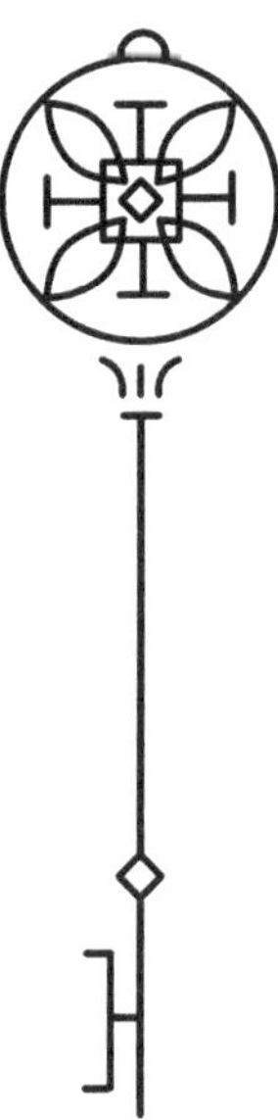

CHAPTER 9

The official holding Karl pushed him onto the platform. The middle-aged man might have a few gray hairs in his mustache, but he was strong. He shoved Karl toward Sauermann, who still had his pistol out and was breathing hard from the chase.

"Here's the criminal," the official said.

Criminal? Was that what Sauermann had told the station officials, that Karl was a criminal?

"We've handcuffs back in my office in the administration building," the official said.

Sauermann nodded. "Fetch them. I'll see he doesn't get away from us. He's not really the dangerous sort."

Karl fumed as the official hurried off, leaving him alone with Sauermann. "I might not be dangerous now, but I will never forget the crimes you've committed. As long as I have breath, I will seek justice—against the man who took my father and against the regime that took my country."

"How very much like your father you are, not just in looks." Sauermann gripped Karl's upper arm, and Karl tried unsuccessfully to wiggle away. Sauermann's mouth turned down in a sneer. "Stubborn. Unable to see the larger picture. It's because I know your father so well that I know I can't let you slip away. He would never stop either, not even in death. Tell me what he was scheming."

"He was trying to take us to freedom. That's all."

Sauermann huffed. "If he was only fleeing, I might have let him go, for old time's sake. But I've searched the manor. All his papers are gone. I don't think words can describe how valuable those are. Where are they?"

Ingrid and Anna had burned all Papa's papers, save the ones in Karl's left pocket, but he said nothing. If the papers were really that valuable, Karl didn't want to risk Sauermann's ire if he knew they'd been destroyed.

"And it seems the most valuable items are missing from Schloss die Punkt Falke. What happened to all the jewelry, the paintings, the artifacts?"

Again, Karl kept his silence.

Sauermann forced him toward the administration building with a grip so tight it burned. "With your father's death, I'm confident I can arrange to have myself appointed as legal guardian for you and your sisters. Cooperate with me and perhaps you can return to school. Life for you can become almost normal again."

"I won't cooperate with the man who murdered my father."

"Murder?" Sauermann made a tsk. "I didn't kill your father. Your father died in a tragic accident."

Karl met Sauermann's eyes. "You may convince everyone else of your lies, but you will never convince me."

"You've no proof, Karl. If you wish to reach your next birthday, you had better let it drop. If I perceive a threat, I will silence it."

Karl heard the promise in Sauermann's steely voice. If Karl spoke, Sauermann would silence him the same way he'd silenced his father.

"Where else have you spread your lies?" Sauermann's fingers pressed harder into Karl's upper arm. "To your sisters?"

Anna. Would she ever learn the truth? And Ingrid—all alone, vulnerable, and in even greater danger if Sauermann found out she knew what he'd done. "They're no threat to you." That was true enough. Ingrid knew of the murder, but Sauermann had influence with all the right people. If he called Leopold Lang a traitor to the Reich, the Reich would be uninterested in justice for the Lang children.

Herr Kaufmann approached. He carried neither a newspaper nor a recovered piece of luggage. Helping Karl and Ingrid had all been part of a deception.

Karl glared. "I knew you approved of the Anschluss, but I thought you still had a conscience. I trusted you—and you've turned me over to my father's killer."

Herr Kaufmann's mouth opened slightly. He turned to Sauermann. "You said the children ran away after their father suffered an accident. Is Herr Lang dead?"

Karl tried to shrug free of his captor. "Yes, because Herr Sauermann shot him."

Sauermann jerked on Karl's arm. "The boy is mistaken. His father is dead, yes, but not by my hand. In his grief, the boy misinterpreted events and concocted this illusion, then stole as many family treasures as he could carry and ran off with his sisters. I fear for the state of his mind. That's why I asked for your help in finding him."

Karl gritted his teeth. "Herr Sauermann murdered my father, and he'll murder me, too, if that's what it takes to keep my silence. He told the rail official that I'm a criminal, and he told you that I'm going mad. But I'm perfectly sane, Herr Kaufmann."

Herr Kaufmann looked between them. The skin above his eyebrows bunched in confusion, as if he didn't know whom to believe. Finally, he turned to Sauermann. "Perhaps you ought to tell me what really happened."

Sauermann forced Karl forward again. "I told you, grief has touched the boy's mind. He's dangerous and delusional."

"You know I'm sane, Herr Kaufmann." Karl turned back to meet his former teacher's eyes. "You remember when my mother died. I loved her just as much as my father, but I didn't go mad with grief for her. My grades slipped, but I didn't come up with delusions. You know me better than that."

Herr Kaufmann seemed to unfreeze. He quickly caught up to Sauermann. "I'm loyal to the Reich—you know that. I want to see all German people united and strong, but we can do that without stooping to ruthlessness. What happened to Herr Lang? The boy seemed perfectly sane last night and this morning. Why does he think you killed his father?"

Sauermann stopped and brought Karl around until they faced Herr Kaufmann. He no longer held Karl quite so firmly, as if trying to appear less threatening. "The boy was overcome with grief yesterday and ran away. His father's death was tragic and no doubt contributed to young Karl's mental instability, but Herr Lang's death did not come by my hand."

While Herr Kaufmann considered Sauermann's words, Karl shoved his whole body into Sauermann, pushing him off balance. Sauermann was bulky and tall, but he hadn't been expecting the full fury of a desperate seventeen-year-old. He tottered and stepped back to catch himself.

Karl ripped himself from Sauermann's grip and sprinted away.

"Karl!"

He looked back at Herr Kaufmann's pleading face and Sauermann's rage, then continued forward.

Whistles sounded from nearby trains.

Passengers stared as Karl raced past them.

Guards chased him.

What Karl needed was another train departure. He could jump on, just as Ingrid had. If only he'd caught that railing. Then they wouldn't have been separated. But Papa had told him time and time again not to dwell on what-ifs and if-onlys. They would never fix the present.

He'd kept ahead of Sauermann before, even carrying his bag and Ingrid's, so he was confident he could outrun Sauermann now, despite the man's longer legs. And Herr Kaufmann—Karl looked behind. Herr Kaufmann wasn't chasing him, but several soldiers were. And Sauermann had his pistol out again.

He'd shot Papa to keep him from leaving, to keep him from ever aiding the enemies of the Reich. He'd threatened to kill Karl to keep him from telling the truth. Karl believed he'd carry out that threat, but would he shoot on a public train platform? They were away from the crowds but not out of sight.

Bang.

Karl flinched as the pistol blast echoed through the station. He looked back to see if Sauermann had shot into the air as warning or if he'd aimed.

The pistol still pointed toward Karl.

It was a good thing running targets were so hard to hit.

CHAPTER 10

A TRAIN HUFFED TOWARD THE station, slowing in preparation to stop. Karl looked from the locomotive to the streets beyond the station. Which way to run? If he left the station, Sauermann could set up a checkpoint to catch him if he came back. And he'd have to come back because he couldn't stay in Vienna, and a train was the best way for him to escape.

He wanted a train that was leaving, not one that was arriving, but he could make this work. He darted closer to the oncoming train, still running as fast as he could. Maybe Sauermann wouldn't shoot at a train full of passengers. As the last carriage rumbled past, Karl turned, crossed the track behind the train, and started running again, catching the train with greater and greater ease as it slowed further and further.

The passengers would all detrain on the other side of the tracks, toward the platform. Karl ran between the rail lines. Before the train came to a stop, Karl jumped on. In the rush of passengers getting on and off, he might slip by unnoticed.

A swelling crowd appeared through the windows as the train chugged to the center of the station. Sauermann directed his men, organizing a search. No doubt they'd board the train when everyone disembarked.

Karl made his way toward the baggage car and grabbed the first hat box he saw. Inside was a women's hat, so he tried the next one. Good. Something different. He covered his blond hair in a brown homburg and hoped the owner wouldn't mind too terribly when he found his hat replaced with Karl's gray fedora. He kept his father's coat but added a black scarf that someone had left on an empty seat. He exited with the last of the passengers, several cars down from where Sauermann waited.

A guard spoke with a rail official as Karl walked past. "We'll need to board the train and search it before you can allow new passengers on."

Karl kept up with the crowd in front of him, then turned at the last moment toward the ticket counter. He glanced at the schedule. Where was that train going? He wanted to be on it, regardless of its destination. Salzburg. That seemed to be the next departure.

"The next train to Salzburg, please." He managed to get the words out without letting his voice shake.

A man with round glasses and mousy brown hair took some of Karl's precious money. "Boarding should begin in ten minutes."

Karl nodded and tucked his ticket into his pocket, next to his false passport. His real one was with Ingrid now. He supposed that was lucky, in a way. He'd get farther with the fake one.

Sauermann was still visible, ordering his men onto the train to search for Karl. They'd scrutinize everyone who boarded, at least from the platform. Karl took a tip learned from his sister and locked himself in a lavatory stall—one in the men's room. He'd wait out the search.

While he waited, he took inventory of his belongings. The clothes he wore, books and papers, and a very little bit of money. Then he took inventory of his options. Papa had told Karl to take care of his sisters. He'd done a poor job of that, but he'd helped them get away from Sauermann, away from the Reich. That was something. He could try to catch Anna before she made it to Istanbul, but she had help. He was more worried about Ingrid; he had no idea where she was headed.

He felt his father's notebook, full of information, still tucked into the pocket of his coat. He had enough money for a ticket to either Paris or Zurich but not both. One couldn't buy a ticket from Salzburg to Paris while France and Germany were at war, so it would have to be Zurich. Karl needed an ally, and his father's friend at the consulate sounded like a good option. He would have connections to other embassies, be able to issue travel visas and search for missing people. Taking the notebook to Zurich might help him find his sisters.

Another desire tugged at him—revenge. It was possible here in Vienna, with Sauermann nearby. Karl rubbed his sore arm where Sauermann had gripped him so tightly. He wanted that coldblooded murderer punished. Physical vengeance was unlikely when Sauermann was armed and Karl wasn't, and justice was unlikely when Sauermann had the regime on his side. Karl could stay and fight, but he was unlikely to win.

Was it cowardly to flee when he knew he couldn't win? He wanted to be courageous, like Papa. But sometimes courage wasn't about fighting. Sometimes courage was about letting go of what was most wanted for oneself and, instead, fulfilling one's duty. Maybe when it came to Sauermann, a far better revenge would be taking the book his father had sacrificed so much for to the enemies of the Reich. And so, for now, Karl would hide.

He waited until the stated boarding time, assuming it would be late because of Sauermann's search. Karl then left the men's room and walked back to the ticket counter. "Excuse me?"

"Yes?" the same man as before greeted him.

"The train that left about a half hour ago. Where was it headed?"

The man shrugged. "I'm not sure which train you mean. We've had recent departures for Venice, Belgrade, and Berlin."

That meant Ingrid could be headed several possible directions, and from those destinations, she could go anywhere. Would she try to follow Anna to Istanbul, or would she try to get to London more directly? The variety sealed his decision. He didn't have the money to chase Ingrid to Venice, Belgrade, and Berlin, so he would have to trust her to make it to London on her own.

Karl nodded his thanks and strode to the platform. He needed to be careful, but looking cautious would make him seem suspicious. He had to walk with purpose. He wished it were colder—then he could use the scarf to hide part of his face instead of using it simply to change the appearance of his coat.

Boarding passengers were bottlenecked through a single checkpoint, and Sauermann stood there watching. Karl wouldn't make it through. He went past it, keeping his distance. He would simply board from the other side, as he'd done before.

No one seemed to be watching him. He walked past the engine, then cut in front of it. A mechanic checked the wheels, but he didn't look up when Karl stepped around him. Passengers who had already boarded might see him from the windows, but if they pointed him out to a rail official, he had a ticket. He was safe if he could just keep away from Sauermann.

He climbed aboard and made his way to a third-class seat, one on an aisle, where he would be more difficult to see from the windows. He leaned back into the seat and pulled his hat low over his eyes. He wanted to keep an eye on the checkpoint, to watch Sauermann's every move, but someone might notice if he showed too much interest.

Exhaustion should have lulled him to sleep, but knowing Sauermann was out there looking for him kept him tense and alert. Finally, the train whistled, and he breathed a little easier. His problems weren't over, not by a long shot.

Sauermann probably had contacts in Salzburg, and they'd no doubt be looking for him. But they would have only a description. Maybe he could find shoe polish and change the color of his hair before the train's arrival.

He waited for the train to move forward, but it didn't. He tilted his hat up just a bit to see why their departure was delayed. The reason was instantly clear. Sauermann had boarded—they were checking the train again, starting in Karl's carriage.

CHAPTER 11

KARL SHIELDED HIS FACE WITH his hat, stood, and walked to the rear of the carriage.

"Stop!"

He recognized the voice, and he ignored it. Sauermann had shot at him in a mostly empty part of the station, but he wouldn't shoot him down in the middle of a full passenger train, not without verifying it was really him. Karl kept his stride steady until he left the carriage. Then he sprinted through the next one and the one after that. He slipped out the vestibule at the end of the car and huddled at the side of the train, away from the doorway.

He tried to calm his rapid breathing, tried to ease the panic still racing through his veins. Sauermann hadn't seen him leave, so he'd keep checking the carriages. Footsteps rushed past inside, barely audible over the sounds of the station. Karl crept along the train, low and close enough that he wouldn't be seen by passengers. After a few cars, he straightened so he wouldn't look suspicious. The mechanic near the engine was packing up his tools.

"Excuse me. Do you know the reason for the delay?"

The man squinted and put a hand to his ear. "What's that?"

Karl repeated his question.

The man shook his head. "Nothing on my end. Engine's in top shape."

Sauermann might hold the train until he found Karl. He could hide again and try another train, but too many people knew his face in Vienna. The longer he stayed, the greater the risk.

One of Sauermann's soldiers came around the train and spotted him.

Karl ducked behind the mechanic. "Don't shoot!"

The soldier didn't even have his weapon aimed, but ducking to the ground gave Karl access to the mechanic's toolbox. He grabbed something heavy and slipped it up his sleeve. He'd lost track of how many plans he'd thought up and failed at, but as long as another lay before him, he wasn't beaten.

"Stand up." The soldier issued his orders with a deep, throaty voice.

Alarm showed on the mechanic's face. He raised his hands and stepped farther from the train so he was no longer in the middle of the confrontation.

The soldier glanced at the mechanic. "Find *Sturmbannführer* Sauermann. Tell him I've found the criminal."

The mechanic moved more quickly than Karl would have thought the man's old limbs capable of.

Karl locked eyes with the soldier. His rifle was aimed now, at Karl.

"I'm not a criminal," Karl said.

The soldier's stance didn't soften. "I don't care what you are or aren't. I've orders not to let you leave on that train."

The tension mounted as they stood there waiting in the shadows of the train. Soon Sauermann came around the front of the engine with the mechanic trailing behind.

"Well done, *Rottenführer*. You may give the train permission to leave." Sauermann took out his pistol and pointed it at Karl, so even though the soldier slung his rifle over his back, Karl still had a firearm aimed at him from only a few feet away.

"Yes, sir." The soldier rushed off. The mechanic picked up his toolbox and left too. No doubt he didn't want to be involved in SS affairs.

Karl had edged away from the train during the transition. He wanted the passengers to see his form. Their eyes might keep Sauermann from doing anything rash because he seemed to prefer committing his murders in far-off manors with no witnesses.

Karl motioned to the weapon still in Sauermann's hand, though it was less noticeable than before. "Are you going to kill me now?"

"Maybe. Or maybe not, if you tell me what happened to your father's papers and all the treasures at Falcon Point."

Karl's mind caught on the last part of Sauermann's demand. "Which do you want more? Falcon Point or the knowledge my father had?"

Sauermann's lips pulled into a line. "What is best for the Reich has always been my first goal. But if your father couldn't see the Führer's vision, then perhaps he isn't worthy of an estate like Falcon Point. And if you don't cooperate, you'll deserve the same as him."

Papa would tell Karl that his life was worth more than the things they'd buried in the cellar. Karl could barter away the family's treasures, but he suspected

Sauermann would shoot him anyway. Karl wasn't ready to die. He had a mission: take Papa's papers where they could do the most harm to men like Sauermann. He had to play for time. "Passengers are at the windows. Would you kill me while they watch?"

Sauermann's smile sent a shiver down Karl's spine. "The last five cars are freight. No one will see anything while they're between us and the station, and they'll pass slowly enough that I'll have time to walk away before they're gone."

The train whistle blew, and soot swirled along the tracks. "They'll connect it with you. All your soldiers know you're looking for me. Herr Kaufmann, too, and the rail officials."

Sauermann frowned. "This is your last chance. Tell me where your father hid his things or die. No one will stop me. Those you've spoken with so far will be kept in line either through fear or loyalty. For everyone else, I'll spread a rumor that you and your father were gunned down by outsiders. Whom should I blame it on, Karl? British agents? Crazed Jews? Communists, perhaps? See how generous I can be—I'm willing to let you be remembered as victims, martyrs even. But we both know you're traitors."

Karl thought of his father's words as steam from the engine poured from the smokestack and the wheels squealed, moving forward. "Which is worse? Betraying your conscience or betraying your country?"

Sauermann sneered. For a moment, Karl thought he would shoot him then, while the air was thick with smoke and steam, but Sauermann seemed content to wait until the passenger cars passed.

"You're just like your father," Sauermann said.

Karl inched closer, to within an arm's length. Four cars had passed, and he wasn't sure how many cars with passengers remained. He didn't dare risk a glance in their direction. He let the wrench he'd taken from the mechanic slide into his hand. "If you kill me, will you at least leave my sisters alone? My father didn't share his secrets with them. They're too young. They didn't see you leaving the study. They didn't even see my father's body."

Sauermann shrugged. The smoke and steam made him seem like the dragon from the family story. "They could be useful alive, while they're minors, if I'm appointed their guardian and if they prove more cooperative than you and your father."

Would Sauermann use the girls to control Falcon Point and then kill them when they came of age? Anna and Ingrid had to be protected.

Rage burned through Karl's chest, and that anger helped him grip the wrench, bring it up, and propel it into Sauermann's head.

The pistol exploded, and Karl felt something tug at his hat.

Sauermann collapsed. Karl's hat tumbled to the ground with a hole through the upper crown. He didn't reach for it. Nor did he bend over Sauermann to see if the man was still conscious. He ran to the train and hopped on the running boards of the last car as it pulled from the station.

CHAPTER 12

When the train slowed on the approach to Salzburg, Karl jumped off. If Sauermann was alive, he would have found the train's destination and called or telegraphed the station. Security would likely check detraining passengers for someone of Karl's description. So while he planned to use the station, he took his time getting there. On his way, he stopped at a bakery for bread and at a butcher's shop for salami so he could make his own sandwiches. He needed to stretch his remaining money.

He hoped Anna and Ingrid were all right. Frau Davies would take care of Anna, but his youngest sister would worry and might feel as if she'd been abandoned. And Ingrid . . . The jewelry sewn into her coat was no doubt valuable enough to get her to England. Ingrid was capable, and she'd have the means, but she would be scared and alone, just like Karl was.

By the time Karl walked to the station, the train from Vienna had long since cleared out. Any sweep organized by Sauermann had given up and dispersed. He went to the ticket counter. "One third-class ticket to Zurich, please."

They checked his identity papers twice as he boarded, so perhaps Sauermann was alive still and directing the increased security. Regardless, no one suspected that Karl Eckerstorfer was really Karl Lang. When the train pulled from the station with no last-minute boarding from Nazi guards, he could finally breathe without feeling like his lungs were constricted.

He slept, he planned, and he mourned. Sorrow was a constant companion now. His parents were dead, and his sisters were lost. Or maybe he was lost. Regardless, the last few days had changed his life, changed him, and he had a feeling things would never be the same.

After arriving at Zurich and passing customs, he washed up as best he could in the train station's men's room, but there was little he could do about his unwashed clothing. He asked for directions to the British consulate. It was several kilometers away, but there were still a few hours of daylight left. He walked, both to stretch his legs and because he wasn't sure he had enough coins for the taxi fare.

He went inside the consulate and approached a stocky, middle-aged male clerk, who looked up at him with a hint of displeasure. "May I help you?"

"I'd like to see the defense attaché, please."

"Are you a British citizen?"

"No, sir." Karl had studied English, but his accent wasn't good enough to claim he was British even if he'd wanted to lie.

"Do you have an appointment?"

"No, sir."

The clerk removed his glasses and polished the lenses. "Mr. Cleary can't see every bedraggled refugee who comes across the border. If you wish a travel visa, I can provide the necessary paperwork for you to fill out. Our defense attaché is a very busy man. There's a war on, if you haven't noticed."

"That's why I wish to see him, sir. I have information that can help."

The clerk put on his glasses. "Hmm. And what might that be?"

Karl forced politeness into his voice. "If you would be so kind as to tell him that Leopold Lang has sent information for him, via his son, I think he'll agree to see me."

The clerk didn't look convinced, but he gestured for Karl to sit in one of the scattered wooden chairs.

Karl complied. The clerk continued working for a minute or two, then slipped down a hallway. The room he'd been left in reminded Karl of Falcon Point a little. The same quality in the wood paneling, the same type of art hanging on the walls, but the atmosphere was far less welcoming.

After a few minutes, the clerk returned. "I'll take you to see Mr. Cleary now."

Mr. Cleary proved to be a tall man with a trim, red-tinted mustache. "Ah, you look every bit the son of Leopold Lang. Those blue eyes. Quite distinctive. How is your father?" Mr. Cleary motioned to a chair across from his sprawling mahogany desk.

Karl sat. And then he was blunt. "He's dead, sir. Killed by an old friend who used to work with him."

The man looked out the window. He seemed sad, so perhaps he had known Karl's father well enough to be a friend. "I'm sorry to hear that."

"You knew him well?"

Mr. Cleary leaned back in his seat. "Well enough to appreciate his talents . . . and his integrity. Nothing I hear from Germany surprises me anymore, but he'll be missed. He wasn't working for me, but he hinted that he was not particularly enthusiastic about the Nazi regime."

"No, sir. He didn't approve of Hitler and preferred that Austria keep its independence." Papa's last words echoed through Karl's head. *Red-white-red until we're dead.*

"And he gave you my name?"

Karl nodded. "Your position at the consulate. He wanted you to have this." He pulled out the spiral-bound memorandum book his father had given him. He'd looked through it on the train, but he couldn't read it. "I believe it's in some type of code."

Mr. Cleary took the notebook and leafed through the pages. "It may take a few days, but I'm sure we'll find out what he wanted to tell us. He hinted that he might send something like this, so I know where to start. You have sisters, don't you?"

"Yes."

"Are they in Zurich? When your father was here last, he set up an account with Vontobel. I imagine he left enough for all of you to enroll in the best sort of schools."

"My sisters and I were separated. I believe Anna is making her way to London. Ingrid will try to make her way there too, but she's all alone, and she's only fifteen."

Mr. Cleary frowned. "Do you know which route she'll take?"

"No, sir. I thought you might be able to send a message to the other consulates to make sure they help her if she comes to them. If I can get access to my father's account, I'd be happy to reimburse the consulate for any expenses."

"It's a numbered account, I imagine. Do you have the number?"

Karl shook his head. Papa hadn't left any information about numbered accounts. The money might as well be on the opposite side of the globe for all the good it would do him.

"No matter. I'll do what I can to help. But your sister would have to come to a British consulate or embassy. Will she seek us out?"

"I don't know. She'll have to eventually, won't she, to get an entry visa?"

Mr. Cleary nodded. "I can make sure she's approved when she requests it. And for you? Is England where you would like to go, for now?"

Karl leaned forward. "Yes. I'd like to join your army, sir, and fight against the Nazis." On his most recent train ride, Karl had thought long and hard about his next step. He was ready to be a soldier. The last few days had made several things clear: he wasn't young enough to count on mercy from anyone, and he was capable of overcoming challenges. It was time to fight against the Reich. He was also out of money, but the army would clothe, feed, and shelter him. He assumed he'd be sent to England for training, and he could find his sisters from there, then help support them.

"How old are you?"

"Almost eighteen, sir."

Mr. Cleary frowned. "Your father mentioned more than once how precious his children were to him. I can't very well repay him for sending me his secrets by letting his son join the army while underage. I would, however, be happy to help you travel to England. Something tells me this war will last long enough for you to get into it, but I'll not help you do it while you're but seventeen."

Karl felt his face heat. "I think I've proven myself as an adult." But had he? He'd delivered his father's secrets, but he hadn't kept track of either of his sisters. He'd gotten them away from Sauermann, but he'd lost them. "Please, sir, allow me to fight. I want to help defeat the Nazis. And I need to provide for my sisters when I find them."

"If you find them." The words were soft, and Karl wondered if Mr. Cleary hadn't meant for him to hear. But that fear was strong. What if he never found Anna? What if he never found Ingrid?

Mr. Cleary opened a desk drawer and handed Karl some money. "It's getting late, and I have plans I can't rearrange. Get some food, get a room for the night, and come back to see me tomorrow. I'll make sure your visa is approved, and I'll pay for your passage. It's the least I can do for Leopold Lang's son."

"I'd prefer to be a soldier, not a refugee."

Mr. Cleary stood. "I'm sure you'll be a valiant soldier when the time comes, but you'll have to wait until you've had a birthday."

CHAPTER 13

KARL KNEW HE SHOULD BE grateful to Mr. Cleary. The defense attaché's respect for Karl's father was comforting, and he'd given Karl a generous amount of francs. But frustration nibbled at him. Why couldn't he join the army now? He was just as large as the average eighteen-year-old, probably better educated, and he had a burning hatred for the Nazis. What did a few months of age matter?

From the consulate, he went to a secondhand clothing store. He wanted to be in uniform soon, but in the meantime, he needed more than one pair of trousers, more than one shirt, more than one pair of socks and drawers. He made a few purchases and went to a dimly lit, unornate hotel that didn't cost him too much. Exhaustion pulled at him—he almost went right to sleep but dragged himself to the shared bathroom down the hall instead. While he washed away all the grime from traveling and running, he realized he was hungry, so he would have to go out again.

The new-to-him trousers he pulled on were a little long. Maybe he'd grow taller and they'd fit him better in a few months. The cuff of his newly purchased shirt was worn, but his father's coat hid it, even if it was a little loose around the shoulders. He glanced in the mirror. He was the same, and yet, he was different too. No clothing tailored to his frame, no carefree smile. Just grief and regret and an uncertain future.

He didn't look like an heir of Falcon Point, not any longer.

He found a café a few streets from the hotel. It was warm, and the dish of raclette reminded him of meals with his father after a long day of skiing. He ate slowly, thoughtfully, wondering what he could do for the next six months until he was old enough to enlist. He took out Karl Eckerstorfer's passport. He was a little older than Karl Lang. Five months until he joined the army.

The passport was still in his hand when a feminine voice caught Karl's attention. "Excuse me."

He looked up to see a young woman with glossy brown hair and red lips standing near his table. She had a folded newspaper tucked under her arm and held a pencil between her fingers. She lifted the pencil, showing a broken tip. "You don't happen to have a spare pen or pencil you might lend me for a few minutes, do you?"

Karl reached into his coat pocket and pulled out his father's penknife. "I don't have any writing utensils, but I could sharpen that for you."

"Thank you." She handed over the pencil, slid into the chair across from him, and set her newspaper on the table, open to the crossword puzzle. "I've only three more clues to solve."

He concentrated on sharpening the pencil, shaving the bits of wood onto a spare napkin. When he finished, he handed it back to her.

"Thank you." She took the pencil but didn't stand.

Karl had attended an all-boys school, so he wasn't used to making conversation with beautiful young women. And she was beautiful, even with the small lipstick smear in the upper left corner of her mouth. "Would you like me to order something for you?" That was what Frau Davies had told him to do in situations like this, wasn't it? All her lessons on decorum and etiquette seemed far in the past, part of a different life.

She smiled. "That's very kind, but no thank you. I've already had coffee and *biberli*, and soon, I'll be off to a dreadfully dull supper. My father and I are just waiting for my mother to finish her shopping." She nodded toward a middle-aged man who sat reading a newspaper a few tables away.

"He didn't have a spare pencil?" Karl didn't think Sauermann had contacts in Zurich, but after being betrayed by Herr Kaufmann, suspicion lingered. The girl didn't look like a spy and nor did her father, but competent agents would look innocent.

She held up the pencil Karl had just sharpened. "I already borrowed it."

Her German was good, but some of her words sounded off. "Are you Swiss?" Maybe she was from a French- or Italian-speaking canton.

She shook her head. "American. My father works at the consulate. You?"

Karl hesitated. "I don't have a country, not currently."

Her animated lips moved into a sort of frown, making a line between her mouth and her cheek. "Did you just come from Germany?" she asked.

Karl nodded. "I'm Austrian."

"I've never been to Austria. I'm Millie, by the way. Millie Stevens."

"I'm Karl." He needed to give a last name but couldn't decide on Lang or Eckerstorfer. She seemed to be waiting for more, so he rushed on. "And I've never been to America, but it's a pleasure to meet you, Miss Stevens."

"It's a pleasure to meet you—and your penknife—Mr. Karl."

"Just Karl will do." His eyes caught his fake passport. "Karl Eckerstorfer." Strange, how telling Millie his phony name felt wrong. Karl could suspect everyone he met of harboring Nazi sympathies, or he could take a risk and trust and hope that someday he wouldn't be alone. He'd been foolish to trust Herr Kaufmann, but Millie was just an ordinary young woman working out the crossword puzzle. Papa had always loved those, flown through them. Sorrow hit Karl again, hard.

Millie tapped the newspaper with an elegant, newsprint-smudged finger. "Well, Mr. Eckerstorfer, I think this clue is wrong."

"Is it?" Karl pushed his grief to the side and embraced the risk and the opportunity that came with it. He tried to get a better look at the crossword puzzle. The words were English, but since it was upside down, he couldn't read it properly.

"The answer is *melancholy*, but the clue says *somber*. I think it should have read *the young man sitting across the café*." She switched to English for the clues and answers and looked to see if he followed. She glanced at the paper again. "No, that wouldn't work, because *mysterious* would fit in the same spot—and both would be suitable descriptions."

No one had ever called him mysterious before, nor had he been accused of being melancholy, other than those months after his mother had died.

Millie's eyes went back to the paper. "Do you know what *wiener hofoper* might refer to?"

"It's an opera house in Vienna. Is that one of the clues?"

Millie nodded. "*Opera house* is too long, but *theater* would . . . No, that doesn't work either. The *r* is in the wrong place."

"Try the British spelling."

She scribbled it in with an approving nod. Then she looked up at him and sobered. "Why did solving that clue make you seem even gloomier than before?"

"Did it?" He hadn't thought his feelings were quite so obvious.

"It certainly seemed to. But perhaps I'm looking for puzzles where none exist. Or maybe you're frowning because I'm interrupting your meal, and your food is getting cold."

He smiled without meaning to. "No, I'm glad you broke your pencil and needed it sharpened." Even if Millie was a stranger, it was nice not to feel so alone. "My parents met at the Court Opera House. State Opera House now. One of those happy accidents that no one could have planned."

"If that's how your parents met, why does it make you sad?"

Karl thought for a moment, deciding how much to say. "I miss them."

"Are they still in Austria?"

Karl swallowed. Trusted the sincerity on Millie's face. "They're dead. And Papa's death was recent."

Her eyes widened. "I'm so sorry. I never would have teased you about being melancholy if I'd known the reason."

Karl sighed. He was in Switzerland now, where the Nazis had no power, so he could say whatever he wanted. "You didn't do anything wrong, just caught me in a mood, I guess. I've lost my home, my father, and my sisters all within the last few days. So I thought I would join the British army because it might help me find my sisters, and it might help me get revenge on the Nazis. They've taken everything from me."

Millie studied him from across the table. "I've seen a lot of refugees these last few years. A lot of them broken, frightened, beaten. Your spirit and your courage seem to be intact, so the Nazis haven't taken everything from you. You still have those."

"Courage isn't doing me much good right now. A man at the British consulate told me I was too young to join their army." Karl leaned back in his chair and folded his arms. "Too young by five months."

"Is that when you turn eighteen?"

"Something like that." He doubted Mr. Cleary knew his real birthday, so he could use the one from the Eckerstorfer passport. It still lay on the tabletop.

"May I see them?" She reached for his papers.

Trust or caution? He'd already shown the passport to countless Nazis, and it wasn't his real name anyway. What harm could come from showing it to the daughter of an American diplomat? He handed it over.

"I imagine you could get into the Royal Navy at age seventeen." Millie looked between him and his passport.

"I've no parent to give consent."

"That might not matter, depending on whom you speak with. Most recruiting officers will take your word for it and not bother to check for proof." Millie handed his papers back to him, brushing his skin in the process. A pleasant tremor ran along the back of his hand, but that was silly. He'd only just met her. Equally silly was how much he wanted to wipe at her smeared lipstick—not because it bothered him but because he found the shape of her mouth fascinating.

Millie continued. "I turned eighteen a few months ago. Nothing really changed. I didn't wake up that morning feeling any more like an adult." She nodded at his passport. "July wouldn't be so hard to change into January. It's an easy puzzle to solve, just a matter of changing a seven into a one."

He opened the passport to where it listed 23/7/1922. If he could somehow remove the ink forming lines at the top and center of the seven . . . Mr. Cleary knew he wasn't eighteen yet, but he doubted Mr. Cleary was in charge of accepting and rejecting refugees who volunteered for the army. Navy or army? If his passport said he'd already turned eighteen, he could have his choice.

"If you could choose between joining the navy or joining the army, which would you pick?" he asked.

Millie glanced at her father. "Navy, because that's what Daddy did in 1917. But he joined the American Navy, not the Royal Navy."

Papa had done codes. That was the type of work needed in a navy or in an army. Karl glanced at his passport again. Perhaps he could scratch some of the ink off with his penknife or a razor, then fill it in with paper pulp.

Millie leaned forward. "I can help, if you like."

"Have you ever done it before?"

She gave a smile instead of an answer. She used her pencil to write something in the newspaper's margin, then tore it off. "That's my address. I think we have everything we might need there. You could come by tomorrow for breakfast, and then we'll work on making you eighteen."

He took the address. He didn't know Zurich, didn't know what part of the city it was. He could probably change a seven to a one on his own, but he caught Millie's eyes. Brown and warm with a hint of mischief. And something else that he couldn't quite pinpoint. They were the type of eyes he wanted to see again. They reminded him of what things had been like before, back when he wasn't running for his life, back when everything hadn't seemed so hopeless, back when he'd been happy.

Only an hour before, he'd thought happiness had vanished forever. Karl had left on one train. Happiness had left on another. But maybe that wasn't the case—maybe his future held something other than grief. What had Papa told him the night before he'd died? Something about life being full of hardships and surprises. Sauermann had provided plenty of hardships. Millie, currently tapping her pencil against the last clue of the crossword puzzle, seemed a surprise of the best sort. One of those happy accidents no one could have planned.

Papa had also talked about plans that night, and it was time for Karl to make some. Plan the first—Karl would join the Royal Navy, find his sisters, and get to know Millie a little better. Maybe a lot better.

CHAPTER 14

Present Day

GUNNAR SAUERMANN TYPED THE LATEST projections into the sleek laptop that rested on the antique library table. The new and the old. The combination of the two was about to make him a very wealthy man. The upcoming payment from the railway for easement rights along the edge of the property would provide the funds needed to convert Falcon Point into a luxury resort. He'd have money, prestige, and independence. Everything he had ever dreamed of was finally within reach.

In today's political environment he could hardly admit that his good fortune had arisen from his grandfather's association with the Nazis during World War II, but that didn't change the fact. While estates all over Europe were being returned to their rightful owners, his grandfather had maintained possession of Falcon Point as trustee. That role had fallen to Gunnar upon his own father's death ten years earlier.

Barring any claim from the Lang family descendants in the next fifteen years, the terms of the Lang Trust would allow Gunnar to take ownership. His meeting today would ensure that he would live quite comfortably regardless.

A knock sounded on the library door.

"Herr Wagner to see you, sir," his butler, Henning, announced.

"Yes, yes, of course." Gunnar stood and studied the new arrival. Lean, with dark hair, gray at the temples, Herr Wagner appeared to be within striking distance of his own fifty-two years.

"Thank you for agreeing to meet me here." Gunnar shook Herr Wagner's hand. "As you can imagine, my schedule has been quite full since the renovations on Falcon Point began."

"Of course."

"Please sit." Gunnar motioned at the chair across from him and reclaimed his seat. "Do you have the final paperwork for me?"

"I do; however, we have a glitch with the money transfer."

A sense of dread rose within him. "What kind of glitch?"

"When we filed our permits with the building authority, we learned that an old protest was on record over the ownership of Falcon Point."

"I don't know anything about a protest."

"I took the liberty of bringing you a copy." Herr Wagner produced a paper from his briefcase and slid it across the table to Gunnar. "The letter states a duplicate was mailed here to this estate. I'm afraid we're missing the second page, but the first provides sufficient information to conduct an investigation."

A handwritten letter dated August 23, 1946. Though Gunnar hadn't ever seen this particular letter, he recognized the handwriting as well as the name in the introduction. Ingrid Lang Hendriks. One of the heirs to Falcon Point.

Gunnar skimmed the contents. In it, Ingrid claimed Falcon Point belonged to her and her two siblings, Anna and Karl Lang. He read the bottom line, and his hands tightened on the page.

> *I sent a copy of this letter to Falcon Point; however, you should be aware that the Nazi who shot and killed my father was*

The page ended before the killer was named, but Gunnar suspected the name would be one from his family tree. If that second page was found, the trust would be dissolved, and he would lose everything. Everything he had, everything he'd promised his wife, everything his father and grandfather had entrusted to him, would be gone.

"As you can see, Frau Hendriks has made a claim to this estate. We cannot release the easement money until we are certain this issue has been resolved," Herr Wagner said.

"You can't be serious. I am the trustee for the Lang family estate." Gunnar dropped the letter onto the table. "Besides, this letter is dated almost eighty years ago."

"That doesn't change the facts. According to land records, this property is still owned by the Lang family. If there are living heirs to this estate, my company is honor bound to find them."

"I can save you a great deal of time," Gunnar said. "The last owners of this estate were Leopold and Liselotte Lang. She died before the war, and he died in 1940, which is why this trust was created."

"This letter indicates there were three children."

"That's correct. All three of them disappeared after their father's death. All indications are that Karl and Anna died during the war."

"And Ingrid?" Herr Wagner asked. "Clearly, she survived."

"Yes. From what I understand, my grandfather tried to contact her after the war but was unable to find her. In our searches since that time, we have no evidence that she is still living or had any children," Gunnar lied.

"I appreciate this additional information. I will pass it along to our investigator."

A new wave of desperation rose within him. "Your investigator?"

"That's right. He will verify the information you have given me. If indeed there are no living heirs, the monies for the easement will be paid to the trust."

"How long do you anticipate this investigation will take?"

"A few weeks." Herr Wagner stood. "I assure you, we want this matter settled as quickly as you do. We are scheduled to begin the tunnel in front of the lake this time next month."

"The new train line will certainly benefit us all."

"That it will."

The train glided slowly to a halt at Salzburg Central Station just inside the Austrian border. Anna Cavendish watched idly from her window in business class while passengers disembarked and queued for luggage.

Prickles of anticipation swirled inside her. Within an hour, she would reach Linz, where a driver would collect, then transport her to Falcon Point.

She rubbed her finger along the edge of the snapshot in her lap. The black-and-white photo had been taken a few years before the war, when Granny had been a small child. Anna had pried off the back of the tarnished silver frame before she'd left London to bring the picture with her on this momentous trip.

The photo's yellowed condition had worried her. To assure the old black-and-white's safety, she had scanned both sides to preserve her grandmother's one tangible connection to her past, then returned the yellowed original to its frame and packed it carefully inside her luggage, keeping the copy inside her purse. Already, she had dog-eared the new print with her constant rubbing.

She shifted in her seat, unable to find a comfortable position.

Today, the photo returned to Falcon Point without its mistress. A sentimental journey—one which took only a few hours in comparison to the lengthy escape the original Anna had endured to reach Great Britain. If only Granny had lived to see this day, a day she had longed for all her life.

Anna blinked away the sudden sting of moisture in her eyes as memories of her grandmother flooded her. Granny had spoken of her home and told a wonderful story each night about an Austrian princess when she had tucked Anna into bed.

Movement outside the train window distracted Anna from her musings as new passengers climbed aboard, stowed their luggage, and settled into their seats. A few minutes later, the high-speed locomotive pulled out of the station and headed for Linz, her final destination.

As the train picked up speed and passed thickly forested mountains covered in black pine, her thoughts spun back three weeks to when her employer, Genskal, an international architectural and interior design firm, had posted hospitality design openings for a four-season resort in Austria.

Anna had taken one look at Genskal's memo with the attached picture, a stunning mansion—the same one in Granny's black-and-white photo—and had stared in disbelief. Genskal's project was Granny's former home. Contrary to what her family had always believed, Granny was Austrian—not German. No wonder they had never found her records.

Shortly after Granny had arrived in England, she had been sent to a girl's academy in the country, far from the German bombs that had landed on her London flat.

Almost giddy at her discovery, Anna had filled out Genskal's application for the hospitality job. Her chance of selection was a long shot, but she had applied anyway. How could she not when the chance to discover Granny's early life had presented itself?

A week later, Anna had received Genskal's congratulatory email for her selection on the Falcon Point resort team. She'd been absolutely gobsmacked. Even though she had the right credentials, she lacked field experience for a project of such magnitude.

Why she, a junior designer at Genskal, had been chosen for such an ambitious venture, she had no idea, but she refused to question her good fortune. Too much depended on the outcome. Now she intended to find out about Granny's family—if records still existed.

The only hiccup in her coup was Beckett Campbell. Anna's heart had filled with dismay when she'd heard, via office gossip, that Beckett, the company's decorated architect, was Falcon Point's project manager. She and Beckett went way back. But even her ex-boyfriend's presence at the future resort couldn't deter her. She doubted much could.

If Beckett made life difficult, she would bear it because nothing and no one were going to keep her from this job. This was the first opportunity Anna had been given to find her grandmother's people—if any had survived the war.

Anna uncrossed her legs as the Alpine landscape outside her window gave way to gentler peaked hills broken by occasional meadows and farmland. She checked her watch as the train began to slow, and the buildings of Linz, the capital of Upper Austria, encompassed both sides of the tracks.

The train halted at Central Station, and she put away her photo. HR had informed her a driver would pick her up. She imagined a man in uniform, with a dark hat and a sign bearing her name, standing outside the terminal when she disembarked.

Nothing was further from her reality.

She hadn't expected Beckett, but there he was, waiting on the platform, his mouth pressed together in a horizontal line as he scanned the disembarking passengers. She hadn't laid eyes on him in four years, but she would have known him anywhere. Her throat tightened as Anna studied the man she had once thought she would marry.

Beckett held his hat, displaying thick brown hair, a square jaw, and an aquiline nose. Several women passed him and turned back to stare. He ignored them, his concentration solely on the travelers leaving the train.

He was a handsome man, quite devastating when he remembered to smile. His eyes held that glint of determination she remembered of old but looked greener today than blue. He glanced down the line of windows and pinned her with his stare.

Half wishing she could go on to Vienna, she rose shakily from her seat to collect her luggage at the back of the car. Her heart battered her ribs when she went down the steps, rolling her suitcases in front of her to provide a physical barrier between herself and Beckett Campbell.

Beckett came forward, then stopped a dozen feet away to take her in. She halted as well, swallowed, and attempted a calm she did not possess. The sharp spring breeze ruffled his hair. He had filled out, not running to fat but looking as though he spent a good deal of time at the gym pumping iron.

"Hello, Anna." He did not smile in greeting.

"I wasn't expecting you; I was told a driver would pick me up." It was abominably rude, and she blushed when the unplanned words tumbled out of her mouth unchecked.

"I gave him the afternoon off and came instead. I hope you don't mind." Beckett didn't appear the least offended. He relieved her of her suitcases and tilted his head in the direction of the car park. "Right this way."

She didn't exactly walk beside him across the road to his car but lagged behind until she reached the dark-blue BMW. He opened the passenger door for her, then loaded her luggage in the boot. Climbing behind the wheel, he fired up the engine and flashed a smile in her direction. Tingles broke out all over her arms. She glanced away.

"Hungry?" he asked.

"Not especially." She fiddled with the clasp on her handbag.

Beckett set the hand brake and let the engine idle. "Lass, I picked you up on purpose. Things need saying between us. You must know I specifically requested you on this team."

Beckett rarely responded with his native Scots; it was a rare show of emotion when he did.

"Why?" She reached inside her handbag and drew out Granny's photo to remind her why she had applied.

He tapped the steering wheel. "Because things ended badly between us, and I wanted . . ."

Her chest tightened. If Beckett believed making a grand gesture by offering her this job would eradicate the guilt he carried for his past behavior, he was utterly mad.

He raked a hand through his hair and swore under his breath. "I don't want things awkward on this team."

"You needn't worry. What was between us is ancient history."

His eyes swept over her. "I haven't forgotten a thing. It seems like only yesterday." He appeared as though he was going to say more, but his eyes dropped to the black-and-white photo in her hands. "What's that you have there?"

"What?" She glanced down at her lap. "Oh, just a picture."

"It looks old."

"The original is quite old. This is a copy."

"Care to tell me about it? It must be important if you brought it all this way."

Glad to speak of other things, she grasped the lifeline he had thrown her. "I suppose it is. My grandmother's family once lived at Falcon Point. She was born on the estate."

"How extraordinary."

"Granny was quite young when the Nazis took control of Austria. As far as I know, all she had left of her family was this picture. Granny was never sure where she was from, which made it impossible to find out if any of her family had survived the war. When I saw Falcon Point on Genskal's memo, you can only imagine my feelings. I hope to find out more about her people while I'm here."

"Falcon Point has an entire room dedicated to the history of the house. The lead designer, Tanja Mueller, has set up our work stations there. Perhaps you can research the property's historical documents after hours to find any mention of your family."

Anna's heart leapt inside her. "Thank you. I will."

He put the car in gear and started up the road, heading toward the Nibelungenbrücke Bridge. In silence.

Anna pretended a fascination outside her window as they crossed the Danube while she overtly studied his reflection.

Beckett always had an ulterior motive. He wanted something from her; she was almost certain of it. Why else would he have requested her for this team? She smelled a rat. And because it was Beckett, she planned to keep a wary distance.

Anna's hair was longer than Beckett remembered, the thick, shiny waterfall now reaching halfway down her back. He itched to touch the silky brown strands as he had once before. But Anna had set up barricades—castle-wall high—and he had no idea how to scale her battlements.

Four years melted away as though no time had passed, her presence as intoxicating as ever. When he had reviewed her application and requested her on the team, he had wondered if the old attraction between them had died. He needn't have worried. The air fairly crackled between them.

He had purposely requested that his name as project manager on the four-season resort not appear on documents until after Anna had signed her contract. But between then and now, someone had shared the news. Her reaction at the train station was not one of surprise so much as of dismay. He supposed he deserved it.

The silence between them hung thick and awkward in the air. Never one to equivocate, he addressed the issue at hand. "You knew I was on the team, yet you accepted the offer. Why?"

She lifted her chin. "Any designer would give their eye teeth to be part this project. Don't get bigheaded, but your reputation precedes you. Working on Beckett Campbell's team is a feather in any designer's cap and a great addition to my portfolio."

Okay, so she wasn't openly hostile, but she'd certainly let him know her decision had nothing to do with their past.

Some egos needed stroking; good thing his didn't. Hard work had gotten him where he was. His talent and willingness to put in the time allowed him to achieve what he'd accomplished in so short a career. But he wasn't buying her twaddle about being on his team.

"Have you visited Austria before?" He lapsed to idle chitchat to draw her out.

"No." She didn't elaborate but crossed her legs and stared out the passenger window.

Internally, he chuckled. Anna was not going to give an inch. This could be fun.

"Did you attend Lady Tilington's spring fling?"

"Yes."

"I'm surprised she asked you."

Anna turned a delightful pink but did not comment.

Lady T disliked Anna for upstaging her unfortunate daughters at their debutante ball. She only tolerated Anna because of her father's title. His and Anna's families inhabited the same social circle, aristocrats all. Personally, Beckett found the endless string of who's who events a dead bore and opted out whenever possible.

He let the silence lengthen, tempted beyond belief to pull the car onto the nearest verge and level with her then and there. But that wasn't the way to win Anna back.

"Are you attending RCA's tribute to Professor Billington?" He and Anna had attended the Royal College of Arts, where Professor Billington's retirement ceremony would be held.

"Yes."

"Care to fly out together?"

Anna darted a look at him, then fiddled with the clasp on her purse. "I hardly know."

She was so ill at ease, he gave up teasing her.

How foolish to believe all he and Anna needed was a bit of time together and things would go back to the way they once were.

All his life, he'd played a long game to achieve what mattered most. He had eighteen months to prove himself to Anna. If he failed—och. He couldn't fail. Too much hung in the balance.

CHAPTER 15

Anna kept her eyes forward and her focus on the scenery outside the windscreen. Unfortunately, her body, the traitorous thing, prickled with awareness, like radio waves homing in on Beckett's station. Why had he collected her?

She stared out the window at the dark-purple columbine, trumpet gentians, and hawksbeard in the grassy meadows but was too distracted to appreciate their natural beauty. The road twisted and curved, climbing ever higher into thick forest broken by an occasional pasture. The mountains that enfolded both sides of the motorway were not the barren-tipped Alps of southern Austria but were less steeply proportioned, opening here and there to the occasional turquoise lake.

She sucked in as the car drove over a rise. Below stood a spire-topped church on a spit of land surrounded on three sides by water.

"A bonnie place," Beckett said, breaking the silence and slowing the vehicle so she could get a better look.

"I love the alpine forests near Salzburg, but this is lovely too. Is the countryside around Falcon Point similar?"

"The mountains are a wee bit taller and better for skiing, but the loch is similar in color."

"And the manor?"

"It needs a good hospitality designer." He winked at her, then asked, "Anna, lass, will you be able to work with me?"

"If you are afraid I'll create a scene, I assure you I am a professional. What was between us is long over."

"Good."

But he frowned at the road and didn't look as though he appreciated her response in the least.

Beckett said no more, keeping his attention entirely on the roadway until they went through a tunnel and entered another small valley. The mountains were taller here and more rugged, and another picturesque lake filled the basin floor. A church, or kirche, the small chapels she had read about, adorned the village with its pointed spire.

A great deal of construction appeared in progress, and the two-lane road merged into a single gravel lane. Beckett braked, and the car stopped in front of a flashing red light.

"This light takes a while. Railroad construction has made a mess of things." Beckett nodded to a village on the far side of the lake whose shops and eateries were situated on the water's edge. "It was too expensive for the Austrian transit system to put a station in Gildenstatt. So they bought up the few remaining homes of an old hamlet on the near side of the lake and are in the process of constructing a train station and a car park not ten minutes from the resort entrance."

"I'm sure the resort will profit from that," Anna said.

"Aye." Beckett made a sweeping motion toward the peaks above Falcon Point. "That's one of the ski runs. The estate also boasts a natural hot spring and small loch at the top of the mountain not far from where they are putting in the runs."

Anna leaned forward in her seat to get a better look. Heavy equipment on the slope had knocked down a vast swath of trees. "I had no idea Falcon Point had so many natural resources."

Beckett gave her a genuine smile; it began with an almost reluctant tugging of lips that warmed his eyes and skittered her heart. Anna rubbed Granny's picture feverishly and glanced away.

"A number of venues on the estate will appeal to a wide range of holiday-makers. It's illegal to tear down the preexisting goatherd huts on the hillsides, so we are transforming them into self-catering cottages. We've also added a number of reproductions to increase the amount of rentals."

"Aren't the huts nationally protected landmarks like they are in Switzerland?"

"Only their exteriors. Our general contractor is in the process of digging basements for sleeping quarters and converting the ground level into kitchen/lounge combos."

Once again, Beckett's creativity had transformed what one might term an eyesore into a trendy source of profit.

The red light continued to flash as the slow-moving grading equipment made its way up the single-lane road.

"Our only real hindrance on the project is Gunnar and Petra Sauermann," he continued. "Herr Sauermann is a third-generation trustee for the estate and behaves as though the place belongs to him."

"Didn't the Sauermanns initiate the resort build?"

"Aye."

"Then why would they cause issues? That seems a little contradictory."

The construction light changed, and Beckett let his foot off the brake and pressed down the accelerator. "Some people are born agitators."

Beckett steered around the southern tip of the lake, approached a pair of pillars, and turned onto a narrow drive that climbed the hillside in a series of zigzags to its zenith.

"We're working on a new entrance closer to the train station that will bypass this narrow road altogether," Beckett told her.

And provide fewer accidents and lower insurance premiums, no doubt.

With Granny's photo clutched tightly in her hand, Anna squinted, trying to see through the screen of shrubbery as the car reached the summit. The lane swung wide, and the trees thinned as Falcon Point in all its majesty came into view.

Well-manicured lawns stretched out before a three-story mansion of pale limestone capped with a series of pointed turrets and a peaked slate roof. The manor was a perfect blend of French Renaissance chateau and baronial architecture.

Warmth enveloped Anna and filled her with a sense of homecoming unlike that of the English estate she had grown up on. She hugged the sensation to herself with the special knowledge that Granny had lived in this beautiful place. For the first time since Granny's passing, Anna felt tethered to something solid and warm.

"It's so much lovelier than I imagined," she whispered after she could speak.

"Aye. 'Tis," Beckett agreed, his voice rumbling with obvious satisfaction. "When we finish the conversion, this will be one of the premier resorts in Austria."

If not Europe. Anna's imagination soared, and she couldn't wait to see the blueprints for what Beckett had planned.

Beckett retrieved Anna's suitcases from the boot and carried them up the steps to the porch, where she waited. The large door stood ajar, and raised voices carried outside to where he and Anna stood.

The words were in German, and Beckett had a fairly good idea of who spoke them. Gunnar and Petra Sauermann should have vacated the premises last week, but the trustee of Falcon Point and his wife had dragged their heels until Beckett had entirely lost patience with them. Early this morning, he had ordered Rudolph Gruber, the general contractor over the project, to start demolition on the bedroom wing with or without the Sauermanns in residence.

Sauermann had insisted that he had a right to remain on site even though area building codes and Genskal's contract stipulated that nonessential personnel and residents were not allowed on the premises.

Beckett set Anna's suitcases down. "Why don't you wait here for just a moment." He turned abruptly and pushed the door wide, leaving a startled Anna on the front steps.

"What seems to be the trouble?" Beckett asked.

"This. This," Herr Sauermann began in English. He gestured toward Rudolph. "He is tearing down our bedroom wall."

Beckett refused to meet Rudolph's eyes to avoid laughing.

"You must fire him. We cannot have men like this showing such lack of respect. You were to wait until we vacated the premises to start the demolition."

"I understand your frustration Herr Sauermann, but I gave those orders."

"You?" Herr Sauermann's brows knit together above his piercing gaze.

"Yes. If you will recollect, your deadline to leave was seven days ago. We are now a week behind schedule because of your delay, and the contract fines are starting to add up. When I spoke to you last evening, you told me you would not pay any fines due to your late departure. That left me two options: abandon the project entirely or move forward on the remodel. I chose the latter, as Genskal has invested heavily and would come out the loser if we withdrew."

Petra Sauermann, an attractive woman of average height and pale-blonde hair, sputtered with indignation. "How dare you treat us in such a way. My father was vice-chancellor of Austria. We are not accustomed to such cavalier behavior."

Beckett pulled out his mobile. "I assure you a grace period of seven days is much longer than Genskal allows without seeking restitution. Perhaps you would like to explain to the president of the company why you have broken your contract before we have fully begun?"

He pressed the dial button and held the mobile out to Herr Sauermann.

"That won't be necessary. We are leaving. I'm sure it was all a misunderstanding." Herr Sauermann lowered his voice and said just to his wife, "Did you get everything you need, Petra?"

"Yes, but I resent being treated in such a rude manner." Frau Sauermann huffed and started out the door, almost running slap into Anna on the portico.

Anna's blue eyes, clear as Scottish lochs, took in the scene, her expression betraying little. The Anna he had known despised confrontations. The desire to shield her from further unpleasantness welled inside Beckett.

He stood in the doorway as the Sauermanns strode out to their car, followed by their personal manservant with their luggage. Anna said not a word, just twisted her upper body as the Sauermanns climbed into their vehicle and drove off.

Slowly, Anna turned back to face him. Her eyes were still wide, but her mouth twitched. Before she reached for the handle on one of her bags, he saw a quick smile touch her lips. He went over and removed the cases from her hands.

She met his eyes. "Remind me never to get on your bad side. Wherever did you learn to work with people like that?"

"You've never dealt with an ugly customer before?"

She shrugged. "You outflanked him before he knew what was coming. What would have happened if he had spoken to Paul?"

Beckett grinned unconcernedly and shrugged. "I didn't call Paul. I dialed another team member."

"You did?"

"Aye. We set up a relay system to deal with Sauermann when he becomes difficult."

"By impersonating Paul Symonds, the vice president over Europe?"

"Normally, Genskal denies contracts with difficult customers."

"Then why did they accept the Falcon Point project to begin with?" Her blue eyes mirrored her puzzled tone.

"I convinced the board of directors this four-season resort would open the door to the Austrian market and that the site was an advertisement for the corporation. Besides, I can handle Sauermann."

"I'm sure you can."

Anna set her suitcases on top of the narrow twin bed and began to unpack. The austere room contained a bed, dresser, sink, and desk, with a couple wall pegs on which to hang her clothes. Genskal's five-man team was housed in the old servants' basement quarters for the duration of the resort construction.

The no-frills room took her back to her uni days when she had shared a tiny flat with three other girls. This time, she was grateful for the privacy of her own room. She ran a comb through her hair, then went to locate the team.

A makeshift kitchen had been provided for them in the butler's pantry downstairs along with the use of the turquoise salon while the staff was on extended release during the renovations.

Reaching the first floor, she was struck by the absolute quiet. Having grown up on a large estate, Anna had some idea of how vast these homes could be, but she had still assumed she would easily locate her colleagues.

Setting off, she took note of the dark paneling, the ceiling frescoes, and the red and gold wall coverings that had gone out of fashion almost a century ago. The wide hallway ran along a series of public rooms. She poked her head through the doorway of a library at least sixty feet in length and half again as wide. The enormous fireplace would make a wonderful gathering place after a day spent on the slopes.

Adjoining the library, a much smaller room painted in dark ocher with heavy leather sofas and chairs had Anna wrinkling her nose from the smell of long-spent cigars. A massive dining room across the hall had truly beautiful ceiling plasters and chandeliers. One wall of windows faced east, framing Kristall Lake, and oils of people from bygone eras stared down at her from the walls.

Her shoes echoed on the marble squares as she passed the entrance hall and floating staircase. A laugh rang out, and she followed the sound to the next public room.

The vast space's sash windows, gilded plasterwork, and Louis XVI furniture in pale cream spoke of wealth and affluence. The elaborate moldings were a foil for walls covered in soft turquoise silk. Everything in her sighed at the light and airy atmosphere.

Three men, including Beckett, and a woman were seated near the fireplace on the upholstered sofas and chairs.

"Anna." Beckett rose to his feet, and the two other men followed suit. "Come meet the team."

Anna caught sight of her reflection in a massive pier glass above the white veined mantel as she crossed the room. The woman smiled at her, her gray eyes assessing. She was dressed in trendy, upscale clothes and looked very toned and put together.

"Anna Cavendish, Tanja Mueller, our lead designer," Beckett said.

Anna had heard of Tanja, a talented designer whose bad-girl image often made society news.

"Welcome to Austria." Tanja's ash-blonde bob swung freely about her shoulders.

Anna murmured appropriately as both men came alongside Beckett to be introduced.

"Gary Smith, our woods preservation expert."

"Enchanted. Welcome to the team." Gary wasn't much taller than Anna's own five feet five, and his New York accent proclaimed his nationality.

She hadn't heard of him, but he must be every bit as skilled as Tanja, or Beckett wouldn't have him on the team.

"Rudolph Gruber, our general contractor," Beckett said with real warmth in his voice, as though he and Mr. Gruber were friends as well as colleagues.

"Rudy," the contractor corrected and took Anna's hand in his and gave it a shake.

"How do you do?" Anna asked, assessing the man.

Rudy was a good three inches shorter than Beckett's six feet and was several years older. If Anna had to guess his age, she suspected Rudy was on the other side of thirty. He had kind eyes and a hard jaw, a unique juxtaposition.

"So, Anna, what part do you play in the resort?" Rudy asked.

"I have no idea, but I'm sure Tanja will fill me in tomorrow."

"That I will," Tanja said, then turned back to Beckett and Gary. "When does the resort website go live, Beckett?"

"A few more days. The marketing department is working out the kinks."

"That's a little soon, isn't it?" Tanja challenged, a furrow between her brows.

Beckett shrugged. "Not my decision. Our lot needs to focus on meeting deadlines. Genskal's marketing department handles the publicity for the resort."

The group nodded.

"What's the timeline on our geothermal installation?" Gary asked, knocking back his drink.

"Another two weeks," Rudy interjected. He shifted to face Anna fully. "Beckett has not only utilized the hot springs for thermal baths for the spa, but he's also designed a restaurant that overlooks the small mountain lake that will be used for skating in the winter."

The man was brilliant. Too bad Beckett couldn't apply that bright mind to his personal life.

Anna glanced at Beckett just as Tanja laid a hand on his arm and kept it there. Anna gritted her teeth and would have given anything for Granny's picture to remind her why she had come.

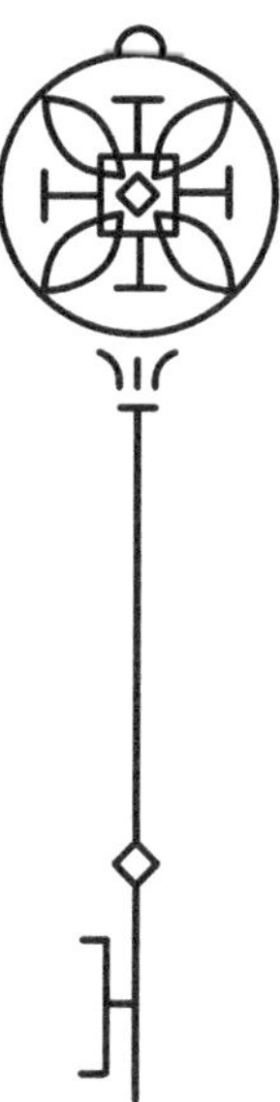

CHAPTER 16

Early the next morning, after she had bathed in an old-fashioned bathroom, Anna tossed on a jacket and slipped outside to explore the grounds. She clattered down the front steps, the crisp spring air stroking her skin. Beside the drive, an intriguing path that disappeared into the lush vegetation beckoned.

The manor itself stood in approximately fifty acres of parkland before the hillsides, covered in larch and pine, rose steeply and joined the mountain beyond. Through the trees, the peaked roofs of goatherd huts showed here and there.

A fork off the main path soon brought her to a formal rose garden with three life-sized Grecian goddesses at its center supporting a pergola of newly leafed climbers. In another month, the garden would be filled with their heavenly scent.

The path skirted a pond. Anna stopped to admire the silver-bodied Golden rudd swishing their gold-and-rose tails under the glassy surface.

She checked the time, then spun on her heel and started back toward the manor. She had no desire to arrive late to work on her very first morning.

When she reached the drive, her eyes swept over Falcon Point's symmetry and pointed, capped turrets. A curious warmth cocooned her. She savored the welcoming emotion, having never experienced this phenomenon growing up on her father's estate.

Anna scraped the soles of her shoes before she entered the vast entry hall. Beckett stood in the foyer, a thick stack of folders under his arm, while Tanja spoke to him, her head tilted to the side, her proximity much too close.

An odd little dart pricked Anna's heart, but she pasted on a smile and chose to ignore it, dismissing it as nothing more than an echo of her past.

"Good morning." Anna greeted both of them while she unzipped her jacket.

Beckett shifted, his face giving little away. "Morning, Anna. I see you've been out and about already."

"After last night's discussion, I realized that if I wanted to get any exercise, I'd better do it before I report to work."

"We certainly put in long hours." Tanja's eyes took in Anna's gray trousers, Hermes scarf, and blue jumper, settling at last on the tanzanite pendant at her throat. "Come this way. I'll show you where your workstation is."

Anna followed Tanja and Beckett down the hall and up a smaller, more serviceable staircase to a room with one entire wall dedicated to floor-to-ceiling, wire-fronted bookshelves. Three tables ran down the center of the room, one loaded with multisized copiers and a fax machine. The remaining tables were set up as workstations—two apiece, one on each side.

A straight-fronted desk with a recessed center cabinet, a massive relic from the Victorian era, stood isolated from the other workstations at the far end of the room, facing the door. Three sizeable monitors shielded the desk's occupant from the room at large. Rolls of blueprints filled a wire bin beside it. It didn't take a rocket scientist to figure out who sat there.

"We're just here," Tanja said, indicating the library table closest to Beckett's desk.

Anna pulled out a chair in front of the unoccupied workstation and draped her jacket over the back. Beckett passed her on the way to his desk, picked up a folder off the top of a stack, and was immediately immersed in work.

"Until I know what you can do, I will preview your work before we submit it to Beckett," Tanja informed her.

Anna nodded. Fair enough. She had expected no less.

"Good," Tanja continued without the slightest notice. "Your resumé said you have experience with kitchen design. Ours is a mess and needs streamlining to meet the needs of a full-fledged resort. I'd like you to focus on that and the dining room, which has similar issues." Tanja jotted numbers on a sticky note and passed it to her. "This is the internet password and key code to the schematics. I'll check on you later." She turned away. "Beckett," she called.

"Yes?" He looked up from his folder, a frown in his eyes.

Anna knew that expression. Tanja wasn't winning any points by interrupting him.

Tanja wove between the furniture in what Anna could only describe as feline grace, a she-cat on the prowl, with dinner in her sights. Anna had to admit Tanja did it well.

Anna looked away, fighting the sudden spurt of indignation, and reminded herself that that ship had sailed long ago. Beckett had cut himself free and could do as he pleased. She was here to do a job and find out what had happened to Granny's people.

Taking a seat, she typed in the passcodes, then waited for her AutoCAD program to boot up.

Beckett's only response to Tanja's overtures were grunts as he continued to scan his reports. Anna ducked her head and bit back a smile when Tanja spun around and started for her workstation.

"*Guten Morgen.*" Rudy wandered in, a cup of coffee in his hand. He set his mug beside his computer and went to speak with Beckett. The two held a low-voiced discussion before Rudy nodded curtly. Then catching sight of Anna, he approached her desk. "I trust you slept well?"

"I did, thank you."

"Our little Anna has already been outside for her morning constitutional," Tanja cut in. "She must have risen with the larks."

Rudy leaned his hip against the table beside Anna's computer. "What has Tanja tasked you with?" He reached over and spun Anna's monitor in his direction. "The kitchen?" He shot Tanja a black look. "You'll have a headache before the end of the day and will definitely need reviving. Come with me to the tavern tonight and try the schnitzel. It is especially good."

Anna could practically sense ears stretching to catch her response. She looked up into Rudy's eyes and saw only kindness mirrored there.

"I'd be delighted."

"Seven?"

Anna nodded. "I'll be ready."

Rudy went back to his station.

As Anna watched him go, her gaze collided with Beckett's and locked. Something flashed in the hazel depths and was gone. He closed his file folder and strode out of the room without a word to anyone.

Gunnar paced the small living room of his rental cottage, his anxiety rising. He needed to research the Lang heirs, but with his wife, Petra, milling about, he couldn't get a moment's peace without her looking over his shoulder and questioning what he was doing.

He had rented the cottage in Gildenstatt two weeks ago, since the village nearest Falcon Point was little more than a construction site for the railroad and didn't have any rentals available. Petra hadn't wanted to move any sooner than necessary, and after his meeting with the railroad official, Gunnar had agreed to his wife's demands that they postpone their move as long as possible. He needed to find the copy of that letter. Everything he wanted was in his reach, and yet, one piece of paper from two lifetimes ago could ruin everything. And how dare the design team kick him out. He had secrets to protect.

His family had been the trustees of Falcon Point for more than eighty years, but the fact remained that they did not own it. Not yet. As trustee, he had the authority to improve the manor that had been his home his whole life, but he needed the railway money to repurpose his house and turn it into something that would bring in money rather than drain what little soluble assets remained from the Lang family.

Gunnar should have been more diligent in searching through the files in the archive room, but he had never seen the point. After all, he had the documents that mattered to maintain and ultimately improve his lifestyle. Or so he'd thought. He would make a point of finding some excuse to return to the estate tomorrow. Perhaps a little more searching would reveal what he needed to find.

If the railroad found the heirs, Gunnar would not only be out the ten million euros being paid to the trust for granting the railway access across the property, but he would also lose his position as trustee, his home, and all the future profits the new Falcon Point resort would bring in.

Gunnar had never considered that someone might not only be aware of Ingrid Lang's survival but also have a clue of how to find her descendants. With Ingrid's married name listed on the letter to the land authority, the investigator had a starting place. For all Gunnar knew, the man might also have an address.

His latest information indicated the troublesome woman only had two surviving descendants: Lars Hendriks and his younger sister, Tess, both of whom were living in the Netherlands, the same country their grandmother had escaped to after fleeing Austria.

Gunnar had assumed Ingrid's move and the name change from her marriage would break the investigative string before it even started. She should have been impossible to trace, especially more than eighty years later. If it hadn't been for the letter.

Petra walked into living room. "Darling, I'm headed to bed. Are you going to be working much longer?"

"I have a few more things to finish up." Gunnar kissed her good night. "You go on."

"Don't stay up too late."

"I won't." Gunnar waited until she disappeared upstairs before he unlocked his briefcase and retrieved the letters he already had from Ingrid Lang Hendriks.

The first had arrived only a month after the conclusion of World War II. Addressed to her brother Karl, Ingrid had shared details of how she had escaped to the Netherlands and eventually married. More importantly, she had written that she'd used the last of her savings to go to London in search of Karl and Anna only to learn Anna had been killed in the Blitz. Unable to locate her older brother, she had written to Falcon Point in the hopes he had returned there.

The subsequent letters had built upon the first: more details about Ingrid's financial difficulties due to her husband's health issues after the war and her continued plea that he respond. The last had been addressed to the trustee of the estate, begging for information about her brother.

Gunnar read through each of the letters again, but nowhere did Ingrid ever mention her desire to reclaim her family's property. He set the copy of the letter Herr Wagner had given him with the others. The date was two months after her last letter to Falcon Point, two months after she wrote of the birth of her first son, a child who ultimately passed away in infancy.

Gunnar's grandfather and father had kept track of the woman and her subsequent attempts at having a family. It wasn't until she was well into her thirties that she finally managed to birth a child who survived past his first birthday.

Whether Ingrid had sent the claim in because of her finances or her desire to share her heritage with her child, he didn't know, nor did he know how his grandfather had prevented the estate from being returned to the sole surviving Lang heir. However he had managed it, Gunnar now found himself in a similar position. Somehow, his grandfather had created this inheritance for him, and Gunnar wasn't about to let anyone take it away.

With a new sense of determination, he turned on his laptop and retrieved the latest report from his private investigator about Lars and Tess Hendriks's whereabouts. A photo had been included in his most recent correspondence. The Hendriks siblings were an attractive pair, both still in their twenties.

He typed a new email to request an update on their locations, then moved the cursor over to the Send button. He hesitated when a new thought struck. It wasn't whether the investigator found the brother and sister. It was whether they were alive when he did.

Gunnar deleted his original email and opened his portal into the dark web. He didn't need a private investigator. He needed services of a different kind.

Anna's ears throbbed to the techno music that blared through the speakers. Magenta and neon-blue lights lit the dance floor inside Elektro, a restaurant-bar-club Rudy had taken her to in Gildenstatt. After a stressful day filled with Tanja's subtle jabs at her novice status, Anna was ready for some fun.

She had eaten a late lunch, so she'd ordered a salad, but Rudy had still insisted she try the schnitzel. She had given it the old college try, but she was too full to finish, and half of her supper lay congealing on her plate.

Remembering the continental fashion, she laid her fork and knife together, parallel at the eleven o'clock position, tines facing down, a signal to the wait staff that she was finished. In England, the tines faced up.

"I never would have taken you for a techno kind of man," she said, glancing at the couples on the dance floor.

"You'll find it hard to go dancing in Austria without a good dose of techno." Rudy looked at her plate. "Didn't you like your dinner?"

"I wasn't that hungry, but thank you for inviting me out."

"My pleasure. Care to dance?"

"Love to." She could use the exercise after sitting far too long at her computer today, reworking the professional kitchen's schematics.

Rudy led her onto the brightly lit floor, where they danced and laughed and danced some more. He was an attentive date, and Anna had to admit it had been years since she had enjoyed herself so much.

"So, Anna, I don't see any rings on your fingers. Is someone back in London missing your company?"

Beckett's image flitted through her mind—the only fellow she had ever let her guard down for. "I'm not seeing anyone seriously."

Rudy's teeth flashed pale magenta in the atmospheric lighting. "*Gut.*" He pronounced it "goot."

His question filled her with disquiet, as did his response. She had sensed his interest in her sharpen throughout the evening. She liked Rudy, but she had no intention of starting a relationship. That could make things tricky on a jobsite. With his Austrian nationality and she based in London, he could only be looking for a fling—something strictly taboo in her book.

When it grew late, they left the club and walked back to the car park, the chilly night making her zip up her jacket.

"I'm off to Vienna this weekend. Would you be interested in going with me? We could stay at my place." Rudy's eyes were hopeful.

Anna shook her head. "I'm sorry, I can't, but I had a lovely evening tonight."

They reached his car, and she waited for him to open her door.

"I knew I shouldn't have asked. You're a dying breed, you know."

Confusion swirled inside Anna.

He laughed at her obvious bewilderment. "You aren't the type for weekend getaways. You're the kind of woman people take home to meet their parents."

Rudy, in his diplomatic way, was letting her know he understood. A little devil spurred her to goad him into full disclosure. "Is that your long game, then, taking me home to meet your parents?"

Rudy goggled at her for one quick beat, her inner imp letting her know she had completely taken him off guard, then he tossed his head back and laughed. "Did I mention that I like you, Anna Cavendish?"

"I believe it was implied. Friends?"

"At the very least." He opened her car door.

She slid onto the seat before he closed it behind her. She could do a whole lot worse than Rudy, but despite the bitter past, no one ever compared to Beckett. Over the last four years, he remained the high watermark she compared all her dates against. Her connection to him had been instantaneous; their minds immediately attuned to each other's with a constant crackle of attraction just under the surface.

Anna slammed the door on her memories before they got the better of her.

"You've gone quiet on me. Regretting our evening out?" Rudy said.

"Not at all. I hope you aren't."

Rudy started the car, but he turned in his seat to face her. "I give you fair warning. I don't give up easily, Anna Cavendish."

Her heart sank, and she looked out the passenger window. *Lovely.* Rudy had taken her as a challenge.

CHAPTER 17

Unable to unwind after work, Beckett tossed on a coat and headed outside to walk the lighted grounds, tucking his hands inside his pockets against the night chill. It had been a long day. Excavation work had slowed to a crawl due to backhoe issues. He had sorted that with the operator and Rudy. He had to pry Rudy from the office so he'd quit ogling Anna.

Beckett hadn't anticipated Rudy's response to Anna. Most men didn't notice her looks right off. She wasn't flashy like Tanja and was happy to avoid the limelight and let others take center stage. But she possessed a classic beauty that would endure long after Tanja's looks faded.

Anna's shiny fall of brown hair and big blue eyes had first captured his attention at a royal garden party when she'd been in her teens and he a first-year architectural student. Her timeless looks had appealed to him, and he had overtly studied her facial bone structure and feminine form.

His attraction for her had been immediate, but he had held back, reminding himself of his goals. Then during his last year in college, they had crossed paths at the Royal College of Arts, and he, whose ambitions had dominated his focus, had stumbled into love.

From a child, Beckett had known what he wanted and had determinedly set his course to obtain it. Anna's appearance in his life had come out of sequential order with his plans. When he was accepted to a graduate program in Sheffield and Anna had another three years of undergraduate studies, he'd done what made logical sense. Cut the connection.

But Anna had had plenty to say about that. She had a sassy mouth on her when riled, and she wasn't afraid to use it. Beckett smirked, remembering past incidences when she had called him out for behaving in a pigheaded fashion. That mouth of hers had stolen his heart—aye, and turned his brain inside out when she had pressed her lips to his.

Beckett walked on, the toe of his loafers dislodging a pebble. He kicked it down the path.

He had accomplished much of his workload today, mainly because Petra and Gunnar Sauermann had left the premises. The pair had interrupted meetings and long-distance calls for the last two weeks with their demands and questions. The conversion should pick up speed now with them out of the picture.

Taking the path through the east gardens, Beckett skirted the pond and tennis court before he circled back to the front of the manor. He checked his watch and frowned at the late hour. Anna and Rudy must be making a night of it.

He had requested Anna's presence on the team for two reasons: one, she had an abundance of talent. And two, he firmly believed all they needed was time together, and everything between them would sort itself out. But Anna, though cordial, seemed determined to keep their relationship distant and polite.

He jingled the euros in his pocket. When Rudy had asked her out this morning, it was all Beckett had in him not to disrupt their private conversation.

Climbing the portico steps two at a time, he let himself in and turned off the main lights. His shoulders slumped. He might as well lock up for the night. Anna and Rudy had a key.

With his thoughts elsewhere, he pivoted and ran straight into Tanja.

"I beg your pardon, Tanja. I didn't see you there."

"No?" She tilted her head and gave him a wicked smile. "I must be losing my touch."

The tiresome female had spent the entire morning chasing him around the office and treating Anna like an intern.

"See you in the morning." He was tired and wanted his bed.

"Turning in so soon?" She pouted.

"It's been a long day."

"Here's something to give you sweet dreams." Tanja ran her hands up his arms and plastered her mouth to his just as the front door opened and he heard Anna's soft voice.

"Where's the light switch?"

Anna reached inside the door and fumbled for the switch, but she had no trouble seeing the silhouette of two people kissing. Tanja's shoulder-length bob was easy to spot. The man . . .

Anna's heart stuttered when she recognized the shape of the man's head. Without a proper good night to Rudy, she skirted the edge of the hall and clattered down the servants' staircase. When she reached her room, she closed her bedroom door and leaned against it for support, her knees trembling.

Beckett and Tanja?

She shook her head and called herself all kinds of fool. Beckett was not hers—not after the cruel way he had broken things off between them. She doubted he ever had been hers. Deep down, her heart had clung to a hidden fantasy that someday, sometime, Beckett would come crawling back to her.

Her brain had accepted the facts years ago, just as it accepted what she had witnessed tonight. But her heart had ignored the memo. The silly organ must be illiterate, because four years was certainly long enough to get with the program and move on.

Anna prepared for bed, using the sink in the corner to brush her teeth and wash her face. She climbed under the covers and turned off the lamp, fully determined to push Beckett from her mind. But her mind was as stubborn as her heart, and it was a long time before sleep claimed her.

Beckett rose early the next morning after a night of fitful tossing. Tanja had ruined everything. How would he ever get Anna to listen to him after witnessing that lip-lock? She must think only the worst of him.

He had thrust Tanja from him last night, but it had been too late. Anna had already reached the stairs. Rudy had chuckled, slapped him on the back, and followed Anna downstairs to his room.

As for Tanja . . . Beckett had turned on her with barely suppressed anger. "Genskal has strict sexual harassment policies. See that this never happens again, or I will file charges against you. Is that clear?"

Tanja had apologized, but Beckett doubted anything could fix the damage she had caused.

His mobile beeped with a text. He was needed at the spa and restaurant site. Tugging on his boots, he went outside and climbed into his 4x4, then headed up the steep construction road.

The day was unusually warm, so he rolled down his window, and the pine-scented breeze wafted through the cab. The outdoors did much to ease his inner angst after last night's fiasco with Tanja. Pulling into a turnout, he soaked up the view of Falcon Point and Kristall Lake on the valley floor.

He eased the 4x4 back onto the track and continued up the mountain, slowing when he came alongside the backhoe driver and Rudy. Both were bent over the scoop, Rudy using a welding torch.

When Rudy saw him, he turned off the flame and lifted his face shield.

"You're up early." Rudy gave him a cheeky grin. "After last night, I wasn't so sure you would make an appearance."

"What you witnessed wasn't initiated by me."

"*Ja. Ja. Ja.*" Rudy wiggled his brows, clearly not buying it. "Cisco needs you at the hot springs. We have a hitch with the plumbing."

Beckett nodded toward the backhoe. "How soon before we're operational?"

"Two hours tops."

"Excellent." Beckett scanned the felled trees that ran vertically down the mountainside. With the trees and small scrub knocked down, the future ski slope resembled an overgrown fire break. Once they got the backhoe up and running, the excavators could smooth things over, then they could seed the slope to prevent erosion.

Putting the 4x4 in drive, Beckett waved and continued up the track to the hot springs. Hopefully, this new glitch wouldn't set back their geothermal installation timeline.

After lunch, Beckett found himself alone with Anna in the office. She appeared to be doing her level best to ignore him as she sorted through a box of books and files. But her color was high, and he could tell last night's scene with Tanja was still upon her.

While he debated with himself how best to approach her, he approved the most recent expenditure report and verified lead times for the en suite, jetted soaker tubs. He glanced at her over the top of one of his computer monitors. The longer he let this fiasco drag out, the harder it would be to clear up. He clicked out of his spreadsheet and pushed back his chair.

Gunnar Sauermann entered the office. His eyes landed on Anna, and he approached her makeshift workstation.

"What are you doing?" Sauermann asked in English, lifting a book from Anna's neat pile and examining its spine.

Anna craned her neck up at Sauermann from where she sat in her chair. "Researching the historical antiquity of the house to add authenticity to the dining room design."

"I did not give permission for this." Sauermann pointed at the book.

"Herr Sauermann, the contract specifically stated that you did." Beckett removed the document and crossed to Anna's workstation, flipping pages as he went. "On page twelve, it specifically states—"

"I do not care what I signed. These people of yours cannot go through private papers." Sauermann snatched a folder from Anna's table and shook it under her nose.

"What brings you here today, Herr Sauermann? More changes?" Beckett took the file from Sauermann's hand and placed it on the library table beside Anna.

"I—" Sauermann looked at Beckett in surprise. "Petra would like to make an adjustment in the master bath. She wants to place an Austrian crystal chandelier over the tub instead of the brass and chrome one formerly selected."

"Very well, but the change fee will cost you three times the price of the chandelier."

"This is highway robbery."

"I already ordered the lighting package for the en suite WCs." Beckett walked back to his desk and added the change to Herr Sauermann's growing list.

"Companies take returns."

"They do, but they charge us a restocking and shipping fee. Those we will pass on to you, with an additional fee for extra staff hours and the surcharge agreed upon when you first signed the contract."

Herr Sauermann tapped his thigh. "No one is to go through our histories."

"To provide authenticity, the history of the house must be verified for design content. I assure you, my team will not misplace paperwork," Beckett said evenly, despite the fact that his patience was beginning to fray.

"Gunnar?" Petra Sauermann entered the room, her blonde hair flawlessly coiffed and lacquered. "Let these people do their job. It is perfectly fine for them to access historical records. We want this house returned to its former glory, don't we?"

Herr Sauermann appeared to struggle, his eyes shifting to Anna. "I will think about it. For now, I want those papers returned where you found them."

Anna glanced at Beckett, her expression an obvious quandary on what she should do.

"As you wish, Herr Sauermann. But that will cost you for slowing down the project," Beckett gritted out, his smile lacking any genuine warmth.

"As for the fees, I will discuss them with your corporate office." Sauermann stormed out.

"I will work on him," Petra said. "He is not always so unreasonable. But please see to it that the lighting is changed for the master bathroom."

"As you wish." Beckett gave a slight nod.

Frau Sauermann followed her husband out of the room. At first, the Sauermanns had driven him mad with their constant changes, but their accrued fees had mounted to €50,000 in the last few weeks. If the Falcon Point trustee kept going at this current rate, Beckett estimated Genskal would make a total of €600,000 in fees alone.

With Rudy in the field and Tanja and Gary examining the ballroom floor, Anna was safe to approach. She had returned to her CAD drawing. Though she had set down the Falcon Point papers, she had left the pile of historical records beside her, no doubt to be returned when convenient for her.

Tanja's kiss still rankled. He doubted Anna would believe it had nothing to do with him. He had to explain. Her opinion of him mattered too much to simply leave it be.

He cleared his throat. "Are you finding the job to your satisfaction?" he asked, keeping the table between them.

Anna looked up, her face slowly registering her surroundings. "I beg your pardon?"

Beckett held back a smile. This most definitely was the Anna of old, wholly absorbed in a project, tuning everything out around her.

"Are you satisfied with the project?"

"Very much so." Her cool response discouraged idle chitchat.

Too bad. Beckett was tired of being pushed aside. If he didn't seize the moment, he might not get another. "Anna, is there a place where we can speak privately? I'd like to explain what happened last night."

Her eyes roved the empty office, then met his gaze. "I believe this is as good as anywhere."

"I was thinking somewhere we would not be interrupted."

"Why?"

"I'd like to discuss what you witnessed last night." Anna certainly wasn't making this easy.

"You don't owe me an explanation. Whatever you do on your own time is your own business."

"But that's just it. I was more waylaid than participant."

Anna raised her brows, clearly disbelieving his words.

"Anna, about our relationship . . ." He raked a hand through his hair.

"There is no relationship between us, Beckett. Remember? You made sure of that four years ago. Now, if you will excuse me, I have a job to do."

He locked his jaw and ground his back molars. Anna picked up the stack of historical books and files off the table and brushed past him, heading toward the bookcases.

The blame for their breakup lay squarely on his own witless shoulders. He'd been selfish and stupid, angry that she had disrupted the order of his plans. After ending things, he'd headed off to Sheffield, anxious to complete his graduate work. Clever Scot that he was, he hadn't recognized the constant ache around his heart, the sleepless nights, and the memories that stopped him in his tracks for what they were—proof positive of how deep his feelings for Anna had gone. By then, it was too late. Anna had locked him out of her life.

Anna yanked open one of the grilled door fronts and thumped the first book onto the shelf with more energy than necessary. The file under her arm dislodged, and papers fluttered to the floor.

"Oh no." Anna knelt on the rug and began to gather up the contents.

Beckett rounded the table to ensure nothing had been damaged. The last thing he needed was Sauermann breathing down his throat.

Several snapshots had landed facedown. Anna flipped one over and gasped, her eyes enormous.

"Are you quite all right?" Beckett asked. "You look as though you've seen a ghost."

Anna held up the black-and-white snapshot. "I think I have."

CHAPTER 18

Anna's knees wobbled, and she sank into the office chair. "Beckett, my grandmother is in this picture. What does it say on the back? I don't read German." Nor did she have the energy to mess with Google Translate.

Gently, he pried her fingers loose from the photo and smoothed out the creases. "Helen Davies, das Kindermädchen, Liselotte, und Anna. Helen Davies, the nanny, Liselotte, and Anna."

"That can't be right." Anna shook her head. "All Granny's school forms had Davies as her surname."

"Are you sure, Anna? This picture says Helen Davies was the nanny. That seems quite definite to me."

"Granny told us she lost her mother when she was very young. Helen brought her to England when they fled the Nazis. She was killed during the Blitz, right after Granny went to a girls' academy in the country when she was seven."

"That's verra young."

"I know. I can't imagine how she felt. Only her school records survived the war, and they had Davies on them. It just goes to show that family stories might not be very accurate."

"Your father didn't know?"

"Dad inherited his father's title when he was in his teens, along with the responsibility of learning how to run the estate. He was inundated. I was always more interested in finding Granny's family than he was."

"What happened to your grandmother after Helen died?" Beckett asked.

"One of the governors at the girls academy was assigned as her trustee along with a court-appointed guardian. They determined that Granny should live year-round at the school instead of being sent to an orphanage. Evidently, Helen had paid all Granny's school fees. With the war on, I assume the academy was in desperate need of funds."

"A tough life for a child, never experiencing life outside the school walls."

"Granny said her trustees were very kind, and she was quite fond of her professors." Anna touched the photograph. "How could I have gotten this so wrong?"

"Your grandmother died when you were so young, Anna. You said it yourself, family stories rarely have more than a grain of truth in them."

"You're right. Granny seldom spoke about the war years. I think she wanted to put it behind her. By nature, she was a cheerful, lively person—the life of every gathering. I adored her."

"Where's that picture of yours? Do you have it on you?"

"Yes." Anna retrieved the black-and-white photo of Granny's family from her purse.

"There's Granny; she's the little one. I think she was five here."

"She looks similar in age to the other photo." Beckett compared the two pictures.

"I agree."

"Who are these other people?"

"It's a picture of her family before they left Austria."

"That woman in your photo looks a lot like the one in this picture."

A chill washed over Anna as she compared the photographs. Beckett was right; the woman in both pictures looked similar. To make sure, she got out her mobile and took a picture of it, then enlarged the photo with her fingers.

"If Helen was desperate to remove Anna from London, she might have enrolled her at the academy, acting in place of a parent, to ensure her safety," Beckett suggested.

"I suppose. But how did a mere nanny leave so much wealth behind? Granny inherited a substantial sum after Helen's death."

"Good question. That's a mystery you may never solve."

A burning curiosity to find the answers engulfed Anna as she stared at the photograph of her grandmother. She glanced up at Beckett and tried to gauge if he would let her do what she was about to propose.

"I need to access the documents in this room. I told you that was why I applied for this job." Well, it was one of the reasons anyway. "You said that Herr Sauermann signed a contract that gave our team permission to access those documents. Surely Genskal wouldn't mind, would they?"

Beckett's eyes took on a remote expression, and Anna had the distinct impression he was doing some sort of mental gymnastics.

"Aye, Sauermann signed a legal contract, but you've seen the man. He's the very devil to deal with on a daily basis. I'd prefer not to rile him."

She opened her mouth to beg, to plead, anything to find out who Granny's birth parents were.

Beckett held up his hand, effectively stopping her. "I will let you research the property records on one condition."

Everything inside Anna went on high alert. Beckett was up to something; she could tell. Her eyes narrowed, and she tried to read his meaning.

"You may only search the records after hours, when the rest of the team has left for the day—"

"Oh, thank you." Like an incoming tide, relief flooded her body. It was always better to have permission than to sneak behind Beckett's back, which was what she intended to do if he turned her down.

"I'm not finished."

"Sorry." A blush heated her cheeks.

"You may only investigate Falcon Point records after hours when I am with you. That way, if Herr Sauermann shows up at an unpredictable time, as he is wont to do, I am there to deal with him."

"I'm not afraid of Herr Sauermann."

"You should be. Sauermann can make your job verra difficult if he chooses. He could insist Genskal let you off the team or drop the contract altogether."

The fight went out of Anna when she realized Beckett was trying to shield her from any unpleasantness. "Genskal would do that?"

"This Austrian contract is a jumping-off point and will open doors to the Eastern European market. Genskal is, first and foremost, a business. You, my dear, are a very junior designer in the grand scheme of things."

"That's rather disheartening."

"That's business." He handed her back her photo. "Do we have a deal?"

"Yes." She eyed him for an instant. "I hope you are up for a number of late nights, because I intend to search regularly."

"Trust me. The Falcon Point website went live today. I will have plenty to do." He indicated his desk, which was buried under blueprints, file folders, and several colorful sticky notes dangling off the bottom of his monitor.

A male laugh sounded in the hall, joined by a woman's. Seconds later, Tanja and Gary entered the room, their heads bent close over a board covered in sample stains.

"Tonight, then?" Anna whispered.

"Yes. After supper?"

She nodded.

Tanja stopped at Anna's workstation without acknowledging Beckett. "I'd like to see what you've done today with that kitchen design."

Anna opened her screen to the series of schematic floor plans and elevation designs she had put together, then scooted back from her computer so Tanja could have a closer look.

Her eyes slid to Beckett. He had returned to his desk and was already absorbed in a sheaf of papers.

Cole Bridger typed on his computer in the CIA's Vienna office and wished he were anywhere else. He had taken this assignment as a way to get closer to his family heritage, but sitting in an office had never been his thing. Put him in the field and he was one of the best agents in Europe. Throw him behind a desk and he might as well be the pumpkin from *Cinderella*—useful when magic hit and ornamental in all other cases.

"Cole, where are we on the translation of the chancellor's speech this morning?"

Cole glanced up at Gwendolyn Hatch, his current supervisor. "I'll have it for you in ten minutes."

"Good." Gwendolyn continued past his desk to hound Zoe, the finance officer. Even though Gwendolyn knew how to use her human resources, she wasn't satisfied to let her employees do their jobs without her knowing exactly what they were working on. Maybe that was why he hesitated to share his real reason for accepting this assignment. Even if Gwendolyn allowed him to do some digging on his own time, he knew from past experience that no one in the CIA believed in the proverbial pot of gold at the end of his family's rainbow.

Hidden treasure. Cole had been dreaming of it since he was four years old on his grandfather's knee. The story his grandfather had told him of an Austrian princess had seemed like a girl's story until he had added in the escape from a dragon. Then there were the hidden family jewels that had been left behind. Or had it been paintings?

The story had changed from one telling to the next, but it had entertained him during his summers spent with his grandparents throughout his childhood. It wasn't until his father had passed away, when Cole was seventeen, that he had learned how firmly the story had been anchored in reality.

Two days after the funeral, his grandfather had handed him a box filled with letters from his great-grandfather, Karl Lang. Within those letters had been the story his own grandfather had told him for so many years. The box also contained an old passport and an old leather-bound copy of the New Testament with letters in the margins. The map to his treasure, his grandfather had called it. Cole had been searching for Falcon Point and his Lang family heritage ever since.

Gwendolyn passed into his view, and he quickly finished the translation of the chancellor's speech. He attached the file to a secure email and forwarded it to his boss.

At the next desk over, Zoe spoke into the phone, her voice filled with frustration. "When will you have it?" She paused. "I needed that report yesterday."

Cole waited until she hung up before he asked, "Everything okay?"

"Not really. One of our assets passed off some new information, but it's coded. I've been waiting for it to be decrypted for two days now."

"Why would a finance officer be dealing with coded information?"

"I'm tracking some suspicious funding through a bank here."

"Can I take a look?"

Zoe handed him a file. Cole flipped it open and scanned through it. He shook his head. The code was one he had used many times before to send information back to headquarters.

"I'll be right back." Cole returned to his desk.

"What are you doing?"

"Decoding this for you."

"You can do that?"

"Yeah." He grabbed a pen and some paper. After trying six different variants of the code, he identified the right one. He translated the message into English.

Once he finished, he shredded his failed attempts and carried Zoe's file and the translation back to her desk. "Here you go."

"You figured it out?"

"It's a pretty common code for field agents."

Zoe read through the message. "Thank you so much. This is exactly what I needed."

"Glad I could help." Cole motioned to the exit. "I'm going to grab some lunch. Do you want me to pick something up for you?"

"Thanks for the offer, but I packed a lunch," Zoe said. "I had a feeling I'd be chained to my desk today."

"Okay. Good luck."

"Thanks."

Anxious to get away from his own desk, Cole headed for the door. He stopped at the security desk to reclaim his cell phone that he had checked in this morning. He thanked the guard and left the building. Time for some lunch away from the office.

Following his typical protocol, he checked his surroundings and circled through the district before making his way to his intended destination. He chose a seat outside a sidewalk café, deliberately opting for one where he would have a solid wall rather than a window behind him.

As soon as he gave the waitress his order, he checked his phone for messages.

He deleted several junk emails before he noted one from a search engine he often used. He opened it to discover a hit on an internet alert he had set up years ago. Falcon Point.

Suspecting it was another false lead, he clicked on the link included in the email. He sucked in a breath when the website filled his screen. A resort in Austria. Could this be the location he had been looking for all along?

CHAPTER 19

Late afternoon sunlight streamed through the large basement windows when Anna entered the kitchen, her schematic drawing in hand. Construction dust opaqued the air as Rudy's workmen pried upper cabinets from the walls.

Beckett and Rudy were due any minute, but Anna had arrived early to inspect the space. She didn't want their remarks to cloud her creativity if an idea should strike.

With Rudy's men ignoring her, she picked her way around the demolished cabinets littering the floor to examine a recently exposed corner more thoroughly. Hmmm. At the far end of the kitchen stood an identical build-out.

She thumped the bump-out closest to her. If the wall was hollow, she could open it up and use the extra square footage in her design. Her mind swirled with possibilities.

"What are you doing, Anna?" Beckett asked from the doorway.

She pivoted. Rudy and Beckett stood observing the disaster that had once been the Falcon Point kitchen.

"Rudy, give me your hammer." She held out her hand for the tool hanging from Rudy's construction belt.

Beckett's lips quirked, but she didn't have time to try to figure out what was so amusing, not when she had a hunch about that corner bump-out. Taking the hammer, she hit the wall good and hard, cracking plaster and sending chunks of it into the air.

She coughed from the dust but swung back and hit the wall again. This time, she broke off enough plaster to expose the lath beneath. Setting down the hammer, she peeked between the narrow wooden slats.

"Hah! I knew it. Rudy, do you have an electronic tape measure?" She fairly danced with impatience.

Rudy removed the measuring device from his toolbelt and handed it to her, a half grin lighting his features.

"Thanks." Anna marched to the far wall and shot the red laser across the room, careful to send the beam between the slats of lath. She compared the reading with her schematic measurements and repeated the process on the adjoining wall.

"What are you up to, Anna?" Beckett asked again.

"Give me a minute. I'm on to something." Excitement rolled off her in waves as the professional kitchen took shape inside her mind.

"Rudy, is this corner protrusion load-bearing?" she asked, her hand patting the wall she had just attacked.

"I doubt it." Rudy joined her and examined the walls. "No, you're good to go."

"At first, I thought these corner protrusions were created to hide air ducts or drain pipes, but this one is entirely empty. I have a hunch the other one is too. Why would they do something like that?"

"My guess is they wanted a seamless appearance, so they boxed up the open spaces," Rudy said.

"Well, for whatever reason, it's good news for my design." She took out her mechanical pencil and sketched her ideas on the back of her schematic printout. When she finished, she handed Beckett the electronic measuring tape. "Can you measure this wall for me?"

"Tanja's already measured the kitchen." Beckett indicated the schematic drawing that contained the kitchen measurements.

"A good designer always double-checks," Anna reminded him.

He raised a brow at her sassy tone. "I assure you Tanja triple-checked those numbers."

She flushed and glanced away. She might report to Tanja, but Beckett was the big boss. How had she forgotten? "Sorry."

"It's okay. I remember how you get when an idea takes hold of you." His voice was smooth as silk.

Her heart accelerated at his tone. She turned away just in time to catch Rudy's quick double take between her and Beckett. *Brilliant.*

She cleared her throat and changed the subject. "Can we include this pantry and open area with that second protrusion?"

"Of course," Beckett said.

He wandered the room, shooting the laser and calling out measurements while she made notations.

"With the extra twenty-four inches from removing that bump-out, I can move the professional ranges to this wall and install a spice cupboard between them."

Anna stared at the dividing wall between the pantry and scullery. "If we remove the second bump-out in that corner, we can expand the pantry and convert the scullery into a walk-in freezer. That will cut down on supply orders and allow the kitchen staff to up food production, not only for those staying at the resort but for a full-time catering service for those in the valley. This adjustment could increase staff jobs."

Beckett nodded, his expression filled with admiration. "Your design is much more efficient by placing the appliances into work-friendly triangles."

Rudy scratched his head. "I thought Beckett was crazy when he added an untried designer to the team. You increased employee productivity and provided a way for the kitchen staff to maintain full-time status. Where did you learn to think like that?"

Heat suffused Anna's face, but she was too honest to lie. "An associate of mine at university taught me to think outside the box."

Beckett met her eyes, and a smile broke out across his face. A bevy of tingles exploded inside her. She tore her eyes away from her ex and watched Rudy cross the room to assist the workmen as they pried another cabinet from the wall.

Wood and nails screeched, and the cupboard crashed to the floor, dust filling the already clouded air.

"When will you have the updated schematics finished?" Beckett asked, getting back to the business at hand.

"Sometime this evening or tomorrow morning," Anna said.

Beckett nodded. "Brilliant design, Anna. I knew you'd be an asset to this team."

Warmth spread through her at his praise. Then she remembered. This was Beckett, the man who had almost destroyed her. She sobered immediately, but the glow remained. If she wasn't careful, she might lose her heart to him all over again.

Anna clicked her computer mouse and added the walk-in freezer's dimensions. She needn't have been nervous working after hours with Beckett in their makeshift office. He was entirely consumed with business and paid her little attention. Only the top third of his head was visible over the massive monitors on his desk, but every sound that emanated from his corner of the room jangled her nerves.

By 11:00 p.m., she had updated the kitchen floor plan and was ready to get cracking on Falcon Point's historical records. She rolled her neck to remove the stiffness while her eyes fastened onto the bookcases. The contents were sorted by decade, so she carted a step ladder to the appropriate section not far from Beckett's desk and began her search.

The binding on a book dated 1938 caught her attention. She leaned out, her arm stretching to reach it. The ladder teetered under the uneven weight distribution, and Anna grabbed for the shelves to save herself, but her fingers slipped. Beckett lunged and gripped her around the waist to keep her from falling.

"Thank you. I'm normally not so clumsy," she said a little breathlessly.

"Glad I was here."

He helped her down but didn't step out of her personal space when she reached the floor. Instead, he pinned her with his intent blue-green gaze.

Anna's stomach flipped, and she swallowed noisily.

"What is that you have there?" he asked, stepping back long after he should have.

"Oh." She blinked and reined in her unruly emotions. "Since the Third Reich absorbed Austria in March of '38, I thought it would be best to start looking around the latter end of the 1930s. That would make Granny about five."

"How old was your grandmother when she left the area and traveled to England?"

"Barely seven."

"It would help tremendously, Anna, if we knew her surname. What do you know about her family? Is there anything special about them that would help us find her?"

"I know very little. Granny did say she was born on the estate in her picture. We now know that is Falcon Point."

"Okay, so we know she was born at Falcon Point." He cocked an eyebrow, his expression seemingly asking if she had more information.

"Her older siblings were Karl and Ingrid. The three of them fled the estate together."

"Just her siblings? Helen wasn't with them?"

Anna stared at him. Trust Beckett to point out something in Granny's story that she had never noticed before. "Until this minute, I always assumed the entire family fled the estate, but Granny only mentioned leaving with her siblings. What if the children left the estate alone?"

"Did your grandmother remember anything else about her escape?"

"She and her siblings were separated at the train station."

"And the nanny took your grandmother to England," he finished for her.

"Yes."

"Those two pictures were taken a couple of years prior to your grandmother's escape. So if she was born at Falcon Point, her records should be here somewhere. The Nazis didn't damage the manor house, nor the local kirches."

Anna climbed back up the step stool.

"Let me. I have a longer reach and can access those top shelves." Beckett switched places with her and perused the 1930s section before he removed a file box. He lifted the lid and grunted with apparent satisfaction.

She stood on the bottom rung to make sure he didn't pitch headfirst onto the floor.

"Thanks," Beckett said when he reached the bottom rung.

Going back to his desk, he set down the box, then borrowed a folding chair from the adjoining table and placed it beside his own. Anna rounded Beckett's barricade, as she liked to call it, and helped him unload the box onto his desk.

"I'll take the bottom half; you take the top?" he questioned with his eye on the stack.

"Sounds good to me."

They split the pile and worked in tandem. She hadn't sat this close to Beckett in four years. His sage and musk aftershave invaded her senses. Every time he so much as twitched, her insides leaped.

As much as she pretended otherwise, his nearness had the same effect on her as in years past. She determined to work at her own desk in the future.

The next file she opened was filled with receipts, and she almost closed it again, but the thought struck her that somewhere on those receipts were names. And names would lead to records.

The top bill was for two hundred schillings for perennials along Falcon Point's drive. Seven hams, two turkeys, one hundred kg of potatoes, and sixteen cabbages. Anna checked the date. December 1937. The signature on the bottom was Heinrich Pichler.

She made note of the name and thumbed through more receipts, most of which were bills from the local green grocer, a seamstress for holiday dresses, and wine. Nothing out of the ordinary. Heinrich Pichler's signature appeared several more times. Was he the owner, butler, or steward?

With a house the size of Falcon Point, the staff and their wages must be in a separate ledger. Closing the folder, her arm brushed against Beckett's. She froze when their eyes met and held. Something stirred in the blue-green depths, and Anna looked away, her skin overly heated.

Holy moly. The man was potent. Anna wanted to fan herself but refused to acknowledge the effect he still had on her equilibrium.

She grabbed the next file and flipped it open, none too gently. Several photos spilled out onto the desktop. She immediately recognized Karl, Granny's brother, dressed in Lederhosen. She flipped the picture over.

Karl Lang.

Goosebumps broke out along her arms. The family name was Lang.

Just to make sure, Anna bent over the other two pictures. A tall man with light-colored hair and a straight nose. No name was listed on the back, but Karl had the same jaw and nose. Was this Karl and Granny's father? He had light-colored eyes, like Granny and her siblings.

The furnishings in the next snapshot clearly identified the turquoise salon. Ladies in drop-waisted dresses had gathered, tea cups on their laps. A woman stood in front of the fireplace, heavy with child. Anna checked the back of the picture.

Liselotte Lang. 1924.

A floorboard groaned in the hallway outside the office. Beckett stiffened beside Anna and motioned for her to get under the desk. She did as she was told. Above her, Beckett unfurled a set of blueprints before he rose to his feet and went around the side of his desk.

"Herr Sauermann? What are you doing here so late? It must be past twelve."

Sauermann was here? At this late hour? Anna's heart flutter-slammed, and she scrunched even smaller into the tight space.

Footsteps came across the room, then halted not far from where Beckett stood. Anna could see the soles of both sets of their shoes from her position under the desk.

"I couldn't sleep. Petra and I were rushed the other morning, and we left several items behind in our suite."

"So you returned in the middle of the night to retrieve them?" Beckett's voice held a note of incredulity. "What if someone had taken you for a prowler?"

"Like I said, I could not sleep. When I arrived, I saw the light and wondered who could be up so late. It appears you and I both suffer from insomnia."

"Sleep is a luxury I often cannot afford when working in the field. I have deadlines to keep, Herr Sauermann. When we hit snags in our production, as we did today, I must make up the difference."

"What is that you are working on?" Herr Sauermann asked, taking another step toward Beckett's desk.

Beckett didn't move out of his way, which effectively blocked Sauermann's progress. Paper rustled. Anna assumed Beckett lifted the full set of blueprints on his desk and showed it to Sauermann.

"I'm very sorry to interrupt your work." Sauermann sounded disconcerted.

Beckett did not budge, nor did he exchange further pleasantries with Herr Sauermann.

His stonewalling methods were notorious. Anna had seen him use that technique before; it always worked to his advantage.

Eventually, Sauermann's footsteps retreated, but Beckett did not give her the green light to climb out from her cramped quarters until the hall was quiet once again.

Why had Sauermann been sneaking about the place in the dead of night? If Anna didn't know any better, she'd swear the man was hunting for something he didn't want them to find. If that was true, it must be something important.

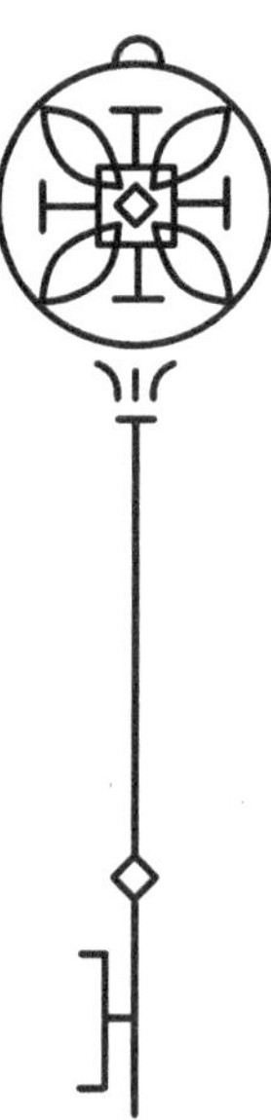

CHAPTER 20

Gunnar slipped off his shoes and took the back staircase. Silently, he doubled back to the archive room and positioned himself outside the open door. Beckett Campbell might have claimed he was working late, but Gunnar had glimpsed a file box between the man's computer monitors, and it appeared to be one of his. What was the man up to?

Beckett's voice carried to him. A woman responded. Gunnar strained to make out the words.

"I can't believe we found it," the woman said. Was that the pretty little designer? What was her name? Amy? Abby? Anna?

"I can't believe your grandmother was a Lang."

Anna. Like her grandmother. The girl everyone thought had died in the Blitz.

"Anna Lang," Anna said. "All these years, I thought her maiden name was Davies."

Gunner's chest tightened, and a pain speared through him as real as if a dagger had pierced his heart.

Another heir. How was this possible? As much as he didn't want to face the facts, the truth lay before him. If her grandmother was a Lang, she was a Lang.

Did this Anna understand the ramifications of her discovery? Did she have proof of who she really was? And was she the original Anna's only descendant, or were there others?

"You know what this means?" Beckett asked.

"No. What?"

"Take a look at this contract. This section here." Papers shuffled against wood.

"The Lang Family Trust?" Anna asked. "I thought the Sauermanns owned Falcon Point."

"No. Gunnar Sauermann is the trustee. This property still belongs to the Lang family."

"Which means whoever this trust benefits would be a relative of mine."

Gunnar's jaw tightened. This resort was supposed to give him financial freedom, not threaten the possessions he already controlled. One thing at a time. As soon as he sold another painting from the estate, he would have the funds to pay the hit man to take care of Ingrid's grandchildren. As for Anna, surely she knew how dangerous a construction site could be.

He made his way to the storage room where the most valuable artwork and antiques were being housed during the current phase of the renovation. After he put his shoes back on, he opened the protective crate that held the last truly valuable artwork from the original Lang estate. These early sketches by Rembrandt should do the trick. A private collector had been asking about them for months. With the money that would come in, Gunnar would be able to pay for the contract on Lars and Tess Hendriks four times over.

Gunnar located the desired artwork and ensured the protective covering was intact. He turned off the light before he opened the door slowly and peeked into the hall. Once he was certain it was empty, he hurried to the back exit where he had parked his car.

He stored the sketches in the trunk and climbed behind the wheel. If Beckett and Anna were working this late every night, when would he be able to get into the archive room to make sure there wasn't any documentation lurking there that could create doubt about the ownership of Falcon Point? If Anna really was a Lang, she could be more problematic than he thought. If a copy of the letter to the land authority had been sent here, where was it? Did other letters exist? More importantly, had Anna found any of the old correspondence from Ingrid Lang?

The 4x4 roared up the mountainside, hitting every pothole in sight. Anna bounced in the passenger seat, grateful for her seat belt as Rudy downshifted and continued up the construction road. More trees had been downed since the last time she had visited the future ski slope. With newly felled pines and hardwoods covering the landscape, it was hard to imagine a smooth slope and chairlifts carrying holiday makers to the top of the run.

Rudy stomped on the brakes and halted beside the caterpillar to speak to the operator.

Anna climbed out and slammed the door. "Thanks for the lift."

She had hitched a ride partway up to the hot springs this morning. Tanja wanted her selection of paint samples and finishes for the spa and restaurant by the end of the day.

"Text me if you change your mind about a ride back to the manor house," Rudy said. "I'll be here for an hour, at least."

"I will. Thanks, Rudy."

He waved her off as she swung her rucksack over her shoulder and started up the track to the hot springs. She inhaled the pine-scented air and took in the birdsong around her. Inside her rucksack, she had packed her binders of paint samples and a lunch in case her selections took some time.

A gentle breeze wafted through the trees, singing through their needles. A swallowtail landed on a clump of wildflowers beside the trail, its wings opening and closing. Anna climbed over the last hillock to reach the bubbling spring.

She wrinkled her nose at the sulfuric odor and moved quickly toward the meadow overlooking the lake a half mile beyond. Not used to such altitudes, she was winded by the time she reached the small body of water and found a grassy seat.

The soft wind lifted the hair off her neck like a lover's hand. While far below, the turquoise waters of Kristall Lake shimmered in the sunlight. She could just make out the newly laid railroad line and heap of gravel where the train station would be built.

All was quiet on the mountain. Bees droned as they darted from one wildflower to the next, and the sun's warmth pressed upon her. If not for the silent caterpillar and backhoe farther down the slope, she might have believed she was the only human alive.

Removing her sample books from her rucksack, she got to work, matching swatches with the nature around her. The sun rose higher in the sky, but Anna hardly noticed. When she played with color, time ceased to exist. She didn't hear the hillwalker until a shadow blocked the sunlight on her selection of samples.

Startled, she glanced up, her heart racing, and met Beckett's amused gaze.

"You always were oblivious to everything around you when you worked with swatches."

She placed a hand over her chest. "What are you doing up here?"

"I check the construction site almost every day. Rudy said he dropped you off so you could choose paint colors. I was curious to see your selections." He sat beside her, uninvited. Nudging her hand aside, he removed the sample sheets from her lap. "Where will this go?" he asked with a nod at the pale-turquoise square.

"The spa rooms overlooking Kristall Lake."

He nodded, then flipped a soft green square toward her. It was similar in shade to the meadow in which they sat. "And this one?"

She took the sample away from him. "The massage rooms overlook the meadow and hillside. I'm not sure if the muted green, taupe, and amethyst I'm thinking about using provide enough zen for that atmosphere."

"Why wouldn't they? They're restful and harmonious."

"Thanks. I always second-guess myself."

"What's this for?" He nodded toward the golden-yellow and warm-orange papers she had set beside her.

"The restaurant interior. I went through the landscape package. They plan to seed the meadow with wildflowers in those shades."

He fingered the warm orange and yellow sheets. "And those ambient colors also encourage harmony and appetite."

She shrugged, secretly pleased he remembered his color therapy courses at RCA.

By the time he finished going through her choices, the sun had reached its apex. Her stomach growled and reminded her she had skipped breakfast.

"I brought lunch. You're welcome to share it with me," Anna offered.

"I have my own, but I've got a couple of bottled waters cooling in the stream under the pines. Would you like one?" He rose to his feet and looked down at her.

"That would be great. Thanks."

He nodded and started for the trees.

She watched him go and marveled at the easiness she experienced in his company after such a long separation. Being in his presence over the last few days had crumbled her defenses, and she was afraid of falling right back in love with him. All right—of tumbling right back into a relationship. She knew from experience how foolhardy that was.

He returned, handed her a water bottle, and opened his lunch. They ate without talking, their eyes on the view. When Beckett finished, he sprawled on the long grass beside her and covered his eyes with his forearm.

"Two weeks after I left you, I realized what a colossal mistake I had made," Beckett said abruptly.

Anna stiffened and glanced away from him, battling down a rising panic. He was going to bring up their past now? His timing was impeccable. No one was on the hillside, and she couldn't escape this conversation until they reached the manor.

"It took me another year to realize you were the only one who mattered to me on this planet."

What did he expect her to say? I'm sorry you were hurt? She had no sympathy for the man, not after how callously he had broken things off with her.

"I hired on with Genskal instead of opening my own firm because I remembered it was your end goal," Beckett said.

What? She dropped her water bottle but hastily snatched it up and screwed on the cap. Beckett had hired on with Genskal because of her? It would have served him right if Genskal hadn't offered her a job.

"You don't believe me?" He leaned up on his elbow and studied her expression.

She didn't bother to respond.

"For the last two years, I have stalked you on social media under a different name," he confessed.

Her eyes widened in utter astonishment. Beckett detested social media, had insisted it was a huge waste of time.

"I did." He plucked a piece of grass, tore the seeds off the end of the stalk, and opened his palm to let the breeze scatter them. "I was mad to find out what was happening in your life. We worked for the same company, but you refused to so much as acknowledge my presence."

"As any normal person would do after what you did. We were talking marriage, Beckett."

"Correction. You were talking marriage."

"Oh ho. And you didn't mention who our children would resemble or where you would take our family on holiday each year?"

"As I recall, I said I doubted our children would inherit Uncle George's bulbous nose." Beckett's eyes gleamed.

"And what about the holidays?"

He glanced at her, then looked away, the humor draining from his face. "I did mention that, more than once, as I recall, along with which public schools I intended to enroll them in."

"We had a rather long conversation about the merits of Eton versus Fettes," she agreed.

"We did." He pressed her hand and kept it there. "I'm sorry, Anna."

Her flesh burned at his touch. Her stomach fluttered as her hand lay passively in his. She wanted to pull away but couldn't quite manage it, so she let it stay there, neither accepting nor rejecting his overture.

This side of Beckett—humble, remorseful, and repentant—was new to her and filled her with confusion.

"I'm sorry I hurt you the way I did. I've reflected on that day thousands of times. If I could, I would go back and beat some sense into my imbecilic self."

Anna lowered her eyes and trembled as his fingers stroked hers. She was shaken at the power he held and resented herself for her weakness. His touch had always thrilled her, yet at the same time, it felt as natural as though her hand had always belonged in his.

Was Beckett telling the truth? Had he really placed his career in neutral to work for the same company just to be near her? He had admitted to social media stalking as well. Anna couldn't imagine the proud Beckett Campbell lowering himself to do so.

Curious to see if that was true, she asked, "Where did I go on holiday last summer?"

"Crete. You blistered that fair skin of yours badly and peeled like a snake afterward."

That wasn't proof. He could have heard about her trip through contacts in the London office.

"Who did I go out with last?"

"Richie Malvern. I wanted to throttle him when I saw pictures of the two of you hillwalking the Peak District."

Anna blinked. She had only posted those photos a few weeks ago, just before she had packed up her flat.

"If you hired on with Genskal to see me again, why didn't you ever stop by my department and chat me up?"

"Anna, lass, I was afraid to approach you."

"Me?"

"Yes, you." He squeezed her hand. "Because if I laid my heart bare and you turned me away—the way I did you—I dinnae know if I would survive. At least by not approaching you, I could fantasize what it would be like if you did take me back."

Her eyes stung, and her heart jackhammered so painfully against her ribs that she was positive it would burst from her body.

He let go of her hand and wiped a tear from her face.

She saw it then. The worry. The fear. All of it laid bare in his eyes. "If you were so concerned, why bring it up now?"

"Because I cannae look at you another day, lass. Being this close to you is nigh impossible. I almost wrung Rudy's neck the other night."

"The night we came back and caught you kissing Tanja?"

"I assure you, I had no interest in kissing Tanja," he growled.

"That wasn't how it appeared."

His skin turned the color of a newly boiled lobster.

Anna took pity on him and laced her fingers with his. The joy that lighted his eyes told her what she needed to know. He had changed. The proud man of her past had loved her, yes, but his profession had been the main thrust of his life. She had assumed it always would.

"You took a terrible gamble telling me this, Beckett."

"I thought I was going to have a heart attack on the way up here. But I simply couldn't go another day without voicing how I felt. Despite the way I treated you, will you forgive me and have me back?"

"I'm taking it under consideration."

"Then while you are taking it under consideration, would you be willing to spend time with me outside of work—to see where this leads?"

Beckett might have changed, but so had she. She wasn't the same carefree girl who had given her heart so easily. She had suffered, and because of it, she kept part of herself back, not wholly capable of giving him her trust.

She ran her free hand through her hair, unable to wrap her tongue around the necessary words.

"Anna?" Her name was the merest sigh, but so much yearning spilled out into those two syllables.

"I need time, Beckett."

"Aye, lass. Take as much as you need." He gazed at her. "I'll wait forever if you are the reward."

As always, he was a gentleman. But she saw the hope tethered inside his eyes, tugging at its lead, a lead held firmly in place by his indomitable will.

"And if it doesn't work out?" Anna had to ask—not to be mean but to make him realize there were two sides to this.

"Then I will live on hope between now and the time you decide."

His humility stunned her again and drove home the truth of his earlier confession about hiring on with Genskal. That, more than anything, proved that he was willing to wait for however long it took.

Though four years had passed since their split, her heart remained raw around the edges, leaving the negative seeds of doubt that had decimated her more recent romantic relationships. Could she work through her doubts and fears and learn to trust Beckett again?

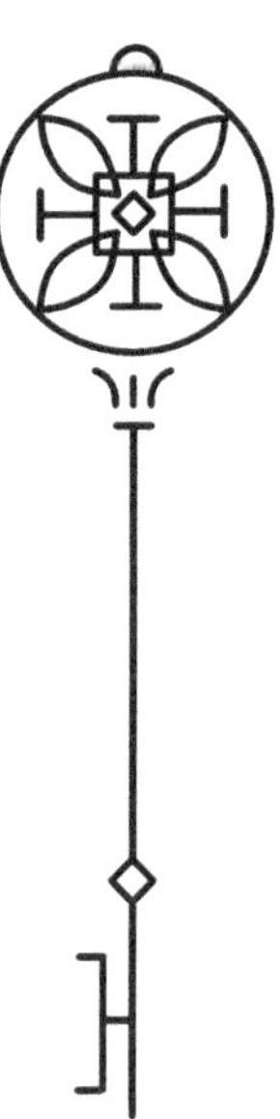

CHAPTER 21

Cole sat on the train that would take him to his apartment on the outskirts of Vienna, his mind racing. He still couldn't believe it. Falcon Point.

For years, his grandfather had searched for his biological father's home, and Cole had joined in the quest throughout his teenage years. His grandfather had given up after Cole's father died of a sudden bout of pneumonia, ultimately passing the legacy on to Cole.

Cole stood as the train rolled to a stop. He moved to the exit and pushed the button beside it. The doors whooshed open, and he stepped onto the platform, then made his way to the street before he glanced around to ensure he was alone. Five minutes later, he entered his third-floor apartment and went straight to the firesafe where he kept his most valuable possessions.

He unlocked it and drew out the contents. He set aside the top tray, which contained a pistol, three fake passports, and ten thousand dollars' worth of various currencies. The contents in the bottom half were what he was after.

He removed the New Testament that had once belonged to his great-grandfather. For years, he had tried to decipher the codes scrawled in the margins, without success. He had even scanned the pages with writing on them so he could have them with him wherever he went, but he had yet to find the hidden meaning. The letters had to be one half of a cypher code, but without the key, it would never be anything beyond gibberish.

The various family papers came next: a Reich passport for his paternal great-grandfather Karl Eckerstorfer as well as his military record from World War II and the death certificate that documented Karl had been killed while serving in the British navy. Following those were the marriage certificate of Karl Eckerstorfer to Millie Stevens and the birth certificate of their son, Cole's grandfather. A second, amended birth certificate lay beside the first. Recorded four years later, this one reflected Cole's grandfather's adoption by Millie's second husband, Henry Bridger. With the stroke of a pen, Glenn Lang Eckerstorfer had become Glenn Lang Bridger. Talk about a genealogical nightmare.

His heart picked up speed when he drew out the letters his great-grandfather had written his great-grandmother. The love they had expressed during Karl's time at sea gave Cole hope that someday he would find a woman who could inspire him to love so deeply. Though he wasn't about to admit the love letters were among his favorites in the collection, he skipped forward to the letters from late 1942, right after Millie learned she was pregnant.

Karl told the story of his escape from Falcon Point after his father, Leopold, was murdered by an old family friend, Wilhelm Sauermann—the Nazi who altered the Lang family history forever.

Cole tried to imagine being in that situation but couldn't. He had a number of cousins on his mom's side, but he had been an only child, as had his father before him.

Still, despite his lack of siblings, he ached for his great-grandfather as he read of his separation from his two younger sisters and his heartache after discovering his younger sister had died. He spelled out every detail as well as his desire to reunite with what was left of his family someday.

Within the same letter, Karl annotated the names of his parents and grandparents, as well as his parents' birth dates and death dates. He also added the progression of how and why his last name changed from Lang to Eckerstorfer. The truth was spelled out in that one document.

Wilhelm Sauermann's treachery had forced Cole's great-grandfather to adopt the alias of Karl Eckerstorfer when he escaped from Falcon Point. Karl's death and Millie's second marriage had changed Cole's grandfather's name from Eckerstorfer to Bridger. If not for the twisted chain of events that dated back to the 1940s, Cole's last name wouldn't be Bridger. It would be Lang.

An inner urgency spurred Anna to seek answers about her grandmother and her family. The pictures she had discovered tantalized her. Who were the people in the photos, and what had become of them?

For the next several days, she spent every evening hunting for records. Beckett's presence across the room had at first unsettled her after their time on the mountain, but true to his word, not once had he pressured her for an answer. If it had been anyone else, Anna would have assumed he had given up. But Beckett, as she well knew, always had a long game. She attributed it to his stubborn nationality, because no one could convince her that he had the patience of Job.

"Anna, can you help me examine the floating staircase?" Rudy asked one afternoon. "I need someone to take notes while I poke around."

"Of course." Anna grabbed her binder and followed him into the foyer.

He knelt and examined the first few treads. "We need to replace this wool runner. It's threadbare in places."

Anna clicked the end of her pen and made a notation in her binder. She glanced up to find Rudy watching her.

"Is something going on between you and Beckett?" Rudy asked as he unscrewed the brass stair rod that held the bottom of the runner in place.

Anna kept her chin down, unwilling to meet his eyes. Had her behavior betrayed something to the team? "Why do you ask?" She attempted to keep her tone casual.

"Because every time I look at you, I can almost hear Beckett growl."

She laughed, entirely disarmed by his comment. "Nothing's going on between us."

"Did something occur in your past?" Rudy fished, not giving up.

Anna stifled a flash of irritation. "Rudy, you're treading into personal territory."

"Sorry." Rudy threw up both hands, palms out. "You can't blame a man for trying. Especially one who is highly interested himself."

"That's very sweet of you, but I already told you I don't do flings. Remember?" She knelt on the next step and checked the wooden riser for wear.

"Loud and clear. How would you respond if I said it's not a fling I'm interested in?" Rudy's eyes had lost their twinkle.

Anna opened her mouth, paused, then shut it again as she searched for an appropriate way to let down a good man in the kindest possible way.

"It's like that, is it?" Rudy gave her a sad smile.

"Like what?"

"You really are taken." He pushed for a definitive answer.

"I just don't see us happening, Rudy." Whether Beckett existed or not, Rudy would never be more to her than a good friend. It was best to let him know without giving him false hope.

"You've dashed my heart to pieces." Rudy placed both hands over his chest as though she had mortally wounded him.

"Very funny."

His behavior put them back on friend status, for which she was most grateful.

"How many stair rods need replacing?" she asked.

"Just two, but we'll need to change out the lot because of the difference in patina. That would stand out like an eyesore for anyone below."

"Righto." She jotted that down.

Looking up, she caught Rudy's intense gaze. Disquiet filled her, and her muscles tightened. Rudy wasn't going to push his ridiculous infatuation, was he?

"If it can't be me, Anna, I think you ought to give Beckett a chance."

"Why?" Anna couldn't keep the surprise out of her voice.

"He's a good man. You won't find many better."

She tapped her mechanical pencil against the clipboard in her hands. "I'll keep that in mind. Anything else?"

"No. That about sums it up." He knelt on the next step and used his drill to remove the brass stair rods, leaving Anna with the distinct impression she had just been manipulated.

"See you, Anna," Gary said from the office doorway.

Anna waved absently to Gary and Tanja as they joined Rudy in the hall. The three of them had invited her to go clubbing in Linz. Having no desire to chat up strangers, fight off pawing drunks, or fend off Rudy's teasing overtures while Tanja hooked up with someone new, she had opted to stay behind.

She faced the bookshelves, hands on hips in the sudden quiet. Beckett had flown to London yesterday for corporate meetings and was due back late tonight. Since she had promised not to search the office without him, she removed two boxes from the bookcases and carted them to her bedroom. She wasn't breaking her word—not precisely. She wasn't in the office.

Other than the two pictures she had randomly found in a mislabeled file from the wrong year, no additional information about her grandmother or her family had surfaced. It was almost as though their presence at Falcon Point had been wiped clean.

With the entire evening ahead of her, Anna changed into sweats and warm, fuzzy socks, then climbed onto her duvet and pulled out the top item in the file box. She read the gold-lettered spine: *Kristall Lake.*

It was doubtful a book about the local lake would have information. Anna set it aside. The book tumbled forward and fell open to a highlighted page. She picked it up, her mouth twisting at the corner.

If someone had taken the trouble to highlight a section, perhaps the book was important after all. Anna determined to use her Google Translate app to translate the highlighted section later.

Several more books followed the first, all in German. A leather-bound volume dated 1930–1940 appeared to record the servants' wages. Curious, she flipped to the first page. The writing was neat and precise.

As her eyes skimmed through the names, Anna marveled that so many had once worked on the estate. Helen Davies's name jumped out at her. Anna paused and reread it. *Helen Davies, das Kindermädchen.*

She touched the neatly spelled name with her fingertips. This dear woman had helped her grandmother reach London, then had lost her life shortly thereafter in the Blitz. Granny owed Helen so much.

Anna moved the book and dislodged two letters wedged behind the cardboard flap inside the box. Curious, she lifted out the yellowed paper. Absently, she checked the return address on each. Both were from the same residence in Amsterdam.

One of the letters appeared to be a duplicate of one sent to the Upper Austrian land authority. The stamp on the envelope read August 23, 1946. The other letter was in German, but she recognized Karl Lang's name on the envelope.

Anna opened the first letter, smoothed out the pages, and clicked the Google Translate app on her phone.

> *To whom it may concern,*
>
> *My name is Ingrid Lang Hendriks. I am the daughter of Leopold and Liselotte Lang, the owners of Falcon Point, an estate in Upper Austria, that was confiscated by the Nazis in 1940. I understand the Sauermann family has retained possession of the estate for which I lay claim with my siblings, Karl Josef Lang and Anna Elizabeth Lang. I sent a copy of this letter to Falcon Point; however, you should be aware that the Nazi who shot and killed my father was*

Anna flipped to the second page and stared at the familiar surname.

> *Wilhelm Sauermann.*

Sauermann. Goosebumps broke out across Anna's skin like a dozen ants had crawled over her body. Surely Gunnar Sauermann was one of his descendants. Was the younger Sauermann aware that his ancestor was a Nazi as well as a murderer? Sending a copy of this letter to Falcon Point was a bold move on Ingrid's part. Perhaps she had expected one of her siblings to return after the war. Anna scanned the rest of the letter into Google Translate.

Please advise how I may regain my family's property.

Sincerely,
Ingrid Lang Hendriks

Anna lay back against her pillow and stared sightlessly at the ceiling.

Wilhelm Sauermann had killed Leopold Lang, then taken possession of Falcon Point. Ingrid's letter made a powerful accusation against the Sauermann family. If it fell into the wrong hands—or more precisely, the right hands—the Sauermanns could lose all rights to the estate. No wonder Herr Sauermann didn't want her snooping through Falcon Point records. He must be aware of this letter's existence.

She shifted restlessly as something dark stirred within her, like a ripple across still water. The thought filled her with disquiet. Wilhelm Sauermann had been a murdering Nazi. How much did his grandson know about the Sauermann family legacy?

Despite the disturbing news, a growing elation sprouted and bloomed within her. Ingrid Lang had survived the war and had married. Ingrid and Granny had beaten the Nazis. Was it possible Karl had survived as well?

Anna sat up on the bed and hugged her knees. Perhaps somewhere out there, she had relatives, people related to her beloved grandmother. She might even—

Steps sounded at the far end of the hallway. Had Beckett caught an earlier flight? She hopped off her bed, opened her door a crack, and peeked out. A tall man dressed in dark clothing opened Tanja's door at the far end of the hall. Not Beckett.

Sauermann.

The hair on the back of Anna's arms rose. Gunnar Sauermann stepped inside Tanja's room and closed the door behind him. Anna could hear him mucking about inside, undoubtedly sorting through Tanja's possessions.

Anna eased her door shut and leaned against the wall, her heart galloping like a runaway horse. What was Herr Sauermann doing? This part of the house was designated for Genskal's design team. Another door opened, and a second later, the entire process repeated itself.

Sauermann was searching their rooms!

Anna's gaze landed on the boxes, their contents spread across her bed. She tiptoed across the room and frantically refilled them, then placed the boxes on the floor and covered them with an open suitcase.

She folded both letters and placed them inside her pocket, slung a towel over her shoulder, then reached for her shower bag. If Sauermann searched her room, fine.

Anna couldn't explain away the archive boxes. Their presence might get her fired, but if Ingrid's letter to the land authority proved accurate, Herr Sauermann had no claim to Falcon Point.

Anna hadn't considered how Ingrid's letter affected her, but the reality of the situation dawned with blinding clarity. As a descendant of Anna Lang, she had a right to the estate too.

Squaring her shoulders, she yanked open her bedroom door and started down the hall toward the bathroom, hoping her primary school acting chops weren't as rusty as she feared.

A door opened behind her. Anna spun on her heel, caught sight of Sauermann, dropped her shower bag, and let out an ear-splitting shriek.

Sauermann stopped cold. "I—"

Feet pounded on the stairs, and Beckett's voice called out. "Anna? Are you all right?"

Beckett rounded the bottom of the basement staircase. Sauermann stood outside Beckett's open bedroom door.

"Herr Sauermann." Beckett raised a brow. "What are you doing down here? This is a restricted area."

The older man's face flushed. "I'm missing a piece of artwork that is going up for sale. I can't find it anywhere."

"He was searching our rooms," Anna said, enjoying the flash of fear on Sauermann's face perhaps a little too much.

"This is my house."

"It's my understanding you're just the trustee," Beckett countered.

"And as such, it's my responsibility to oversee all the belongings within the manor."

"Yes, but according to our contract, you are not allowed to set foot on this floor without prior consent," Beckett said, his voice like iron. "If you give me a description of the painting, my team will be happy to look for it."

"Thank you." Sauermann nodded and headed for the stairs without another word. Anna said nothing until his footsteps faded. She exhaled slowly as her body released the coiled tension Sauermann's presence had supplied.

She retrieved her shower bag from the floor. "You're back early."

"We finished ahead of schedule, so I checked the internet for tickets and got lucky."

"I've never been so happy to see anyone."

"You enjoyed my sixth cavalry charge?"

"More than you know." Her body ached for the comfort of his arms, and she took a tentative step in his direction.

Beckett watched her progress but made no move to accommodate her. "What do you really think Herr Sauermann was looking for?"

Anna withdrew the folded envelopes from her pocket and handed him the one written to the land authority. "I think it was this."

Beckett scanned the letter and whistled. "Do you realize what this means?"

"Yes. I am a descendant of Anna Lang, and Falcon Point belongs to my family."

CHAPTER 22

Cole reread his great-grandfather's letters. He studied the Falcon Point website and searched Google Earth to gain a visual of the estate and the surrounding area. For the past few days, he had researched and analyzed, his hope blooming with each passing hour.

For years, he had thought his family's lost estate was in the Austrian Alps, but if this really was the Falcon Point that had once belonged to the Lang family, it was in a completely different region. No wonder his family had never found it.

He zoomed in on the manor, the view demonstrating that his great-grandfather hadn't exaggerated the grandeur of the home where he had spent his childhood. Cole shifted the view, circling outward. The lake, a village nestled across from Falcon Point, the rooftop of a smaller structure on the mountainside a short distance from the main grounds. His great-grandfather had written that the family treasure was buried beneath the gamekeeper's house.

A new excitement bubbled inside him. This really could be it.

Hoping for verification, he did an internet search for land records in Austria, but even after fifteen minutes of looking, he couldn't figure out how he would send a request for ownership records. Too bad his CIA resources weren't available to aid in his quest. Using those channels, he could have the information by tomorrow, but this was entirely personal.

Cole went into his bedroom to retrieve his cell phone and pulled up his favorites to dial his grandfather's number.

"Cole, my boy. Is that you?"

He smiled at the sound of the familiar voice. "It is. How are you, Grandpa?"

"Doing fine. Not much new here," he said. "Tell me about Austria. Is it everything you expected?"

"The job is boring, but I did find something that might make up for that."

"Oh?"

"I think I found Falcon Point."

"What? *The* Falcon Point?" His grandfather's astonishment rang through the phone. "*Our* Falcon Point?"

His excitement rose alongside his immense satisfaction. "That's the one."

"How did you find it?"

Cole described the website of the planned resort, with its enhanced drawings and planned grand opening. "From what I can see, the website just went up. There isn't a lot of information on it yet."

"You need to make a visit to see the place for yourself."

"I've thought about it," Cole admitted. "I want to know who owns the property first. I hoped you might be able to help."

"How?"

"You mentioned when I got this assignment that you had a friend in banking over here. I thought your friend might know where I would go to request the land records."

"Yes, Isabelle Roberts. I can put you in touch with her, but the owner would have to be one of Ingrid's children or grandchildren," his grandpa said. "According to my mother and all the letters my father wrote, since my aunt Anna died during the war, Falcon Point belongs to us and any other descendants from my aunt Ingrid."

"You don't expect me to put in a claim for ownership, do you?"

"No. I expect you to find our family. My father's greatest wish was to see his sisters again," his grandpa said. "He never got that, but you can give us the next best thing. Find your cousins. Find out what happened to them."

"And find the treasure?"

"That too."

Anna was just drifting off to sleep when her mobile buzzed with an incoming text, the screen lighting beside her. She rolled over and glared at her cell before she picked up the offending contraption.

It was Beckett. *I found a few genealogical websites.*

Did the man never sleep?

She blinked a few times and texted back. *Thank you for the information.*

Snuggling back under the covers, she drifted into the cozy nirvana just before sleep, but her mobile beeped again. Her eyes blinked open, and she stared at the branches patterning her bedroom ceiling from the light of the waxing moon.

She groaned and checked her mobile screen.

Another text from Beckett. *Dinner tomorrow night at The MahaRaja?*

The MahaRaja? Even she, who had been here for no time at all, had heard about the upscale Indian restaurant across the lake. People as far away as Vienna and Salzburg drove out to dine at its exclusive tables. The place was booked weeks in advance. How had Beckett managed to get a reservation?

She texted back. *Yes.*

Afterward, she stared wide awake at the ceiling until the moon set. She didn't know what to think about the new Beckett, a man who laid his heart bare and invited her to exotic dinners.

She rolled onto her stomach and buried her face in her arms, but slumber proved elusive. By 3:00 a.m., she would have given anything for a sleeping pill . . .

Beckett Campbell was driving her utterly mad.

When Anna arrived at the office that morning, Beckett brushed past her on the way to his desk. "How is the kitchen design coming along?"

"It's starting to click. I think you'll be pleased," she said.

He nodded, picked up a blueprint, and was immediately absorbed in the design. Throughout the day, he worked at his desk, behaving as though he hadn't asked her to take him back or made a date with her hours before. Was his self-control really that good? Or was this Beckett's idea of being patient?

Twisting her mouth in concentration, she scrolled through several pages of cabinet makers before she clicked on a link.

Someone came up behind her. She caught a whiff of sage, amber, and musk, Beckett's signature aftershave.

He bent over her shoulder, his eyes on the monitor. "Looking forward to tonight," he whispered, his voice rumbling in her ear.

Anna's heart fluttered at his nearness, and tingles skittered across her skin, starting at her core and shooting to her fingertips.

He moved away to speak to Gary before she spun her chair to face him. Tanja met her eyes over the top of her monitor. A smirk lifted the corners of her lips and was gone.

Anna ducked her head. A smile broke out on her face, and she glanced across the room at Beckett. He was still speaking to Gary but had turned so he could face her. Casually, he tapped his mouth with a forefinger as though listening to the woodworker.

Anna swallowed convulsively and turned back to her computer, her fingers idle on the keys. Tanja called her name three times before it broke upon her consciousness.

"Sorry. I was woolgathering." Anna clicked on her keyboard to bring up her screen.

"Could you send me the latest kitchen elevations?"

"Of course."

"How are the lead times on the cabinets we discussed?" Tanja tucked a strand of hair behind her ear.

"Back-ordered. We'll need to go with a different manufacturer."

"What do you suggest?"

"I found a Swedish company that looks promising. Italy had some lovely ones as well." Anna steeled herself and gave Tanja the bad news in a rush. "The walk-in freezer is giving me fits. The earliest delivery will take four months."

"We don't have four months."

Anna twiddled her fingers. "I did find a local restaurant that recently closed. The place was open less than a year and has a freezer close in size to what we need."

Tanja frowned. "When can they deliver?"

"Tomorrow, if Rudy can spare a couple of men to pick it up. The specs are online. With a few minor tweaks to the pantry dimensions, we'll be operational in a matter of days. And the owner assures me the unit is still under warranty."

"Send me the link, and I'll take a look. What about the appliances for the self-catering cottages?"

Any hopes Anna had entertained of knocking off early to doll herself up died. Tanja kept her hopping for the rest of the day.

To top everything off, whenever Beckett passed Anna's workstation, he met her eyes and smiled, causing her nerves to jump with awareness each time he did.

Beckett had promised he wouldn't demand an answer, but he had launched a subtle campaign that was driving her nearly bonkers.

Indian music piped through unobtrusive speakers. Beckett placed his hand on the small of Anna's back as they followed the sari-clad hostess to their table.

Despite the evening chill, he had called ahead for a terrace table close to the water.

Multicolored party lights strung across the railing reflected in the lake's dark surface. Tall evergreen junipers in large containers shielded them from the other guests. No one else had requested the terrace, but with the patio heater on full, he and Anna were very comfortable.

After they ordered, Beckett faced Anna, not bothering to hide his admiration. Her blue eyes were dark in the dim light, and the shadows brought out the sculpted bones of her face. He couldn't take his eyes off her.

She played with her water goblet.

"How was your day?" he asked.

"Busy. And disruptive. I had a hard time concentrating."

"Why is that?" He gave her a sly grin.

"A coworker kept distracting me." A small dimple appeared in the side of her cheek.

"Do I need to talk to him?"

"I doubt he'd listen."

"Why is that?"

"I don't think he was interested in a conversation."

The food arrived, and the server set out the rice and naan, followed by their main dishes. Anna had ordered butter chicken, which smelled divine. He had gone for the chicken tikka masala.

Beckett leaned back in his chair and idly watched Anna, making her blush until the server left. Picking up where she left off, he asked, "If he wasn't interested in conversation, what exactly was he interested in?"

"That's an intriguing question." She scooped up a spoonful of fragrant Indian rice with fresh curry leaves. "One that needs further investigation."

He set down his fork. "How do you propose to accomplish that?"

The server returned just then and refilled Anna's water, then his own.

"Thank you," Beckett said, his eyes never straying from Anna's.

Anna swallowed, then took a sip of water and dabbed her mouth with the linen napkin in her lap. "Oh, I don't know. Do you have any ideas?"

"I do." He stood and methodically moved his dishes, utensils, and chair beside hers. He took his seat and lifted her hand to his lips. "Anna, I love you."

Her eyes softened, and she pressed her hand to her stomach.

Was that an invitation? Had her feelings for him changed? Tentatively, he leaned forward, making sure she had room to back away if he had misread her. She didn't withdraw, and hope speared through him. His lips were only an inch from hers when his mobile went off inside his pocket.

He groaned. "Perfect timing." He had forgotten to put the blasted thing on silent. He removed it to do just that when he saw Genskal's corporate number flashing on the screen.

"What is it?" Anna's voice sounded husky.

"Corporate. I'm dreadfully sorry, Anna. I've got to take it."

"By all means."

He rose from the table and slipped around the wall of junipers. Why couldn't he have left the irritating device inside his car?

The dark waters of Kristall Lake lapped gently against the shore and pylons of the restaurant decking. Anna picked up her fork and took a bite of her butter chicken. Even lukewarm, it was delicious. Faint sounds of the sitar reached her ears.

What was keeping Beckett? Corporate must have had something weighty to call him after hours. She glanced around the outside seating to see where he had gone, but the tall rocket junipers were spaced tight to create outdoor rooms for the waterfront tables, and she couldn't see past them.

She tore off a piece of naan, folded it inward to make a pocket, and scooped up a portion of butter chicken. She took a bite and let the spices explode on her tongue, then closed her eyes and chewed.

A sudden gust swept across the lake and fluttered the tablecloth, making her shiver. She slid her arms into her dress coat and adjusted her chair closer to the heater. The waning moon crested above the water, its silvered reflection distorted by the breeze. The sitar notes picked up in volume.

Anna tore off another piece of naan as a low-pitched male voice speaking in English reached her through the junipers.

What was Herr Sauermann doing here? Anna hadn't seen him in the main dining room when she and Beckett had arrived.

Trying not to eavesdrop on what sounded like a private conversation, she spooned another small helping of rice onto her plate. The word Hendriks jumped out and made her forget her manners. Wasn't Hendriks Ingrid Lang's married name? She reached for her glass and took a sip.

"Lars and Tess Hendriks. Brother and sister. I need you to remove them immediately."

Anna's hand tightened on her glass, and she froze in her seat.

"Dump them in the canal, for all I care. Just do it. Both of them are in Amsterdam—Tess works at the Van Gogh Museum. Lars is a photographer for Royal Coster Diamonds."

Anna could barely hear the words over the wild pounding of her heart, the blood pumping in her ears.

"I've done half the work for you already," Sauermann said in a furious whisper.

Silence reigned for the space of six beats.

Anna closed her eyes and willed her heart to slow. Tess and Lars had to be Ingrid's relations. Why else would Sauermann want them gone? They stood to inherit the estate if they laid claim to it. And Sauermann was going to see to it that they never would.

"Send me the evidence. I'll wire you the money when the job is complete."

Footsteps stomped off. The faint sound of the opening of the restaurant's terrace door reached her. The music increased in volume, then grew faint as the door closed behind him.

She pawed through her purse for her mobile and googled the museum. It had been easier to remember than the other place. She touched the green button. A recording came on, and she pressed the number for English.

"We're sorry. Please call back during our hours of operation, which are daily 9:00 a.m. to 6:00 p.m. and Fridays until 9:00 p.m."

Anna hung up and tucked a long strand of hair behind her ear, then set the alarm on her phone to call the museum in the morning. Part of her still shied from what she had overheard. This couldn't be real. She'd wake up any minute and find it was all a bad dream. *But if it isn't?* her mind persisted in asking. Could she stand back and do nothing? Deep down, Anna knew she had to act. If Sauermann had hired a hit man to kill Ingrid's offspring, Anna needed to do something now. But what?

The slap of shoes on the deck. Beckett came through the opening in the junipers. His dark hair was ruffled as though he had raked a hand through it. The normalcy of his presence made what she had just heard all the more surreal.

"Anna, I'm so terribly sorry." He retook his seat and turned to her. Two indentations immediately scored the area between his brows. "Are you quite all right?"

"No. I'm not." Her voice cracked with emotion. "Beckett, you believe I'm a sane person, don't you?"

"Aye. Though sometimes it's debatable when your temper's up." His attempt at humor did not lighten his eyes.

"Will you believe me when I tell you that I just overheard Herr Sauermann hiring someone to kill a man and woman in Amsterdam who are descendants of Ingrid Lang?"

"You what?"

"Herr Sauermann came onto the terrace and called someone on his mobile. He spoke in English on the other side of those junipers. I heard every word." Her hands trembled, and she folded them together in her lap. "What do we do? I tried calling the Van Gogh Museum where he said the woman works. They were closed."

"We need to call the local police station and make a statement so they can pay Gunnar Sauermann a visit."

"But what about the Hendrikses? They're in danger."

"I'm sure the local constable will contact the Amsterdam police."

Beckett rang the police. As he waited for them to answer, Anna stiffened as the sudden realization struck her.

If Sauermann found out who she was, he would want her dead too.

CHAPTER 23

Someone was watching her. Under normal circumstances, the sensation would not have given Tess Hendriks cause for concern. Quite apart from the fact that her long blonde hair and piercing blue eyes often turned heads, her position as museum educator at the renowned Van Gogh Museum in Amsterdam frequently made her the focus of attention. She was used to having all eyes on her while she gave tours and trained docents. But this—this discomforting awareness—felt different.

Uneasiness crawled up her spine, tightening her shoulders as she surveyed the museum's main lobby from her position behind the information desk. To her right, one of the museum's student employees was patiently explaining the correct way to use the audio guide to a loud, disgruntled American tourist. The man's companion—a plump woman with artificially red hair—listened to the interaction with barely disguised indifference. Tess couldn't help but wonder if the woman would spare Van Gogh's paintings the kind of attention she was currently giving her purple nails.

Two teenage boys loitered close to the cloakroom, but their eyes were riveted to their respective phones. A young couple walked past, adjusting their newly issued headsets as they entered the nearest gallery. Close behind them, a harried father speaking in rapid French herded his children toward the staircase. One of the children glanced at Tess as she passed. Tess smiled, her instinctive reaction faltering the moment she noticed the man standing in the shadow of the pillar at the base of the stairs. He shifted slightly, and his eyes met hers. Even from this distance, she felt the icy animosity in their depths, and she stiffened.

In her pocket, her phone vibrated. She blinked, and the man turned away, heading for the main doors. Watching his retreating form, she repressed a shudder and reached for her phone. Even if he were not wearing the same torn jeans and black leather jacket over an olive-colored T-shirt, she would know him again. The lank brown hair that hung to his shoulders, his hollow eyes, and his pocked face were indelibly imprinted in her mind.

Tess glanced at her phone screen. It was a text from her brother, Lars.

We need to talk. Can you meet for lunch?

Surprised, she read it again. There was no mistaking the urgency in his message, but she could not imagine what had prompted it. Even though they worked within walking distance of each other, they rarely met during the week. Lars's job as the lead photographer and videographer at Royal Coster Diamonds meant his hours were completely unpredictable. More often than not, his photo shoots went over their allotted time, and between lighting or technical issues and working around the models' schedules, his time was rarely his own.

My next tour ends at 12:30. Would that work?

His response was immediate. *Yes. Bagels and Beans at 12:45?*

Tess smiled. She could have guessed the location even if he'd not mentioned it. Lars might be an artistic genius with a camera, but he was completely predictable when it came to food. If he found something he liked, he stuck with it. A Bagels and Beans smoked chicken bagel was a Lars Hendriks staple.

See you soon.

She slipped her phone back into her pocket and glanced at the clock. Her next tour began in seven minutes, and already, some of the museum visitors were gathering at the designated meeting spot outside the Self-Portraits Gallery. Reaching into the top drawer of the desk, she withdrew the cordless mic and attached it to her floral blouse. She clipped the battery pack to the waistband of her black trousers and picked up the clipboard displaying the names of those who had signed up to take the tour. One last glance at the three people working beside her reassured her that they had things well under control, so she moved out from behind the desk. Mentally switching gears from her native Dutch language to English, she approached the rapidly increasing crowd with her smile in place.

"Good morning," she said. "And welcome to the Van Gogh Museum."

Tess hurried out of the museum's employees' entrance and into the Museumplein. The vast public square was bathed in warm sunlight and filled with tourists. Paths cut across the grass, and rows of parked bicycles lined its perimeter. A large rectangular water feature separated the Van Gogh Museum from the magnificent Rijksmuseum beyond.

Turning away from the Rijksmuseum and weaving through the line of people waiting to enter the Van Gogh Museum, Tess crossed the redbrick walkway to the Stedelijk Museum. She took the path that ran alongside the museum of modern art until she reached the road. Van Baerlestraat was humming with multiple lanes of traffic. Bicycles of all shapes and sizes sped alongside the cars, and pedestrians gathered in a straggly group at the street corner, waiting their turn to cross.

The traffic light changed, and as the vehicles and bicycles came to an impatient stop, the pedestrians surged across the road. Tess ran to join the tail end of the crowd. Stepping over the tram tracks, she made it to the other side of Van Baerlestraat just as the lights changed. The hydraulic breaks of a nearby bus hissed, and all the vehicles pressed forward again.

Continuing a few meters farther down the pavement, she reached the café. Four small, round tables were set up outside. There were two chairs at each table, and although every one was occupied, there was no sign of Lars. Tess pushed open the café's heavy wood-and-glass door and walked inside.

A bell rang as she entered, but neither of the women behind the counter looked up. They were fully occupied, serving the half dozen people already in line. Tess took her place behind a young man in a business suit who was talking on his phone. She glanced around the narrow room. There were half a dozen mismatched tables nearby, and even though there were still a few empty chairs, each table had at least one diner. Beyond the counter, three wooden steps led to the rear of the café, where a few more tables were pressed against the walls.

Straining her neck to see around the line of customers, she scoured the café for any sign of Lars. He was tall enough that he usually stood out in a crowd, even if he was sitting. She pulled her phone from her pocket to see if she'd missed another message. Nothing. Behind her, the doorbell rang to announce the arrival of another customer, and a familiar voice reached her.

"I should have known you'd arrive before me."

Her lines of worry dissolved into a smile. "And I should have known you'd be late."

Lars gave her a brief hug, and Tess was relieved to see his blue eyes—that were so like hers—sparkle with humor. Surely that meant whatever had prompted his unexpected invitation could not be so terrible.

"How are you?" she asked.

"Oh, you know, still taking the best photos in Amsterdam one click at a time."

Tess laughed. "And still working on developing humility."

Her brother grinned and placed his hand on her back, pushing her gently toward the counter. "Place your order," he said. "I'll pay."

Once they'd made their selections and the lady had returned his credit card, Lars used his height to survey the room for an empty table.

"Right at the back," he said. "It looks like the couple there is getting ready to leave. See if you can nab their spot before anyone else does. I'll bring the coffee."

Tess wove through the handful of people standing at the counter waiting for takeout orders and reached the table just as a middle-aged couple stepped away from it. Dropping onto one of the recently vacated chairs, she watched as Lars claimed the seat across from her. He offered her one of the two steaming mugs in his hands.

"It's not that I don't love having lunch with a tall, handsome man." She took the mug and gave him a winning smile. "Especially when he pays for it. But seeing as you visited me in Haarlem last week, I was a bit surprised to get your invitation. What's up?"

Lars placed his elbows on the table and leaned toward her. "I made a discovery this morning." His eyes shone. "And if I'm right about it, it's a really, really big deal."

"Right about what?"

He shook his head. "First, I need you to tell me everything you remember about Oma Hendriks."

"Oma Hendriks?" Their father's mother had died of cancer when Tess had been young. "You're older than me. I'm sure your memories of her are better than mine."

"I don't believe that," Lars said. "Not only are you female—which, by definition, means you remember every little detail anyone ever tells you—but you also loved to sit on her knee and listen to her stories."

Tess smiled softly at the memory. "She did tell marvelous stories."

"Did she ever tell you where she grew up?"

"I thought it was Haarlem." She frowned, searching her memory for anything more. "I remember Pap saying that Oma and Opa worked for the resistance during the war and that it took Opa years after being released from the concentration camp before he was well enough to work."

"Yes," Lars said. "And then he took a job in Rotterdam, where he and Oma and Pap stayed until he died."

"But then Oma brought Pap back to Haarlem," Tess said. "Surely she wouldn't have done that if it weren't her home."

"She may have considered it home," Lars said. "But I'm not convinced it was where she grew up. Neither she nor Pap ever talked of any other family members there. Opa had family in Utrecht, but Oma had no one." He looked at her pointedly. "At least, she didn't have anyone in the Netherlands."

"Where else would they be?"

Lars paused. "Think hard, Tess. Do you ever remember Oma speaking German?"

"She worked for the resistance. I'm sure she spoke German. Most Dutch people do."

"Of our generation, yes, but not Oma's generation. And I'm not talking about speaking enough to get by if a German soldier approached you after curfew. I'm wondering if you ever heard her speaking it fluently."

Tess shook her head. Where on earth was Lars going with this convoluted conversation about a grandmother who'd passed away over twenty years ago? "I only ever heard her speak Dutch," she said. "She told me Dutch fairy tales and sang Dutch . . ." Her voice trailed off as a faint memory nudged its way past the others.

"What is it?" Lars pressed. "What have you remembered?"

"There was one story she sometimes told about a young princess in the forests of Austria. I asked her once why the story made her so sad. She didn't tell me, but afterward, she sang a little German folk song."

"It was an Austrian forest. You're sure of that?"

"Yes, but why—"

"I have something to show you." Excitement radiated off him as he reached into his pocket and withdrew his mobile phone.

"An order for Lars?" A young woman stood at the table, carrying two plates. She smiled prettily at Lars, who accepted the dishes with a slight nod.

"Thank you," Tess supplied.

"Of course." The waitress looked at Lars hopefully. "Would you like a refill on your coffee?"

"No. No, thank you," he said, managing a smile this time.

The waitress had barely turned away before Lars pulled a picture up on his phone and slid it across the table to Tess. "Take a look," he said.

Tess lifted the phone and studied the image on the screen. It appeared to be a photograph of an old black-and-white picture. A pair of earrings lay on a dark fabric cushion. The large pear-cut diamonds were surrounded by two rows of smaller stones, and each hung below a darker gemstone mounted to the finely crafted gold clips.

"A double halo pear earring setting suspended beneath two sapphires is unusual enough," Lars said quietly. "To create it with flawless diamonds is almost unheard of."

"They look just like Oma's earrings," Tess said, studying the picture more carefully.

As a child, she'd stumbled upon her grandmother sitting alone in her bedroom, gazing at earrings just like these. The old jewelry box had been battered and torn, but Tess had been captivated by the sparkling jewelry within. She'd immediately wanted to try them on her own small ears. Her grandmother had run her worn hand across Tess's cheek and told her the earrings were far too fancy to wear while playing but that one day, perhaps she could wear them to a ball. Tess had asked to see them many times afterward, and soon before her grandmother died, Oma had given her the faded jewelry box with the admonition that she keep it safe until she was grown.

"Please tell me they're not still in the back of your sock drawer at home," Lars said.

"Why not? They've been there for years."

Lars ran his fingers through his hair and groaned. "I should have taken a better look at them long ago. It never crossed my mind that they could be anything more than costume jewelry."

Tess tensed. "What do you mean?"

He pressed a key on his phone, and the black-and-white picture sprang to life again. "Royal Coster is producing a line of vintage jewelry for the fall. In preparation for the photo shoot next week, they asked that I go through some old catalogs so we can simulate the way they used to display jewelry back then. I found one book that itemized some of the unique pieces that were never recovered after the war." He pointed to the photo. "This one is listed as handcrafted, five-carat-diamond-and-sapphire earrings commissioned by Leopold Lang of Falcon Point, Austria, for his bride on their wedding day in 1921."

"They can't possibly be the same earrings," Tess said.

Lars leaned forward again. "Tess, look at the filigree work on the clips. I've been photographing diamonds for almost eight years, and other than the ones sitting in your sock drawer, I've never seen anything else like that. Ever."

The café suddenly seemed too warm. "It makes no sense," she said. "All that time when Opa was recovering from being in the concentration camp and Oma was struggling to make ends meet, why wouldn't she have sold the earrings if they were that valuable? They barely had enough to get by their whole married lives."

"I don't know." Lars put his phone back into his pocket and picked up his bagel. "But my gut tells me there's something to it. We know nothing about Oma's life before the war. If she really did come to the Netherlands from Austria, she would have kept that hidden."

"Even after the war was over?"

Lars bit into his bagel and chewed slowly. "Maybe she had a good reason."

Tess wished she'd had the opportunity to ask her white-haired grandmother what she'd endured during her lifetime. If their parents were still alive, perhaps they could have filled in some of the gaps in the fabric of Oma's life. As it was, she and Lars were the only remaining members of their small family, and when it came to family history, it felt as though they were groping around in the dark.

"You'd better come over to the house and look at the earrings," she said.

Lars nodded. "I can't leave the city until Sunday, but I'll come first thing that morning, and I'll bring a loupe. With some magnification, it shouldn't be hard to tell if the gemstones are the real things."

"And if they are, then what?"

"I can offer some suggestions," he said, "but ultimately, it's your call. Oma gave the earrings to you."

"Hi, Lars."

At the unexpected interruption, Tess and Lars looked up to see a stunningly attractive woman standing at their table. Her hair was similar in length and color to Tess's, but her eyes were velvety brown, and she stood at least three inches taller.

Lars instantly straightened in his chair. "Marit! It's good to see you."

The woman laughed. "I believe you are scheduled to see me all afternoon. Meeting you in the café has simply bumped our meeting time up by half an hour."

The color seeping up Lars's neck deepened when he noticed Tess watching him with raised eyebrows. It wasn't often that she saw her brother unnerved, and she was more than happy to make the most of it. He must have caught the humor in her eyes because he offered her a brief frown and then cleared his throat.

"Marit, this is my sister, Tess. Tess, this is Marit Jansen. She's one of Royal Coster's top models."

"Hi, Marit," Tess said. "It's nice to meet you."

"You too." Marit's smile was warm and genuine, and Tess found herself unexpectedly drawn to the beautiful woman. "Do you live here in Amsterdam?"

"In Haarlem," Tess said. "I ride the train in each morning. I work at the Van Gogh Museum."

"Ah. I love that place."

Tess laughed. "Me too."

Lars rose from his chair. "Are you heading over to Coster right now, Marit?"

"Yes. I need to change before the photo shoot."

"I'll walk over there with you, then."

Marit's gaze flitted from Lars to Tess and back. "Oh, but I didn't mean to—"

"You'll actually be doing Tess a favor." Lars grinned. "I've already arranged to see her again on Sunday, and over the years, I've learned that she can only take me in small doses."

Tess laughed. The way Lars was acting, he really liked this girl. "He's all yours, Marit." Before Marit could respond, Tess's phone started to buzz. She took it out of her pocket and glanced at the screen. "I'm sorry," she said. "This call's being forwarded from my work phone, and it's an international number. I'm expecting a call from one of the London galleries, so I'd better take it."

"Of course," Marit said.

Lars placed his hand on Marit's elbow to guide her out of the busy café. "I'll see you Sunday, Tess."

Tess nodded, accepting the call as she waved them off. "Hello. This is Tess Hendriks."

"Thank goodness, I've found you!" The relief in the woman's voice almost masked her English accent.

"I'm sorry," Tess said. "Have you tried calling before?"

"No. I'm just grateful I reached you before it was too late."

"Too late?" Tess frowned. As far as she knew, they were weeks ahead of schedule on their plans to transport three Van Gogh paintings to their temporary home in London.

"Yes. Forgive me for being blunt, but before I say anything more, are you the granddaughter of Ingrid Lang Hendriks?"

Tess's breath caught. Wasn't Lang the name of the Austrian Lars had mentioned not more than ten minutes ago? She rose to her feet. Lars and Marit had almost reached the café's door.

"Who is this?" she asked, grabbing her handbag and hurrying after them.

"My name is Anna Cavendish," the English woman said. "My grandmother was Anna Lang—one of three siblings who disappeared from Falcon Point in Austria at the beginning of World War II. I'm at their former home now, and I recently found some letters from my grandmother's sister, Ingrid, and they led me to you."

The voice on the other end of the phone paused, and Tess squeezed past two heavyset women and their grocery bags in time to see the door close behind Lars and Marit.

"I can't say much over the phone." Her caller's voice had lowered, and Tess strained to hear her over the noise of the café. "I know you have no reason to believe something a total stranger tells you, but I have to warn you. I'm not the only one who has made the connection between you and Ingrid Lang. You and your brother are in grave danger."

The café door opened again, and from outside, Tess heard the blare of a horn followed almost immediately by the roar of an engine, screams, and the squeal of tires. All around her, customers pushed back their chairs and came to their feet to stare through the café windows as a dark-blue van barreled across the road and onto the pavement in front of them.

Cars screeched to a halt, the crunch of metal and glass accompanying the van's progress. Bicycles fell, their riders thrown to the ground in a tangle of frames and wheels and bodies. Messenger bags, groceries, and packages scattered as pedestrians ran for cover. But for some, there was nowhere to go. The van was too fast, the chaos too great. Tess saw Lars thrust Marit aside seconds before the van hit him, swerved, and then hit her.

"Lars!" Tess screamed, pushing her way through the frozen onlookers and yanking the door open.

"Wait!" A businessman who'd been seated closest to the door reached for her arm. "You're safer in here."

She brushed his hand off. "That's my brother!" she cried.

The man stepped back. "Has anyone called 112?" he yelled.

Tess didn't wait to hear the reply.

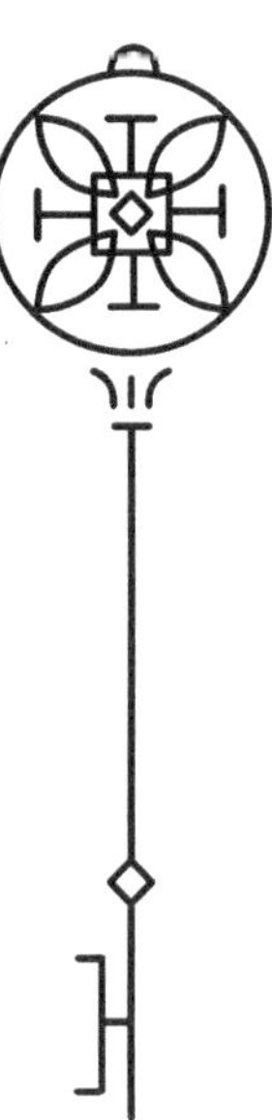

CHAPTER 24

Glass was everywhere. The air smelled of burnt rubber and exhaust fumes and fear. With her heart pounding, Tess ran toward Lars's limp form. All around her, people were crying, some were staggering to reclaim fallen bicycles; others were standing numbly beside their damaged cars or reaching to help those still lying in the road. A clang sounded, and the tram rounded the bend.

"Stop the tram!" someone yelled, and four men broke away from the crowd and began running toward the oncoming vehicle, arms waving.

In the distance, the wail of sirens began, and Tess dropped to her knees beside her brother. "Lars! Lars!" She reached out and touched him. Blood covered one side of his face, running from a cut on his forehead. His eyes were closed, and he made no response. She saw his chest move, and a sob of relief escaped her.

His trousers were torn and bloody, the unnatural position of his left leg suggesting that it was broken. His mobile phone lay beside him, its smashed screen blending in with the thousands of shards of glass littering the pavement. Beside Lars's phone, Marit's large handbag was on its side, its contents spilling onto the ground.

Seizing a silk scarf from among Marit's possessions, Tess wadded it up and pressed it against Lars's wound, panic clawing at her as the pale-green fabric rapidly turned red. She turned slightly. Marit was lying a couple of meters to her left, but only her feet were visible behind the wall of people separating them. A young man broke away from the crowd gathered around the model and moved toward Tess.

"She's awake but in a great deal of pain," he said in answer to her unvoiced question. He crouched down beside her. "What about him?" He carried a cracked bicycle helmet, and his arm bore the angry red scratches and dark grit of road rash.

"I . . . I don't know." Mindlessly, Tess wiped the tears from her cheeks with her free hand. She'd not realized she was crying. "His head is bleeding, and I think his leg is broken, but I—"

"But he's alive?" the young man said.

She nodded. The sirens were getting louder, and she took Lars's hand in hers, praying that the medics would reach him in time.

The injured bicyclist rose to his feet as the emergency vehicles poured onto Van Baerlestraat. Blue lights swirled, and Tess's ears rang from the cacophony of alarms on the police cars and ambulances. The emergency vehicles screeched to a halt in the center of the road, and their doors swung open.

"Over here," the man beside Tess shouted, waving his broken helmet in the air with his uninjured arm. A man with slightly curly brown hair, wearing the distinctive turquoise-and-yellow uniform of a paramedic, exited the nearest ambulance and loped toward them, a black bag in hand. "He took a direct hit," the stranger said as the paramedic drew closer.

"Thanks." The paramedic dropped to his knees on the glass-strewn pavement and began pulling equipment out of his bag. "What more can you tell me?"

"He . . . he was hit on his left side," Tess said. She lifted the blood-soaked scarf so he could see the wound on Lars's head. "And I think that leg might be broken."

The paramedic's head jerked upright, and his hazel eyes met hers. "Tess?"

Tess's heart missed a beat. Bram. It had been years since she'd seen Bram Dekker. They'd gone to primary and secondary school together, but afterward, they'd lost touch. She'd left Haarlem to attend university in Utrecht, and he'd gone to The Hague to study nursing. She'd no idea he'd returned to Amsterdam or that he'd gone on to become a paramedic.

His gaze swiftly returned to his patient. "Is this . . . ?"

"It's Lars," she said, her voice choking on his name. Her brother's face was now so badly bloodstained it was barely recognizable. "Help him, Bram. Please help him."

With a grim look, Bram placed his stethoscope in his ears and leaned over Lars. Tess watched as Bram checked one thing after another. She was vaguely aware that others were standing nearby, some of them silently observing, others talking softly. People hurried past. Shouts mingled with the growl of cars and the clank of bicycles. Tess barely noticed. Her sole focus was on her brother and the slight but regular movement of his chest that reassured her he was still breathing.

Leaning back, Bram pushed the button on the small radio attached to his shoulder and turned his head to speak into it. "Dirk, I'm going to need a stretcher right away."

Tess waited until Bram received a crackly response before speaking again. "How is he?"

Bram met her eyes, and she saw the worry there. "The bad news is he's broken his femur, and we won't know the full extent of his internal injuries until he's had some scans done; the good news is that despite his blood loss, his vitals remain stable."

Tess nodded numbly. As long as Lars was alive, there was hope.

"What have you got, Dekker?"

Tess swung around as the handful of people lingering nearby parted to make way for a burly man dressed in a black-and-yellow police uniform.

"Broken femur, severe head laceration, possible internal injuries." Bram looked up at him. "Victim's name is Lars Hendriks." He pointed at Tess. "This is his sister, Tess Hendriks. Tess, this is Inspector Gerrit Visser."

"Nice to meet you," Tess said automatically. Truthfully, there was nothing nice about it at all.

"Can I ask you some questions, Ms. Hendriks?" Inspector Visser held a pen and notebook in his hand and looked at her expectantly.

The ambulance driver arrived on the run, carrying an orange plastic stretcher. Bram immediately gave his colleague his full attention, and realizing that she would need to move out of the way to enable the men to do their job properly, Tess reluctantly rose to her feet. She brushed some broken glass off her trousers. As if from a distance, she noticed that there was blood on her sleeve. It was Lars's blood.

Swallowing hard, she faced the police officer. "What do you need to know?"

The siren wailed as the ambulance neared the hospital. Tess clutched the edges of the collapsible seat she was using in the back of the vehicle and braced herself as the driver barreled through another set of traffic lights. Across from her, Bram was monitoring the machines attached to Lars's body. The steady bleep of the heart monitor matched the drip, drip, drip of the liquid running into her brother's vein from the bag suspended above his head. Tess matched her breathing to its rhythm, silently praying for Lars and for Marit and for the strength to make it through this nightmare no matter what lay ahead.

She'd answered Detective Visser's questions as best she could. Other than positively identifying her brother and Marit, she considered it unlikely that she'd added anything further to the information he'd already gathered from the other witnesses.

The blue van's tinted windows had prevented anyone from getting a good look at the driver, and the man had made his escape before anyone had fully grasped the enormity of his crime. Unfortunately, if he followed the example of most criminals in Amsterdam, his vehicle was now submerged in one of the city's many canals. It would not matter if any eyewitnesses had had the wherewithal to take a photo of the number plate, the van—with all its indicting dents, broken headlights, and fingerprints—would be almost impossible to find.

"Tess." Despite the noise within the ambulance, Bram's voice startled her. She met his gaze and saw compassion there. "I'll be going in with Lars," he said. "Things might be a bit crazy at first, but someone in the ER will tell you where you can wait, and I'll come out and find you as soon as I can."

She shook her head, fighting back her seemingly endless supply of tears. "Don't worry about me. Just knowing you're with Lars is enough."

The ambulance lurched to a stop, and instantly, the back doors burst open. Voices, firm and insistent, issued commands, and hands reached for the stretcher. Bram unhooked the monitors and released the break on the gurney.

"I'll find you," he repeated, then he jumped out of the vehicle.

Tess scrambled out after him. By the time her feet reached the pavement, he was already running alongside the gurney toward the open hospital doors. A siren wail announced the approach of a second yellow vehicle with the distinctive red and blue stripes and flashing blue lights. It peeled up to the hospital entrance. Tess guessed that this ambulance carried Marit, and although she desperately hoped the young woman was all right, her priority was Lars.

Hurrying after the emergency room staff, Tess entered the redbrick building. Floor-to-ceiling windows illuminated the small lobby. The gray tile floor was polished to a shine, and modernist white plastic and metal chairs circled a small sitting area to the right of the doors. Tall concrete pillars broke up the open space, but the harshness of the sterile environment was softened by a large green fern that overflowed down the sides of a rectangular planter box beside the receptionist's desk.

An elderly man sitting in the far corner of the waiting area lowered his newspaper to watch as the staff pushed Lars's gurney through a wide set of swinging doors on the left, but the other three occupants of the room barely acknowledged the activity. The weary looks on their faces suggested they had seen this happen too many times already.

Eyeing the bold *No Admittance* sign posted above the swinging doors, Tess slowed her footsteps. Was this as far as she could go? Behind her, the main doors whooshed open, and Tess moved aside as the gurney carrying Marit entered. The model's long blonde hair hung limply off the side of the stretcher, and blood stained the white blanket covering her body.

"Oh, Marit," Tess murmured, her nails digging into the palms of her hands. "Please be okay."

The medic pushing the gurney spared no one a second glance. Tess waited until he and the nurses surrounding Marit disappeared down the restricted hall, and then she approached the reception desk.

Tess had lost track of how many people had come and gone through the emergency room lobby before Bram reappeared through the swinging doors. She rose to her feet and took a few steps toward him, her chest tightening as she searched his handsome but inscrutable face. He spotted her immediately, but his expression gave nothing away as he crossed the room toward her in long, fluid strides.

Tess's mind instantly went back to the many times she'd watched him compete in track-and-field events at school. They'd been part of a tightknit group of friends back then, and although her interests had been primarily focused on the arts, she'd enjoyed attending the school's athletic events to cheer on Bram and his teammates. His youthful, lanky frame had filled out considerably in the intervening years. It was obvious that his work as a paramedic kept him in excellent shape.

He offered her an apologetic look. "Sorry I kept you waiting so long."

"How is he?" she asked.

Bram took her hand and guided her back to the chairs. She hadn't seen him in over five years, and yet, the action felt completely natural and brought her more comfort than she could have imagined.

"He's stable," Bram said. "I stayed back there long enough to hear the results of his scans. There's no sign of internal bleeding—which is huge. His leg's a mess, but that appears to be his only break, and they're taking him in for surgery right now."

"Is he awake?"

"He came round long enough to answer the medical staff's questions. I'm sure his head's pounding, but he was lucid."

Relief caught in her throat, and her tears began again. She bowed her head to hide them, but Bram was not fooled.

He tightened his grip on her hand. "He's going to be okay, Tess. A broken femur is nothing to joke about, and he's in for a long, painful recovery, but he'll make it."

She nodded. "Thank you," she whispered.

"Hey, what are friends for?" He smiled—a slightly crooked, wonderfully familiar smile. "Well, other than cheering you on in the 100 meters or swimming together in the canals or arguing over which is the best crepe at Crepe Affaire."

"Strawberries and cream," Tess said.

He chuckled. "Nutella. No question."

For the first time since she'd left Bagels and Beans, Tess managed a smile. "How did we lose touch with each other?"

Bram shrugged. "Going to universities in different cities can do that. I hear from Evi and Markus every once in a while, but other than that, my only news of old friends comes through my mother." He paused. "I was sorry to learn about your parents. It must have made what happened today even harder."

It had been three years since her parents had died in a car accident, and even though the severe pain of that loss was now more of a dull ache, it was still there. The thought of losing Lars in a similar way—of being left with no family whatsoever—was almost more than she could bear. And even though Bram's news about Lars's condition had given her the hope she desperately needed, she knew she did not have the emotional strength to discuss either accident now.

"How do you do it?" she asked. "How do you go from one emergency to another without cracking under the weight of it all?"

"It's not easy," he admitted. "The first few car accidents I attended shook me up pretty badly." His eyes glazed over slightly, and Tess guessed that he still struggled with those memories. "I quickly learned that I have to separate the awfulness of the situation from the people I can help. Doing that goes a long way toward enabling me to keep a clear head when I need it." He glanced at her. "It's definitely harder to do that when the patient is someone I know though."

Tess could only imagine. "I'm glad you were there today, Bram," she said.

"Yeah." He squeezed her hand again. "Me too."

The radio at his shoulder crackled to life, and Bram stilled, turning his head slightly to listen to the woman on the other end. When she finished speaking, he pressed the reply button and spoke into it. "Understood. We're on our way." Releasing Tess's hand, he rose abruptly. "I'm sorry, Tess."

"Go," she said.

With a grateful nod, he turned and ran for the main doors. Tess stood. Through the large windows, she watched him jump into the waiting ambulance. The lights and siren turned on, and the vehicle entered the traffic, rapidly picking up speed and disappearing from sight within seconds.

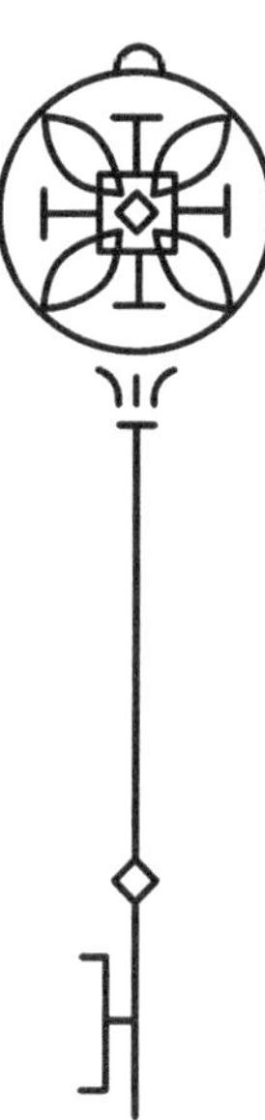

CHAPTER 25

Anna paused while Beckett opened the door to Gildenstatt's local Amt, a two-room police precinct with a single barred cell. Her mind drifted to Tess Hendriks, and her worries increased. Their call had dropped, but why? Had Tess hung up on her?

Just before the call had ended, a chaotic sound of what seemed like shattering glass and crunching metal had reached her through the line. Had Anna reached out too late to save her? Anna had called Tess back—twice. But no one had answered.

The officer on duty approached the counter in his pristine uniform. "May I help you, *fraulein*?"

"I called last night and was told to come in and file a report," Anna said.

"What sort of report?" he asked politely.

"I overheard a man hire someone to commit a murder."

In the blink of an eye, the officer's attitude changed to one of concern. "This is serious indeed. Please, come this way."

Beckett went to accompany her, but the officer raised his brow. "Did you overhear the same thing?" he asked Beckett.

"No. But I'm with her." Beckett gently squeezed the back of Anna's arm in a gesture of support.

"I'm sorry, sir, but you will need to stay here. Please take a seat." The officer indicated a row of hard wooden chairs before he ushered Anna into the other room and handed her a form.

"Did you only hear the conversation, or did you catch a glimpse of this man?" the officer asked after they were settled.

"I can identify the person who ordered the murder," Anna said, her index finger tapping the paper.

"By just an overheard phone conversation?" The policeman's lips compressed, his disbelief obvious.

What did he take her for, a tourist who had sampled too much Austrian beer?

"*Fraulein*, if you only heard a conversation, how can you possibly identify the man?" he asked, his tone overly reasonable. "I can hardly round up every person in Gildenstatt so you can listen to them speak."

"I have met this man before," Anna huffed, her temper rising. "That's how I recognized his voice." Why wouldn't this man take her seriously?

"And who might that be?"

"He's a local. His name is Sauermann. Gunnar Sauermann," Anna said, recalling Sauermann's first name from the documents on her desk.

For three full seconds, the policeman didn't respond. He didn't do anything—just stared at her. Turning without a word, he selected a form and handed it to her. "Please fill this out, and I will file your report." The policeman left the room and closed the door behind him.

Anna glanced at the German form and pulled out her mobile. This was going to take Google Translate.

Tess stood in the empty emergency room lobby, staring sightlessly out of the window. It had been over three hours since she'd arrived at OLVG East with Lars in the ambulance and almost two hours since Bram had joined her in the waiting room to tell her that Lars was going in for surgery on his broken leg. The hands on the waiting room clock had seemed to slow more with every passing quarter hour, and with no update on Lars's condition, Tess's anxiety was steadily climbing.

Half a dozen ambulances had come and gone since Bram left, but because the emergency personnel served all the hospitals in Amsterdam, it was quite possible that he would not return to OLVG East today. Her feeling of regret at that thought surprised her. She could not have anticipated how much strength and comfort she had drawn from having him there.

Her stomach growled, and she pressed her hand against it. She'd left her uneaten bagel at the café, and breakfast felt like a millennia ago. The receptionist had taken pity on her after she'd been waiting for two hours and had offered her a cup of weak coffee. Tess had managed to drink half of it before it turned into something that resembled cold, muddy water. Despite her stomach's complaints, she had no desire to eat anything.

She'd called the museum director. Somehow, she'd managed to articulate without breaking down the reason she would not be returning to work for the next few days. Her call to Royal Coster had been even more difficult, especially because she could give the receptionist no update on either Lars's or Marit's conditions. The receptionist had promised to contact Marit's parents to let them know what had happened. But no one had entered the emergency room asking about the young woman yet.

The main doors opened, and for a moment, the sounds of Amsterdam and the warmth of early summer entered the lobby. Stifling a sigh, Tess turned away from the passing cars and bicycles, vaguely aware that the man who'd entered the lobby was now standing at the front desk. Tess started back toward the chairs.

"May I help you, sir?" the receptionist asked.

"Yeah." The man sounded young. "I heard my cousins were in a bad accident. Someone on Van Baerlestraat said the ambulances brought them here."

Tess froze. Had anyone else been brought in from the accident after Lars and Marit? She glanced across the room. The man had his back to her. He was no longer wearing his leather jacket, but the lank hair brushing the top of his olive-colored T-shirt was horribly familiar, as was his diffident stance. With her heart pounding so hard Tess could barely think, she slipped behind the nearby concrete pillar and leaned her back against it. Taking deep, controlled breaths, she strained to hear the remainder of the conversation.

"I'm afraid I can't give out that information, sir."

"You don't understand." There was a hint of anger in the man's voice. "I'm Lars and Tess Hendriks's cousin. They're the only family I have."

"Then I assume one of them will contact you as soon as they can," the receptionist said calmly.

"So they're still alive?"

Tess pressed her fingers against the pillar. Who was this man, and how did he know her and Lars?

"I can't tell you anything more, sir."

"I want to speak to your boss," he spat.

"I'm afraid she's unavailable at the moment." The receptionist was unflappable. "But you are welcome to take a seat in the lobby if you'd like to wait for her." A telephone rang. "If you'll excuse me one moment." There was a slight pause. "Emergency room."

The man swore, and as the receptionist continued to talk into the telephone, Tess heard the staccato echo of his footsteps crossing the tile floor toward the main doors. She shifted two small steps to the left to keep the pillar between her and the stranger. The door closed behind him, but she stayed where she was, counting seconds in her mind.

"He's gone." At the receptionist's voice, Tess jumped. The woman had left her desk and was tidying the magazines lying on the nearby table.

Tess moved away from the pillar. "He . . . he isn't my cousin."

"I guessed as much when I saw you hiding back there."

Tess took an unsteady step toward the chairs. "Thanks. I appreciate you not giving me away."

"We get angry exes in here all the time." She gave Tess a wry smile. "The cousin line isn't new."

Tess nodded. It was easier to let the woman think the creepy man was her ex than to try to explain something she didn't understand herself. "I just hope he doesn't come back."

"I don't suppose you'll be here if he does." The woman glanced at the doors leading to the restricted area. "It shouldn't be too much longer."

Tess dropped into the closest chair and tucked her trembling hands between her legs. What did all this mean? She had pretty well dismissed the phone call she'd received at the café as a crank call, but now, it seemed that she had a stalker who not only knew her name, but he knew Lars's too. Was he in any way connected with the woman on the other end of the phone? And if so, was he working with her, or was he the person the woman had been trying to warn her about?

She'd not thought about that call since the accident. Had she even hung up the phone? She took her mobile out of her pocket and pulled up her recent calls. A number repeated with the international area code listed. Tess closed her eyes, trying to remember. Anna. The English woman had said her name was Anna Cavender, Cavendish, or something like that. Tess's thumb hovered over the call button as indecision tore her in two. Would making contact give her answers, or would she simply be playing into an elaborate and terrifying hoax—one that had left Lars and Marit fighting for their lives and her feeling more alone and vulnerable than she'd ever felt before?

A middle-aged woman wearing scrubs entered the waiting room through the swinging doors. "Ms. Hendriks?" She looked at Tess expectantly.

"Yes." Tess picked up her handbag, dropped her mobile inside, and rose to her feet. Gripping the bag's handles so tightly she could barely feel her fingers, she faced her fears. "How is he?"

The nurse smiled kindly. "He's still in the recovery room, but he's awake and is asking for you."

Relief washed over Tess, making her knees weak. "Can I see him?"

The nurse nodded. "Come this way."

Tess followed her through the swinging doors and down a wide corridor. Doors lined their route. A few of them were ajar, and she caught sight of hospital beds—most of them occupied—and all sorts of medical equipment. Signs hung from the ceiling, showing the way to the radiology department, labor and delivery, and the cafeteria. The murmur of voices ebbed and flowed as she passed the patients' rooms, and the smell of cleaners surrounded her.

The nurse stopped opposite the door to a lift. She pushed the button on the panel, and the doors opened immediately. Tess followed her in and watched silently as she pushed the button for the third floor.

"I'm Emilia," the nurse said. "I'll be your brother's nurse until I go off shift this evening."

"How's he doing?" Tess said. "Did the surgery go okay?" After being kept in the dark for so long, the questions tumbled over each other.

Emilia gave her a sympathetic smile. "He's doing as well as can be expected, given what he's been through. The surgeon attached a rod and plate to your brother's femur to stabilize the bone. I believe the procedure went well, but the doctor will meet with you to give you more details."

The lift rose quickly, and within seconds, the door opened in front of a nurses' station. Two women in scrubs were seated behind the desk. A man in a white coat was standing behind them, flipping through a file.

"I'm taking Ms. Hendriks back to see her brother," Emilia said.

Both nurses offered Tess brief smiles, but their attention quickly returned to their computer screens. Emilia led her down a hall to the left, past a series of doors signposted as surgery rooms. The whisper of soft voices she'd heard on the lower floor had disappeared, replaced by the hum of fluorescent lighting and the beeping of a distant heart monitor.

At last, Emilia stopped opposite a closed door. She knocked softly, then she turned the handle and stepped inside.

"Your sister is here, Mr. Hendriks," she said, walking around a pale-green curtain and pushing it back a couple of feet to reveal a hospital bed surrounded by several monitors and an intravenous drip line.

Tess entered the small room, her eyes on the man lying in the bed. Lars stirred slightly. A wide bandage swathed his head, and traces of dried blood still clung to his hair. His eyes were closed, his face pale and scratched. A blanket had been pulled up to his chin, but various wires and tubes protruded out from under it, connected to the machines beside the bed. She reached out to touch his hand through the blanket, and his eyelids flickered open.

Turning his head slightly, he managed a weak smile. "Hi, Tess."

"Hi yourself." She swallowed the lump in her throat. "How are you feeling?"

"Hammered."

"It will take a little while for the effects of the anesthetic to fully wear off," Emilia said. She pointed to a red button on the arm of the bed. "I'll be back to check on you soon, but push that if Mr. Hendriks needs anything before then."

"Thank you," Tess said.

Emilia nodded and walked out of the room, closing the door behind her.

Tess reached for one of the two plastic chairs in the room, moved it closer to the bed, and sat.

Lars's gaze followed her. "How's Marit?" he asked.

"I wish I could tell you. I called Coster, and the receptionist said she'd contact Marit's parents. But that was hours ago, and no one came into the ER asking for her."

"Marit's parents live in Maastricht. It will take a while for them to get here." A spasm of pain crossed his face, but Tess was not convinced that anything physical had caused it. "I tried to push her out of the way. I tried . . ." He cleared his throat and started again. "I need to know if she's okay, Tess."

Tess rose to her feet again. "I'll go down to the nurses' station and ask. They may not tell me anything, but I'll try."

"Thanks. I appreciate it."

She squeezed his hand through the blanket. "I'll be right back."

Tess was halfway down the hall when she heard a ping announcing the arrival of the lift. Moments later, a man's voice reached her.

"Which room is Lars Hendriks in?"

Her feet froze to the floor as visions of the man she'd first seen at the museum filled her head. Surely he hadn't reached this part of the hospital. Her pulse quickened. She didn't dare wait to find out if it was him. Turning on her heel, she started running back toward Lars's recovery room.

"Tess."

At the sound of her name, she turned her head and staggered to an unsteady halt. Bram, still wearing his brightly colored uniform, was hurrying toward her. In an instant, her panic ebbed, leaving her limbs shaking.

"I'm sorry I didn't get back here sooner," he said. "I had to take a couple of patients to OLVG West before my shift ended." He paused, his brow furrowing as he studied her more closely. "Tess, what's wrong?"

"I thought . . ." She shook her head. She should not be winded after running five meters down a hall. "I thought . . ." she began again.

Bram reached out and took her arm. "Steady," he said. "Take a deep breath."

She did as he said, willing her trembling to subside. "I thought you were someone else."

"Someone who frightens you this much?" Concern filled his eyes.

"Yes." In that single word, Tess acknowledged her fears. "I . . . I don't know who he is, but he was watching me at the museum this morning, and he came to the hospital a little while ago, asking about me and Lars. He . . . he knew about the accident."

Bram's frown deepened. "Let's find you a chair, and you can tell me about him from the beginning."

Grateful that he wasn't brushing off her concerns as the wild imaginings of someone who'd recently experienced significant trauma, Tess managed a shaky smile. "Okay. But first, I promised Lars I would ask about Marit. We haven't heard anything about her."

"Let me take care of that," Bram said. He had yet to release her arm. "I want you off your feet until your shaking is under control."

Embarrassed that he'd noticed, Tess shook her head. "I don't need a chair."

He raised an eyebrow, obviously unconvinced.

"Really, Bram. I'll wait here while you go and ask about Marit. The nurses are more likely to tell you how she's doing." When he still made no move, she added. "I'll lean against the wall, and if I feel bad enough, I'll sit on the floor."

Bram rolled his eyes. "How did I forget how stubborn you are?"

"Not stubborn," she said. "Determined. Lars is desperate for news about his friend, and I cannot give my attention to why the man at the museum followed me to the hospital until I have that information for him."

She recognized the reluctant acceptance in Bram's eyes.

"Sit," he said, pointing to the floor. He waited until she was sitting with her back against the wall, then he jogged back down the hall toward the nurses' station.

Tess pulled her knees up to her chest and rested her head against them. Her trousers smelled of dust and hospital and blood. Her stomach roiled. If Bram did not return with good news about Marit, she didn't know how she would break it to Lars. She raised her head, straining to hear the voices at the end of the hall, but they were too indistinct to make out any words.

Tess stayed on the floor until Bram reappeared. By the time he reached her, she was standing again.

"Any better?" he asked.

She nodded. "What did you find?"

"First, they've given no information on Lars's condition or location to anyone else—and they won't. Second, Marit just came out of surgery."

Relief and anxiety vied for dominance. "How bad is she?"

"She had significant internal bleeding." His voice was grave. "They've removed one of her kidneys, and she's been given a transfusion."

Tess pressed her back against the wall, glad for its support. "Will she make it?"

"Her chances for a full recovery are good. I didn't talk to anyone who was in the operating room, but Emilia seemed to think the procedure went well."

"What do I tell Lars?"

"The truth," he said. "Marit will have to focus on her own recovery for five or six weeks, but after that, she should be well enough to visit him. Maybe seeing her will help motivate him to push through his rehab."

She managed a small smile. "You noticed how pretty she is too."

He took her elbow and steered her toward Lars's recovery room. "I noticed how much she looks like you."

CHAPTER 26

Cole tapped on his computer keys until he found what he was looking for. He supposed he shouldn't be hacking into the employee database of a London-based design firm without proper authorization, but he couldn't help himself. He had to know who was working on the remodel of Falcon Point. With any luck, someone on site would be an easy source of information.

After several minutes of searching, he uncovered the list of the design team headed up by Beckett Campbell. He kept reading. Rudolph Gruber, the general contractor. Tanja Mueller, lead designer. Cole jotted down the names before checking into the personnel files. He scanned through the photos and personal information for each. The image of a junior designer popped up, and Cole paused. Anna Cavendish's blue eyes were the same shade and shape as his own. Strange. He'd never seen anyone with quite that color of blue outside of his family.

Cole checked the time and set aside his notes. As much as he wanted to keep researching, he had a visitor to prepare for. He moved into the kitchen, wiped down his counters, and disposed of the last week's takeout containers. When the pizza box didn't fit into the trash can, he slid it into the oven. No one would see it there.

When his grandfather said he would put him in touch with his banker friend, he had expected a text message with her phone number, not an appointment to meet at his apartment. Most likely, his grandfather would receive a report on Cole's living conditions within an hour of the woman's leaving his apartment.

"Beggars can't be choosers," he muttered to himself. He finished wiping down the kitchen as a knock sounded. He tossed the dishrag into the sink and checked his phone to view the feed from the surveillance camera he had planted above his door.

The woman appeared to be in her late twenties. Expressive green eyes, deep auburn hair, gorgeous skin. This was his grandfather's friend? At best, Cole had expected some rotund woman in her fifties. At worst, he worried the friend might come with a set of hearing aids.

Cole pocketed his phone and pulled the door open.

"Cole Bridger?" The woman's accent tagged her as a fellow American.

"That's me. You're from the States."

"Yes. I'm Isabelle Roberts." Her head tilted slightly, and curiosity and humor peeked out from behind her professional exterior. "Your grandfather asked me if I could help you with something."

"Please, come in." Cole motioned her inside and led her into the living room.

As soon as Isabelle sat down, she said, "Mr. Bridger wasn't very specific about what kind of help you needed."

"I'm trying to identify the owner of an estate here in Austria." Cole sat beside her. "I hoped, with your experience in banking, you might be able to steer me in the right direction."

"That should be easy enough." Isabelle opened her oversized bag and withdrew her laptop. "Perhaps it would be easier to work at your kitchen table."

"It might be, if I had two chairs."

Amusement flashed in Isabelle's eyes. "You're quite the bachelor, then."

Even though the observation was accurate, Cole said, "I haven't lived here long enough to buy anything beyond the necessities."

Isabelle opened her laptop. "Where is the property located?"

"It's about an hour outside of Linz. It's called Falcon Point." Cole pulled up the resort's website. "This is it."

"A resort?"

"It looks like it's going to be one, anyway. According to the website, the ski slopes will open this November, but the rest of the resort won't be complete until next year."

Her voice turned wistful. "It's beautiful."

"Yeah, it is." Cole tried to envision living in such a place but couldn't. For him, home was wherever his keepsake box was stored. "Any ideas on how to figure out who currently owns the place?"

"I can put a request in to the land authority for you. It should only take a day or two to get a response."

"That would be great. Thank you."

"It's not a problem. My bank access will cut through the red tape a lot faster than if you tried to request it yourself." She typed in the information for the estate and took down Cole's phone number. When she finished submitting her request, she closed her laptop. "That should do it."

"Thank you again for your help."

Her expression softened. "Anything for Mr. Bridger."

"How do you know my grandfather?"

Her face lit up as though warmed by happy memories. "He and my grandpa worked together years ago."

Cole read between the lines. His own grandfather had worked intelligence. Was it possible both he and Isabelle had followed in their grandfathers' footsteps? He could hardly ask her if she was CIA without revealing his own association with the agency.

Intrigued, Cole opted to sidestep the possibly awkward conversation and asked, "Have you already eaten dinner?"

"No. I was going to pick something up on my way home."

"Or you could let me take you out." Cole noticed her surprise. Although, why a woman who looked like her would be surprised by a dinner invite was beyond him. "It's the least I can do to thank you for your help."

She let a slow smile form. "I guess we could do that."

"Great. There's a fantastic little place down the street." Cole collected his laptop. "Let me put this away and grab my wallet." He carried his laptop into his room and secured it in his safe. When he returned a moment later, Isabelle waited by the couch.

"Ready?" she asked.

"Yes." Cole opened the door for her and followed her into the hall. "How long have you lived in Vienna?"

"A couple years."

"And before that?"

"I worked in New York for a few years after I graduated college."

"Did you go to college in DC, or did you used to live there?"

"How did you know I lived in DC?"

"Because you know my grandfather." Cole noted the way she sidestepped his question, and his curiosity heightened. "I'm surprised this is the first time we've met. I used to spend all my summers with my grandparents."

"That must have been amazing. Your grandfather is an incredible man."

"I couldn't agree more."

Tess rolled her shoulders in a faint attempt to relieve the ache that had settled there hours ago. Lars had finally fallen into a deep sleep. He had flitted in and out of consciousness in the recovery room, waking long enough to recognize Bram as one of Tess's school friends and to hear the update on Marit's condition. Tess need not have worried about his reaction to the news. He would undoubtedly have more questions once he was thinking clearly, but for now, he was content to know that she had survived.

Soon after the surgeon had met with them, Lars had been moved to another room on the fourth floor, where he would likely stay until he was well enough to be released from the hospital. Bram had made the trek to the next floor with them, and along the way, he'd stopped to talk to the staff at the nurses' station again and had learned that Marit's parents had arrived and that she was being moved to the same floor as Lars. The news came as an unexpected relief to Tess; she had not realized how much Marit's situation had been worrying her.

Perhaps her concern stemmed from the fact that she understood what it meant to feel alone. She'd experienced it acutely in the waiting room—and would still be feeling it if it weren't for Bram. She glanced at him now, wondering where the time had gone since secondary school, why they'd not reconnected before this, and more especially, why he was still with her in Lars's hospital room.

As though he felt her gaze, Bram turned from the news he was watching on the television and raised his eyebrow. It was a quirk he'd had for as long as she could remember, and it made her smile.

"Are you ready?" he asked.

She gave him a puzzled look. "Ready for what?"

"Ready to tell me about the man who has you so scared." He inclined his head toward the bed. "It looks like Lars has settled, and in a few minutes, I'm going to persuade you to go home for the night." He raised his hand as she began to object. "Tess, you need your sleep as much as Lars does. The hospital staff is perfectly capable of looking after him. You can be back here first thing in the morning." A teasing glint appeared in his eyes. "And as naturally lovely as you are, grit and blood are not your best look."

Tess glanced at her stained clothing and caught her lower lip between her teeth. He was right. She was a mess. But she didn't want to leave Lars, and the thought of taking the train home looking like this filled her with dread. She'd be the object of everyone's stares, and she didn't want to answer anyone's questions—no matter how well meaning they may be.

"I don't want to go," she said. "By the time I reach the train station—"

"I'm driving you."

She stared at him. "Bram, I live in Haarlem."

"I figured as much. Are you still in your parents' home?"

"Yes."

"Great. I'll drop you off, and then I'll go stay the night with my mother. She'll be thrilled. She's been after me to come home for a visit for weeks. I have to be back at work by 8:00 tomorrow, so I can pick you up and drop you off at the hospital on my way."

She stared at him, the question she'd asked herself moments before resurfacing. "Why are you doing this?"

"We're friends," he said simply. He shifted in his seat so he was facing her more fully. "Soon after I started my course at The Hague University, my parents called to tell me they were getting divorced. I should have seen the warning signs, but I didn't. I was blindsided. I was miles away from anyone I knew, and I had to go through those dark days and come to terms with a gutting new reality alone."

"I'm sorry, Bram. I had no idea."

He sighed. "I didn't tell you that to make you feel bad; I just wanted you to know that along with seeing people experience the worst kind of shock and pain through my work, I've been there myself. You shouldn't have to face the things you've gone through today on your own—not if I'm here."

His understated empathy brought a lump to her throat. "Thank you."

"You're welcome. Now let me be a listening ear while I take you home. Stalkers are not something to ignore."

Tess glanced at Lars. Despite the large bandage around his head, he looked relaxed, and his breathing was steady and deep. He was sleeping soundly.

"Here." Bram reached into the pocket of his uniform, pulled out a small pad of paper and a pen, and offered them to her. "Leave him a note. Tell him you'll be back first thing tomorrow."

She eyed the paper, rapidly considering her options. No matter how she looked at the situation, Bram's offer was by far the most sensible and convenient. "You really don't mind taking me home?"

"I wouldn't have offered if I didn't want to do it." He pressed the pad into her hand. "Start writing."

The decision was made. She wrote her note and left it propped up against the cup on the bedside table. Bram turned off the television, and she dimmed the lights, then they slipped out of Lars's room together. After a quick stop at the nurses' station to tell them they were leaving for the night, Bram led Tess into the lift and pressed the button for the ground floor.

Even though the hour was late, the emergency room was busy. A different receptionist was sitting at the desk, helping an elderly man fill out some paperwork, and a young woman was sitting in the chair Tess had occupied all afternoon, holding a crying baby. The main doors opened as she and Bram approached, and Tess stepped outside.

The daytime temperatures had dropped, and darkness enveloped the city. Lights coming from the hospital bathed the pavement, and a steady stream of headlights zipped by, proving that Amsterdam never slept.

"Where are you parked?" she asked. The downtown hospital did not have a dedicated car park, and vehicles were lined up along both sides of the busy road.

Bram pointed to the right. "This way." He smiled. "It helps to have an emergency personnel parking pass."

"Do you always drive to work?"

He snorted. "I'm a Dutchman, Tess."

She smiled—and after a day of fear and worry, it felt rather wonderful. "Forgive me. I should have asked if you're still riding your magnificent black-and-yellow bike." The ten-speed had been his pride and joy when he'd been in school. "Don't tell me the famed bumble bee is no longer."

"I'll have you know that bike saw me through college and my first year in Amsterdam without a single repair. It was a very sad day when I had to retire it in favor of a bike that didn't clank louder than the tram."

Tess took one look at Bram's solemn expression and started to giggle. Pretty soon, he was grinning.

"Come on," he said, stopping opposite a small Renault and unlocking the front door. "Get in."

Tess took her seat and put on her seat belt as Bram started the car. Only after he'd merged into traffic did she voice the question that begged asking. "If you ride your bike to work, why was your car at the hospital?"

Bram kept his eyes on the road. "I had Dirk drop me off at my flat at the end of our shift so I could pick it up. I took a guess that you come into the city from Haarlem by train. It's an easy daytime commute but not so great late at night, after a long day at the hospital."

Tess found herself inexplicably lost for words.

He glanced over at her with a worried look. "You okay?"

She gazed out the car window at the glow of the city—the individual lights that represented so many people all going about their own business. And yet, somehow, mercifully, Bram's path and hers had intersected just when she'd needed him the most. She turned to face him again. "I'm glad you and Dirk responded first to the emergency on Van Baerlestraat."

"Yeah." He offered her an understanding smile. "Me too."

There were fewer bicycles on the road at night, which made navigating the city streets easier, and it wasn't long before they were heading west on the N200, with the countryside reaching out in a vast flat expanse before them.

Tess shifted in her seat, her muscles unwilling to relax as they usually did when she left the city behind. It was no good. She could not ignore the specter hanging over her any longer. "I first noticed the creepy guy at the museum," she said. Bram did not respond, but his grip on the steering wheel tightened, and she knew he was listening. "It might sound weird. I was getting ready for my English tour, and I just felt his stare." She shuddered.

"When did this happen?"

"This morning." Had it really been only today that she'd first seen him? It felt like a lifetime ago.

He nodded. "Does he know you spotted him?"

"I think so. He was standing by one of the pillars. Maybe he could tell I was looking for someone because when I caught his eye, he turned and left."

"Did you see him leave the building?"

"He went out through the main doors, but then I left to lead a tour, and I don't know if he came back in." She fiddled with her seat belt. "I didn't think about him again until he walked into the emergency room, and instinct kicked in. I just knew he mustn't see me. When I heard him ask the receptionist about me and Lars, my sense of self-preservation went into overdrive. He told her he was our cousin and he'd heard about the accident on Van Baerlestraat and wanted to know if we were still alive."

Bram's expression was grim. "You're sure he asked about Lars too? I can see him making up stories about your relationship if he's fixated on you, but why would he bring your brother into it?"

"I don't know. It . . . it made his question all the more scary."

He glanced at her with a frown. "Why?"

Bram would likely think she was nuts, but if he really wanted to be her sounding board, he needed to hear everything. "Because right before the accident, I had a phone call from an English woman I didn't know who told me my life and Lars's were in danger."

The car swerved slightly, and Bram released a hissing breath. "For goodness sake, Tess! Why didn't you say something before? Start again at the beginning. And this time, don't leave anything out."

She did as he asked. After describing her brief encounter with the man at the museum, she reviewed her discussion with Lars about the photo of the earrings and his belief that the ones she'd received from her grandmother were the same pair. She then told him exactly what the woman named Anna had said on the phone and described the car accident from her perspective. Finally, she reviewed her second encounter with her greasy-haired stalker in the ER.

When she finished, Bram was silent for a full ten seconds.

"It's a lot, isn't it?" she ventured.

"Yeah. I'd say so."

"Do you think I'm imagining things? Maybe it was just a crank call. Someone could have done it on a dare. Maybe the creepy guy is someone who knows Lars? Or maybe—"

"Tess, you were top of our class in writing. If your imagination could come up with something like this on its own, you'd have a literary masterpiece by now."

It was Tess's turn to be silent. He was right. And that terrified her. "What should I do?"

"Talk to the police. Tell them what you told me."

"But what can they do? The guy hasn't actually done anything other than be creepy."

"Unless he's connected to whoever drove the van into Lars and Marit."

Shock hit her like a fist in the stomach. Marit's hair was similar in length and color to hers. And from a distance, no one would notice the difference in their height or eye color. "You think the driver thought Marit was me?"

Bram's jaw tightened. "I hate to say it, but given your phone warning, it seems likely. If the driver was expecting you and Lars to come out of the café together, he wouldn't even have questioned it."

"Then it's my fault Marit is in the hospital," Tess said. "If I'd run out there faster and he'd seen me instead—"

"Don't even go there, Tess," Bram said sternly.

Tess stared numbly out the window. They'd reached Haarlem. Every landmark they passed—from the windmill to the cathedral to the corner shop—was familiar, yet she'd never felt more lost. As if from a distance, she watched Bram take the turn onto the street where she lived. He drove slowly alongside the canal that fronted her parents' house, pulling into a parking spot about ten meters from the front door.

The moment he turned off the ignition, he jumped out of the car and ran to open her door. Reaching for her hand, he pulled her to her feet beside him.

"Look at me, Tess," he said. "*None* of this is your fault."

She raised her eyes to his. The lamplight hummed a few feet away, and she could see the concern in his face. "It wasn't my fault," she said softly.

His shoulders sagged with relief. "Say it again."

"It wasn't my fault."

"Good girl." He gave her an encouraging smile. "Where's your key? It might be easier to get it out while we're by the lamppost."

She rooted through her handbag until she found it. Lifting it out, she showed it to him.

"I'll walk you to the door," he said.

They started down the pavement. In this part of Haarlem, the homes were built in the traditional Dutch style, tall and narrow with steep, pitched roofs and front steps that led directly onto the pavement. Lights shone in a few upper windows of the tightly packed houses, and music from a café across the canal floated in the air. A car honked, and a dark cat with glowing eyes slipped through the railings outside the nearest house. Tess flinched. Bram reached for her hand, wrapping his warm fingers around her cold ones. He was a safe anchor in a tempestuous sea, and she clung to him, her feet slowing as they reached her door.

She paused at the first step and turned to face him. And then she felt it. Like a swarm of ants crawling across her skin, the prickling sensation raised her hair on end. Her heart began to pound, and she did not need to see or hear anything unusual to know that someone in the shadows was watching her.

"Bram." Her voice was barely above a whisper, but somehow, it managed to communicate everything.

He tensed. "Is he here?"

She gave a slight nod.

"Any idea where?"

The other side of the road ended at the edge of the canal. Other than her direct neighbors, the nearest buildings were on the opposite side of the water. There were no mature trees wide enough for a man to hide behind, but vehicles lined the pavement all the way down the street.

"He must be in one of the parked cars."

Bram pulled her closer. "Walk up the stairs ahead of me," he said. "I'm going to stay between you and the road. Unlock the door. I'll follow you inside, but I don't want you to go any farther than the entry until I've checked the rest of the house." He released her hand and stepped behind her. "Okay. Let's go."

Tess had the front door open in seconds. She stepped inside and made room for Bram to follow her in. He closed the door behind him and slid the bolt into place. “Don’t move,” he said, turning on the hall light. “I’ll be right back.”

CHAPTER 27

GUNNAR CHECKED HIS BEDROOM AND then the butler's quarters to ensure everyone was asleep. Once satisfied, he paced back into his temporary office and retrieved the prepaid phone he used when contacting the people he would rather not admit to knowing. He didn't want to make the call, but he couldn't stand it anymore. The man he'd hired had assured him the Hendriks siblings would be in the morgue by the end of the day. The end of the day was nearly here, and so far, he hadn't heard anything.

Gunnar pulled up the contact and dialed. The phone rang twice before a gruff greeting sounded.

"Have you taken care of it?" Gunnar asked, deliberately keeping his comment vague even though he had already ensured both his wife and his butler had retired to their rooms.

"The brother survived the accident. I haven't been able to get a status on his condition yet."

"And the other one?" Gunnar asked.

"She just got home," Jac said. "As soon as her friend leaves, I'll take care of her."

"Good, but what about the brother?" Gunnar asked. "It doesn't do much good to take care of one without the other."

"One thing at a time."

Irritation simmered. "You assured me you would have it completed by tonight."

"And I will. As soon as I take care of the girl, I'll go back to the hospital. The night staff won't know me."

"Do you even know where he is?"

"This is my job. I'll get it done."

"You'd better. I'll wire the rest of your payment as soon as I receive confirmation that your job is finished."

"You'll hear from me shortly."

"Excellent. Best of luck tonight."

"I don't need luck."

The line went dead. Gunnar lowered his phone. He paced across the room again, struck by its minuscule size. How did people live in these tiny houses with their boxy rooms? He was ready for the design team to be finished with the remodel so he could move back into Falcon Point.

First, his other employee needed to take care of the newest Lang descendant, Anna Cavendish. She and the Hendriks siblings were all who stood between him and the future his grandfather had entrusted to him.

Tess attempted to quell her rising panic as Bram's footsteps sounded overhead. Thankfully, her house was not large, and he finished his sweep in a matter of minutes.

"I've checked every room," he said, rejoining her in the entryway. "I don't see any sign of someone having been here, but you're the only one who'll be able to tell for sure."

She nodded. Despite the solid door that separated her from the man outside, his disturbing presence still hovered over her. The thought that he—or anyone else, for that matter—may have attempted entry into her house was even more chilling.

"I'm calling the police dispatcher," Bram said. "I've helped out with Haarlem's emergency services in the past. It's time to call in a favor."

"What will you tell them?" They had no more proof of any misconduct now than they had before. "We don't even know where he is."

Bram led her into the dark living room. "I turned on the light upstairs. See if you can spot him while he thinks you're up there."

Tess stood partially hidden by the curtain and gazed out the window. Lights from the buildings on the other side of the canal reflected off the water. A couple of cars, including Bram's, were bathed in the pale-yellow glow of the lamplight, but the other vehicles parked along the road were simply dark smudges against an equally dark backdrop. Straining to see any sign of movement, she allowed her gaze to move slowly from one shadowy form to the other along the road.

"It's impossible," she said. "I can't make out anything."

Bram had his phone to his ear, and she could hear it ringing on the other end. A woman's voice answered.

"Hi, Angela," he said. "This is Bram Dekker. I have a possible stalker sighting on Kampervest. Do you have any officers in the area?"

While Bram listened to the dispatcher's response, Tess kept her eyes on the road. At first, she thought she'd imagined a tiny spark of light in the car immediately opposite her house. But when it transformed into a glowing dot that moved in a steady arc—much as a cigarette would travel when moved in and out of a man's mouth—her heart began to pound.

She grasped Bram's arm with one hand and pointed with the other. "There," she mouthed.

The moment he saw the burning cigarette, Bram's eyes narrowed. "That's right." He was still speaking to the dispatcher. "Tell him the suspect is parked opposite number . . . ?" He raised his eyebrow at Tess.

"Twenty-six," she said.

"Twenty-six," he repeated. He listened to her response. "Thanks, Angela. I'll watch for him."

Bram disconnected and looked at Tess. "She's sending a patrol car down Kampervest. It should be here in the next couple of minutes."

"What will the officer do?"

Bram had moved to stand right behind her. His attention was on the road, but his nearness shored up her flagging strength. "I think the bigger question is what will the creeper do when a police car pulls up beside him?"

They did not have long to wait. Bram spotted the vehicle coming from the direction of the bridge seconds before the blue lights turned on. As it approached, the police car slowed to a crawl, and the parked cars turned from black to gray in the swirling azure light. When it reached her house, the police car stopped, effectively blocking the cars parked nearby from leaving. Tess watched as the officer behind the wheel spoke into his radio.

A car door slammed, and Bram tensed. "He's making a run for it!"

Bram already had the front door open when a shadowy figure slipped between the parked cars. Taking the steps in one leap, Bram tore down the street in pursuit. By the time Tess reached the door, the police officer had also taken up the chase, and Bram was rapidly closing in on his quarry.

A car turned the corner at the end of the street and started toward the men. Tess's stalker wove in and out of the headlights, attempting to outmaneuver Bram.

The driver slammed on his brakes, the screech rending the air as he fought to control his vehicle. Bram darted right, narrowly missing being clipped by the car's front fender. He pivoted, setting his sights on the fleeing man once more.

Tess's stalker had taken advantage of Bram's close call, but his increased lead made no difference. At age eighteen, Bram had been the fastest sprinter in the school district; it appeared little had changed since then. Bram's shoulder connected with the man's back. Bram wrapped his arms around him and tackled him to the ground. There was a thud and a muffled curse. Their tussle continued for the few seconds it took for the police officer to reach them.

The solid click of handcuffs engaging echoed down the street, and suddenly, it was over. Bram was standing, brushing dirt off his uniform. The policeman was hauling the man to his feet, and up and down the row of houses, spectators stood on their top steps—most of them in their pajamas—watching the officer escort the stranger to the police car.

A cool breeze tugged at Tess's hair, and she shivered. She stood on the doorstep while Bram consulted with the policeman. Locked inside the car, the man they'd caught was shrouded in shadows once more, but she felt his glare, and her shivering intensified. The scream of brakes echoed in her head, and visions of Lars being slammed to the ground by a navy van merged with Bram being pinned in the headlights of an oncoming car.

Tess's breathing became ragged, and she stepped back from the doorway. She reached for the end of the banister rail, her hand barely able to grasp the worn wooden knob. Rapid footsteps sounded on the stairs, and she swung around.

"Tess!" Bram pushed the door closed behind him. "Are you okay?"

"N . . . n . . . no."

He closed the distance between them and wrapped his arms around her. "It's all right," he said softly. "It's over."

Tess had no idea how long she and Bram stood in the hall together. He continued to hold her long after her shaking stopped and her tears dried. Standing with her cheek against his chest, she closed her eyes, and he gently smoothed his hand across her hair until the fear that had so consumed her was replaced by an unexpected calm.

At last, she raised her head. "Thanks."

His eyes met hers. They were bonded by years of shared memories, but tonight had taken them somewhere new. Amid the raw emotions of the evening, something indefinable had changed between them.

"You can't stay here," he said. "Go upstairs and pack an overnight bag, and I'll call my mother to tell her she has another guest coming."

Relief that she would not be left at the house alone filled her. "You're sure she won't mind?"

"I'm sure. And if I'm lucky, she'll make such a fuss over you she'll completely ignore me."

Tess smiled, and he responded with a soft chuckle. "You remember what she's like."

"She'll make me miss my mother."

He leaned over and pressed his lips to her forehead. "Go pack." With her forehead tingling from his touch, she turned to go up the stairs. "And, Tess," he added, "if you have your grandmother's earrings in the house, put them in your bag too. We'll take them to the hospital tomorrow to see if Lars can tell if they're the real thing."

"They're upstairs," she said. "But I don't have a jeweler's loupe."

"We'll figure it out."

Tess nodded. "I'll be right back."

By the time she reached the top of the stairs, Bram was talking to his mother on the phone.

It took her only a few minutes to throw some pajamas and a change of clothing into a bag. She added a few items from the bathroom before returning to her bedroom and opening her sock drawer. Reaching into the back, she pulled out a small box. The red satin covering had faded to a pale-rose color. A brown stain marred one corner, and the fabric was pulling away around the tiny metal hinges. Releasing the clasp with her finger, Tess opened the box and studied its contents.

The earrings sat on a black velvet cushion. The diamonds sparkled in the light, and Tess was instantly transported back to the very first time she'd seen them in her grandmother's old hands. An unexpected wave of longing for her oma washed over her, and she snapped the box closed. She'd shed enough tears for one day. Tomorrow would be soon enough to study the jewelry and determine its worth.

Adding the jewelry box to her overnight bag, she slipped the strap over her shoulder, and with a last brief glance around her room, she turned off the light and hurried back down the stairs.

Bram was waiting for her at the bottom. He reached for her bag. "Ready to go?"

"Yes." She took the house key out of her handbag.

Bram opened the door and stepped outside, waiting until she'd locked the door behind them before taking her hand. "When I told my mother you were coming, she hurried off the phone to make *stroopwafels* for us."

"But it's past eleven o'clock."

"It's never too late for *stroopwafels* and nutella."

She rolled her eyes. "I should have known you'd put nutella on them."

He grinned. "Of course. As I've told my mother a million times before, there's no reason to limit such a marvelous condiment to bread and crepes."

Tess chuckled and thought back on her memories of Bram's mother. Tess should not be surprised that the rather unconventional woman would consider cooking for them this late at night. Mrs. Dekker had always welcomed Bram's friends into their home and had been willing to feed them anytime. Her laid-back attitude meant that her house was usually cluttered and untidy, but she was rarely ruffled by anything.

"Did you give your mother a reason for my unexpected visit?"

"I told her I'd been on scene at an accident involving your brother and that although I'd persuaded you to leave the hospital long enough to get some sleep, I didn't think you were ready to go home alone."

They passed the stalker's parked car, and Tess averted her eyes. The unnerving sensation that she was being watched was gone, but the empty car was an unfortunate reminder of the man who'd been inside.

"What will happen to him now?"

Bram's thoughts must have paralleled hers because he responded to the abrupt change of subject without missing a beat. "He'll be taken to the police station for questioning. I told the officer that he'd been seen in the Museumplein area about the time of the Van Baerlestraat accident and that they should speak to the officers over that case before they let him go." He gave her a troubled look. "You need to file a temporary restraining order, Tess. If they have nothing they can pin on him, he'll be released."

Logically, Tess knew Bram was right; emotionally, she could not cope with one more thing. "Can we talk about it tomorrow?"

"Of course."

They'd arrived at Bram's car. He opened the door for her and put her bag next to another bag on the back seat.

"You came prepared," she said.

"I grabbed it when I picked up the car," he said, getting in on the driver's side and starting the engine. "My parents sold their house when they divorced.

Mam lives in one of the newer flats on the south side of town. It won't take more than ten minutes to get there."

Just as Bram had said, it wasn't long before they turned onto a road bordered on either side by two large blocks of tan-brick flats. He took a turnoff on the right that led to a small car park. There was one vacant parking spot left. As soon as he claimed it, Bram grabbed the bags from the back and led Tess to the far side of the nearest building, where a welcoming light shone outside a ground-floor flat.

He gave a light knock and opened the door. Mrs. Dekker, whose purple pajamas were partially covered by a large apron depicting windmills from around the Netherlands, flew out of the kitchen to greet them. Her hair had grayed since Tess had last seen her, but it was spilling out of the loose bun on the top of her head as it had always done.

"Bram!" she cried, wrapping her arms around her son and squeezing him tightly. "It's so good to see you." She turned to Tess. "I'm so glad you brought Tess back to visit." Tess braced herself as Mrs. Dekker enveloped her in a big hug. "She's even lovelier than I remember."

"Thank you for letting me come on such short notice, Mrs. Dekker," she said.

"Nonsense." Bram's mother beamed. "You're welcome anytime." She slipped her arm through Tess's. "I was sorry to hear about your brother. I hope he'll recover quickly."

"I hope so too."

Mrs. Dekker smiled kindly. "Well, come on into the kitchen. I have hot *stroopwafels* ready for you." She leaned her head a little closer but made no attempt to lower her voice. "There's no harm in trying to bribe Bram to visit more often, is there?"

Tess caught Bram's wink right before he picked up her bag and headed for a room on the left. "I'll put Tess's things in the guest room, Mam. Go ahead and give her the first *stroopwafel*. I'll be right there."

Half an hour later, Tess had eaten two syrupy *stroopwafels*, and Bram had eaten close to half his weight in them, along with half a jar of nutella.

Mrs. Dekker took off her splattered apron and hung it over the back of a chair. "It's time for me to go to bed," she said. "There are clean towels in the bathroom, Tess, but if you need anything else, don't hesitate to ask." She turned to Bram. "I left a pillow and a couple of blankets on the sofa for you."

"Thanks, Mam. And thanks for feeding us so well. No one makes *stroopwafels* like you."

Mrs. Dekker smiled happily. "Sleep well."

"Thank you, Mrs. Dekker," Tess said. "Good night." She waited only until Bram's mother had disappeared down the hall before confronting him. "You gave up your bed for me."

"It's not a big deal. I've lost track of how many nights I've spent on a hospital cot. Believe me, my mother's sofa is luxury bedding compared to that."

"Let me take the sofa. You're so tall, you'll hang off the end."

Bram laughed. "I'm used to it." He stepped closer and brushed some hair back from her face. His fingers touched her cheek, and all trace of humor left his face. "You're exhausted, Tess. Take the bed, and get some sleep."

His gaze moved to her lips, and Tess's breath caught. She sensed his hesitation; she understood it. Before today, she'd not seen Bram in years, but after all they'd been through during the last few hours, it felt as though they'd been together forever.

"Bram," she whispered.

His lips found hers, and then he was pulling her close. Her arms snaked up around his neck, her fingers finding his soft brown curls as he deepened the kiss. The fear and heartache that had consumed her all day receded, replaced by a feeling of joy and belonging.

With a soft moan, he pulled away.

Tess felt the loss immediately and wrapped her arms around herself.

Bram ran his fingers through his hair and let out an unsteady breath. "You'd better go to bed."

Tess might have questioned his feelings and second-guessed her response to his kiss if the look in his eyes had hinted at any kind of regret. It didn't. Not at all.

"Good night, Bram," she said softly.

"Good night, Tess," he replied.

And then she walked into the guest bedroom and locked the door behind her.

CHAPTER 28

Anna unlocked the door and glanced over her shoulder at Beckett. They had yet to hear anything back from the police since she had filed a report against Herr Sauermann. The single bulb from the manor's basement entrance lit the planes of Beckett's face and cast everything else into shadow. His eyes looked black in the uncertain light, and his hair was ruffled from the chilly breeze.

The last few days had borne home to her that Beckett had truly changed. In her heart of hearts, she knew he was ready to commit. And when Beckett committed himself to something, his course was set.

During their walk by the lake tonight, Anna had come full circle—her heart and mind finally in agreement. She had forgiven him and was ready to take him back. But after his full disclosure up on the mountain, he deserved more than a rushed acceptance through chattering teeth, so she'd held back the words and waited for a more opportune moment.

Long after the lights had gone out at the manor, the cold had driven them indoors.

"Would you like a cup of tea before you go to bed?" she asked, keeping her voice to a whisper so as not to wake the team.

"As much as I'd love to say yes, I've a few reports to submit before I call it a night." He touched her cheek, his hand warm against her chilled flesh. He picked up the stack of files they had placed inside the basement door before they had taken their impromptu walk on the shore. He removed several from the bottom of the stack that belonged to him and handed her the rest.

"Looks like you have a bit of homework yourself, lass." He motioned to her pile of paperwork with the thrust of his chin.

"I do rather." She stood on tiptoe and kissed his cheek.

"Good night." He ran his thumb over her jaw, then headed upstairs, his footsteps echoing up the stairwell.

Turning, she started down the corridor, passing her room to reach the old butler's pantry, where the team had set up a makeshift kitchen with a hotplate, fridge, microwave, and sink.

Anna set the kettle on to boil, leaned against the worktop, and faced the hall. A light glowed under the kitchen door. *Odd*. She had turned it off before she and Beckett had gone down to the lake. Perhaps Rudy had checked the newly installed walk-in freezer and had forgotten to switch it off.

Her mobile pinged with a text. *Miss you already. Sweet dreams.*

She smiled at Beckett's text. Adjusting the files under her arm, she walked toward the kitchen, texting Beckett as she went. The man kept impossible hours. She didn't know how he found enough time to sleep at night.

Pressing her shoulder against the swinging door, she entered the kitchen. The door closed behind her, and she reached for the switch, but the pantry light was on as well. Shaking her head, she crossed the floor to turn out the light.

She stopped beside the switch and finished her text, then hit Send. She turned off the light. A slight sound and a displacement of air made her stiffen. She was not alone.

Click.

The kitchen plunged into darkness.

"Who's there?" Anna's voice wavered. She spun on her heel and started for the door. "That's not funny. Turn the light on this instant," she demanded as the first prickles of fear rippled over her body.

"I don't think so," a man's unfamiliar voice whispered in English, his tone full of menace.

Anna dropped her phone. Her files slipped from under her arm and fell to the floor. This wasn't a game one of her coworkers had pulled on her. In a flash, the conversation she had overheard at the Indian restaurant with Herr Sauermann replayed in her mind.

Had Sauermann figured out who she was and sent someone to get rid of her? Sweat broke out on her back, and her mouth dried out like cotton. She swallowed convulsively and strained for any sound that might give away the man's location.

All was dark except for the swath of gold seeping under the door from the hall and the green point of light from the walk-in freezer. Anna didn't need the hall light. She knew the layout of the room like the back of her hand. If she could locate the man's position, she could work her way to the far side of the room and slip out through the butler's pantry.

A soft noise directly behind her. A hand clamped on her shoulder. Cold metal brushed against her neck.

Anna sucked in a lungful of air, ready to scream.

"Scream and I cut your pretty throat."

The call for help died on her lips.

His body quivered against her back, taut as a strung bow. She sensed anticipation coiled inside him, daring her to move.

She whimpered and hated herself for giving him the satisfaction of feeding off her fear. He laughed, and the blade nicked her neck. She inhaled loudly through her nose, her fear eclipsing the pain.

Blood, warm and sticky, beaded on her flesh, then trailed down her neck. She trembled, her mind filled with bright-red images.

He wanted to kill her and would do it if she gave him the least excuse.

His arm locked around her, and he dragged her toward the room's interior.

How could she fight him? If she so much as moved . . .

He opened a door, and a whoosh of icy air sluiced over her body.

The blade left her neck, and she offered a silent prayer of gratitude.

"Get in."

He shoved her in the middle of her back and sent her staggering forward onto her knees. Anna threw out her hands and saved herself from bashing her face against the frigid metal floor. Before she pushed herself to her feet, a metallic snick reached her, and the lock latched.

No.

She rushed in the direction of the noise, her fingers clawing the air as she blindly sought for the handle to let herself out. At last, her hands encountered, then gripped the long, horizontal lever. She used her weight and shoved against it, but the door refused to budge. Nothing could open it—the thick metal door was locked from the outside.

A sense of helplessness surged through her. She was entombed inside the walk-in freezer. No one would hear her if she screamed—or look for her until morning.

She had to fight this. She had to stay warm. She took a step away from the door and jogged in place. She couldn't keep it up indefinitely; eventually, her body would tire and grow cold. Then she would freeze.

Her mind swung to the things she wished she had done, the things left unsaid. Her greatest regret was that she hadn't told Beckett she loved him. Now he would never know.

Beckett pulled up his cost analysis spreadsheet and entered Falcon Point's weekly expenditures. Despite his proven track record, corporate insisted on weekly updates. Between Herr Sauermann and corporate's babysitting tendencies, Beckett's wings were clipped. He stifled his growing impatience to branch out on his own like he had always planned. Anna was worth any sacrifice.

He had sensed a softening in her tonight. Her eyes had been less guarded, and he had allowed himself to dream that one day she would forgive him.

Focus, Campbell. He had spent the majority of the day arguing with the geothermal installation tech about the impossibility of his design. Beckett had sketched the format so the tech could understand that his design incorporated the goatherd huts as well as the spa and restaurant.

Did no one think outside the box? Walls of innovation were made of glass—not concrete—and were, therefore, easy to break through. What he had planned was doable. He just needed someone with vision to make it happen.

He moved to the spreadsheet with Sauermann's adjustments and accrued fees, printed off a hard copy, and filed it away. He opened the next folder, and his eyes fell on Anna's kitchen elevations. What were her schematics doing with his paperwork? And where was Tanja's drapery order? He rifled through the stack on his desk, looking for the missing folder. He must have picked up Anna's by accident. He glanced at the clock. No way could he put off this report; corporate needed it first thing in the morning. He rose from his desk and started for the stairs. Hopefully, Anna was still awake.

The basement hall light was still on. He smiled to himself. Anna's considerateness was typical of her personality. Doubtless, she had left it on so he could navigate his way to his room.

When he reached her bedroom, Anna's door was partway open, the bed still made. She had mentioned a cup of tea. He continued down the corridor to the butler's pantry. No sign of Anna. The hotplate was still on and the kettle was dry.

He turned off the hotplate, raked a hand through his hair, and glanced around. Unease settled over him. Anna would never leave a burner on, not in an old place like this. Was she sick?

His footsteps echoed in the empty hall. The bathroom door stood wide, the light off. She wasn't upstairs, of that he was certain. Perhaps she had gone outside?

But when Beckett turned, he found the kitchen door slightly ajar. No light shone beyond. He poked his head inside to check. Papers lay scattered on the floor, illuminated by the glow of the hallway lamp. Pushing the door open farther, he flicked on the switch. The overhead lights clicked on, and the room sprang to life.

"Anna?" he called out. "Anna, are you in here?"

When he saw the papers were hers, something dark crawled up his spine and stirred his blood. She'd never leave those lying about. He snatched up a worker's crowbar from the neatly stacked tools inside the door and examined the room with greater care. Had Sauermann found out who Anna was and hired someone to harm her too?

Beckett turned on the pantry light, but the area was empty. Where could she be?

"Anna?"

His uneasiness grew. He left the pantry, passed the walk-in freezer, and entered the staging area. Piles of cardboard-wrapped cabinets lined the floor, ready for installation. He rubbed his neck and frowned.

He went back and gathered up her CAD drawings and shoved them into one of the empty folders. The freezer kicked on, the quiet hum filling the room. As he started for the kitchen door, a small black object caught his eye.

A mobile. He picked it up, noting the cracked screen. He pressed the icon, and his number showed on the caller ID. Her papers *and* her mobile? Everything inside him stilled.

His eyes fixed on the blinking green light of the freezer as he puzzled over the disturbing facts before him. Where could she be? Time slowed.

The blinking light continued to flash. Beckett's eyes sharpened.

Why was the freezer running? The temperature should have stabilized in it by now. Since the unit was under warranty, the manufacturer had calibrated the thermostat after the install. All had appeared fully operational at the time.

A sudden terror ripped through him. He dropped the crowbar and lunged for the freezer door. The lever was locked. His hands fumbled with the dial, then threw the bar and swung the door wide.

Huddled on the floor near the threshold sat Anna, her lips blue, her body shaking spasmodically.

Beckett thanked God she was still alive. He scooped her into his arms; her skin was cold to the touch. Leaving the freezer door open, he rushed into the corridor, bellowing at the top of his lungs, "Rudy! Tanja! Gary!"

Gary stepped into the hall and blinked owlishly.

"I need hot water bottles. Hurry!" Beckett shouted.

Gary appeared to take in the situation, then stumbled half asleep down the hall to the butler's pantry, where the water bottles were stored.

"What's going on?" Tanja emerged from her room, belting her robe.

"Anna was locked in the freezer. We need to warm her body temperature."

Tanja's eyes darted to Anna's shivering form in his arms. "There's a space heater in one of the spare bedrooms. I'll get it."

"Thanks."

Beckett carried Anna to her room. Laying her in the middle of her down-filled duvet, he wrapped her tight, much like a swaddled baby, then placed her on his lap and locked his arms around her.

"I k-knew y-y-you'd come." Anna's teeth chattered, and she pressed her chilled face into the warmth of his neck.

His heart constricted, and he rested his head against hers. "I'm here, lass. I'll always be here for you."

Anna shook even harder. A good sign, surely? He kissed her hair. "You're going to be all right, lass. We'll get you warm." He tightened his grip around her and kissed her temple as the reality of her near loss swept over him again.

Tanja entered Anna's room, pushing the rolling space heater in front of her. "How is she?"

"I think she'll be okay. We just need to warm her up."

"If someone locked her in the freezer, we need to call the police," Tanja said.

"You're absolutely right," Beckett agreed. "Make the call. The police need to be apprised of what Sauermann has been up to."

"Sauermann?" Tanja repeated.

"Aye. Sauermann." He was sure of it.

CHAPTER 29

Sunlight streaming in through the curtains woke Tess the next morning. She lay in the unfamiliar bed and gazed about the room. She'd been so emotionally drained the night before, she'd basically collapsed on the bed and taken no time to survey her surroundings. It was a small bedroom with minimal furniture. Apart from the bed, there was a dresser and a bedside table.

Tess assumed that the small door in the corner led to a cupboard, but the limited storage space must be full because boxes were stacked in uneven heaps around the perimeter of the room. Some of the boxes were labeled with large stickers that said things like *Photos*, *Christmas*, *Stamps*, and *Yarn*. But the contents of most of them remained a mystery, and Tess could not help but smile that Mrs. Dekker's propensity for disorganization had spilled so fully into her guest room.

Climbing out of bed, she picked up her overnight bag and opened the bedroom door a crack. No sound came from anywhere else in the flat, so she slipped down the hall and into the bathroom. A little while later, with her hair still wet from the shower, but wearing clean clothes and minimal makeup, she exited to the smell of coffee percolating. She took the time to make the bed and replace her belongings in her bag, then she headed to the kitchen.

Bram had his back to her. Like yesterday, he was wearing a paramedic uniform, but this morning, his shirt and trousers were without the stains he'd sported yesterday. Just the sight of him caused a ripple of nervousness to course through her. After what had happened between them last night, she didn't know quite what to expect.

"Good morning," she said.

Bram swung around. His smile was instant, and her tension eased.

"Good morning, yourself," he said. "Would you like some coffee?"

She nodded and stepped closer. "Is your mother up yet?"

"I haven't seen her." He poured her a mug full of the black, steaming brew and set the cream and sugar on the counter beside her. "I can guarantee she'll be out here any minute wanting to cook eggs for us before we leave." He glanced at the clock on the wall and grimaced.

Tess understood. The very reason she rode her bike to the station and took the train to the city and back every day was to avoid the traffic on the road at this time in the morning.

"Coffee is all I need," she said. "My bag is packed, so I can leave whenever you're ready."

"You're sure?"

"Absolutely."

"You're up already," Mrs. Dekker bustled into the kitchen, still wearing her purple pajamas.

"Yes, Mam," Bram said, bending to place a light kiss on his mother's cheek. "And we must leave right away if I'm to make it to work on time."

"But what about your breakfast?"

He raised his mug. "Tess and I have both had coffee, and I think I ate enough *stroopwafels* last night to keep me going until this evening."

His mother frowned. "I don't like you leaving without me feeding you."

"It's fine. Really." His expression became thoughtful. "There is one thing you could help us with though."

"Something for lunch?"

He shook his head. "A loupe? You don't by any chance have a jeweler's loupe in one of your many boxes of long-forgotten hobbies, do you?"

Tess had completely forgotten about their need of a loupe. Was it possible that Mrs. Dekker owned such a specialized instrument?

"A loupe?" Mrs. Dekker pondered her son's request a moment. "That's another name for a magnifying glass, isn't it?"

"Yes," Tess said. "A small but powerful one."

"I may have just the thing," Mrs. Dekker said, hurrying to the guest bedroom. "It will be in my stamp-collecting box."

Thankfully, the stamp-collecting box was labeled, and within minutes, Bram's mother located a black-handled magnifying glass.

"Will this do?" she asked, holding it up.

"It's perfect," Tess said. "Thank you so much."

"I'll bring it back next time I come," Bram said, taking it from his mother and giving her a hug.

"And if I tell you I need it by next week, will you come back sooner?"

He laughed. "I won't leave it so long between visits next time."

"I'm glad to hear it," she said.

Bram picked up Tess's bag and slipped the magnifying glass inside before going back into the living room to grab his own bag.

"Thank you again for letting me stay," Tess said.

"I hope you'll come back soon too." Mrs. Dekker leaned in to give her a hug. "And give your brother my best wishes for a speedy recovery."

Tess glanced at the clock on the dashboard as Bram pulled into the parking spot outside the hospital.

"You've got three minutes," she said.

He flashed her a smile. "I'll make it. I only have to go as far as the ER, and I've run that distance in less."

She laughed, twisting to reach her bag on the back seat. "Then I'd better get out of your way."

"Actually, I'm kind of hoping the opposite is true."

She dropped her bag onto her knee and looked over at him. Behind the warmth of his gaze hovered a hint of uncertainty.

"Can I meet up with you when I get off work?" he asked.

"I'd really like that."

He smiled. Opening the car door, he jumped out and arrived on the other side of the vehicle in time to close the passenger door behind her. He hit the lock on his key fob and turned to face her. His hazel eyes held hers.

"I know your creeper is out of the picture for the time being, but take care of yourself today, okay?"

"I will," she promised. "I plan on being in Lars's room the whole time."

"I'll join you there as soon as I can," he said and then he leaned closer and pressed his lips to hers.

Tess's heart soared, but before she could so much as catch her breath, he was jogging down the pavement toward the emergency room entrance.

Hitching the strap of her overnight bag higher onto her shoulder, Tess walked through the hospital's front doors and into the lobby. This part of the building was far more spacious than the emergency room area. A vast skylight brightened the entry and the wide hall beyond. Gray tile lined the floor, and the shape of the semicircular reception desk was echoed in the circular configuration of the public seating.

Not wanting to wait her turn to speak to one of the women behind the desk, Tess studied the signs hanging from the ceiling for one that would indicate the location of the lift. She spotted it a few meters down the hall, and it wasn't long before she was on her way up to the fourth floor. The lift pinged, and the door opened to reveal the nurses' station. One of the nurses standing behind the desk looked up and smiled.

"Good morning, Ms. Hendriks."

"Hi, Emilia," Tess said, glad to see a familiar face. "How's Lars?"

"He claims to have had a reasonable night's sleep," she said. "He's finishing up his breakfast right now, but I'm sure he'll be happy to see you."

Tess hurried down the hall to her brother's room. Raising one hand, she knocked lightly on the door.

"Come in."

She pushed it open and stepped inside. Lars was sitting up in bed surrounded by cushions, his half-eaten tray of food sitting on a bedside table before him. His blankets lay bunched over a rectangular object that covered his leg, and a fresh gauze bandage was taped to his forehead.

"Good morning, big brother." Now that his arms were outside the blankets, Tess could see the many red scratches crisscrossing his skin. "You look like you've been in a fight."

"I feel like I have too."

She took the chair closest to him. "Are you in a lot of pain?"

"Some," he said. "It would be a lot worse without the meds they have me on."

She offered him a sympathetic smile. "I'm so sorry, Lars."

He sighed. "Yeah. This wasn't exactly how I planned to spend the rest of the week."

"Have you seen the doctor yet?"

"He came in about an hour ago." He pointed to a pile of papers on the other chair. "It looks like there's a lot of rehab in my future."

Tess picked up the stack and flipped through the pages. She understood why Lars seemed so despondent; she felt overwhelmed by what lay ahead, and she wasn't the one who would have to go through it all.

"I'm just glad you're still here. It could have been so much worse."

"I know." He shook his head slightly. "Why would anyone drive straight into pedestrians like that?"

"I don't know. None of it makes sense."

"How's Marit?"

"She was moved onto this floor yesterday, so I'll see if I can find out."

"Now?" he asked.

Tess smiled. "You really like her."

"What's not to like?" he said evasively. "It will just make me feel better to know that she's okay."

"All right." Tess rose. "I'll be back in a few minutes."

She'd taken only a few steps toward the door when a crisp knock sounded.

"Come in," Lars said.

The door opened to reveal two police officers. Both men were tall and heavy-set, and when they entered, their presence filled the small room. Tess backed up a couple of paces and dropped into her chair again.

"Mr. Hendriks," the older officer said. "My name's Chief Inspector de Wit, and this is Sergeant Vinke."

"Nice to meet you," Lars said. He gestured toward Tess. "This is my sister, Tess."

"We're glad to hear that you and Miss Jansen are recuperating from your recent injuries."

"What can you tell me about Marit's condition?" Lars said.

"Not much, I'm afraid." The chief inspector took a notepad and pen out of his pocket. "But she's expected to make a full recovery."

It was probably more information than Tess could have gathered, and she was glad for the good news.

"I'd like to ask you some questions, if I may," Chief Inspector de Wit said. He nodded at Sergeant Vinke, who produced a mobile phone from his pocket and brought up a picture. "Take a look at the man in this photo and tell me if you recognize him."

The sergeant shifted closer to Lars and handed him the phone.

Lars studied the picture and shook his head. "I don't remember seeing him before."

"How about you, Ms. Hendriks?" the chief inspector asked.

Lars passed the phone to Tess.

Even after bracing herself for seeing him again, she could not repress the shudder that coursed through her when her stalker's hollow eyes stared back at her from the screen. "Yes," she said. "I've seen him before." Lars gave her a puzzled look, but she kept her attention on the chief inspector. "The first time was yesterday morning at the Van Gogh Museum, then again at the hospital after Lars was admitted, and finally outside my house in Haarlem last night."

Lars was now openly staring at her, but the policemen did not seem at all surprised.

"I understand someone called in a tip to the Haarlem police last night that led to his arrest," Chief Inspector de Wit said.

"Yes. My friend Bram Dekker called. He was concerned about my safety."

"He had reason to be," the policeman said. "The man's name is Jac Mesman. He already has a long list of infractions and misdemeanors to his name and was arrested for armed robbery a year ago."

If it was possible, Lars's complexion was even paler than it had been before. "Why was he after my sister?"

"That's what we'd like to know." The chief inspector took the phone from Tess and scrolled to another photo. He showed it to Lars and then to Tess. "This was taken by the traffic enforcement camera on the corner of Van Baerlestraat and Paulus Potterstraat. It's the best picture we have of the driver who caused the accident yesterday."

The picture was grainy, but there could be no doubt of the identity of the man with the long brown hair and olive-colored T-shirt behind the wheel of the blue van.

"Tess was still in the café when he came across the road," Lars said. "If she was his target, why did he make his move then?"

Tess clasped her hands together and willed her racing heart to calm as Bram's theory replayed in her head. "He may have thought Marit was me. From a distance, it would be hard to tell us apart."

Lars stared at her. "You think Marit was specifically targeted by this guy?"

Tess looked at him miserably and shrugged. "I don't know."

The chief inspector cleared his throat. "Can you think of any reason why Mesman would be trailing you, Ms. Hendriks? An angry ex-boyfriend? Money issues? Trouble at work?"

"No," Tess said. Not even her overactive imagination could conjure up a reason for all this madness. "Up until yesterday, I would have put my life in the ordinary-bordering-on-boring category."

The chief inspector pursed his lips. "Very well. I'd like you to talk us through every encounter you had with Mesman yesterday, and if you're willing, I'll have Sergeant Vinke record it."

Tess nodded, and the sergeant took charge of the phone again. At a signal from the chief inspector, the sergeant pushed the Record button, and Tess forced her mind back to the first time she became aware of someone watching her at the museum.

When she finished speaking, she was completely drained. It had taken every ounce of courage she'd possessed to relive her encounters with Mesman.

No matter that he was currently behind bars, her lingering fear of him remained horribly real.

Perhaps her distress showed on her face, because when Sergeant Vinke stopped the recording, the chief inspector gave her an understanding smile. "Thank you, Ms. Hendriks," he said. "That was excellent. Your eye for detail in your professional work enabled you to give us a very thorough account." He turned a page in his notepad. "Now, if you'd each be good enough to give me a contact number, we will leave so Mr. Hendriks can get some rest."

"I haven't seen my mobile since I left the café," Lars said.

A vision of Lars's broken phone lying amidst the glass on the pavement filled Tess's mind. She should have picked it up. Perhaps someone had added it to Marit's belongings.

"I saw it on the pavement," she said. "It was so badly damaged, I don't think it would be of any use to you now."

Lars grimaced. "It looks like you'll have to call the hospital if you need to talk to me, Chief Inspector."

There was another light knock, and Emilia popped her head around the door. "I apologize for the interruption, but the doctor has asked that I check Mr. Hendriks's incision."

"No problem." The chief inspector raised his eyebrows at Tess. "Would you be willing to step outside with us so we can take down your number, Ms. Hendriks?"

"Of course." Tess rose. As much as she loved her brother, she had no desire to see his wound so soon after surgery. "I'll come back in when Emilia has finished," she told Lars.

He nodded, but his attention was on the nurse who was already uncovering his injured leg. Tess averted her eyes and followed the policemen out of the room.

The officers were conferring quietly in the hall, but Chief Inspector de Wit looked up as she approached. He was still holding his notepad and pen. "Your extension at the museum along with your mobile number, if you don't mind," he said.

As Tess recited the numbers, her thoughts turned to the call she'd received in the café right before the accident. Should she mention it to the policemen? Other than its unfortunate timing, she had no reason to link it to Mesman. But what if it was somehow connected?

"I don't know if this is important," she began hesitantly, "but right before Lars's accident, I received a strange phone call. It wasn't a threat exactly; it was more like a warning."

Chief Inspector de Wit's look sharpened. "Tell us about it."

Tess relayed the short conversation she'd had with the unknown English woman. The policemen's expressions remained unchanged, but their increased tension was palpable.

"Is the number still on your mobile?" the chief inspector asked.

Tess scrolled through her calls, pulled up the international number, and showed it to him. He made note of it before slipping his pen and notepad into the pocket of his yellow-and-black jacket.

"Thank you once again, Ms. Hendriks." He gave her a grim smile. "We'll make some inquiries and will be in touch."

CHAPTER 30

Cole made it only fifteen hours before he couldn't stand it anymore. He had to know if Isabelle was intelligence or simply intelligent. Their dinner together had revealed her resumé matched the position she currently held. An undergraduate at the University of Virginia, followed by an MBA from Columbia. The woman was brilliant. She also skillfully sidestepped any topic she didn't want to discuss. At least he had managed to get her number.

His brief attempt at internet stalking her had further enhanced his suspicions. No Facebook or Instagram. No Twitter or Snapchat. Either this woman was very private, or she was deliberately keeping a low profile.

Though he was tempted to verify her academic achievements, Cole opted instead for a phone call to a friend with access. Using his secure line, he dialed the senior intelligence officer he had previously served with in Frankfurt.

A thick Southern accent came on the line. "This is Jasmine."

"Hey, Jazz. It's Cole."

"Cole? What are you doing up in the middle of the night?"

He grinned and leaned back in his chair. "It's morning where I am."

"So your last transfer didn't take you home after all."

Cole thought of Falcon Point. "That remains to be seen. I ended up in Vienna."

"Why didn't you tell me? You're practically around the corner."

Cole didn't mention that even though Germany bordered Austria, Frankfurt was more than seven hours by car or public transit. "It was an unexpected transfer. I need a favor though."

She chuckled. "You always do."

"Can you run a name for me? I may have crossed paths with one of ours, and I need to know if she's cleared to help me with something."

"Sure. What's the name?"

"Isabelle Roberts. The story I have on her is she's a UVA graduate, MBA from Columbia, and currently works for a bank in Vienna."

"You think she's a NOC?" Jasmine asked, referring to a nonofficial cover officer.

"Possibly," Cole said. "I'm pretty sure at least her grandfather was intel."

"Let me make a call, and I'll get back to you."

"Thanks, Jazz." Cole gave her his secure number and hung up. Afraid he might miss her return call, he dug a protein bar out of his center drawer and sat back to eat his lunch at his desk.

With nothing else to do but wait, he read through the morning's cable traffic. Suspected arms dealer spotted in Curacao, a terrorist cell in Cleveland, the sale of missing Rembrandt sketches in Zurich. He continued through the tidbits from around the world.

Twenty minutes passed before his phone finally rang. "This is Cole."

"Hey, I found what you were looking for," Jasmine said.

"And? Is she one of ours?"

"I'm sorry to ask this, but why do you need to know?"

Cole grappled for an honest answer. "My grandfather sent her to help me with a project that may spill into work. I don't want to inadvertently expose her to intel if she isn't cleared."

"Your grandfather sent her? Is she pretty?"

"Yeah. Why?"

"Then why are you asking me this question?" Jasmine laughed. "You should know your grandfather wouldn't put an attractive woman in your path unless she was one of ours. You know how he is about the family business."

"Sometimes I forget you used to work with him."

"He was one of the best communications specialists I've ever served with. Your father, too, God rest his soul."

"Thanks."

"I'm still surprised you never went into coding like the rest of your family."

"When you start learning how to break codes at the age of three, it gets pretty old by the time you're fifteen."

"You always were one who preferred to be in the field."

"Yeah." Cole tapped his fingers on the desk he was currently chained to. "What can you tell me about Isabelle?"

"Only that she's one of ours."

Pleased by the answer, Cole straightened in his chair. "Thanks for the info, Jasmine. I appreciate it."

"You take care. And give my best to your grandfather next time you talk to him."

"I will." Cole hung up and thought back to his grandfather's first mention of his friend in Vienna. Had his grandfather planned to set him up with Isabelle? He hadn't thought anything odd about the conversation at the time, but if anyone could hide an ulterior motive, it was Grandpa. And Cole certainly wouldn't put it past his grandfather to throw a beautiful, interesting woman into his path. The man was so ready for great-grandchildren he could hardly stand it, and a chance to pair Cole up with an intelligence operative was all the better.

If the stories were true, his grandfather was the third generation of intelligence officers in the family, which would make Cole the fifth. Although Cole might have gone into what was most decidedly the family business, he wasn't like the others. He had spoken the truth to Jasmine. His father and grandfather might have taught him about how to create and decipher codes, but that wasn't the career for him. Put him in a dark alley to sneak around anytime. It was a heck of a lot more satisfying than punching computer keys all day.

"Why didn't you tell me about the stalker?" Lars asked.

Emilia had left, though she'd promised to return soon, and Tess had barely taken two steps into his hospital room before he'd turned on her.

"When exactly would you have had me do that?" she said. "When you were barely coherent after your surgery or in the one and a half minutes I had with you before the officers arrived?"

He ran his fingers through his hair. "I'm sorry, Tess. I just hate that I wasn't there for you, that you had to deal with that creep all by yourself."

"Bram was there last night. He walked me to my door."

Lars released a short breath. "I have a lot to thank him for."

"Yeah, well, here's another one." Tess lifted her overnight bag off the floor and rifled through it until she found the jewelry box and the magnifying glass. "I brought Oma's earrings for you to look at. We didn't have a loupe, so Bram borrowed this magnifying glass from his mother."

Lars carefully lifted the lid on the battered box, withdrew one of the earrings, and held it under the light. Sparkles danced across the hospital room wall as he raised the magnifying glass to study the gemstones.

"Well?" The suspense was killing her.

"I see one tiny inclusion on the diamond and two on the sapphire," he said. "Hand me the other one."

Tess gave him the other earring, and he lifted it to the magnifying glass. "One inclusion on that sapphire, none on the diamond," he said.

"What does that mean?"

Lars lowered the magnifying glass and stared at the earrings in wonder. "That means we're likely looking at the missing Lang earrings."

"But you said they were flawed." Tess wasn't sure her heart could take much more pounding.

"Any diamond or sapphire that is completely flawless is probably a fake. Nature doesn't make gemstones like that. These are about as perfect as they can be for having been mined out of the ground, and they would be listed as flawless."

Tess slowly lowered herself into her seat. If these really were the Lang jewels, was it possible that the woman who had called her in the café knew something she and Lars didn't know about Oma? Was their grandmother's maiden name Lang? And was she in some way related to the affluent Austrian family?

"There's something else I need to tell you," she said.

Lars looked up from his continued study of the earrings. He must have shifted slightly because the empty jewelry box slid across his blanket-covered leg and dropped to the floor. Tess moved around the bed to retrieve it. The velvet cushion the earrings had sat on for so many years had fallen loose, and when she picked it up, she felt something hard. Turning it over, she discovered an old fashioned key sewn onto the back of the cushion.

"Lars, look." She held it out to him.

Lars set the earrings down and took the cushion. "It looks like it's made of brass." He ran his finger along the length of the key's shaft. "I wonder what it unlocks."

"And how long it's been hidden there. Someone must have considered it pretty important to sew it onto the back of the cushion in the jewelry box."

Their conversation was interrupted by another knock on the door. Lars immediately pressed the velvet cushion back into the box and set the earrings inside. Closing the lid, he slid the box beneath his blanket just as Emilia entered.

"I've come to collect your breakfast tray." She picked it up as she spoke. "How are you feeling? Do you need more pain meds?"

Lars shook his head. "The pain's there, but it's manageable."

"All right. Be sure to press the button when you notice a change. It's best not to wait until the pain is too intense."

"Thanks, Emilia," Lars said.

She smiled. "Another visitor just arrived. Can you handle one more?"

Tess glanced at the door. It was ajar, and through the narrow opening, she caught a glimpse of someone wearing turquoise and yellow. Bram. Her heart lifted. They'd been apart for only a couple of hours, and yet, she'd missed his steadying presence more than she cared to admit.

"Another policeman?" Lars asked.

"A paramedic," Tess said, rising to her feet and hurrying to the door. She opened it wide and stepped into the hall.

Bram greeted her with a warm smile. "I had a short break, so I thought I'd run up and check on Lars."

"I'm so glad you're here."

His eyes met hers, and his smiled dissolved. "What's wrong? Has he taken a turn for the worse?"

"No." She took a deep breath. "The police were here."

She didn't need to say anything else; he instinctively knew how difficult it had been for her. He took her hand and held it tightly. "I may only have a few minutes before I get called out again. What can I do?"

"Come in and see Lars," she said. "I need to tell him about the phone call, and I could use some moral support."

Emilia exited the room, carrying the breakfast tray. She gave Tess and Bram a friendly smile before continuing down the hall, and Tess led Bram inside.

Lars was watching the door. "Good to see you, Bram."

"You too." Bram moved forward and shook Lars's hand. "How's it going?"

"I think I'll survive—and if I'm not mistaken, that's in large part due to you."

Bram smiled and shook his head. "Nah. I just got you off the pavement. I think the surgeon deserves most of the credit."

Lars chuckled. "I'll have to remember that when I'm in rehab cursing the new hardware in my leg."

"You do that." Bram pointed at the familiar object lying on the bed. "Did the magnifying glass do the job for you?"

"Yeah. Thanks for that too." Lars glanced at Tess, and she nodded. Bram deserved to know what they'd found. He pulled the jewelry box out from under his blanket. Opening the lid, he turned the box so Bram could see its contents. "It looks like we have the Lang earrings on our hands."

"Wow." Bram bent over the bed to get a better look, then he turned to Tess. "Does this give the phone call more credibility?"

"What phone call?" Lars said.

Tess sighed. "That's what I was going to tell you before we found the key and Emilia came in."

Her brother glared at her. "How many more things haven't you told me?"

This was not the time to mention her rapidly growing feelings for Bram. Especially with the man standing not more than a meter from her. "I think this one will bring you up to date on the stalker-accident, Lang-jewelry events of yesterday," she said.

"All right," he said. "Let's hear it."

Tess reclaimed her seat, wondering where to start. "Do you remember my phone ringing right before you and Marit left the café?"

"Yes. You said it was an international caller."

"It was," Tess said. "But not the one I was expecting." Bram had taken the chair next to hers, but she kept her focus on Lars. "It was from an English woman named Anna. She was calling from Austria to warn me that because of our relationship to Ingrid Lang Hendriks, we might be in danger."

Lars's eyes widened. "Ingrid Lang Hendriks?"

"I don't even know if Lang was Oma's maiden name, and coming out of the blue like that, it seemed like a crank call, but you'd just been telling me about the Lang jewelry, so I tried to catch up with you . . ." Her voice trailed off, and she swallowed hard. "You were hit before I reached you."

Bram's hand reached for hers, and she clung to it.

"She warned you that our lives were in danger?" Lars was having difficulty taking it in.

"Yes."

It was Bram who broke the uncomfortable silence. "Is it possible that your grandmother's earrings are worth killing for?"

With a dazed expression, Lars picked up the earrings and laid them across the palm of his hand. "I have no doubt they're valuable, but is anything worth that price?"

"Not to most people," Bram said. "But to Tess's stalker, perhaps."

"His name is Mesman," Tess said to Bram. "This morning, the police identified him as the driver of the van."

The significance of her statement hung in the air between them.

"There's too much we don't know," Lars said. "You need to talk to the English woman. She wouldn't have reached out to you if she didn't have a reason to believe we're being targeted. She has to have some kind of proof."

Releasing her hold on Bram's hand, Tess picked up her handbag and pulled out her phone. "I have her number," she said.

"Call her," Lars said.

She stared at the number on the screen. Surely nothing bad could come from reconnecting with the woman. The police had not prohibited Tess from calling her back.

"You need to know what you're dealing with, Tess," Bram said.

She nodded and pressed the number. There was a brief pause, and then she heard an unfamiliar ring. Lowering the phone, she pushed the speaker button. Ringing filled the small room, followed by a click, and then a woman's voice.

"Hello."

"Hello," Tess said. "Is this Anna?"

"It is." The English woman's voice was guarded.

"This is Tess Hendriks. You called me yesterday." Had it really only been twenty-four hours?

"Tess! Are you all right? I wasn't sure what happened yesterday. There was a loud noise, and then you were gone."

"Yeah. Sorry about that." Tess was not about to explain anything to this complete stranger. She was returning her call to get information, not to give it. "I've spoken to my brother since then, and we'd both like to know why you feel that we are in danger."

She glanced at Lars. This was it. Would the woman turn out to be an extortionist, or would she provide them with some credible information?

"Because you're Ingrid Lang's direct heirs," Anna said.

Ingrid Lang's direct heirs? What on earth did she mean by that? "What does Ingrid Lang have to do with any of this?"

"Do you know anything about her family?"

"What do you know about it?" Tess hedged.

"Enough to know that we're related."

Tess exchanged a wary look with Lars. The English woman had hinted at this in her first phone call. "How?"

"The Lang family has lived at Falcon Point for generations. Leopold and Liselotte Lang owned the estate in Austria during the 1920s and '30s. They had three children: Karl, Ingrid, and Anna. Liselotte died before the war broke out, Leopold soon afterward. But the children escaped, each ending up in a different country and not knowing what had become of the others. I still don't know what happened to Karl, but Anna ended up in England and is my grandmother."

"And you believe that my grandmother is her sister, Ingrid."

"Yes." There was a rustle of papers on the other end of the phone. "I'm at Falcon Point right now, helping with a huge remodel. The estate is being developed into a resort. I found some letters and photos in the archive room that helped me piece together our family connection."

Tess could barely think through the pounding of her heart. Anna had documentation. They had the Lang earrings, and now Anna was claiming that not only were they related to the original Langs of Falcon Point, but they were also related to her.

"So we're cousins?"

"Second cousins, to be exact," Anna said. "Which is thrilling for me, but the worst possible news for Gunner Sauermann."

"Who's that?"

"The man acting as trustee for the Lang family estate." She paused, her voice dropping slightly. "He stands to lose a great deal if any member of the Lang family steps forward to claim Falcon Point."

"Enough to kill for?"

"Yes." There was no trace of doubt in Anna's voice.

"Do you have proof?"

"Last night, I was forced into a walk-in freezer at knifepoint and left there to die."

In the stunned silence that followed, the steady bleeping of Lars's monitor filled the room—an unnerving reminder of how close he'd come to death. Surely things like this didn't happen outside a Hollywood film. "Are you okay?"

"I will be," Anna said. "My boss found me before it was too late, and he's had me wrapped in a quilt in front of a space heater ever since."

"So you're still at Falcon Point?"

"Yes."

Tess was having difficulty processing all of this. "What . . . what is it like?"

"Rather wonderful, actually." Anna's voice warmed. "And I'm going to do everything in my power to prevent it from staying in Sauermann's hands."

"Which means you must stay alive."

"Yes. And so must you and Lars. Do whatever it takes to stay safe until we have things taken care of here."

Was this the time to tell Anna that she was calling from Lars's hospital room? Even though it sounded like she had enough to cope with at Falcon Point, Anna should probably know what had happened in Amsterdam.

"Someone may have already tried to eliminate Lars and me," Tess said.

"What happened?" There was no mistaking the tension in Anna's voice.

Tess gave her an abbreviated version of what they'd experienced during the last twenty-four hours. When she finished, the phone was silent. Tess glanced at Lars. Had she said too much?

"Sauermann *has* to be behind the accident." Anna's voice rang with conviction.

"Can you prove it?"

"Not yet. But we will."

"And until then?" It seemed to Tess that if Sauermann could orchestrate attacks on multiple people in different countries, there was no limit to what else he might do.

"I've spoken to the police," Anna said. "Sauermann should be taken into custody soon, if he hasn't been already."

"You'll keep us updated?"

"Of course." Anna paused. "At some point, we'll need to hire a solicitor to sort everything out, but this is our grandmothers' home, Tess. It's worth fighting for."

Our grandmothers' home. Tess stared at her phone and blinked back her tears. Sweet Oma, who had suffered so much during the war and had lived her life so humbly afterward, what would she make of all this?

"Thank you, Anna."

"I'll be in touch," the English woman promised. And then she was gone.

Lars released a tense breath. "Wow. That didn't go the way I expected."

At her side, Bram stirred, but Tess fixed her gaze on her brother. "I'm going to Austria."

"No way," Lars said. "If Sauermann was willing to hire a hit man in Amsterdam, there's no telling what he'd do if he discovered you at Falcon Point."

Tess rose and started pacing across the two-meter-wide room. "I wouldn't have to go to the house itself. I could meet Anna somewhere nearby, and Sauermann need never know. I may not be familiar with the area, but my German is fluent, and if there's any question about the value of paintings and other artifacts in the house, maybe I can help." She clenched her fists. "I must do this, Lars. Not for you or for me, but for Oma."

"You cannot go into a situation like that alone." Lars glared at the blanket covering his injured leg. "And we both know I can't travel right now."

"I'll go with Tess," Bram said.

Tess swung around to face him.

"It's good of you to offer, Bram, but that's not necessary," Lars said firmly.

"I hate to break it to you, Lars," Bram said, "but I think it is. I recognize that look in Tess's eyes. I once made the mistake of calling her stubborn, and she quickly corrected me. She's *determined*. Like it or not, you're up against a determined woman set on going to Austria." He winked at Tess, and she bit back a smile. "I'm overdue for taking time off work. Spending a few days in the Austrian mountains sounds like a good way to use it."

Tess watched the conflict rage in Lars's eyes. She knew he was frustrated by the helplessness of his current situation and was likely just as aware as she was that Bram had purposely downplayed the danger involved in making the trip.

"I'll not do anything rash, and I'll check in with you whenever I can," she promised.

Her brother gave a defeated sigh. "You'd better." He handed her the jewelry box. "Who knows what that key is for, but take this with you in case you need proof of your connection to Oma. I'd tell you to put it in the hotel safe, but your sock drawer has worked well for years."

Tess smiled. "Thanks, Lars."

"No, thank Bram," Lars said. "I wouldn't have caved if I didn't know he'd be with you."

"I'll let you believe that would have stopped me," Tess said, smothering a grin.

The radio on Bram's shoulder crackled to life. He got to his feet immediately and was at the door by the time the message ended. "I've got to go," he said apologetically. "Book the flights, Tess, and let me know how much they cost so I can pay you back." He exchanged a final look with Lars. "Don't worry. I'll take care of her." And then he was gone.

As the sound of Bram's running footsteps faded down the hall, Tess pressed the jewelry box to her chest. She was taking it back to Falcon Point.

CHAPTER 31

Gunnar stared at the latest profit projections for the Falcon Point resort. The small office in his temporary quarters was little more than a shoebox with a desk and a bookshelf, but for the moment, he'd suffer the inconvenience knowing what would come next. The flow of money from the resort would be steady, and his trustee fees would triple. Not to mention all of the upkeep of the estate could come from the trust, which would allow him to siphon profits from the resort for his personal use. Would his plans come to fruition, or was he going to lose everything? He hated not knowing.

He hadn't heard from Jac Mesman since late last night, despite his promise to call as soon as the job was finished.

Why had Jac not checked in with him?

The other Lang heir would hopefully be eliminated by week's end. Though he had come to an agreement with one of the work crew a couple days ago, that death would need to look like an accident. He couldn't very well have the police investigating a murder in his soon-to-be luxury resort.

Gunnar opened his desk drawer and drew out his burner phone, tempted to call Jac again. He hesitated. Maybe he shouldn't be using it after all. If Jac had been arrested, would the police be able to trace Jac's calls back to him?

Gunnar stuffed the phone under a stack of files in the drawer. If he didn't hear from Jac by tonight, he would get rid of it after everyone went to bed.

A knock sounded on his office door. Gunnar slammed the drawer shut. "Yes?"

Henning opened the door. "I'm sorry to disturb you, sir, but Officer Baumgartner is here to see you."

Gunnar fought a rise of panic. Had Mesman been caught? Did the police know of Gunnar's involvement?

"Sir?" Henning said.

Gunnar shook himself out of his stupor. "Show him in."

Henning disappeared down the hall and returned a moment later with the police officer.

Gunnar stood. "Officer Baumgartner, what brings you out at this early hour of the morning?"

"I apologize for disturbing you, Herr Sauermann, but I'm afraid I have a delicate matter to discuss."

Gunnar's palms dampened. He motioned for Baumgartner to close the door. "Please. Sit down."

As soon as they were seated, Gunnar forced himself to ask the question he wasn't sure he wanted answered. "What is this delicate matter? I hope my contractors at Falcon Point haven't been causing you any trouble."

"Not exactly, but I'm afraid we did have an incident last night."

"What happened?"

"A member of the design team was locked in a freezer. She nearly froze to death."

Gunnar fought his disappointment at the word *nearly*. "But she's okay?"

"Yes." Baumgartner cleared his throat. "The woman involved came into our office yesterday and filed a report. She insisted that she overheard you two nights ago speaking on the phone about killing someone."

Gunnar transformed his panic into indignation. "You can't be serious."

"I'm afraid so. Technically, I should have visited you immediately after her complaint was filed, but knowing what an upstanding member of the community you are, I brushed it off as a misunderstanding."

"And now you think because she had some accident on my property, I'm trying to kill her?" Gunnar shook his head. "This is preposterous. I haven't been near the estate in days."

"I'm relieved to hear you say that, sir, but I do need to see your cell phone to check your most recent calls."

"My calls? I just told you I wasn't involved."

"I'm sorry, but I am obliged to follow up on the report."

"Fine." Gunnar retrieved his personal cell phone from his pocket and unlocked the screen.

The officer scrolled through the call log. Once satisfied, he handed the phone back. "Thank you, sir."

"Is there anything else?"

"I'm afraid I will also need to speak with anyone who can account for your whereabouts last night."

"My wife, my butler, the boy who delivered our dinner." Gunnar waved a hand to brush aside the officer's concerns. "Those are the only people I had contact with yesterday. I do expect that when you speak to them, you will be discreet."

Baumgartner shifted in his chair. "Of course."

The other man's obvious discomfort gave Gunnar the courage to take the offensive. "Now, about this report, I can't have such documents lying around that might negatively affect my reputation or the reputation of the resort I'm creating."

"I am the only person who is aware of the young woman's claim."

"What is to keep someone else from finding it in your files or through an internet search?"

"I assure you, Herr Sauermann, I will keep the file private." Baumgartner stood. "Thank you for your time. I'm sorry to have disturbed you."

Gunnar stood as well and shook the man's hand. "I appreciate your discretion."

As soon as the policeman left his office, Gunnar sank back into his chair. Anna Cavendish had survived. He hadn't heard from Jac. What was going on? He had paid good money to take care of these lingering problems.

He blew out a frustrated breath. Apparently, it was time to look for someone new to help him. Hopefully, the third time would be the charm.

Cole would not make it two years in this job without going insane. Monitoring intelligence coming and going, translating, sitting, typing, daydreaming.

With the possibility looming of finding Falcon Point, of finding his extended family, he suspected he would fall victim to a few daydreams regardless of where he was working. Technically, his grandfather would be the legal heir to the property, but to be able to give him the gift of knowing what became of his father's family would be beyond anything Cole could imagine.

He glanced at the clock. Only another hour before he could leave for the day. Could. Had he really transformed from the employee who had to be reminded it was time to leave into the one who watched the clock? Something had to change.

He pushed back from his desk and strode to Gwendolyn's office, where he rapped a knuckle on her open door. "Got a minute?"

"Yeah." Her eyes still on her computer screen, she waved him in. "Did you hear Jac Mesman was arrested in Amsterdam?"

"We've been trying to nail him since he took a shot at Congressman Whitestone in Athens. Do you think the arrest will stick?"

"Looks like it." She looked up and motioned toward a chair. "He was picked up outside a woman's house for stalking, but earlier in the day, that same woman's brother was hit by a van. A traffic camera caught a glimpse of Mesman fleeing the scene behind the wheel of the vehicle in question."

"Who were his targets?"

"That's the interesting part. Two people were injured in the hit-and-run, Lars Hendriks and Marit Jansen. The authorities think Jac Mesman mistook Marit Jansen for Lars's sister, Tess Hendriks."

"Who do the Hendrikses work for? Are they intel?"

"Not that we can tell. Lars is the lead photographer for Royal Coster Diamonds."

"Sounds like the sister was the real target," Cole said. "What does she do?"

"She works at the Van Gogh Museum."

Cole's eyebrows lifted. "And someone paid to get rid of her? There's more to the story."

"I agree. One of our field agents in Amsterdam is working with Interpol, but the chief of station messaged me a few minutes ago, asking for our assistance."

"Why?"

"When our man went to speak with the Hendrikses, he overheard them talking in the hospital. Seems he thinks the Hendrikses found some jewelry that disappeared from an estate here in Austria during World War II."

Instantly intrigued, Cole straightened. "Let me look into it."

"I have field agents who can handle this."

"I know, but I've spent my whole life studying World War II." He tilted his head toward his work area. "I may have signed on as an analyst here, but I could use a break."

Gwendolyn leaned back in her chair and studied him for a moment. "You know, you're very good at what you do."

He was afraid she would say that. "Thank you, but . . ."

"But you hate every minute of it."

Relieved she understood, he nodded. "Yes. I hate every minute of it."

"Okay. It's yours." She hit a button on her keyboard, and the printer beside her whirred to life. She retrieved the single page it produced and handed it to Cole. "Here's the summary report. I'll email you the rest of the details."

"Thanks." Cole took it and skimmed the contents. When he reached the line about the jewelry, his gaze shot up. "The jewelry they found belonged to the Lang family?"

"Yes. How do you know about the Langs?"

Cole's eyes met hers. "I'm one of them."

Now that Cole had an active case connected to his family heritage, he tapped into his CIA resources to dig up whatever he could on Falcon Point. Even though his workday was nearly over, the workday at CIA headquarters still had hours left in it. Plenty of time for his associates on the European desk to do some legwork for him.

With any luck, Isabelle would also succeed in finding some of the missing pieces that would turn his search into a success. The prospect of seeing her again sent a ripple of anticipation through him that rivaled what he experienced when he learned of the Lang family connection. A little surprised at his eagerness to spend more time with Isabelle, he struggled to concentrate on the possibility of finding Falcon Point.

Was there a connection between his old family estate and Lars and Tess Hendriks? Or had they just found jewelry that once belonged to his ancestors?

He accessed the siblings' personal information. His initial internet search revealed their names as survivors in the obituaries for their parents after a car accident three years ago. What was it with this family and cars?

Noting that Lars and Tess were the only surviving relatives, he continued his search of obituaries, but this time he searched for the parents as surviving relatives. As he hoped, he discovered the grandparents' obituaries. He read through the first two and noted the names on their family tree. When he reached the third one, the name jumped out at him. Ingrid Hendriks, born 1924. Could this be the sister his great-grandfather had written about in his letters?

A new search, this one of marriage records, took longer to find, but the results gave Cole the answer he was looking for. Ingrid Hendriks's maiden name was Lang. If this information was correct, Lars and Tess Hendriks were his cousins. Or second cousins. He never was good with those distant relations. Either way, they were all Langs.

An uncomfortable scenario formed in his mind. The website for the Falcon Point resort had hit the internet only last week. If Tess and Lars had possession of jewelry from the Lang family, could lost treasures from World War II be the reason his cousins had been targeted? And if so, were they innocent victims, or were they dealing on the black market? With Tess working in a museum and Lars working as a photographer for jewels, they certainly had the contacts in the art world to be on either side of the equation.

Cole did a quick search for their numbers and picked up his desk phone. He called the brother first. No answer. When he dialed Tess's number, it went straight to voice mail.

"Great," he muttered. Only one thing to do. If he couldn't get them on the phone, he would do his investigating the old-fashioned way. He stood and noticed the finance officer packing up for the day.

"Hey, Zoe, could you wait a minute? I'm going to need a last-minute travel order processed."

"Sure. Who's it for?"

"Me. I'll be right back." Cole started toward Gwendolyn's office but stopped when she rushed out her door.

Cole spoke at the same time she did.

"I need to go to Amsterdam."

"You need to go to Amsterdam."

Cole's surprise that they'd said the same thing was overshadowed by the urgency in Gwendolyn's voice.

"Has something happened?" Cole asked.

"One of our operatives uncovered a funding stream to Jac Mesman," Gwendolyn said. "It looks like a payoff for the hit."

"That's good info."

"That's not all. The Berlin office has tied him to the group that has been smuggling artwork confiscated during World War II into the US. I don't know who these two Dutch nationals are, but we need to find out why Mesman was after them," Gwendolyn said. "Another transfer was sent this morning."

"You think whoever hired Mesman is sending someone else?"

"Yes. With everyone in the middle of transfers and vacations, the Amsterdam office is shorthanded. They could use another operative with field experience until they identify who received the payment." Gwendolyn handed him one of the papers she held, along with a cell phone. "Here's your itinerary and a secure cell phone. You're booked on a nine o'clock flight."

"Thanks."

Gwendolyn turned to Zoe and handed her a signed travel order. "I'm glad you're still here. Can you process this before you leave?"

"Of course." Zoe took the paper and sat back at her desk.

"Once Zoe has that processed, she can give you a cash advance. You already have a travel credit card, don't you?" Gwendolyn asked.

"Yeah. I'm all set." Cole looked at his itinerary. "Wait. You have me traveling under my real name?"

"Yes. It will simplify things since you could very well be related to the intended victim."

"What cover story am I using? That I work at the embassy, or that I'm a tourist?"

"Better go with working at the embassy," Gwendolyn said. "You'll need to be able to explain how you know your cousins are in danger."

"True."

"Good luck."

"Thanks." Cole gathered his notes and shut down his computer. Ten minutes later, he had a thousand euros in his wallet, his personal cell phone back in his pocket, and he was only a quick stop at his apartment away from tracing his family roots.

Cole stepped off the train at his stop and checked his phone for the fourth time since sending a text to Isabelle twenty minutes ago. Still no response. He had hoped she had come up with the information on the land ownership by now. He had also hoped to spend time with her tonight, but obviously, that was no longer an option.

He traversed the short distance between the station and his current apartment. The last thing Cole expected to find when he arrived home was Isabelle waiting outside his door.

Her eyes brightened when he approached, and she held up a manila envelope. "I found what you were looking for."

"Seriously?" Cole asked. "I tried texting you a little while ago, but when you didn't respond, I figured you didn't have anything yet."

"I must have left my phone on silent after I got off work."

Cole retrieved his keys and unlocked the door. "Come on in. I can't wait to see what you found." He led the way inside and closed the door behind her.

"The ownership wasn't hard to find," Isabelle began. "The entire estate was put in a trust during World War II."

"A trust for whom?" Cole ushered her into the living room.

Isabelle drew a set of papers out of the envelope she held. She skimmed over the top sheet before answering. "The Lang family."

"My family," Cole whispered.

"What?" Her eyebrows drew together.

"Nothing." He stepped closer so he could look at the documents. "Who manages the trust?"

"Gunnar Sauermann."

"Sauermann?" Cole snatched the papers out of her hand. "You can't be serious."

"I gather you know him."

Cole skimmed over the trustee documents. Was the current trustee related to the man who had murdered Leopold Lang?

"Cole?" Isabelle's voice broke into his thoughts. "Do you know Gunnar Sauermann?"

"I don't know him." Cole looked up. "But I know of his family."

"How?"

"If I'm right, one of his ancestors murdered my great-great-grandfather during World War II."

Both elegant eyebrows lifted. "Does this all have something to do with Falcon Point?"

"Yeah." Cole glanced at the time on his phone. He could spare a few minutes. "A man named Wilhelm Sauermann murdered Leopold Lang, the man who owned Falcon Point during the war."

"And he would be your great-great-grandfather."

"That's right." Cole pulled his cell phone from his pocket and retrieved a scan of one of his great-grandfather's letters. He showed it to Isabelle. "This is the letter that describes what happened the night of my great-grandfather's death."

Isabelle leaned forward for a closer look. "You keep old family letters on your phone?"

"I know, it's weird, but I scanned them so I would have a backup, and it's nice to be able to refer to them when I don't have them on hand." Cole held up the documents she had brought him. "Based on the information you found, it looks like the Sauermanns gained control of my family's property and never let it go."

"Why didn't you make a claim before now?"

"No one could find Falcon Point," Cole said. "All we had to go on were the letters my great-grandfather wrote to his wife while he was serving in the British Navy. His letters mentioned Falcon Point, but my family assumed it was located in the Alps. We've been looking in the wrong part of the country for decades."

"For generations."

"Yes."

"Sounds like the Sauermanns aren't going to be very happy when you show up and tell them their services are no longer needed."

"You're right." An uncomfortable thought surfaced. Could Sauermann be involved in the assassination attempts on Tess and Lars Hendriks? If the current trustee didn't know about the existence of Cole's grandfather, the Hendrikses would be the only descendants of Leopold Lang who could make a claim on Falcon Point. But why go after them now?

"Cole?" Isabelle laid her hand on his arm. "Are you okay?"

"Yeah." Cole shook himself out of his thoughts. He checked the time again. "I'm sorry. I'd love to talk about this some more, but I have a flight to catch."

"Where are you headed?"

Cole censored his answer automatically. "Just a quick business trip."

"Maybe I'll see you when you get back."

"I'd like that."

Isabelle took a step toward the door before turning around. "I have my car downstairs. Would you like a ride to the airport?"

"That would be great, if you don't mind."

"Go pack. I'll wait here."

"Thanks." Cole walked into his bedroom. He checked the name on his itinerary, a reminder that he would be traveling as himself for the first time in ages. He unlocked his safe, removed the top tray, and retrieved his personal passport. His gaze landed on the New Testament nestled in his family papers. Would he ever uncover the mystery hidden within its pages?

He locked his safe, grabbed his bag, and emerged from his bedroom.

Isabelle's eyebrows rose. "That was fast."

"I travel a lot for work and usually keep a bag packed." Though he was tempted to confide in her that they worked for the same organization, he could hardly admit that he had accessed her cover story without potentially having it blow back on Jasmine. "Ready?"

"I am."

Cole opened the door for her. "Lead the way."

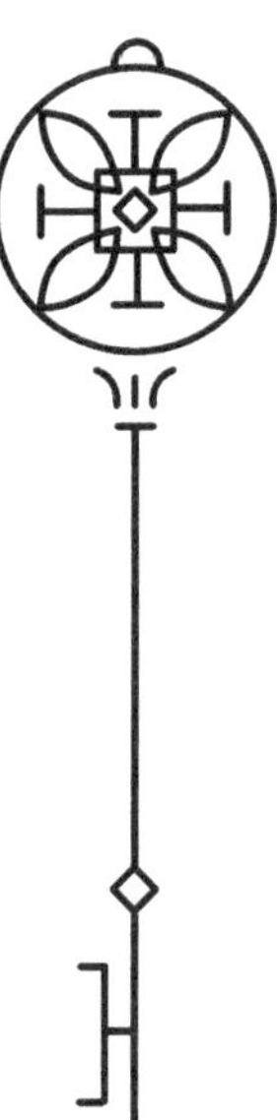

CHAPTER 32

WITH HIS MESSENGER BAG HANGING from his shoulder, Cole strode through the Amsterdam airport. After a quick stop at an automated kiosk to buy a three-day transit pass, he made his way down the escalator to the train station. Despite the late hour, he didn't have any time to waste. According to the latest intel from CIA's Amsterdam office, they had an agent staked outside Tess's house, but he had yet to lay eyes on her. Lars remained in the hospital, reliant on nothing more than the usual hospital security.

Cole had expected the local authorities to keep a police detail on Lars, but according to Cole's latest information, a bomb threat at the Anne Frank house, one of the most popular tourist sites in the city, had pulled all additional units to investigate.

If it were him, that would be exactly the kind of ploy he would use to draw the police away from the real target.

Cole headed straight to the hospital. No better time for an assassin to strike than during the night shift.

Cole found the correct platform and waited impatiently for the train to approach. A quick glance around revealed only a few fellow passengers lingering nearby as well as a handful of airport employees waiting with him, undoubtedly going home for the night.

The rumble of the approaching train reverberated through the underground station a moment before its lights illuminated the tracks. The train whooshed to a stop, and Cole allowed the other riders to enter first before boarding himself. He chose a seat near the door and checked his phone for updates. With the limited signal, he needn't havc bothered.

The train rolled forward, and a minute later, it emerged outside. Cole checked his messages again. Nothing new on the bomb threat, and no sighting of Tess Hendriks. Could she be at the hospital visiting her brother? Surely the locals would have noted it if she had chosen to stay in the city rather than return home.

Gwendolyn's comment about the local office having inexperienced personnel made him wonder if they had overlooked that possibility.

With each passing minute and each passing mile, a sense of urgency churned inside him. He wished he could call the local office, but no one would be in at this hour. He needed answers, and his cousins might very well provide them.

When the train reached Amsterdam Centraal, Cole was the first person off. He quickly left the station and located the tram that would take him to the hospital. After scanning his transit pass, he sat and counted the number of stops until he reached his destination. Almost midnight. Would hospital security deny him entrance? He pulled up the website for the hospital. As he suspected, visiting hours ended long ago. Looked like he was going in a back door.

A heart attack victim brought in by ambulance gave Cole the distraction he needed to slip through the emergency room waiting area and into the main section of the hospital. Since a police report had been filed on the accident, he had to assume the police suspected foul play, which meant the hospital's security protocols would prevent admittance to anyone not already on a visitor list. Under normal circumstances, he could have used his alias to claim law enforcement status, but since he was traveling under his own name, his options were limited.

Cole bypassed an orderly staring at his cell phone and diverted down a side hall when two nurses approached. Once they passed by, he continued to the alcove where the elevators and the stair entrance were located.

Though he preferred stairs over elevators, he didn't want to risk getting locked in a stairwell. He'd learned that lesson the hard way in a secure office building in Minsk two years ago.

Footsteps approached, and Cole debated what story he could use to justify his presence at this hour of the night. The elevator doors slid open as the orderly from the waiting area came into view. Cole quickly stepped inside and pressed the button for the fourth floor. Immediately, he hit the Door Close button, relieved when the other man didn't try to join him inside.

When the elevator slid to a stop on the correct floor, Cole exited and took a moment to read the sign on the wall.

At least his contact in the local field office had provided him with Lars's room number.

That thought sent a new wave of uneasiness through him. If the CIA could gain that information, who was to say someone else couldn't too? With the arrest of Jac Mesman, the local authorities might not even know of the new threat.

Cole shifted his bag from one shoulder to the other and made his way to the correct room. Down the hall, a male nurse entered a patient's room. Or was he a nurse? Throwing on a pair of scrubs would be an easy way to blend in while executing a kill order.

Cole quickened his step.

He reached Lars's room and peeked inside. The blond-haired man lay on the bed. A bandage covered a good portion of his forehead, and the blanket lay askew, revealing a cast covering one leg. He was alone, and his eyes were closed as he lay motionless in the dark.

Concerned that he might be too late, Cole stepped into the room. In the same moment, the nurse emerged from the room next door.

"Hey!" he demanded before saying something in Dutch that Cole didn't understand. When Cole didn't respond, he repeated his words in English. "What are you doing in there?"

Cole's eyes lowered to the man's ID badge. Dean Bakker. The credentials looked real enough, but Cole still wasn't convinced he was facing a hospital employee rather than a hit man. Since the nurse had come out of another patient's room, he was leaning toward the former.

Opting for one version of the truth, Cole said, "I'm his cousin."

"We've heard that before." The nurse grabbed Cole's arm with unexpected force.

Cole tampered the urge to fight back. "I'm serious. Lars is in danger. Someone else is coming after him."

Suspicion flashed on Dean's face. "The last 'cousin' who showed up looking for him ended up in jail. That's where you're going to be when the police get a hold of you."

"I'm not the enemy. I'm here to protect him. I'm family."

"This man doesn't have any family except his sister, and you aren't her."

Lars stirred in his bed. "What's going on?"

Relieved that the man was still breathing, Cole shifted to face him as much as the nurse would allow.

"The person who sent the last hit man after you paid for another."

"What?" Lars pushed up in his bed. "Who are you?"

"He says he's your cousin."

Lars shook his head. "Up until yesterday, I didn't have any cousins."

"We're second cousins," Cole corrected. "Or something like that. My great-grandfather was Ingrid Hendriks's brother."

Dean pulled on Cole's arm. "We'll sort this out with security."

"I'm telling you the truth," Cole insisted. The last thing he needed was to have the authorities run his ID, especially when he was using his real name. Not to mention getting detained wouldn't bode well with his desire to get back into fieldwork.

Cole could break free of the nurse, but then what? He needed the hospital's cooperation to ensure Lars's safety. And he also didn't want hospital security chasing after him when they very likely had a real threat looming.

"Look, I'll talk to your security, but let me stay here." Cole motioned to the phone on Lars's bedside table. "You can call from there."

"Come with me into the hall, and I'll call." Dean pulled a hospital-issued cell phone from his pocket.

"Fine."

Cole stepped into the hall, and Dean followed. He released Cole to dial as an orderly approached.

Cole's eyes narrowed. He was the same orderly he had seen by the emergency waiting room and again by the elevators. Cole's gaze followed the lanyard around the man's neck to the ID badge that hung from it, an ID badge that was flipped the wrong way so it wasn't visible.

"Security?" Dean said. "I need you to send someone to room 417."

The orderly's jaw clenched. Cole continued his assessment of the other man, right down to the slight bulge at his ankle. Was that a holster?

The orderly reached into the back of the waistband of his scrubs in a move Cole had seen more times than he cared to admit. A gun emerged at the same time Cole reacted.

"Gun!" Cole grabbed Dean's arm, yanked him into Lars's room, and sent him sprawling onto the floor. Dean's cell phone dropped from his hand and skidded under the hospital bed.

The silencer on the weapon reduced the gunshot to a puff of air, but the bullet clanged into the metal door frame only inches from where Cole had been standing a moment ago.

Cole darted farther into Lars's room and muscled the door closed behind him.

"What . . . ?" Dean sat up, both stunned and indignant. "Was that . . . ?"

"That was the hit man I was telling you about."

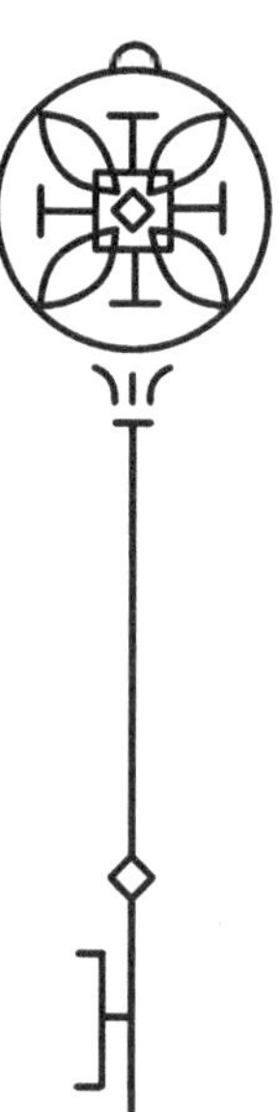

CHAPTER 33

Cole analyzed the room for any means of escape. The window wasn't an option, nor were there any other exits. They were trapped.

Cole grabbed the closest chair and shoved it against the door. An instant later, the door rattled against it.

"Grab your phone and give it to Lars." Cole motioned to where it had fallen. "I'm going to need your help."

Dean did as he was asked.

The gunman tried to break through the barrier again, this time with more force. Cole leaned his full weight against the chair.

"What am I supposed to do with this?" Lars held up the phone.

"Tell security we've got a live shooter." Cole scanned the room. The bed was dangerously positioned in front of the door. A rolling monitor cart occupied one side of the room, and an unused IV stand was tucked in the corner nearest Cole.

The door rattled again, this time jerking Cole back an inch.

With limited time and no choice but to use what he had available to him, Cole said, "Unhook Lars from the monitors."

The gunman pushed against the door yet again. It popped open a few inches, but Cole shoved the chair, and the door slammed closed.

"Okay, he's unhooked," Dean said. "Now what?"

Fully aware that the man on the other side of the door could hear them, Cole said, "Move his bed sideways so he's out of the line of fire."

Dean complied with surprising speed. As soon as he completed his task, Cole waved him forward and motioned for him to keep the chair shoved against the door.

The moment the two men traded places, several shots fired, the swooshes of displaced air corresponding with splintered wood in the door. Dean jerked back.

"Don't let go!" Cole shouted.

Another push against the door. More bullets lodged in the wood. It wouldn't take the man long to break all the way through. Once he did, he would have to take only two steps inside before he would have a clear line of fire between himself and Lars.

Not if Cole could help it.

Cole reached for the cloth screen hanging from the ceiling. Even though it left the two feet of space between the floor and the bottom of the curtain exposed, any barrier right now was better than nothing. He pulled the curtain closed so he and Dean were on one side of it and Lars was on the other.

The little alcove the drawn curtain created by the door only spanned a five-foot diameter, but it would keep Lars from being easily targeted once their opponent made his way through the barrier they had erected.

Even as another round of bullets sprayed into the door, Cole leaned in and whispered to Dean. "Go behind the curtain. As soon as you hear the door open, shove the monitor cart this way as hard as you can."

Dean nodded.

The click of a magazine ejecting from a pistol sounded, followed by a new one being loaded into place.

Taking the reload as his cue, Cole shoved the chair out of the way and sent it tumbling beneath the curtain into the other side of the room. He then lifted the IV pole over his head like a weapon.

An instant later, the gunman burst into the room. Surprise reflected on his face that the previous obstacle had been removed. That surprise multiplied when the monitor cart impacted the curtain, and Cole swung the IV stand at the gunman's arms.

The hit man cried out and stumbled into the cart as it tangled in the curtain, but his weapon remained firmly in his grip. Cole swung the IV pole again, but it banged into the wall behind him. His opponent lifted his weapon and reached for the curtain.

With little space to move, Cole dropped the IV stand and rammed his shoulder into the other man. The man's knee came up, but Cole blocked it. Unfortunately, he didn't manage to avoid the fist that connected with the underside of his jaw.

Cole staggered back and slammed into the wall. His hand blocked the next punch, and he shoved at his opponent. The gunman took a step back to gain distance, and his gun hand lifted.

Cole reacted instinctively. Taking advantage of the close proximity, he grabbed the man's gun hand with one hand and ripped the weapon free with his other. Cole barely had control of the pistol before the other man struck again. He grabbed for the gun, and Cole fired.

Where the bullet impacted, he couldn't be sure, but the man jerked and stumbled back a step. He leaned over, and it took a moment for Cole to realize he was going for his secondary weapon.

"Don't do it." Cole took aim.

The man drew a second pistol from his ankle holster. The weapon flashed into view, and Cole squeezed the trigger. This time, he had no doubt he'd hit his target.

Security arrived only moments before the doctor. While Cole's second shot had incapacitated the gunman, he hadn't aimed to kill. Keeping the man alive long enough to find out who had hired him was worth whatever efforts the hospital staff had to go through.

Dean had tended to the man who had tried to kill them until the doctor relieved him. As soon as the wounded patient was transferred onto a gurney and taken away, Dean moved across the room to tend to Lars.

His cousin's bed was still pushed against the far wall, the IV stand lying on the floor and the chair and monitors situated haphazardly in the center of the room.

"Are you both okay?" Cole asked.

"Yeah, thanks to you." Dean motioned to the bed. "Since you're not shooting people anymore, want to give me a hand and help me move the bed back to where it was? I need to hook him up to the monitors and check his vitals."

"I only shot one person."

Cole grabbed one end of the bed and helped Dean put it back into place, then stepped aside to let Dean tend to Lars.

"How are you doing?" Cole asked Lars.

"Better now that no one is trying to kill me."

"I hate to say it, but that isn't going to last long. Whoever wants you dead is determined to finish the job."

"Who would want me dead?"

Cole didn't answer. While he appreciated the nurse's help in fighting off the hit man, that didn't mean he was ready to bring him into his confidence.

Dean finished hooking the blood pressure cuff up to Lars's arm. "I'll be right back. I need to get my cart."

"While you're at it, can you let whoever is in charge of hospital security know we need to speak with them?" Cole said.

"Sure. I'll make the call."

As soon as Dean left, Lars repeated his earlier question. "Who wants me dead?"

"Best guess, a man named Gunnar Sauermann." Cole picked up the IV stand and put it back in the corner. "This is all hypothetical, but I think it's because you and your sister are heirs to the estate he and his family have been running since World War II."

Lars shook his head. "This is all so farfetched. My grandmother never had much in the way of material things. If there was an estate out there somewhere she had a right to, I have to think she would have made a claim."

"It's possible she tried," Cole said. "Have you heard of the Lang family?"

A flash of awareness appeared on Lars's face but was quickly banked. "I don't think so."

"I hope you don't play poker," Cole said. "You aren't a very good liar."

"Are you?"

"Am I what?"

"A good liar." Lars adjusted the pillow behind his back.

"I am a very good liar, but I'm not lying now."

"Why are you really here?" Lars asked. "My grandmother never said anything about having siblings, but you're the third person in two days to claim to be my cousin."

Alarm bells rang in Cole's head. "The third? Who were the others?"

"One was the guy who was picked up outside my sister's house."

"And the other one?"

"Some distant cousin who called to warn us that someone might be after us. She said she was a Lang descendant."

Uneasiness rose within him. "Something's not right here. I've been researching the Lang family for years. The only living descendants of the Lang family are you, your sister, me, and my grandfather."

"That's not what the woman who called Tess said, but if what you say is true, you would have a claim to the estate too."

"Yes."

"Then why do people keep coming after me instead of you?"

"Because they don't know I exist."

The police arrived first. Cole gave his statement and sat by while Lars recounted his version of the story. This time, he didn't dispute Cole's claim of being related.

The officer jotted down the last of his notes. "I think that's all we need for now."

"What about protection?" Cole asked. "Obviously, my cousin is still in danger."

"We will arrange to have an officer posted outside Mr. Hendriks's door for the next day or two, but once we turn this over to Interpol, you'll have to coordinate with them."

"Thank you." Cole knew the drill. Once Interpol took over, the locals could use their involvement to wash their hands of the problem. But Interpol specialized in investigative work, not protection.

As soon as the officers left, Cole asked, "How much longer are you expected to be in the hospital?"

"A few more days. Then I'll be heading to a rehab facility. I'm hoping Marit will get released at the same time I do, but she's still in pretty bad shape."

"Marit?" Cole pulled at his memories. "The woman who was run down by the same car you were?"

"That's right."

"We need to talk to the doctor about transferring you to another medical facility while you recover," Cole said. "You won't be safe here."

"The police just said they'll post an officer outside my door."

"Yes, but that won't last long. I'm telling you, you need to hide, and you can't very well do that while you're stuck in a hospital bed, especially when it's in the same hospital where you were originally admitted."

"What makes you think this Sauermann guy will come after me again?" Lars asked. "And why can't the police or Interpol arrest him?"

"They have to prove he's behind the funding stream. That takes time." Cole didn't mention that men like Sauermann rarely got their hands dirty. More than likely, the money would be filtered through numbered accounts in some banking haven.

"This is all so surreal." Lars raked his fingers through his hair. "How did you know I was in danger in the first place?"

"I got a tip from a friend." Cole leaned forward in his seat. "If it's okay with you, I'll stay here tonight. In the morning, we can talk to the doctor about transferring you somewhere else under an alias."

"You sound like you know a lot about this kind of stuff."

"I work for my country's embassy, so, yeah, I guess you could say that."

"You work for the embassy here? In the Netherlands?"

"No, in Vienna." Cole offered Lars a sliver of the truth. "The money to pay for the hit men came from an Austrian bank. That's how I got involved."

"I appreciate your help, seriously, I do, but if someone is really after me, won't they be able to follow me to wherever the medical transport takes me?" Lars asked. "Besides, I'd rather not leave Marit here alone. For all we know, someone could still confuse her for Tess."

Cole's gaze landed on Lars's leg. The truth was that moving him would be as risky as setting up a protection detail here, unless . . . "I have another idea."

"What's that?"

"The gunman may survive the night, but if he can't communicate with his employer, no one will know if he was successful."

"You want me to pretend I died?"

"It's better than the alternative."

Lars didn't speak for a moment, clearly contemplating. Finally, he nodded. "You're right. As long as I can make sure Tess and Marit know I'm really alive, you can make up whatever story you want."

"Informing Marit will be easy enough. As a precaution, I can ask the hospital to switch both of your rooms to make sure no one else can find you."

"I like where you're going with this," Lars said. "What about my sister? My cell phone was broken in the accident. I don't have a way to get in touch with her until she gets where she's going."

"What do you mean 'gets where she's going'? I thought she would be at home."

"No. She's on her way to Falcon Point."

CHAPTER 34

Cole didn't waste any time. By seven o'clock in the morning, Lars and his friend Marit had been transferred to new rooms. Marit's record now indicated that she had been released this morning, and Lars's showed he hadn't survived last night's shooting.

The police had agreed to maintain a presence at the hospital for the next twenty-four hours, but ultimately, keeping Lars out of sight would be the greatest defense.

After settling his newly discovered cousin in his new room, Cole sent a message to Gwendolyn with an update and a request to fly to Linz, the closest airport to Falcon Point. The approval and his new flight information came back quickly.

He wasn't willing to deal with public transportation during rush hour, so he took a taxi to the airport. On the way, he pondered his next move.

Cole still couldn't believe Tess Hendriks had left for Austria at the same time he had been flying to Amsterdam. Depending on where she'd spent the night, she could already be at Falcon Point and have no idea the kind of danger that could be awaiting her there.

Was Gunnar Sauermann the person behind the assassination attempts? Cole couldn't be sure. Thus far, all he had were his suspicions, suspicions he could admit were seeded in his deep distrust because of the man's family heritage.

Cole pulled up Tess's phone number and dialed. It went straight to voice mail.

"Great," he muttered under his breath.

He had confirmed her number with Lars before he left the hospital. Was it possible she was on a plane? Lars had indicated she had left last night, but if that was the case, why was her phone off? Unless she had turned it off to avoid being detected while she was sneaking around Falcon Point.

Cole shook that thought away. He was the one who did things like that. Tess Hendriks worked at a museum. Surely she had more sense than to go to Falcon Point by herself.

With a confidence born of familiarity, the taxi driver shifted gears and took the bend in the narrow mountain road with only a couple of feet to spare between his vehicle and the drop-off below. Tess's breath caught, and Bram's grip on her hand tightened fractionally.

"Now I understand why Austrians don't bike everywhere like the Dutch do," Bram muttered.

"Because they'd keep stopping to admire the view?"

Bram rolled his eyes, and Tess laughed. She knew that wasn't what he was going for, but he couldn't fault her reasoning.

They'd flown into Vienna the day before and taken the train as far as Linz. The majestic buildings of the capital city had soon given way to rolling green hills dotted with goats and cream-colored cows wearing bells around their necks. They'd passed quaint farmhouses with wooden shutters and overflowing window boxes and whitewashed churches with turquoise onion-top roofs. And when they'd arrived in Linz, even the glow of the city lights reflecting off the Danube had had a magical quality. Walking hand in hand with Bram through the historic city center had made for the perfect ending to a long day of travel.

This morning, they'd been fortunate to find a taxi driver from Gildenstatt willing to transport them to their final destination. Knowing that the road would take them into the mountains, Tess had anticipated picturesque scenery, but nothing could have fully prepared her for the splendor before her now.

"Have you ever been to Gildenstatt?" The driver spoke, and Tess tore her gaze from the view out the window.

"No," she said.

"Ah." He seemed pleased. "You are in for a treat. You shall get your first proper look at the village in one moment." The entrance of a tunnel cut directly into the mountain gaped wide before them. Without checking his speed, the driver plunged them into the semidarkness. The tunnel curved gently to the right, and suddenly, they were driving into the light once more. "Now you can see it." There was pride in the man's voice. "Gildenstatt, Kristall Lake, and Falcon Point beyond."

All around them, tree-covered mountains reached for the blue sky above. Below, the same azure color reflected in the water of a pristine lake. A cluster of buildings of various shapes and sizes stood close to the water's edge, and on the other side of the lake, a large house with pointed turrets and a slate roof sat surrounded by vast lawns, flower gardens, and trees.

"Look, Bram." Tess pointed at the distant manor, the sudden lump in her throat taking her by surprise.

Bram leaned closer, gazing out the window on her side of the vehicle. "Do you think that's it?"

Tess nodded. She didn't need the driver's confirmation. Somehow, she just knew it.

Bram must have sensed her unexpected battle with emotion because he brushed his lips across her cheek. "You've got this," he whispered before shifting back into his seat.

"A perfect place for a honeymoon, yes?" the driver said, giving Tess what he obviously assumed was a knowing look in his rearview mirror.

"Oh, we're not on honeymoon," she said, studiously avoiding looking at Bram while desperately hoping that the warmth currently creeping up her neck would travel no farther.

"No? Forgive me. I assumed too much. What brings you to Gildenstatt, then?"

She hesitated. She would give him the truth but not the whole truth. "I'm meeting my cousin here."

"Ah. Very nice. There are some excellent cafés and restaurants along the lake. It won't be hard to find one where you can share a fine meal."

"I'm sure you're right." Tess had called Anna from Schiphol Airport to let her know that she was en route and would be arriving in Gildenstatt the next day. Anna had immediately suggested meeting for a late lunch or early dinner in the village. As soon as they checked into the B&B, Tess would call Anna again. She assumed Anna would recommend a suitable restaurant.

The driver stopped at a traffic light, and a large lorry filled with dirt lumbered by in a cloud of dust.

"He's got a point, you know." Bram's low voice reached her over the noise, and Tess braved looking at him again. His eyes were twinkling, but his fingers were still firmly wrapped around hers. "It would be a good place for a honeymoon."

"Yes," she said, her feigned nonchalance completely at odds with her now flaming cheeks. "Especially when the resort is complete."

He chuckled. "Good point. I'll keep that in mind."

The light turned from red to yellow to green, and the taxi inched forward, turning onto a gravel road that led toward the lake.

"This is it," the driver said, pulling up in front of a large house painted a pale-salmon color.

Traditional brown shutters framed each window of the three-story building, and an enormous clematis plant covered a good portion of the wall, long tendrils clinging to the wooden balcony on the upper floor. Baskets of flowers hung below the eaves and sat in stands on either side of the front door.

"It's lovely," Tess said.

The taxi driver gave her an approving smile and opened his door.

"I'll grab the luggage and pay the driver," Bram said. "Why don't you go in and get us registered."

Tess picked up her small shoulder bag and climbed out of the car. Leaving the two men talking beside the car's open boot, she walked into the welcoming B&B. A narrow hallway led directly to a short desk, and behind the desk, a white-haired woman sat studying a computer screen.

"Good morning." The woman looked up as Tess approached and greeted her in German. "My name is Lena. Welcome to Gildenstatt."

"Thank you," Tess replied. "I have a reservation for two rooms."

"Wonderful." Lena was as efficient as she was friendly, and by the time Bram entered with their two small cases, Tess had their room keys in hand. "Breakfast will be served in the dining room through the glass doors on your left between seven and ten o'clock. I'm happy to recommend a local café or restaurant for lunch or dinner."

"We're meeting someone today," Tess said. "But we may take you up on that offer later."

"Of course." The Austrian woman glanced at the clock on the wall behind her desk. "If you have plans this afternoon, I'll let you settle in so you're not late."

"Thank you," Tess said. She reached for her bag, but Bram shook his head.

"I've got it," he said. "You lead the way."

"How long do you need before you're ready to head out again?" she asked as they started up the steep staircase.

"Two minutes tops."

Tess laughed. "I forgot that I'm dealing with a fast-acting paramedic. I'll call Anna, and as soon as I know where we're meeting, I'll knock on your door. If she can't join us right away, maybe we can explore the village a bit."

"Sounds good," he said, coming to a halt outside a white door labeled with a wooden number eight. "Is this you?"

Tess checked the keys and handed him one of them. "Yes. And you're next door."

"Great. I'll see you soon."

Cole jolted awake when the plane touched down in Linz. He had dozed a bit in Lars's hospital room during the early-morning hours, but the lack of sleep had caught up with him by the time he'd made it onto his first flight. He had slept soundly on both legs, relieved the planes hadn't been overly full. With any luck, he'd be able to catch another nap on the cab ride to Gildenstatt.

Though he had made use of the restroom in the Amsterdam airport to freshen up and change his clothes, he followed his typical protocol and changed his clothes again once he deplaned in Linz. The likelihood of someone following him here was low, but that didn't alter his habit of being cautious. The fact that he didn't have any way to access a gun in this part of the country left him uneasy. It was ironic, he supposed, that he wasn't comfortable being unarmed when he was one of the few CIA agents who were permitted to carry in the first place. Most of his colleagues used their unarmed status to blend in, to ensure they couldn't be mistaken for anything other than the civilians they pretended to be.

He had put a call in to Gwendolyn to ask for one of his fellow agents to meet him here in Linz, but she had insisted she didn't have anyone available to make the six-hour round trip from Vienna, the nearest CIA station. Her response was frustrating, but Cole couldn't blame her. He would only be here long enough to find Tess and whisk her away to safety. He didn't need a gun for that.

Fifteen minutes after walking out of the restroom sporting a fresh shirt and a ball cap, he hired a taxi to take him to the little village near the house where his great-grandfather had grown up. As soon as he was settled in his seat, Cole closed his eyes, but the sense of anticipation pulsing through him wouldn't let him relax enough to sleep.

He was on his way. All those years his grandfather had talked about finding Falcon Point and here Cole was, only an hour from seeing it for himself. Okay, it would likely be more than an hour before he could find a way in. After all, he could hardly show up on the front porch and announce himself as a member of the Lang family.

He debated his next move. If Gunnar Sauermann was involved with the assassination attempts, Cole needed proof, which would likely come in the form of a money stream. But that was something he wouldn't be able to find without help.

His thoughts turned to Isabelle. What were the chances she could trace the money transfers? Of course, that was assuming she was the source Gwendolyn was referring to when she passed him the information about the second hit man yesterday. Whether it was Isabelle or some other financial genius, whoever found that payment was responsible for saving Lars Hendriks's life.

Cole glanced out the window and took in the mountain scenery. When the cab entered a tunnel, he retrieved the photos of the letters his great-grandfather had written. It was time to reacquaint himself with the 1940s version of Falcon Point as well as the Sauermann ancestor who had changed the Lang family forever.

With any luck, in the next day or so, Cole would be able to start reversing the Lang family's misfortune and give the Sauermanns what they deserved.

CHAPTER 35

WERE ALL HIRED GUNMEN IRRESPONSIBLE? Or did Gunnar keep ending up with ones who couldn't figure out how to dial a phone? Why hadn't his man called?

Gunnar searched through the international news, focusing on the Netherlands. Ideally, Lars Hendriks's death would look accidental. After all, the man was already in the hospital. Things happened to patients whose health was already compromised.

Tess Hendriks, on the other hand, might very well meet a death worthy of a headline. Gunnar narrowed the newsfeed to ensure only stories that had hit the internet within the past twenty-four hours would appear.

He skimmed through until one popped up that caught his attention. *Shooting at hospital in Amsterdam.* Gunnar clicked on the article and read intently. *A lone gunman shot and killed a patient last night at OLVG East. The gunman was wounded by authorities and is expected to survive.*

Gunnar read the rest of the article, disappointed that no names were given. Clearly, if a patient was killed, it must have been the brother. He noted that there wasn't any mention of the sister.

Had his latest employee already killed her at her home before taking care of the brother? If so, it was possible her body might not be discovered for days, if ever. After all, she lived alone, and the Netherlands had plenty of waterways where a body could be dumped.

Gunnar hoped that was the case because he was tired of chasing these Lang descendants. They were like cats who never seemed to reach their ninth life.

Petra walked into his office. "Are you ready to go to lunch?"

Though Gunnar would have preferred to sit in front of his laptop searching for more clues, he nodded. "Anytime you are."

"I'm ready now. Let's go."

"I'll meet you in the living room in a minute." As soon as Petra left, Gunnar erased his search history and shut down his laptop. After he pocketed his personal cell phone, he joined his wife.

"Shall I have Henning pull the car around?" Gunnar asked.

"No. It's lovely outside. We should walk."

"As you wish." Gunnar opened the front door and escorted his wife outside. They walked the short distance from the rental cottage to the diner that had become their regular spot for lunch.

"How much longer do you think it will be before we can move back into our house?" Petra asked.

"Several more months, I'm afraid."

"I much prefer Trisha's cooking to the chef here."

"I know, but it will be worth the wait." Gunnar followed her inside, and they settled into their usual seats. He shuddered at the fact that they had been here often enough to have a usual table at a local diner. Really. This situation was insufferable.

The waitress approached with menus.

Gunnar held his hand up. "I don't need that." He already had the menu memorized. He ordered his selection and waited while Petra discussed the day's specials with the waitress.

Bored with the conversation, Gunnar glanced out the window. His gaze landed on a young couple walking on the sidewalk a short distance away. When the woman turned her head, his breath caught. The face matched the photo his private investigator had sent him.

Tess Hendriks wasn't lying dead in her house in the Netherlands. She was alive and well and strolling down the street in Gildenstatt.

Cole gazed through the window of the cab at the thick greenery. Any minute, he would reach Gildenstatt. According to the land records, Falcon Point was on the other side of the lake from where he would stay tonight. Would the estate be anything like he had imagined?

The Google Earth images had revealed a sizeable house and several smaller structures scattered along the hillside beyond. Could onc of those be the structure where the family treasure was hidden? His great-grandfather had given the general location, but how much of the landscape had changed over the past eighty-plus years?

The cab turned off the main thoroughfare and followed the sign toward the village. Excitement shot through him. He was so close. The thick trees gave way to the open space dominated by a pristine lake. Cole looked beyond the water, and his heartbeat quickened. There it was—a castle-like home dominated the land overlooking the shore opposite him.

Eagerness rose within him, and he had to remind himself that he wasn't here on family business but rather on agency business. He wanted to find Gunnar Sauermann, but he needed to locate Tess Hendriks first. Whether it was her connection to Falcon Point or a tie to the smuggled World War II artifacts, someone wanted her dead, and Cole had to find out who before it was too late.

The cab slowed and pulled to a stop. Cole grabbed his messenger bag and paid the driver. After thanking him, he stepped onto the sidewalk in front of the bed-and-breakfast where he would stay tonight. According to the information Gwendolyn had sent him, it was one of the few places that took in short-term lodgers that had rooms available. If the stars aligned, Cole would find Tess staying under the same roof, but first, he needed a shower, a hot meal, transportation, and a plan.

Cole found the registration record for Tess Hendriks at the little B&B in Gildenstatt, but he didn't find her.

Unlike at the hospital, the proprietor of the bed-and-breakfast had been more than accommodating when Cole had mentioned he was looking for his cousin.

Lena, the stout woman who owned the B&B, informed him that Tess and her boyfriend had checked in and then left the inn. She had no idea where Tess had gone or when she would return. Since Cole couldn't do anything but wait for Tess to get back, he would use his free time to pay a visit to Falcon Point.

His search for a rental car lasted only a minute. Lena confirmed that no rental car companies existed in the small village. She called the only taxi driver in town to schedule him a ride only to find he was out with a fare.

"He said he can pick you up in a half hour," Lena said in German.

Cole deciphered the thick Austrian accent before responding in her language. "I'll take what I can get."

Lena confirmed his ride. "Can I get you a cup of tea while you wait?"

"No, thank you. I have some calls to make."

"Let me know if you change your mind."

"I will." Cole checked his watch. Three o'clock. "Could I ask a favor?"

"Of course."

"If my cousin returns before I get back, can you call to let me know? I wanted to surprise her."

She offered a warm smile. "I'd be happy to."

After Cole gave Lena his number, he returned to his room and sat at the antique writing desk by the window. He gazed out at the view of the main street. A work truck passed by, and a few pedestrians walked down the sidewalk, but otherwise, the street remained quiet.

He pulled his secure cell phone from his pocket and dialed Gwendolyn. It went straight to voice mail.

"Gwendolyn, I just called to check in. I found where Tess Hendriks is staying but haven't located her yet," Cole said. "I'm heading to Falcon Point in a bit to do some poking around. Let me know if you have anything new on Sauermann." Cole hung up the phone and switched to his personal cell.

He texted Isabelle. *Looks like I'll be back in town by the weekend. Do you have plans Saturday night?*

A text came back a moment later. *I do now. What did you have in mind?*

Encouraged, he replied, *How about dinner and a concert at the Vienna State Opera House?*

Perfect.

A new layer of anticipation hummed through him. He was about to see the family home he had been searching for for as long as he could remember, and now he had a date this weekend with a beautiful, intelligent, interesting woman with a security clearance. What could be better than that?

I'll call you when I get back in town.

A thumbs-up popped up on his message, indicating she liked his text. He smiled as Jasmine's observations replayed through his mind.

Had his grandfather arranged this meeting with Isabelle with the intent of setting them up? If so, Cole would have to thank him.

Dressed in jeans and a plain blue T-shirt, Cole sat in the back of the taxi while his driver slowly crept up the road that led to his ancestors' old estate.

"You working at Falcon Point?" the taxi driver asked.

"Yes." It wasn't a lie. Cole had every intention of working at Falcon Point, just not on construction.

"It's just over the next rise."

Cole leaned closer to the car window as they made the turn. His heartbeat picked up speed when the estate came into view. *Magnificent* was his first thought. *Home* was his second.

Up close, the property truly was incredible. Manicured lawns created a peaceful setting, a three-story mansion nestled in the center of them. The size alone was jaw-dropping.

A work truck similar to the one he had seen drive past the B&B was in front of the main house. A couple other cars were parked beyond it.

Cole took in the open space surrounding the mansion before his gaze followed the land rising above it. Through the thick pine trees, he could make out the roofs of several structures. Could one of those roofs be the structure he was looking for? Was it possible Cole was really only a hike away from finding it?

"Have you brought anyone else up here in the last day or two?" Cole asked.

"Can't say that I have."

If he was the only taxi driver in the area, that meant Tess was still in the village somewhere. As long as she was away from Falcon Point and Sauermann, she was safe, and if she was safe, he had some time to explore.

Though he was anxious to see the main structure, Cole said, "Can you keep going up the road? I think I'm supposed to report in by those buildings up the mountain."

"Ah, the goatherd huts." The driver continued forward until he reached an area that appeared to be a makeshift parking lot and pulled up beside another work truck.

"This good?"

"Yes. Thank you." Cole paid the cabbie in cash. "Can I get your number in case I need a ride back to the village tonight?"

The driver retrieved a business card from off his visor. "Here you go."

"Thanks." Cole opened the door.

From what his great-grandfather had described in his letters, the building he was looking for was near the edge of the woods beyond the manor. Had Leopold and Karl really come all this way? The building in front of him had to be at least a mile from the house.

Suspecting workers might still be inside, Cole skirted past the first hut and started down a dirt path wide enough for a vehicle to drive through. Cole noted the tire tracks and assumed this would eventually become an access road to the guest cottages. He followed the makeshift road until he reached the next hut. A power saw buzzed for several seconds before quieting only to start up again a moment later.

Cole continued past, his forward progress drawing him farther down the mountain. Did the gamekeeper's house look different than a goatherd hut? Cole imagined it would be bigger, but he didn't see any clearings large enough for a structure much bigger than the huts he had already passed.

Flutters of excitement rose within him. All these years and he was walking in the same woods where his ancestors had once trod, the same woods where Leopold and Karl had hidden the treasure his family had been searching for for generations.

Karl's letters had mentioned artwork and jewels, among other treasures. Would Cole find some missing Van Gogh or Monet? Or perhaps some priceless painting by an obscure artist he'd never heard of?

Cole reached a break in the tree line where the road overlooked the sprawling estate. What would it have been like to have grown up here? Playing in the woods, sheep grazing in the pasture, a home so large that you could play hide-and-seek for weeks and never be found.

His imagination took flight as he pictured a home removed from the evils and secrets of the world. Perhaps his ancestors had imagined they were isolated, but Karl's letters proved how wrong that perception had been in the early days of World War II. Despite the idyllic setting and remote location, the family hadn't been able to escape the evils of Hitler and the Nazi party, but at least two of the three siblings had survived.

He thought of Tess Hendriks. Where was she? Lena hadn't called to tell him Tess had returned to the B&B, and the cabbie hadn't brought her to the estate. Had she opted to stay in Gildenstatt for the day and visit Falcon Point tomorrow?

The road took a dip down the mountain, and Cole passed an enormous, sprawling pine. He stopped and peered across the expansive lawn between him and the back of the house. From here, he couldn't be more than two hundred yards from the back door. He hadn't realized the work road had dipped so close to the mansion.

Two men walked outside and retrieved a piece of sheetrock from the back of a truck. Cole waited for them to return inside before he started forward again.

He reached a small clearing and glimpsed another hut above him. Each hut looked like the next, each of them at least a quarter of a mile apart, but he couldn't tell which were original structures that had been renovated and which ones were new.

He let out a sigh. This might take longer than he thought.

CHAPTER 36

A COPPER BELL JINGLED ON the door as Anna and Beckett entered Café Hofbacker, a dark wooden structure with overflowing flowerpots beside the front entrance. The café stood on a steep hill near a string of lovely cottages with views of the lake. Anna had asked Tess to meet her here before dinner crowds clogged Gildenstatt's cobbled streets.

While they waited, Anna took in the quaint seating nooks with chintz pillows and numerous photos on the wall of the Habsburg imperial family. Her palms had turned sticky at the mere thought of meeting her cousin Tess.

"Table for four," Beckett said to the hostess.

The hostess, a heavyset woman in national dress, led them across the dining room to a round table beside a massive brick fireplace. The two-sided affair divided the dining area in half.

Beckett pulled out Anna's chair and set it facing the door so she would see Tess first thing. The café was almost deserted except for a young family of three seated near the entrance, a man whose sole focus was his mobile, and two backpackers at a separate counter for takeaway.

"Would you like something to drink while you wait for your party?" the hostess asked.

"Do you have a selection of herbal teas?" Anna inquired, unable to make heads or tails of the foreign words on the menu.

"We do." The hostess pointed to a selection in German.

Recognizing *haselnuss* for what it was, she said, "I'll take the hazelnut, please."

"And you, sir?"

"Water. Thank you."

The hostess retreated with their orders, and Anna fiddled with the metal clasp on her purse, her body ramrod straight.

Beckett reached over and tucked a strand of hair behind her ear. Since the freezer incident, he had been a man with a mission, and that mission was protecting her. That morning, he had installed a deadbolt on her bedroom door and set up a wireless security system throughout the basement. No one could enter their section of Falcon Point without Beckett's mobile alerting him.

"Relax. She'll come," he said.

"But what if something happened to her?"

The copper bell rang, and a tall, striking blonde woman and a man with light-brown hair entered the café and spoke to the hostess near the entrance. Everything inside Anna went on high alert. That had to be Tess.

Anna pushed back her chair when the blonde turned and headed for their table, her blue eyes the same color and shape as Anna's.

"Tess Hendriks?" Anna asked at the same time the woman said, "Anna Cavendish?"

Anna's British accent contrasted with Tess's Dutch one. Under normal circumstances, Anna would have smiled, but with at least one hit man still on the loose, all she managed was a crooked grimace.

Even though her nerves were stretched to the snapping point, her manners reasserted themselves. "I thought you might prefer meeting somewhere less formal after your trip. Please join us."

"Thank you," Tess said. "This is my friend, Bram Dekker."

Beckett rose to his feet and extended his hand. "Nice to meet you. Beckett Campbell. I'm rather more than Anna's friend."

Ignoring Beckett's comment, Anna indicated the two vacant chairs, and they all took their seats.

"How was your trip? Did anyone follow you?" Anna's words sounded forced despite her best efforts.

"Not that we could tell," Bram said.

They all fell silent when a waitress dressed in a green-and-white dirndl arrived to take their orders.

"Please order for me," Anna whispered to Beckett. "I don't want to pull out Google Translate to read the menu."

Anna waited until the waitress headed back to the kitchen before she asked, "How are your brother and his friend doing?"

"When we left yesterday, they were both stable. Lars had surgery on his leg, and he'll be in rehab for weeks, but he's going to make it. And so will Marit. That's the most important thing."

Relief washed over her. Tess was right. The accident's outcome could have been so much worse.

"What about the trustee?" Tess asked. "Was he apprehended?"

"We reported him to the local police and haven't seen him since," Anna said. "I spoke to a solicitor who deals with property confiscated during WWII. He says I have a strong chance of removing Falcon Point from Herr Sauermann's direction. If you and Lars join forces with me, it's an even firmer case."

"Of course. I think our grandmothers would have wanted it that way," Tess said.

"I do too," Anna agreed. "I have a picture of our grandmothers when they were children. Would you like to see it?"

"I'd love to. We don't have any pictures of Oma when she was young."

Anna removed Granny's photo from her purse and handed it to Tess. "That snapshot is the only thing of Granny's that survived the war. You can see Falcon Point in the background."

Tess touched the outer edge of the photograph, obviously moved. "Oma lived such a humble life after the war. She never once complained, but to know she came from this kind of lifestyle . . ." Tess shook her head. "She used to tell the most wonderful stories. My favorite was about an Austrian princess—"

"Who slayed a dragon?" Anna interrupted, her voice clogged with emotion.

"You know it too?" The photograph in Tess's hand trembled slightly.

Anna nodded. "That was Granny's favorite story. She told it to me every night before she tucked me into bed."

The awkwardness Anna had experienced since Tess's arrival slipped away like darkness in the face of dawn, and an invisible connection stretched between the cousins. The link, though tentative, felt familiar.

Family.

The emotion reminded Anna of the first time she had laid eyes on Falcon Point, a feeling of welcome, of coming home. How could she feel this way about a woman who, despite the same eye shape and color, was from a different culture and whose native tongue was not her own?

But the sentiment persisted until Anna accepted its existence. She and Tess were family, linked by more than blood and tragedy. In her cousin, Anna sensed the same depth of resolve to seek justice for their would-be murderer and a willingness to reclaim the Lang estate from a family who had murdered their great-grandfather. Lurking underneath it all was a desire to explore their new connection.

Tentatively putting her figurative toe in the water, Anna scooted her chair closer to Tess's and pointed to Granny's photograph.

"That's your grandmother, Ingrid. And that's Karl beside her. He's the oldest."

"I wonder whatever happened to him?"

"Ingrid wrote to him after the war. He never answered. Granny said Karl led the Nazis away from her at the train station, and Ingrid helped him." Anna's voice broke a little, and she cleared her throat again. "They were real heroes."

Tess digested the information in silence, her eyes blinking rapidly.

Anna sniffed, and Beckett slid his arm around her and gave her shoulder a reassuring squeeze.

"And this little one, that's your grandmother?" Tess finally asked.

"Yes. I was named for her." Anna pointed to the two adults standing behind the children. "Those are our great-grandparents, Leopold and Liselotte."

Tess squinted at the photo. "Liselotte looks rather frail."

"She died shortly after that photo was taken."

Tess leaned back in her chair. "So, what do we do next?"

"Well, I hope you don't mind, but I took the liberty of contacting a man at the Austrian land authority. He has forms for us to fill out that will lay legal claim upon the estate. I have an appointment with him tomorrow. I wondered if you might want to come?"

"Yes," Tess said with a warm smile. "I'd like that."

CHAPTER 37

Gunnar fumed as he listened to the foursome's conversation. They knew. All of his late-night searching had been for naught. Anna had found the lost letter, and she knew of her heritage.

Gunnar shifted closer. He had opted to stay in town after lunch in the hope of contacting the man he had tasked with killing the Hendriks siblings. The café had the best Wi-Fi and the best coffee in the village, which had resulted in his making this his temporary office for the afternoon.

When he had chosen his seat, he had opted for the table behind the fireplace to avoid interacting with the locals while he pondered what to do next. Little had he known an answer to his question would walk through the door in the form of two of the three heirs. Fate smiled brightly on him when they chose to sit at the table on the other side of the fireplace from him.

Though well concealed from everyone except the woman sipping her coffee at the table behind him, Gunnar could hear every word the two young couples spoke.

The discussion on how to file their claim continued. At least the land office had already closed for the day. That meant he had to do something tonight.

He didn't know how Anna had found the Hendriks girl, but perhaps he should thank her. A quick call to his man at the estate and the last two heirs could be eliminated at the same time. It was about time his employees completed the task without getting caught. From what the Hendriks girl had said, she must not have received the news yet that her brother hadn't survived the night.

Felix, the local taxi driver, walked into the cafe. He spoke in English, his booming voice carrying. "You found your cousin."

"I did," the Hendriks girl said.

"*Ja,* I can see the resemblance." He paused. "Did you have another cousin meeting you here?"

"No, why?"

"I took a man up to Falcon Point today. His eyes were just as blue as the two of yours," Felix said. "Thought he must be related."

Another man spoke now, and Gunnar recognized the voice as Beckett's. "You took someone to Falcon Point?"

"I did."

"Who was it?"

"Said he was working up there."

"When was this?" Beckett asked.

Gunnar's anxiety skyrocketed. Another man who resembled the two Lang cousins? Lars Hendriks was supposed to be dead. Worst case, he should still be in the hospital in Amsterdam.

Felix paused long enough that Gunnar could visualize him checking the time on either a watch or a cell phone before answering. "Must have been about four o'clock. He had me drop him by a goatherd hut a bit up the mountain."

"Something's not right," Beckett said.

"You didn't hire any new workers?" Anna asked.

"No, and I have to authorize any new hires," Beckett said. "The rest of our design team left an hour ago for a wedding in Salzburg. None of them would have had any new subcontractors reporting to work today."

"Then who is up there?" the Hendriks girl asked.

A chair scraped against the wooden floor before Beckett spoke again. "I don't know, but we'd better find out."

Gunnar drew out his second cell phone and sent a text. *Three targets: Anna Cavendish, Tess Hendriks, and a man searching the goatherd huts on the mountain. It might be Lars Hendriks. The women are returning to Falcon Point now.*

Priority?

All of them. It has to be tonight.

Understood.

Gunnar slipped his phone back into his pocket and waited for the door to close behind the foursome before he emerged into the main section of the café.

He'd given his man his assignment, but after so many failed attempts, Gunnar had to be sure nothing went wrong. If the heirs to the Lang estate were going to Falcon Point, so was he.

Cole searched one cottage after another, but he had yet to find a single one that didn't already have a completed basement, each of which was empty. Was it possible the construction crews had already found the treasure? Surely something would have hit his radar if newly discovered gems and artwork had recently been sold.

Then again, maybe it already had. The Rembrandt sketches had surfaced less than a week ago. Could they have been part of his family's hidden artwork?

Cole returned to the construction road where the taxi had dropped him off. The gravel lot that had previously been filled with cars was now empty. With the workers clearly gone for the night, he picked the lock of the hut that appeared to be the headquarters for the construction on this part of the estate.

His suspicions were confirmed as soon as he slipped inside. Unlike the others he had been in, this one was already furnished. He crossed to a desk littered with work orders and blueprints.

He searched through the paperwork, pausing when he found a map that notated the location of all of the huts on the mountain, then checked the descriptions, disappointed when he didn't see any mention of the gamekeeper's house. He looked over the map again, confirming that he had searched all those on the lower part of the hillside.

After completing his search of the hut, again without finding any sign of a previous storage bunker, Cole pulled out his phone and retrieved the scanned image of the letter that best described the day before Leopold Lang's murder. Cole read through the story Karl had related to his wife of helping his father carry paintings and a chest full of jewels and keepsakes to the hidden bunker beneath the gamekeeper's house. The mention of a pine tree beside it didn't help much. There were pine trees everywhere.

He skimmed further, and a phrase jumped out at him with new meaning. *We snuck out the back door to avoid being seen by the servants. The hiding place was beneath what had once been the gamekeeper's house. Even though it was only a few hundred meters away, at times it felt like we were walking much farther.* Now he was getting somewhere. He had forgotten about that specific detail since he'd never had a house to reference before.

He checked the map again. None of the huts appeared to be close enough to the house to fit the location described in Karl's letters.

Cole took a moment to ensure he left everything the way he'd found it and walked back outside. He moved down the mountain far enough to gain a clear view of the main house. No doubt about it. The gamekeeper's house would have been located much closer than any of the structures he had searched today.

A phrase from the letter replayed in his mind. *What had once been the gamekeeper's house.* Cole assumed the house still stood, but maybe he hadn't found it because it had been torn down.

He started back down the road, this time not searching for a manmade structure but a location where one could have been. He went only a few steps before he reached a rack of tools. Deciding he might as well take advantage of the easy access, Cole selected a shovel.

He hiked back toward the main house and stopped when he reached the edge of the trees. Except for one work truck, all of the vehicles that had previously been parked beside the house were gone. A sedan he hadn't noticed before occupied the space beside the truck. With any luck, if Sauermann saw him, he would mistake him for a worker, but the possibility of running into him caused Cole to scan the windows for any sign of life. When he saw none, he took a step forward.

His phone rang, and he took a step back again. "Hello?"

"Cole, it's Gwendolyn."

"You're working late."

"I received some new information," she said. "I don't know if you saw the intel on a recent sale of some Rembrandt sketches."

"I did. I'm not sure, but I think they could have belonged to the Langs before World War II."

"They did. Interpol did a routine check on the source to ensure the artwork hadn't been stolen," Gwendolyn said. "When their agent questioned the man who brokered the sale, he produced documentation that proved ownership by the Lang family as well as the paperwork that identified Gunnar Sauermann as the trustee authorized to conduct business on their behalf."

"That doesn't surprise me. I already knew Sauermann was the trustee."

"Yes, but did you know that a large portion of the funds from the sale of the sketches was funneled to an off-shore account?"

"How did Sauermann manage that? If the proceeds were paid to the Lang Trust, he shouldn't have been able to move it."

"That's an excellent question, one I don't have an answer to," Gwendolyn said. "I sent an agent to Linz this morning to see if she can trace the funds."

His thoughts instantly went to Isabelle. "Anyone I know?"

"No, but I asked her to find out if the money from the railroad has hit the account for the Lang Trust."

"What money from the railroad?"

"Sorry, you must not have seen the latest emails on Falcon Point. We found out the railroad is cutting through the edge of the estate and is paying a hefty sum for it."

"How hefty?"

"In the neighborhood of ten million euros."

"Wow. That's a lot of money," Cole said.

"Yeah, it is. If you're right about Sauermann, it's enough to kill for," Gwendolyn said. "Where are you now?"

"I'm at Falcon Point," Cole said, his concern heightening. "Any chance this agent you sent to Linz can get me a weapon?"

"Sorry. You know standard protocol is to remain unarmed so we can blend in."

"Except in circumstances when there's a high probability of an armed conflict," Cole countered. Had Gwendolyn never been in this kind of situation in the field before?

"You aren't a target. Tess Hendriks is. Besides, you can use the local authorities if you need extra resources," Gwendolyn said. "Did you find her yet?"

"Not yet. I'll go back to Gildenstatt after I take care of some family business here. With any luck, she'll be back at the B&B by the time I get there."

"Don't lose sight of why you're there."

Cole leaned on the shovel he carried. "I won't."

CHAPTER 38

An air of tension hung over the four occupants of Beckett's car. From her position in the back seat, Tess could see the white of the Scotsman's knuckles as he gripped the steering wheel, waiting for the traffic light to turn green. Up ahead, the two-lane road merged into a single, graveled lane, and the cars were stalled behind a large backhoe that appeared to be moving at little more than walking pace.

Beckett released a frustrated sigh. "Normally, it only takes twenty-five minutes to reach the manor from Gildenstatt, but the railroad company's construction has really made a mess of the roads."

"Is this construction connected to the work you're doing at Falcon Point?" Bram asked.

"Yes and no." The light turned green, and Beckett inched his BMW forward. "The railroad company has their own contractors and timeline. As you can see, they've started work on the portion of the new line that goes past Gildenstatt to the former village where the train station will be located, but they're still waiting on approval for an easement that will run across Falcon Point land. Once that happens, we'll have to work a bit more closely with one another."

"I see," Bram said. "So tell me exactly what you're working on."

Beckett began to describe the remodel of Falcon Point, from the changes to the manor itself to the creation of guest cottages that looked like goatherd huts. Showing genuine interest, Bram leaned forward to listen, and it wasn't long before Beckett's expression became more animated and he relaxed against his leather seat.

The backhoe pulled off the road, and immediately, the string of cars that had been following in its wake surged forward. With barely a pause in his description of the spa he was designing, Becket shifted gears. The tires spun on the loose gravel, and the car picked up speed as it started up the hillside.

Anna swiveled around in the front passenger seat, and inclining her head toward Bram, she smiled at Tess. "I'm impressed." She spoke softly so as not to interrupt the men's conversation. "Bram's a good man to have around in a stressful situation."

"He'd tell you it's all part of his paramedic training," Tess said. "But it's much more than that. I'd have been pretty lost without him with all that's happened over the last few days."

"I can imagine," Anna said. "And even though this isn't the best of circumstances, I'm glad you both decided to come to Falcon Point."

"Me too."

Anna's smile widened. "We're getting close. This is the last of the switchbacks. As soon as we turn this bend, you'll get your first good look at the house."

Beckett took the corner slowly, and suddenly, there it was.

"Oh." Words failed Tess. The house was even more magnificent up close than it had been from a distance.

"It's pretty amazing, isn't it?" Anna said.

Tess nodded, struggling to untangle her emotions. The pale limestone walls gleamed in the sunlight, and the many windows reflected the blue skies above. Unbidden, a vision of Oma sitting on her humble bed with the sapphire-and-diamond earrings in her work-worn hands flashed into her mind, and a familiar lump returned to Tess's throat. She pressed her hand against the side of her shoulder bag, feeling the square shape of the jewelry box beneath the bag's soft leather. Now that she knew the earrings' value, she hadn't dared leave the jewelry at the inn.

"There's a special feeling here," she said. "It's stunning in the grandest possible way, but somehow, it still . . ." Tess shook her head. "I can't explain it."

Anna gave her an understanding look. "You don't have to," she said. "I get it. It feels like home."

"Yes." That was it. She hadn't been brave enough to voice it herself because it seemed so ridiculous, but there was something about this place that made her feel as though she belonged.

"As you can see, this driveway leads up to the front of the house," Beckett said. "We'll take you there before you leave, but first, I need to take the back road up to the goatherd huts to check on my equipment. If any of my men are still there, they can tell us if they saw anyone snooping around."

He took a narrow dirt road that wound up the mountainside behind the manor until he reached an area that had been cleared sufficiently to allow several cars to park side by side. Pulling up in front of a small hut, Beckett turned off the engine. "It looks like everyone's left for the day, but we can reach most of the other huts from here." He opened the door and had one foot out of the car before he'd finished speaking. "I'll check this one before we go any farther."

As he disappeared inside the small building, Anna, Tess, and Bram got out of the car. Tess walked to the edge of the clearing, her gaze slowly moving over the tree-covered hillside. The grounds were even more extensive than she'd imagined, and by now, the intruder could be anywhere.

She heard Bram's voice and turned to see that Beckett had reemerged from the hut and was talking to him. Beckett pointed toward a small footpath that took off into the trees, and Bram nodded. It looked like they were headed out.

"Do you think we can find him?" Tess asked as Anna stepped up beside her. "He could be anywhere."

"I won't deny there are a lot of places to hide on the grounds, but Beckett knows the lay of the land pretty well, and when he sets his mind on something, not much gets in his way." Anna's eyes darted to the handsome Scotsman. "Especially when it's personal."

"Like locking you in the freezer."

"Yes," she said, a hint of steel in her voice. "But if this intruder ends up being the same thug I met in the kitchen, Beckett's going to have to take a number after me."

Cole stopped fifty yards from the main tree line and turned in a circle. Based on his great-grandfather's letters, Cole expected the gamekeeper's house to be about three hundred and fifty yards from the manor. From where he stood, only four pine trees fell within that radius. Each encroached the open area where the mountain sloped down into the yard, adding variety to the tall grass that covered the space between the thick trees and the yard proper.

He tried to visualize the grounds as they would have been in 1940. Would the gamekeeper's house have been this close to Falcon Point? He glanced at the tree closest to the center of the yard. It was in plain view of all the windows.

With an estate this size, Cole couldn't imagine Karl and Leopold would have dared haul things out of the house in full view of whatever servants they employed, no matter how loyal they'd thought they were. The second tree could also be seen from the manor. The two closest to the road, however, were far enough to the side of the house to be obscured from view.

Cole approached the tree closest to him. The tall grass swayed in the breeze and covered the area surrounding the base of the thick pine. If anything had ever existed beside it, the evidence had been erased long ago.

Cole pressed his shovel into the ground, put his foot on top, and used his weight to drive the tip through the grass and into the ground. The shovel slid through the dirt the full depth of the shovelhead. He pulled it out and used his foot to repair the disruption he had caused in the yard.

He circled the tree and repeated the process every few feet. He impacted the roots several times but never hit anything that wasn't naturally occurring in the ground.

When he reached his starting point, he stepped back a pace and circled again. The results were the same.

He glanced at the corner of the house. This would have been the most direct location from the back door to carry something out without being seen.

If the information in his great-grandfather's letters was correct, he had only one option left. If the underground bunker wasn't beside the next tree, he didn't have a clue where to look. With a combination of excitement and dread, he crossed to the massive pine that dominated the spot where the hillside rose sharply. Thick roots ran along the surface of the yard, interrupting the grass for several yards in every direction.

His hand tightened on the handle of the shovel. He fought back the fear of disappointment and embraced hope. His great-grandfather had written of Leopold's claim that when they returned to collect their hidden possessions, they would discover the greatest treasure of all. As much as Karl expressed his anguish about losing his youngest sister, Anna, during the bombings in London, Cole suspected Karl's greatest desire had been to reconnect with his remaining sister. With this obvious love of family, Cole couldn't help but wonder, What did Leopold treasure above all else?

Cole took a quick look around to ensure he was still alone. Once satisfied, he pressed the shovel into the ground. He struck a root and took a step to the side to try again.

Disappointment seeped through him when on his second try, the shovel cut through the dirt and slid smoothly into the ground. Six attempts later, he hit another root. His hope fading, he took a step to the side and put his foot on the top of the blade of the shovel. He pressed down. The shovel cut through the ground, but this time, he sensed an interruption, as though the metal met with a brief resistance before continuing. Did he catch part of the root again?

Not bothering to repair the most recent hole, he took another small step to the side and tried again. The shovel only went a few inches before it hit something solid. Cole's heartbeat quickened. He tried a new spot and again met resistance.

Cole used the edge of the shovel to scrape away the top few inches of dirt. Was that wood? He pushed aside more dirt and pine needles but was unable to determine if it was a board or a thick root.

Cole dropped to his knees for a closer inspection. A faint whoosh of air sounded above him. Bark splintered and rained down on his head. A gunshot? With a silencer? Here?

Even though his mind insisted he was imagining things, he instinctively scrambled behind the tree and surveyed the woods and open space behind the house.

It took him only a second to identify the slight movement in the nearby trees. Sauermann? Could he have seen Cole snooping around the grounds? And was this the way people at Falcon Point dealt with trespassers? If so, that was going to change as soon as the estate reverted back to its rightful owners.

Cole took another step to ensure the person in the woods couldn't get a clean shot. The movement must have encouraged the gunman because more bark splintered a second later.

Cole edged around the tree until it was between him and the shooter. Twenty yards of open space lay between him and the cluster of pines behind him. Even though the trees would provide him cover, he couldn't risk running across that much open space.

Unarmed and trapped, Cole only had one feasible option. He'd have to let the gunman come to him.

He glanced at the ground where the shovel lay, then squatted down, grabbed the handle, and pulled it toward him. It wasn't his weapon of choice, but for the moment, it would have to do.

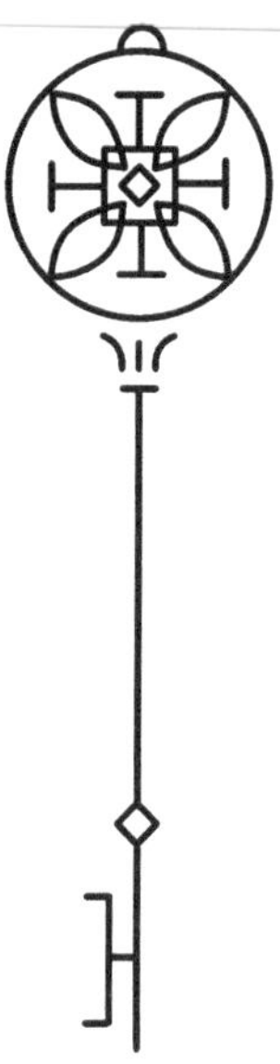

CHAPTER 39

Beckett looked out over the sea of trees, worry gnawing at his gut. Why would an intruder come up here?

"We have a dozen huts to cover," he said. "It's a bit of a hike, I'm afraid." Their Dutch visitors appeared to be in good shape, but neither of the ladies was wearing the right shoes for an activity like this.

"We should probably get going," Anna said. "We have a lot of ground to cover."

She set off down the path, and Beckett hurried to catch up to her. There was no telling what the lass would do if she encountered the man who'd left her for dead. Come to that, there was no telling what he would do either.

He fell into step beside her, with Tess and Bram bringing up the rear. Following the newly cut track, they hiked up the mountain, searching the upper huts and their perimeters. Each structure was an empty shell without upgrades, save for the new basement pours. None of the windows or doors appeared forced, and they could see no fresh footprints.

Doubling back, Beckett started toward the lower huts. Small gullies cut here and there through the track, leaving loose rock and pebbles from the recent rain. Anna's foot slipped, and he grabbed her arm to keep her upright.

"Thanks," she said, regaining her balance.

"Maybe I should hold on to you for a wee bit, just in case." Beckett laced his fingers with hers.

"In case you fall?" Anna asked with a twinkle in her eyes.

"Precisely."

They started down the hill, the formal grounds of Falcon Point in sight. Tree roots crossed the path, and the dense canopy overhead hid the sun, keeping the air cool and the ground damp. A pair of squirrels darted up a tree and stopped to scold them from the upper branches. Behind him, the rattle of rolling stones was followed by a startled cry.

Beckett swung around in time to see Tess reach for a nearby bush as her feet went out from under her. She landed on her side and slid down the incline, stopping against a boulder.

"Tess!" Bram was down the slope in seconds.

"Stay here." Beckett released Anna's hand and scrambled down the hill to join Bram.

"Are you all right?" Bram knelt beside Tess.

Tess gave a shaky laugh. "Yes." She rubbed her dirty hands against her trousers, shifted slightly, and grimaced.

"Is it your leg?" Anna asked, her voice filled with concern.

Tess nodded.

"Try straightening it," Bram said.

She did as he asked. "I'm all right. It's just a bad scrape."

None of them had missed the quick intake of breath that she attempted to hide.

Bram frowned and offered her his hand. "Try standing on it."

Moving slowly, Tess came to her feet. "See, I'll be fine."

"Walk for me. I want to see you put pressure on it."

Tess took a few halting steps. Her trousers were torn, but she was mobile. She looked at Beckett. "Please don't let this slow us down. Really. It's nothing."

Beckett took in the blood seeping through her torn trouser. "How bad is it, Bram?"

"I don't think she's broken anything, but the sooner we can get some ice on her knee, the better."

Beckett nodded. He had intended to lead the group back to the car and drive down to the manor, but they'd already walked so far down the mountain, the journey would be much shorter if they stuck to the path and entered Falcon Point from the rear gardens.

"We can take the trail through the woods to the house," Anna said, her eyes on Tess's bloodied leg. "It's much closer than having Tess hike all the way back to the car."

He should have known Anna would reach the same conclusion. Taking the shortcut made perfect sense. Except for the possibly violent intruder who might be lurking nearby.

Beckett's gaze rested on Anna, a battle waging inside him. "I dinnae think that wise."

"If all three of us stay together, we'll be fine," Anna assured him.

He hated that her words made better sense than the alternative. There was no point arguing. She was spot-on. He'd be better off saving his breath for the long run to the car.

"Right," Beckett said. "I'll meet you at the manor." He pivoted and jogged down the track. It would probably take him twenty-five minutes to reach the car and another five or ten to drive back. If he made good time, they would reach the house only about a half hour before he did.

Cole's hand gripped the wooden handle of the shovel, his senses heightened. The breeze rustled through the pines. The grass swayed in the breeze. A squirrel scampered up a nearby tree. For more than a minute, Cole didn't sense any other movement. Then he heard it. The shooter's first steps interrupted the faint background noise, barely audible.

Cole estimated the direction and took a half step to his right. He visualized a dozen different scenarios of how the next few minutes would unfold, skipping over the ten that would leave him wounded or dead. Even as his operations training pumped through his brain, questions surfaced. Why was this man shooting at him? The idea that someone on the estate would fire on a trespasser without warning was absurd. Did Sauermann know who Cole was? And if so, how?

The gunman took another step forward and then another. Cole had hoped to open a discussion, preferring to talk things out over having the situation end in bloodshed, but the nearly silent footsteps and lack of conversation didn't bode well for an easy resolution.

Either this man was a pro, or he'd watched a lot of spy movies. Whatever he was, Cole had no intention of going down without a fight.

The footsteps veered to one side. Smart. The man wasn't taking a direct approach. Rather, he was circling above him, cutting off Cole's access to the woods while also keeping enough distance to stay out of Cole's reach. Why did Cole always have to go up against the clever criminals? Just once, he'd like someone who would make things simple for him.

His original solution of striking the man with the shovel when he got close enough was replaced with a much riskier option. How would a shovel work as a projectile?

Cole gauged the man's position and walking speed. His grip tightened on the shovel, and he took another small step to the side.

He counted to three in his head, timing each number with the next step. Then he sprang into motion.

Cole burst out from behind the tree, hurled the shovel into the air at the gunman, and sprinted forward.

The man grunted as he jumped aside to avoid being hit. The gunman lifted his weapon to aim, but he wasn't fast enough. Cole launched himself at him. He hooked an arm around the man's waist and knocked him to the ground.

A shot fired. Birds took flight.

Cole grabbed the man's right arm and slammed it against the ground to knock the gun free of his grip. It didn't work.

The gunman bucked beneath him and used his left hand to push Cole off him. When that effort wasn't successful, he curled his fingers into a fist and jabbed Cole in the ribs.

Pain shot through him, but Cole sucked in a breath and held on. He slammed his opponent's hand into the ground again, this time with more force. The man's grip loosened, but the gun didn't fall free. Cole elbowed him in the ribs and tried again. This time the man's grip faltered, and the weapon bounced out of reach.

Cole scrambled after it, but a hand grabbed his ankle and kept him from moving forward.

His fingers came within an inch of the weapon before he was yanked back, his body dragging across the grass.

Cole kicked out with his free leg, and his foot connected with the gunman's torso. That didn't stop the man from pushing to his feet. He took a step toward the gun, but Cole scissored both legs around the other man's ankles and brought him to the ground.

A curse escaped the gunman, and his hand disappeared beneath his pant leg. A split second later, a knife swiped at Cole. The blade cut through Cole's shirt and grazed the skin on his abdomen. Cole ignored the sting of the fresh wound and scampered to his feet.

Balanced on the balls of his feet, he faced the man who now threatened him with a knife. The gun lay in the tall grass somewhere behind Cole's opponent. Once again, Cole was unarmed and had no weapon in reach.

He took his first good look at the man trying to kill him. Dark hair, tall, vicious. If this was Sauermann, he looked a good fifteen years younger than his fifty-two years.

Deciding it couldn't hurt to try a conversation, Cole asked in German, "Why are you trying to kill me?"

The only response was a thrust of the knife toward Cole. Cole jumped back.

"Do you even know who I am?" Cole asked, trying again.

Another lunge with the knife. Another evasive move.

Cole circled toward where he had last seen the gun, but Sauermann or whoever he was cut him off. He jabbed with the knife again.

Cole anticipated his move and grabbed his knife hand. Immobilizing his wrist, Cole jerked the man closer and twisted his arm.

A cry of pain rang out as the knife fell to the ground.

Cole scooped it up. His opponent scrambled back.

It took only a moment for Cole to recognize his intentions. He was going for the gun.

"Don't do it." Cole gripped the knife handle.

The other man straightened, the gun in his hand. He swung it in Cole's direction.

Cole reacted on instinct. He sent the knife flying.

The blade speared into his opponent's chest. The gun and the man fell to the ground.

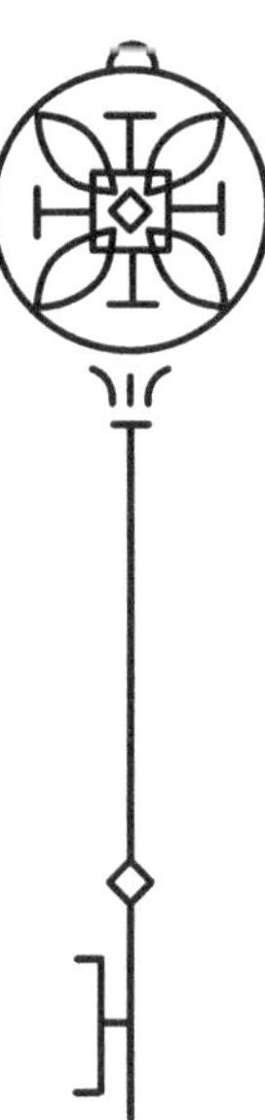

CHAPTER 40

Gunnar peered through the curtains, his jaw clenched. Who was the man standing over Volker? He highly doubted Lars Hendriks could fight like that. Even if he hadn't recently been hit by a car, the man at the edge of the yard wasn't some random person off the street. He was well trained in hand-to-hand combat. Otherwise, he never would have defeated this latest hired gun.

Gunnar had watched the battle unfold as one might watch a boxing match on television, but the stakes for this battle were so much higher. Again, Gunnar came out on the losing end.

Three times. Gunnar couldn't believe he had hired three separate hit men and they had succeeded in eliminating only one of the three Lang descendants.

He couldn't wait any longer. With Anna and the Hendriks girl planning to file a claim tomorrow, he had to act now.

Whether Volker was dead or wounded didn't matter. He wasn't of any use to Gunnar anymore. No, Gunnar would have to do the dirty work himself.

He glanced out the window once more. Then again, maybe Volker could be of use. He could take the blame for the murders Gunnar was about to commit.

Cole's breath shuddered out. He hated killing. Even though the knife had missed the heart, he doubted the man bleeding on the ground would survive without immediate medical attention. In this remote area of Austria, that wasn't likely.

He drew out his phone to call an ambulance, but could he risk it? He was traveling under his own name. He didn't have any protection from the local authorities, and despite his legal claim to Falcon Point, technically, he had been trespassing.

Despite the hurdles he'd face, Cole dialed 112.

When the operator came on, Cole said, "I need an ambulance at Falcon Point. A man attacked me and was stabbed with his own knife."

The questions started, and Cole gave the details of his location and the incident that led to his assailant's injury. He took a step toward the man to further assess his condition.

Cole pressed his fingers against the man's neck and felt a faint pulse beat beneath his touch. "He's still alive, but the paramedics had better hurry."

"We have an ambulance on your side of the lake. It should be there shortly."

Once he had satisfied the operator's need for information, he hung up and straightened.

Footsteps approached, and a woman shouted in English.

"Hey! What are you doing?"

Cole whirled as two women, one blonde, the other brunette, emerged from the woods, followed by a man with light-brown hair. The threesome appeared to be close to his age, ranging from mid to late twenties.

"Who are you?" the dark-haired woman demanded.

Cole debated how to answer, but he was saved from coming up with an explanation when the other woman saw the prone figure in the grass. She gasped and pointed. "Bram. Look."

Bram rushed to the injured man's side, apparently more concerned with issuing first aid than worrying about any danger that might exist. Admirable. Bram stripped off his jacket and pressed it around where the knife still protruded from the man's chest.

Cole let his eyes stray to his attacker. A whirl of motion sounded behind him, and he turned to face the women again. His gaze didn't make it past the tip of the shovel that was now only inches from his throat.

"Whoa!" Cole held both hands up and took a step back.

"Who are you?" the dark-haired woman demanded again.

"Cole Bridger."

Bram interrupted before Cole could offer any further explanation. "We need an ambulance."

"I already called one." Cole took another step back. "It's on its way."

"Did you do this?" the shovel-wielding woman asked.

"Yes, but only because he tried to kill me," Cole said.

"I find that hard to believe." The dark-haired woman advanced, keeping the shovel blade in a threatening position. Her blue eyes flashed with the same determination he often saw in his own reflection. The woman wasn't someone to be messed with, but Cole wasn't about to let her take him down either.

He tugged at his shirt where his attacker had slashed him, the blood stain clearly visible. "I didn't do this to myself."

The other woman pointed at where Cole had been digging. "Anna. Look."

Cole recognized the woman on the other end of the shovel now. He'd seen her on the design firm's website. Anna Cavendish, junior designer.

Anna's gaze scanned the yard until she saw the disturbance in the dirt and grass. Fury and a new wave of suspicion flashed in her expression. "What are you doing here?"

"I'm looking for someone."

"Digging up the grounds is hardly looking for someone," Anna said.

"I can explain," Cole said, even though he wasn't sure how he was going to convince these people he had a right to be here.

"Who are you looking for?" the other woman asked.

Cole took another step back to put more distance between him and the shovel. He glanced at the blonde, this time focusing on her more closely. Recognition dawned. Tess Hendriks. "You. I'm looking for you."

"Me?" Tess asked. "Why would you be looking for me? I don't know you."

"I came here to warn you. Gunnar Sauermann is trying to have you killed." Cole waved at the man lying in the grass. "He tried to kill me when he found me here on the grounds."

"Sauermann?" Tess repeated.

Anna lowered the shovel a fraction of an inch. "That's not Sauermann."

"Where is he, then?" Cole asked.

"He's been staying in Gildenstatt," Anna said.

Sirens rang out as the rumble of an engine approached.

"How did you know about Sauermann?" Tess asked. "And why are you really here?"

The shovel lifted again, and Cole reacted on instinct. His hand came up, gripped the shovel handle, and twisted it out of Anna's hands.

Anna and Tess stepped back, apprehension visible on both of their faces.

"I'm not here to hurt you. I'm here to protect you," Cole said. "I'm your cousin."

Tess's mind flashed back to those moments in the hospital when Jac Mesman had claimed to be a relative. She fought back the fear that surfaced and stood her ground. "Try again," she said. "Up until this week, I had no cousins. You're the third person who's claimed that relationship with me in as many days, and Anna's the only one who checks out."

Shock flared in his blue eyes as he swung to face Anna. "Are you sure Anna is your cousin?"

The sirens were getting louder. Bram turned from his position beside the injured man. His hands were still firmly pressed against the bloody wound. "Did you tell the paramedics to come back here?"

Staring at Anna, the man ignored him. "You're Anna Lang's granddaughter?"

"Hey." Bram raised his voice. "I need an answer. Will they know to come onto the grounds instead of the house? We're talking life and death, here."

"Yeah, we are," the man said, glaring at Bram. "Mine, Anna's, Tess's, and Lars's."

Tess stiffened. "How do you know about Lars?"

"I was with him yesterday. He's the one who told me where to find you." He tossed the shovel aside and faced Tess barehanded. "My name's Cole Bridger, and I'm Karl Lang's great-grandson. That guy"—he pointed to the man lying on the grass—"tried to take me out just like Mesman tried to take out you and Lars." He shifted slightly. "In case you haven't figured it out yet, someone has it in for all of Leopold Lang's direct descendants."

Keeping her eyes on Cole, Anna stepped forward and reached for the shovel again. "Tess, call Lars."

"You can try," Cole said as Tess pulled her mobile out of her bag. "But if you call the hospital, they're going to tell you he's dead."

Tess froze. She'd called Lars's room when she and Bram had arrived in Linz, but there'd been no reply. She'd assumed he was already asleep.

"Another hit man came to the hospital yesterday," Cole continued. "He's no longer a threat, but since he was the second hired gun to target Lars, the easiest way to keep him safe was to hide him behind a fake death certificate." He pointed at Tess's phone. She'd forgotten she was holding it. "Lars gave me your number, and I tried calling to warn you. When I couldn't get through, I took the first flight into Linz."

Tess glanced at her phone screen. Sure enough, she'd missed a few calls. Two were from an unknown international number, and three were from an unknown number in Amsterdam. Had Lars tried calling from the hospital?

Someone shouted, and suddenly, two men in red-and-white uniforms appeared around the side of the house. One carried a large black bag, the other a stretcher.

"Over here!" Bram raised his hand to signal the paramedics.

Cole moved closer to Tess. Anna moved too. Stepping between them, Anna raised the shovel slightly.

"I'm not here to hurt anyone," Cole said, his voice low but insistent. "We are cousins. After Karl Lang escaped Austria, he joined the British Navy. His only son, Glenn Lang Eckerstorfer, is my grandfather. We've been searching for Falcon Point for decades but didn't know exactly where to find it until the resort was posted online last week." He glanced at the paramedics. They had reached the injured man and were conferring with Bram in rapid German. "That's the truth. And now would be a really good time to believe it."

Vaguely aware that Bram was helping the paramedics prepare the injured man for transportation, Tess studied the man before her. He'd been speaking English, but his accent pegged him as an American. Would Sauermann have gone that far afield to find a hit man? And then there was his wound and his uncannily familiar eyes.

"Are you wearing contact lenses?" She sensed rather than saw Anna tense.

"Nope. And I'm guessing you aren't either." Cole raised one eyebrow. "I wonder which one of our Lang great-grandparents the blue color came from."

Anna slowly lowered the shovel. "We'll probably never know. The photos are all black and white."

Cole's gaze sharpened. "You've seen photos?"

"Yes. I've found some here, and I also have one of my grandmother and her family when she was a small child," Anna said. "It's the only thing of hers that survived the war."

"Did she have anything else from when she lived here?" Cole asked. "A letter or a book?"

"No, well, nothing except what was written on the back of the photo."

"What was written on the back?" Cole asked.

"It's a German poem. Some of the words are underlined, but I don't know why." Anna opened her purse and pulled out a worn photograph. "Here. You can see for yourself. This is the copy I made."

Cole took it and studied the photo Tess had seen for the first time only a couple hours ago. Her gaze strayed to where Bram was helping the paramedics lift their patient onto the stretcher. He looked up, and she saw the conflict in his eyes.

"It's okay, Bram," she said. "I'll be fine if they need your help getting him to the ambulance."

"I won't be long," he promised. "They're saying the police have been held up by an accident on the other side of the village."

That seemed like something Cole would want to know, but the American was still staring at Anna's photo.

"I need some paper and a pencil."

"Why?" Anna asked.

"Because this could be the key to a treasure I've spent my whole life dreaming about."

CHAPTER 41

Cole followed Anna into the manor and soaked in the history. After all these years, he was finally here, walking through the house where his ancestors had once lived. He was here with cousins he hadn't known he had.

Finding Lars and Tess had been an unexpected development, but learning that Anna Lang had survived the war made him question what other family stories had been incorrect.

He passed through a wide hallway and glanced through the doorways of the various rooms. Parlors, an enormous dining room with dripping chandeliers, a library. They crossed a black-and-white marble entryway until Anna stopped and motioned toward an open doorway. "You can wait here while I go grab some paper."

Cole followed Tess into an enormous room. A fireplace in white marble, turquoise walls, antique furniture scattered throughout—everything about the space exuded class and elegance. Cole suspected his great-grandfather hadn't spent much time in this room playing cops and robbers or whatever little boys played back in the 1930s.

"This is incredible." Tess ran a finger along the glossy wooden surface of an occasional table on her way to examine a painting on the wall. "Too bad. This is a reproduction."

"How can you tell?"

"I have a degree in art history, but even if I didn't, after working in an art museum for over five years, I've gotten pretty good at spotting what's real and what isn't."

"That's a handy skill to have," Cole said. Even though he had dealt with stolen artwork and artifacts in the past, he always had to enlist an expert to validate what was genuine and what wasn't.

Tess continued around the room, studying each piece of artwork as well as the furniture. "I thought the estate would have more originals. Except for the furniture, everything here is a print or a reproduction."

"Maybe the valuable artwork has been secured somewhere else while they're under construction," Cole said.

"Possibly, but I would think the furniture would be protected too."

Anna walked in holding a notepad and a pencil. "Here you go."

"Thanks." Excitement leapt within him. He took the paper and pencil from her, then sat at a cherry writing desk, laid the paper on it, and pulled out his phone. "Let me see that photo again."

Anna retrieved it from her purse. Cole took it from her and flipped it over. His heartbeat quickened. "This could be it."

"Could be what?" Tess asked.

"The key." Cole held up his phone to show Anna and Tess the image of a scanned book page. "These letters here are a code, but my family never knew what the cypher was to break it."

"You think the words on the back of my grandmother's photo connect to those letters?" Anna's voice rang with excitement.

"I do," Cole said. "I think this is the key to finding the treasure Leopold and Karl Lang hid before Leopold was murdered."

"I never heard about any treasure," Anna said.

"Before Karl escaped from here with his sisters, he helped his father hide their valuables in the cellar of the gamekeeper's house."

"That's what you were looking for in the woods," Tess said.

"Yeah. Unless it was found by the construction teams, it has to still be out there somewhere."

"We haven't found anything," Anna said.

Tess motioned to the paper. "Can you figure it out?"

"Yeah, but it may take a while."

"What kind of timeframe are we talking?" Anna asked.

"North of ten minutes, south of an hour."

"In that case, I'm going to sit down." Tess lowered herself onto a padded chair beside the desk and propped her foot on the one next to her.

"Is there anything we can do to help?" Anna asked.

"Yeah." Cole handed her his phone. "Read those letters off to me."

Anna read through the letters on the first page. "Now what?"

"Go to the next image."

"How many pages are there?" Tess asked.

"Forty-two. Like I said, this is going to take a while."

Beckett sped up the road and entered Falcon Point's main gate. After the lengthy jog back to his car, he'd taken the construction road, which had tacked on another ten minutes, rather than drive his BMW over the uneven track that looped past the goatherd huts.

When he came over the rise, an ambulance was parked in the drive not far from the portico steps. His heart skipped a beat, and his foot pressed down on the accelerator, shooting the vehicle forward in record time.

He slammed on the brakes, and the car skidded to a halt. He opened the door before the vehicle had stopped rocking on its springs and sprinted for the ambulance, rounding its open rear doors. Paramedics, assisted by Bram, loaded a stretcher into the back.

"Anna?" Beckett asked. "Is she all right?"

Bram nodded. "She's fine."

Beckett cleared his throat several times. For an instant, he thought Anna's unknown assailant had attacked her.

"Any idea who that is?" Beckett had never seen the man on the stretcher before.

"I don't know," Bram said as the paramedics hooked the patient to a drip line.

Beckett paced to the opposite side of the ambulance, then pivoted. "Tess?"

"The women are fine. They went inside with their cousin."

"Cousin?" The comment was so unexpected, Beckett stopped his pacing.

"It's a long story."

Beckett raked a hand through his hair while his erratic heartbeat slowed.

"Are you all right?" Bram asked, looking at him with concern.

"Aye. When I came over that rise and saw the ambulance in the drive, it gave me a few bad minutes. What's this about a cousin?"

"Another relation has come to call. This one's an American."

"We've got a regular United Nations under one roof," Beckett commented as both men went up the portico steps and entered the manor. "My guess is that they're in the turquoise salon."

Beckett led the way down the hall, their footsteps making little sound on the carpeted runner. As they drew near the salon doorway, subdued voices reached them. His eyes landed on Anna, and the last of his worries dissipated.

Anna appeared unharmed by the recent events, but the same couldn't be said for the other two occupants of the room. Tess had her leg propped on a pillow, and a blond man Beckett had never seen before sat between the two women, his shirt ripped and tinged with blood.

All three of them glanced up at him and Bram. Two things struck Beckett simultaneously: an air of repressed excitement hung over the room, and all three cousins had the same unique shade of blue eyes.

Beckett crossed to Anna and squeezed her shoulder before he addressed the newcomer. "I take it you're another long-lost relative?"

"Are all you Brits as welcoming as Anna?" the man asked.

His sarcasm was not lost on Beckett, and he looked questioningly at Anna.

"I didn't know if he was friend or foe, so I improvised—just to make sure." Anna shrugged.

"What did you do?" Having seen Anna in action a time or two, Beckett could only imagine.

"She's very handy with a shovel," Tess informed him with a tinge of humor.

"Be grateful," Beckett said blandly to the man. "Last time someone surprised her, it was a Samurai sword. I believe Lady Tilington is still grateful she wasn't decapitated."

The blond man's eyes gleamed with interest.

"That's a story for another time," Anna said. "You've interrupted us, Beckett. This is our cousin Cole, by the way." She indicated the blond man with a flourish.

"I can see the family resemblance."

"Can we get back to breaking this code?" Cole asked.

"What code?" Beckett asked in utter confusion.

"We're looking for the Lang family treasure," Anna said matter-of-factly.

Cole jotted down the last five letters and set down the pencil. For over a half hour, he had decoded the notes written in his great-grandfather's New Testament, and finally, he had reached the end.

Beckett had taken up residence in the spot behind Anna, while Tess remained seated by Cole with Bram beside her.

Cole rubbed the ache out of his hand.

"Did you figure it out?" Tess asked.

"Yeah. Most of this spells out directions," Cole said. He read through what he had written. "I have five characters at the end that don't make any sense to me. I don't know what they are."

Anna and Beckett both leaned closer.

"This writing on the back of Granny's photo really was part of a code?" Anna asked.

"Yes." Cole stood and rolled his shoulders to fight the stiffness that had settled there. "Leopold must have separated the two pieces of the puzzle before his children escaped from Austria."

"I'm surprised Leopold gave the key to my grandmother," Anna said. "It would have been more logical to entrust it to Ingrid since she was older."

"My grandmother was given a different kind of key," Tess said.

"What do you mean?" Cole asked.

Tess opened her purse, retrieved a small jewelry box, and opened it.

Anna edged closer. "Those earrings are stunning."

"Yes, they are." Tess tugged at the inner lining of the jewelry box and produced an antique key. "I found this sewn onto the backing just this week."

"Can I see it?" Cole asked.

Tess handed it to him.

Cole turned the key over as he examined it. "This looks like the key to an old vault door."

"A vault?" Tess asked. "Why would my grandmother have a key to a vault hidden in a jewelry box?"

"I don't know." Cole handed it back. "But you should bring it with you."

"Bring it with me where?" Tess asked.

"Treasure hunting." Cole stood. "What do you say? Shall we go find out where this leads?"

"I'm game," Anna said.

An unfamiliar male voice sounded from the doorway. "So am I."

Cole whirled, his gaze landing on the middle-aged man across the room, a pistol in his hand. The hand trembled.

Cole's hand instinctively went to his waistband where he usually kept his gun holstered, a gun he didn't currently have with him after flying on a plane. His request to Gwendolyn to provide him a weapon didn't seem so silly now, but even he hadn't anticipated running into a potential assassin here at Falcon Point, especially one who wanted to kill him.

He did a quick analysis of the latest gunman. Not a pro. White knuckles from gripping the gun too tightly, a slight tremor in his arm.

"Herr Sauermann," Beckett stepped in front of Anna. "What are you doing?"

Cole didn't know why everyone always asked that question when facing a gun, but he couldn't fault the Scotsman for asking. A little distraction might give him the opening he would need to disarm Sauermann before anyone got hurt. If he could get a little closer . . .

Sauermann waved the gun at Tess. "I'll take that key."

Tess swallowed hard.

"Here." Cole took the key from her. "I'll give it to him."

"No. Let her bring it to me." Sauermann waved the gun toward Tess before he aimed at Cole.

So much for getting close enough to disarm him. Cole noted the terror in Tess's eyes. He pressed the key into her palm. "It's okay, Tess."

Her gaze whipped up to meet his.

"It's okay," Cole repeated. "He doesn't want to shoot you, especially with the police on their way."

"You're bluffing," Sauermann said.

"I'm not. You may have seen the ambulance out front. The police aren't far behind."

"I heard the paramedics talking. The police are still dealing with an accident and a closed road," Sauermann said, but Cole didn't miss the unease that flashed in his expression.

Tess took a step forward, then another.

"Bring those directions with you too," Sauermann said.

Cole picked up the scratch paper he had used to break the code and handed it to Tess. Tess took it but didn't look down to see what he had given her. Her focus was on the gun aimed in their direction. She started forward again, and Cole stepped in front of the desk to hide the decoded message from view.

The paperweight caught his attention, and he took another half step to his left. His fingers curled around the brass falcon. His fist tightened.

"Set them down there." Sauermann nodded at a round occasional table.

Tess did as she was instructed. As soon as her hands were free, she quickly retreated to where Bram stood.

Cole kept his gaze on Sauermann. No way was Cole going to let this man follow in his grandfather's footsteps. Someone might very well die today, but it wasn't going to be a Lang.

CHAPTER 42

Gunnar tried not to think about the fact that he was outnumbered five to one. He had the gun. That meant he was in control.

He should pull the trigger and take care of Tess and Anna right now, but he didn't want to explain how they'd come to be murdered inside his home. No, he would have to take them somewhere else to dispose of the meddlesome Lang descendants and their friends.

His arm trembled, his muscles tiring from the weight of the gun. He took two steps forward and retrieved the key and the paper Tess had set on the table.

For years before his grandfather had died, he had insisted the Langs had hidden their most valuable artwork and jewelry before Leopold Lang's death, but no amount of searching had revealed evidence of any secret storage rooms or hallways where they could have been secured. Based on what he'd just overheard, the reason his grandfather had never found anything was because he was looking in the wrong building.

Gunnar slipped the key into his pocket and lifted the paper. A quick glance, and his anger flared. "Where is it? The real one."

His eyes lifted as a blur of movement flashed in front of him. Something hurled toward him, but Gunnar only had time to flinch before it connected with his gun hand.

Pain shot through him, and he cried out. The gun fell free and thudded onto the carpet. Panic overshadowed pain, and he leaned down to retrieve his weapon. His fingers brushed against the handle, but before he could grab it, the blond man tackled him to the floor and knocked him back several feet.

Gunnar bucked beneath him and stretched his arm in the direction of where his pistol had landed.

"Beckett, don't let him get the gun," the man said.

Beckett must have been right behind the other attacker because before Gunnar could grab his weapon, a foot kicked it beneath a nearby sofa.

Panic snaked through him. What would everyone think if they knew what he had tried to do? He couldn't let the truth come out. The Sauermann family was above reproach. They were pillars of the community. He couldn't let the Langs ruin that.

The man who had tackled him to the ground eased off him and jerked Gunnar to a stand. In less than two seconds, one of Gunnar's arms was twisted behind his back, his other pinned to his side.

"Anna, call the police. Tell them to hurry."

"That didn't do us any good last time," Beckett said. "The police were supposed to arrest Sauermann."

"Then call the police in Linz," the man said.

Anna lifted her phone. "I'll look up the number."

Petra's voice sounded behind him. "That won't be necessary."

Gunnar was still trying to wrap his mind around why Petra would be here and how he would explain why he'd had a gun when she spoke again. "Let him go."

The grip on his arms eased, and Gunnar pushed his way free. He turned, and his jaw dropped when he saw Petra aiming a pistol at his attacker.

"Petra, what are you doing here?" Gunnar asked.

"The same thing you are. I'm ensuring our interests are protected."

When Gunnar only stared at her, dumbfounded, her delicate laugh rang out. "You didn't really think I would let the Lang descendants take everything from us, did you?"

"You knew—?" Gunnar couldn't bring himself to finish the sentence. How much did his wife know? Did she know about the hitmen? Or did she only know the Lang descendants could cost them everything?

"I tried to let you handle this problem on your own, but when I found out Tess Hendriks was in town looking for her cousin, I had to make sure she wasn't going to cause any problems," she said. "I was right to be worried." She motioned to the sofa. "Get your gun."

Gunnar leaned down, lifted the skirt of the sofa, and retrieved his pistol. "How did you know Tess was here?"

"Felix likes to talk. You're lucky I had him give me a ride home from the market today." Petra waved at the others in the room. "Now, tie the men up. We'll let Anna and her cousin come with us."

"Come with you where?" Tess asked.

"To dig up our treasure, of course."

Tess's stomach clenched. This could not be happening. Willing herself to remain calm, she watched as Petra Sauermann kicked a bag toward her husband.

"Take care of them," she said, "and take their cell phones."

Gunnar withdrew a long coil of rope and a knife from the bag. "Where did you get these?"

"The maintenance shed. I'm not about to let you shoot someone here in the manor. Murder at Falcon Point wouldn't be good for resort business," Petra said. "An unfortunate swim in the lake would be much more convenient."

With Gunnar's weapon still pointed at Cole, he motioned to the closest chair. "Hand over your cell phone," he barked, "and sit with your arms behind your back."

Cole dropped his phone onto the floor and slowly lowered himself onto the nearest Louis XVI chair. He kept his eyes on Gunnar, watching silently as the man set down his weapon near the door and approached him with the rope. Tess glanced at Bram and Beckett. The two men were standing a few feet apart, not moving an inch. Would they act now that Gunnar was unarmed?

Behind her, Anna gasped and Beckett flinched. Tess swung around to see that Petra now had one hand wrapped around Anna's upper arm, her gun to Anna's head.

"You may no longer have a weapon pointed at you, gentlemen," Petra said, her voice all the more chilling because of its calm, "but be assured, even after they leave this room, these two women will."

No one spoke. Gunnar cinched the rope around Cole's wrists and then began tying his ankles to the front legs of the chair. The chair shifted, scraping against the floor as Gunnar tightened the knots. The Austrian gave Cole an ugly look before turning to Beckett.

"Your turn," he said, pointing to another chair a few feet away.

Beckett sat, and Gunnar moved closer to begin the procedure again.

Within minutes, all three men were trussed to the furniture, their cell phones confiscated. Gunnar slipped the knife into his belt and reclaimed his gun. "What do you want me to do with their phones?"

"Toss them onto the rug and grab a hammer," Petra demanded.

Gunnar dropped them and disappeared into the hall. Petra claimed Tess's and Anna's mobiles and added them to the pile in the center of the room. Gunnar reappeared, a hammer in hand.

Petra pointed to the phones. "Make sure none of them will be of any use to our friends."

Gunnar gripped the hammer and slammed it onto the first phone. Pieces scattered. He repeated the process again and then again.

When the destruction was complete, he crossed to the desk and grabbed the piece of paper covered in Cole's handwriting. He studied the page briefly before offering Cole a gloating smile. "You have my thanks. Perhaps your unwelcome arrival was not such a bad thing after all."

Cole managed a slight shrug even though his wrists were tied. "Too bad you interrupted me before I was finished."

"Oh, you were finished. I heard you."

"Then you need your hearing checked."

Gunnar's hesitancy was so fleeting Tess wondered if she'd imagined it.

"Hurry up, Gunnar. You have what we need." Petra's tone brooked no argument. "Keep an eye on that one." She waved her gun at Tess. "Anna is coming with me."

Gunnar grabbed Tess's arm, and using the gun in his other hand, he pointed at the doorway.

"Follow them," he said as Petra and Anna disappeared into the hall.

Tess stiffened. She could not bring herself to look at Bram, but she glanced at Cole once more. He gave her an almost imperceptible nod, and an unexpected surge of resolve filled her. She, Cole, and Anna were Langs. And that meant something. She would do as the Sauermanns asked. For now. But they were deluded if they thought she and her cousins had come all this way to simply fall in with their plans without a fight.

Tess stood beside Anna outside the kitchen door. Petra's gun remained trained on them, but Gunnar had put his weapon in his pocket. In one hand, he held the shovel Anna had left leaning against the wall beside the door; in the other hand, he held Cole's decoded instructions.

"Read it out loud," Petra said.

"From the kitchen door, go northwest 350 paces across the garden and into the trees. Turn north at the grove of larch trees, and follow the trail along three switchbacks uphill through the pines. Turn west at the rock outcropping. Walk sixty-five paces. The divided pine marks the way." Gunnar looked up at the sky. The early evening sun was hidden behind the clouds. "Which way is northwest?"

"Toward the mountains, of course," Petra said, impatience with her husband the first hint of emotion she'd displayed since showing up.

Gunnar frowned. "I will count out the paces. You keep your eye on them."

Tess saw Petra's jaw tighten. It appeared that Frau Sauermann preferred giving orders rather than taking them. The Austrian woman had yet to lower her weapon, but her husband had already put away his gun and the knife he'd used in the turquoise room. He was considerably taller and heavier set than his wife, but Tess was beginning to wonder if she and Anna might have a better chance at turning the tables on their captors if she focused her attention on outwitting him.

Gunnar started across the grass, counting out loud with each step he took.

"Move!" Petra urged Anna and Tess forward with a wave of her gun and took her position behind them.

They marched in a straight line toward the trees. To their right, Tess recognized the spot where they'd first approached Cole. The grass was trampled there—evidence of the paramedics' recent presence on the property. They were too far away to see the cuts Cole had made in the turf, but Tess had already caught Anna eyeing the shovel in Gunnar's hand and wondered if her cousin was plotting to wield the tool as a weapon again.

Gunnar's voice droned on, and Tess began muttering random numbers, much as she'd done as a child when she'd purposely tried to confuse Lars while he was counting the number of euros in his piggybank. Anna met her eyes, a small smile playing on her lips.

"Twenty-nine, fifty-seven, one hundred and eighteen, three, forty-five," Anna chanted in English.

"Thirty-two, fifty-one, two hundred and thirteen," Tess continued, speaking more loudly now, and in German.

"Silence!" Gunnar roared.

Petra's gun dug into Tess's back. "Not another word," she hissed.

Tess closed her mouth and kept her eyes forward as Gunnar stormed past them, returning to the back door. Moments later, his tally began again, starting at one. It had been a childish exercise, perhaps, but Tess did not regret it for a moment. If nothing more, she and Anna had bought the men a little more time to escape. Because, of one thing she was sure, Cole, Beckett, and Bram were not simply sitting in the drawing room waiting to be rescued.

CHAPTER 43

Cole flexed his wrists and stretched his fingers. It was no use. The ropes were too tight for him to work his hands free. Why couldn't the Sauermanns have used zip ties? He could have broken out of those in ten seconds flat, but no. They'd opted to tie him, Bram, and Beckett to antique chairs.

Cole suspected Gunnar had taken extra care when tying him up. He wasn't sure what had upset the older man more, being bested by Cole or being saved by his wife.

"We've got to get out of here," Bram insisted for the tenth time in the past three minutes.

"The Sauermanns will kill all of us as soon as they have what they want," Beckett added.

"With any luck, they'll give Anna a shovel," Cole muttered. He didn't know his cousins well, but he doubted either of them would give up without a fight.

Beckett tried to throw his weight and use his momentum to move his chair.

"Where are you going?" Cole asked.

"There might be some scissors in the desk."

"You wouldn't be able to open the drawer even if there were," Cole said.

Frustration filled Beckett's voice. "I've got to do something."

Bram followed Beckett's lead and tried to throw his weight to move his chair closer to the desk.

"Would you two stop that," Cole said. "You're distracting me."

"Distracting you from what?" Bram asked. "You're just sitting there."

"I'm thinking."

"Then think of a way to get us out of here," Beckett demanded.

Cole saw it now, the deep-seated love the man beside him had for Anna and his desperation to protect her.

Fully aware that he would need Bram's and Beckett's help once they broke free, he took the first step toward calming the man beside him. "How long have you been in love with my cousin?"

"I'm not going to sit here and gab. We need to figure a way out of here," Beckett said, his eyes darting around the room.

"Give me a minute of quiet, and I'll help you get your girlfriends back."

"How—?" Beckett started.

"Give him his minute," Bram said. "I've seen his handiwork. I think he has experience in this kind of stuff."

"Shhh." Cole closed his eyes. Bram and Beckett were right. All five of them were going to die if they didn't break free, and as much as he hoped Anna and Tess could overpower the Sauermanns, he couldn't count on it, not when both of the Sauermanns were armed.

Cole visualized himself free of his bonds, and backtracked in his mind to determine how to reach that state. When he opened his eyes again, he looked at the antique chair he was tied to before he glanced up. "I hope the girls will forgive me," he said.

"For what?" Bram asked.

"For this." Cole jerked his body to his right and sent himself crashing to the floor. As he had hoped, the chair broke, but he managed to get only one leg free. The back of the chair remained intact.

"What *are* you doing?" Beckett asked.

"I'm trying to get my hands free." From his position on the floor, Cole said, "Beckett, you try. Throw all your weight to one side, so the chair will break when you fall."

"If this works, we're hiding the broken chairs," Beckett said.

Cole flexed against the ropes. "After we stop the Sauermanns."

"Right." Beckett rocked his body back and forth twice and then grunted as he threw his weight to the side. He crashed to the floor. The back of the chair splintered, as did one of the legs.

"Bram, your turn."

Bram only rocked once before he tipped himself over. Unlike Cole and Beckett's chairs, Bram's shattered. Two chair legs cracked, and the back separated from the seat.

"Now what?" Bram asked.

"Try to free your legs from the chair." Cole demonstrated to Bram and Beckett how to use the floor to push the wooden remnant from the chair out of the ropes. Once they had all freed one leg, Cole said, "Now try to use your foot to break the other chair leg to free yourself."

Bram was the first to succeed. "Got it. What's next?"

"Come over here behind me. Put your hands next to mine, and I'll see if I can untie you," Cole said. "Beckett, if you can stand up, try to open the desk and check for scissors."

As soon as Bram was in position, Cole scooted closer to him until they were back to back with Bram's ropes against his fingers. Cole fingered the knot, visualizing it so he wouldn't accidentally make it tighter rather than loosening it.

He worked his fingers in between two strands and loosened them slightly.

Meanwhile, Beckett stood and hopped to the desk. He turned around and used his hands to open the drawer. When he turned around again, he peered into the drawer. "No scissors."

"Keep working on getting your legs free." Cole forced confidence into his words despite the anxiety rising within him. "It'll take some time, but we'll get out of this."

"Aye," Beckett said, "but will we get free before it's too late?"

Tess's knee was throbbing. The bleeding had stopped long ago, but based on how hard it was to bend, she was fairly sure it was nicely swollen. It seemed like they'd been tromping through the trees for hours rather than minutes. Gunnar was constantly second-guessing himself. The terrain was steep, and they had doubled back more times than she could count. Petra was beginning to lose it.

"How hard is it to count to sixty-five?" she snapped.

Gunnar scowled at her. "It's not the counting that's the issue. It's staying in a straight line. Who knows how many trees have grown along the path since Leopold Lang wrote this."

Petra rolled her eyes. "We found the rock outcropping, didn't we? It shouldn't be that hard."

"Be my guest." Gunnar pointed at the exposed rock. "Sixty-five paces to the west takes you directly into that tree."

Tess glanced at Anna. The longer the Sauermanns argued, the better their chances of escape. At some point, Petra would lower her guard—or at least her weapon—long enough for one of them to act.

"Be ready," Anna whispered, obviously on the same wavelength.

Tess shifted her weight off her injured leg. She needed to be prepared to move in an instant.

"What if that's the tree we're looking for?" Petra asked.

Gunnar raised his head to study the pine. "Then what's next?"

"Cole told you he hadn't finished decoding," Tess said.

Petra jabbed her with the gun again. "I told you, no talking."

Anna glanced at Tess, her eyebrows raised. Tess shook her head slightly. Translating was not an option right now.

"Check the other side of the tree," Petra said.

Gunnar pushed through the tangle of foliage growing at the base of the pine. Ferns and wild grasses fought for space around the thorny blackberry bushes. He snagged his trousers but brushed the branch away impatiently. "There's nothing over here," he said, driving the shovel into the ground. "Just an empty space covered in weeds and pine needles."

Gunnar moved a few feet farther. He raised the shovel and thrust it into the ground again, moved another few paces, and tried again. And that was when they heard it. The solid thud of metal hitting something hollow.

"Petra!" The noise changed. Now it sounded as though Gunnar was scraping at something.

"Go!" Petra yelled, shoving Tess toward the blackberry bush.

Anna stumbled after her, her eyes reflecting the same dread that Tess was experiencing. What had Gunnar found?

CHAPTER 44

The ropes loosened around Cole's wrists. Finally. It had taken him far longer to untie Bram than he'd expected, and the tension in all three men was palpable.

Cole worked one hand free before Bram even finished untying him. "Help Beckett. Hurry."

Bram paused long enough to free his feet from the ropes still tangled around his ankles.

Cole freed his own legs, and his eyes swept the room. "I need a weapon. Are there any guns in the house?"

"No." Beckett turned his head to look at Bram. "Hurry up, man."

"A knife, then." Cole stepped toward the door. "Where's the kitchen?"

"The kitchen is torn apart. We're remodeling it."

"Great," Cole muttered. Two unpredictable gunmen, two hostages, and his only help was two civilians. And he was unarmed.

His gaze landed on a bookshelf along the wall. He darted across the room and grabbed a marble bookend. It wasn't much of a defense, but it was better than nothing.

If he could get Bram and Beckett to create a distraction . . .

Footsteps pounded toward the door, and Cole whirled around. Beckett was already rushing out of the room, a fire poker in hand. Bram was right behind him, carrying a fireplace broom. So much for a coordinated attack.

"Hurry up!" Beckett shouted.

Cole sprinted after them.

Bram stepped outside. "Which way?"

Cole took the lead. "Follow me."

Anger boiled inside Anna, bubbling ever higher. Petra Sauermann stood not five feet behind her with a gun trained on her back while she and Tess knelt beneath the lower boughs of a massive pine tree, their bare hands digging through eighty years of accumulated debris, searching for the Lang family treasure.

She and Tess were going to die—unless they could figure out a way to disarm the Sauermanns. Yet again, another generation of Sauermanns planned to rob and murder members of her family.

Not if she could help it.

Anna shifted to keep a better eye on Petra Sauermann, the real threat of the married pair. Her fingers closed over a branch when she shoved aside another armful of loamy earth. The jagged end felt promising, as did its semipliant length. At least the stick wouldn't snap if she used it. She met Tess's eyes and lifted one end of her find, just enough for Tess to see without rousing Petra's attention.

"Hurry it up," Petra said, reverting to English to get her point across. "We don't have all day."

Anna pushed the stick beside the tree trunk and kept digging. Tess met her eyes and nodded. She understood their need to accumulate anything at hand to fight back.

A few seconds later, Tess passed her a rock, and Anna placed it beside the branch.

She didn't find anything else that could be turned into a weapon until her hand uncovered a semi-rotted piece of planed wood. She started. Had she found the entrance? Her sudden movement must have conveyed itself to Petra because the woman leaned over, pushing a pine bough out of her face.

"What is that?" Petra demanded.

"A piece of wood." Anna shrugged. The thing was three-quarters rotted.

"Let me see."

Anna held up the planed piece, which partially crumbled in her hands.

"Gunnar, this is it." Petra's voice rang with excitement.

Herr Sauermann came forward to inspect the rotted wood in Anna's hand. "I'm surprised it held together this long."

"Clear the rest of that away." Petra kicked Tess in the lower back, directly over her kidneys.

Tess gasped and hunched in on herself.

"Are you all right?" Anna mouthed to her.

Tess nodded, tears filling her eyes.

Anna gritted her teeth. Petra Sauermann was going to pay for that.

Cole spotted a large rock outcropping ten yards beyond where he'd expected it to be. More than halfway there. He slowed his pace, pleased when his companions followed his example.

"Where to now?" Bram asked.

"Sixty-five paces that way."

"What happens when we get there?" Beckett held up the fire poker. "This isn't going to hold up against a gun."

"When we get close, we'll split up." Cole reached the boulder and began counting his steps once more. "I need you two to create a distraction without getting yourselves shot."

"We can do that, but how are *you* going to keep from getting shot?" Beckett asked.

"I'm still working on that." Cole picked up his pace again. He weaved through pine trees and adjusted the directions to accommodate for the changes in landscape over the past eighty years. The low murmur of voices carried to them, and Cole slowed once more. He signaled to Beckett and Bram to stop. Cole edged forward a few more steps and stopped when the Sauermanns came into sight. They both stood beside an enormous pine, a low branch partially obscuring them from view, but Anna and Tess weren't anywhere in to be seen. Where were they? Was Cole too late?

Moving slowly, he took another step to the side. A flash of color appeared at the base of the tree.

"Hurry up," Petra demanded.

Cole moved again until he could see the spot of ground Petra was focused on. Relief swept through him. Anna knelt on the ground, her hands pushing dirt aside. Tess sat beside her, also clearing away dirt. His cousins were alive. They could still save them.

Anna's hands moved aside another batch of earth and encountered a hinge. Pushing dirt as she went, she ran her fingers along the surface of what appeared to be some kind of trapdoor. She judged it to be about four by six feet.

"I found something." Perhaps the Sauermanns would be so interested in her discovery that they would give her and Tess the opening they needed to escape.

"Let me see." Herr Sauermann knelt beside Anna and brushed her aside.

A rustling sounded in the trees, and a branch snapped just up the slope from where she and Tess knelt.

Sauermann stilled. "Shhh."

Another snap, this time even closer.

"Gunnar, go see if someone's there." Petra motioned with her weapon.

Sauermann rose to his feet and headed into the trees, his gun arm extended.

Anna's fingers tightened on the branch. She steeled herself to disarm Petra.

Petra cocked her gun and pointed it at the back of Tess's head. "Open that up. I want to see what's inside. Now."

Exhaling sharply, Anna released the pine branch, and together, she and Tess shoved back the rotting hinged door. Beneath it lay a large metal plate. She and Tess heaved it aside with some difficulty only to encounter another sheet of metal, this one so corroded it buckled in the middle and fell into the hole beneath, clanging and banging as it tumbled down the wooden steps to the earthen floor.

Cole signaled his companions to freeze. His cousins had found the treasure, and it might very well cost them their lives. His stomach clenched, and his mind raced.

The instinct to negotiate surfaced but was quickly pushed aside. He would give up the treasure to save his cousins' lives, but the Sauermanns wouldn't be content with that. They would make sure their secrets were buried, even if that meant killing all of them.

Gunnar approached the spot where a twig had snapped beneath someone's foot a moment ago. Cole's hand fisted around the marble bookend. He could take Gunnar out in one shot, but he couldn't risk it, not with Petra aiming a gun at Tess and Anna.

Silently, Cole squatted and ran his fingers over the ground until they brushed against a pinecone. He picked it up and straightened.

Gunnar stopped ten yards from where he, Bram, and Beckett remained shielded by a cluster of three pine trees. As soon as Gunnar's head turned away from them, Cole sent the pinecone flying into the woods. Like a dog searching for a bone, Gunnar followed the sound.

Cole lowered his voice. "Time to split up. No matter what happens, you have to do exactly what I tell you."

Bram nodded. "We're listening."

Anna peered into the dark, dank hole. All she could make out was the top of a wooden staircase.

"What's inside? Can you see?" Tess whispered, her voice barely audible.

Petra motioned toward the opening with her gun. "Get down there. Both of you."

"Tess is injured. She can't climb those stairs," Anna protested to buy more time. If she and Tess descended into that abyss, she had no confidence that either of them would come out alive.

"Fine. If she runs off, I'll shoot you." Petra moved closer until she was directly behind Anna.

Anna grasped the wooden railing and placed her foot on the top step. When she reached the third step, the wood beneath her foot broke loose from the side supports and fell with a clang on top of the corroded metal covering below. Anna clutched the wobbly rail to keep her balance.

"What was that?" Petra asked.

"Some debris fell." Anna lied without the least remorse.

Not informing Petra about the missing third step, she gingerly descended the rickety stairs until she landed at the bottom.

When Anna reached the cellar floor, Petra told Tess, "You stay where I can see you. I mean it. If you leave, she dies."

"I won't leave," Tess said.

While Petra clung to the railing with one hand and placed her foot on the first tread, Anna snatched the broken step off the floor. A rusty nail stuck out an inch from one end. She grasped the step tread with both hands. And waited.

Petra's foot hit air where the third step had been. She screeched and lost her balance, clinging with one arm to the railing to keep herself upright.

Anna set down her stair tread and grabbed hold of the railing, shaking it for all she was worth in an effort to unbalance Petra. With one hand on the rail, Petra held her gun in the other. Tess appeared at the top of the stairs with a tree branch and hit the older woman between her shoulder blades at the same time the railing pulled free. Petra lost her balance and tumbled down the stairs, her gun flying across the floor.

Petra landed at Anna's feet in a pool of sunlight from the opening above. Not one to lose an opportunity, Anna snatched up the stair tread and swung it, the nail drawing blood from Petra's shoulder.

Petra shrieked and covered her head. "Gunnar!"

The impotent rage Anna had harbored topside broke loose and flowed. She swung at Petra again while her eyes darted around the floor. Where was the gun? She couldn't spot it.

Petra kicked out at her from the earthen floor. Anna dodged the woman's shoe and gained the stairs. A metallic double click sounded above. Anna paused and glanced up.

Herr Sauermann stood at the top of the stairs, the tips of his shoes hanging over the edge. "Hit her again and I'll shoot you from where I stand."

CHAPTER 45

Cole's hand tightened on the marble bookend, and he fought the urge to rush forward. His plan to have Beckett and Bram distract Gunnar while he went after Petra had been straightforward enough, but now that Gunnar was with his cousins, he needed a new strategy. Cole slipped behind a tree where he had ten yards of open space between himself and where Gunnar stood over Tess, his gun in his hand.

Anna and Petra emerged from the hole in the ground. Gunnar aimed his weapon at Anna's head. Cole's stomach clenched. They were out of time.

His heart in his throat, Cole stepped clear of his cover and sent the bookend flying.

"Watch out!" Petra yelled.

Gunnar ducked, and the marble whizzed over his head. Cole raced forward and claimed a new hiding place, this one fifteen yards from where Gunnar currently stood. Though he could see his cousins through the branches, the thick pine created a barrier between himself and Petra. Of the two Sauermanns, she was the one he was more worried about. If the woman could hide her evil nature from her husband, who knew what she was capable of.

Cole searched the ground for anything he could use as a replacement weapon. He picked up a two-foot-long branch at his feet, a splinter cutting into his skin. He ignored the discomfort and shifted to the other side of the tree, where he could again assess the situation.

Anna's and Tess's eyes both searched for the source of the disturbance, but with Petra's gun now aimed at them, they didn't dare move.

Pine needles rustled beneath footsteps, and the white of Bram's shirt flashed into view.

"Their friends must be out there," Petra said. "Kill them."

"What about those two?" Gunnar pointed at Tess and Anna.

"They're our insurance until their friends are taken care of."

Gunnar turned in a circle, searching the dense woods. Cole remained motionless, trusting the shadows to hide him. Gunnar's gaze swept past Cole's position, but he paused when he looked in Bram's direction. The gun came up, and Cole's heartbeat quickened. Had Gunnar located Bram? Or did he sense someone there?

Gunnar continued forward, away from where Petra held Tess and Anna at gunpoint.

They're all civilians, Cole reminded himself. He had to do something.

The signal from his brain to his legs was still in transit when the fireplace poker speared through the air from where Beckett now stood. The poker didn't hit the target, but it caught Gunnar's attention. He whirled to face Beckett and fired off three shots.

A cry of pain tore from Beckett, and he stumbled backward.

Cole's gut clenched, but he fought to keep his concentration on Gunnar. He gripped the branch he held as though it were a spear and hurled it through the air. This time, Gunnar wasn't quick enough. It hit him square in the chest and knocked him back a step. His foot caught on a bulging tree root, and his arms flailed, the gun still gripped in his hand.

Cole burst forward, deliberately keeping trees between himself and Petra. He launched himself at Gunnar and grabbed his gun hand, forcing his arm upward to keep any bullets from strafing into the woods.

A shot fired into the air from Gunnar's weapon. Another shot fired, this time from Petra.

Cole ducked, checked Petra's position, and took a step to his left to keep her husband between them. Cole reached for Gunnar's pistol, but the older man had just enough height to keep it out of his grasp.

Out of the corner of his eye, Cole caught movement. Bram rushed to where Beckett stood beside a tree, Beckett's hand gripping his arm.

"I'm okay. Go!" Beckett insisted.

Bram burst out of the trees, brandishing the fireplace broom over his head like a sword.

"Watch out!" Petra shrieked, but the warning came too late.

Bram raced forward and slammed the metal handle across Gunnar's back. Gunnar grunted, and he pitched forward, taking Cole with him as he fell to the ground. The gun tumbled free and disappeared into the soft pine needles on the forest floor.

"Get the gun," Cole shouted at Bram.

Bram dropped onto his knees to search as another shot fired. Petra. Would she leave Anna and Tess to come to her husband's aide?

Cole pushed to a stand. The trees were too thick between him and Petra for her to get a clean shot, but that didn't stop her from trying. Two more shots rang out, both bullets impacting nearby trees. At least if Petra was shooting at him, she wasn't shooting at his cousins.

Gunnar's hand disappeared beneath his shirt and reappeared an instant later holding a knife. He swung wildly and scrambled to his feet.

Cole jumped back, the knife catching a piece of his torn shirt. He took another step back, nearly tripping over Bram.

Bram jerked to the side, but his hands continued to rustle through the underbrush and pine needles. Urgency filled his voice. "I can't find it."

Cole took another step back. "Don't make me kill you."

"I'm the one with the knife." Gunnar sliced the blade through the air in a show of strength. Madness and greed flashed on his face. His eyes wild, Gunnar lunged forward. Cole jumped to the side and grabbed Gunnar's wrist. In a practiced move, Cole twisted the other man's arm with one hand and wrestled the knife free with the other.

Gunnar pushed away and kicked at the ground near where his gun had fallen.

"Really. Don't make me kill you," Cole said. Explaining one stabbing victim in Austria was bad enough. He didn't want to go for a second.

Gunnar dropped to the ground a few yards from Bram, both of them digging through pine needles in search of the lost weapon. The black gun grip jostled to the surface. Bram reached for it at the same time Gunnar did, but Gunnar was closer.

Gunnar grabbed the gun and whirled toward Cole. With a sense of déjà vu, Cole gripped the knife handle and sent the weapon flying. He hit his target, and this time, the blade pierced straight through the heart.

The gun nozzle pressed into Anna's spine dropped away, and a loud, keening wail emitted from Petra. The woman took two steps toward her husband and screamed, "Gunnar!"

Immobilized, Anna blinked. A dozen yards to the right, Herr Sauermann lay prone with a knife stuck in his chest. Cole stood farther still at an angle. Of Beckett, there was no sign.

"No!" Petra yelled and swung about.

Tess grabbed Anna's arm and yanked. "Get down!"

Petra lifted the gun and fired where Anna had stood only a second before. The woman's face contorted, and she squeezed the trigger again. A hot wind dislodged the hair beside Anna's face, and an explosion followed, the shot pulling Anna from her daze.

She hit the ground and rolled, coming up against the base of a larch where Herr Sauermann had placed the shovel. Anna bounded to her feet.

Tess reached the pine tree and snatched the rock she and Anna had hidden away. Taking aim, Tess hurled it at Petra and hit the woman's shooting arm.

"Ahh." Petra grabbed her arm and dropped the weapon.

Anna was too far away to seize it. Tess was closer. Anna read the determination in her cousin's eyes and knew Tess was going to go for the firearm. But Tess's injury wouldn't allow her to reach it in time.

Tess took two steps forward before Petra picked up her pistol. She couldn't miss from that range.

"Put down the gun," Cole's voice commanded.

The distance was too great to grapple for the gun, but he distracted the woman and bought them time.

Branches snapped. Bram appeared in Anna's peripheral vision. He was alone. A frisson of fear zipped through her. Where was Beckett?

The cry in the woods. Had Herr Sauermann shot him?

Her pulse thundered, and her blood boiled. She grabbed the shovel and pivoted.

Petra raised her gun and aimed at Tess. Tess ducked behind the pine.

Anna took two running steps and swung the shovel. The metal blade arced over her head, much like a catapult, and hit Petra in the back. The force threw the woman forward, face-first onto the ground.

The gun went off, and a bullet embedded itself in the pine where Tess had taken cover. Sulfur soured the air. Petra Sauermann rolled over and blinked in a dazed sort of way.

Anna kicked the gun across the ground in Tess's direction. Her nostrils flared, and she placed the metal blade directly against Petra's throat.

"Ach, lassie, dinnae kill the woman." A firm hand clamped onto the shovel handle from behind.

"Beckett?" Anna's voice shook, and she looked over her shoulder to make sure it was him.

"Aye."

She exhaled, and the tension drained from her body. "I thought you were—" Her eyes landed on Beckett's bloodied arm. "You were!"

Anger clouded her reason. Anna turned back and pressed down on the shovel. Petra gagged, and white showed around her irises.

"Easy, lass. You dinnae need to take off her head."

Anna narrowed her eyes. "Believe me. It's tempting."

Tess picked up the pistol. "I think you need to listen to Beckett. I've got her now."

Cole's breath shuddered out. How he and his new friends had managed to come out of this alive was a miracle in itself. He retrieved the decoded directions and Tess's key from Gunnar's pocket, then stepped aside to make room for Bram, who knelt beside Gunnar.

Cole abandoned his latest stabbing victim and approached Anna, who still held a shovel to Petra's throat. "Remind me to never make you mad."

"Beckett, are you really okay?" Anna asked, the waver in her voice undermining the fury in her eyes.

"I'm okay," Beckett said.

"Let me check your wound," Bram said. He motioned to where Gunnar's body lay. "There's nothing I can do for Sauermann."

Petra whimpered.

"He's dead?" Tess asked.

"He's dead," Bram confirmed before he crossed to where Cole and Beckett had congregated beside the three women.

Cole held the key out to Tess. "I believe this belongs to you."

Tess glanced at Cole before lowering her gaze to the gun she still had aimed at Petra. "Maybe you should hold on to the key for now."

"Maybe you should let me take that." Cole relieved Tess of the weapon and traded it for the key.

Beside them, Bram ripped the torn fabric of Beckett's sleeve and shifted to get a better look in the fading light. "You got lucky. It looks like the bullet just nicked you."

"We need to call an ambulance." Anna kept the tip of the shovel against Petra's throat. "Give me your mobile."

Petra reached into her pocket and held out the phone.

"Unlock the screen," Anna said.

Petra did as she was asked and handed it over. A second later, she gulped when the pressure against her throat eased.

"Anna, you can put down the shovel," Cole said. "I'll take care of our prisoner."

Anna lowered the shovel and tapped on Petra's phone.

"I don't need an ambulance," Beckett insisted. "I'll be fine."

"You were shot," Anna said.

"You heard Bram. I was nicked," Beckett countered. "Besides, I'm not leaving you."

"Bram, what do you think?" Anna asked.

"He'll need a few stitches," Bram said. "If I can get ahold of the supplies, I can take care of that for you."

"I'm sure there's a doctor in Gildenstatt who could do it," Cole said.

"I don't need a doctor."

Despite Beckett's protest, Tess reached out a hand. "Give me the phone. I'll call."

"Call the police too," Cole said. "See if they're on their way yet. It's been almost an hour since I first called emergency services."

Tess called 112. After she requested an update on the police's progress, she looked up the local physician's office and made a call to the doctor's emergency line. She explained the need for medical attention at Falcon Point before hanging up. "The police should be here shortly, and the doctor is on his way."

"How long until the doctor gets here?" Anna asked.

"He said he was finishing a house call near where they're putting in the train station. He should be here in about fifteen minutes." Tess held up her key. "While we're here, should we see what this unlocks?"

Sirens sounded in the distance.

"I hate to say it, but we should probably get these two away from here," Cole said. "We aren't going to want the authorities meddling in our family business."

"I'm pretty sure the police are going to meddle since we have a dead body on our hands." Bram nodded toward Gunnar.

"Yeah, but we don't need that dead body to give them reason to search around up here," Cole said. Though Cole would have preferred to task himself with covering their tracks, he didn't trust the others to handle Petra if she tried to escape.

"I'll take care of Petra," Cole said. "Bram and Anna, I need you to drag Gunnar's body down to the yard."

The sirens grew louder.

"Won't the cops just follow the tracks right back up here?" Beckett asked.

"They would, but you and Tess are going to follow behind us and cover them up."

Bram's eyebrows furrowed. "Should we be worried that you know what to do to hide a crime scene?"

You have no idea. "We didn't commit any crimes. They did."

"How are we going to keep Petra from leading the police right back up here?" Tess asked.

"Who's going to believe her? She just tried to kill us." Cole grabbed Petra's arm and tugged her toward the manor. "Come on."

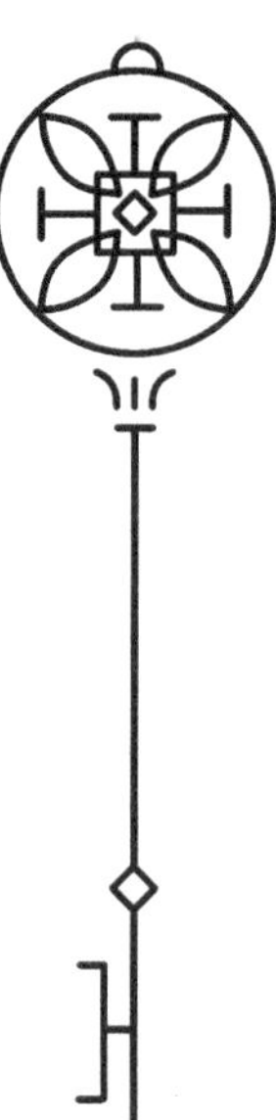

CHAPTER 46

Sirens wailed louder and then cut off when Cole led the way onto the manicured grounds. He angled toward the place where his last stabbing victim had lain. "Leave Gunnar there. We'll let the authorities deal with him."

"Should one of us go tell the police we're back here?" Anna asked.

"Bram, can you go? Anna doesn't speak German, and the other two are injured," Cole said. "I don't want them to see me first while I'm holding our friend here at gunpoint."

Bram nodded. He made it only a few yards before two officers and a woman rounded the corner of the house.

Isabelle?

Cole blinked twice. The last person Cole had expected to see arrive with the police was a fellow CIA agent, yet there she was, dressed in a cream pantsuit, her oversized purse hanging from her shoulder, and a look of determination on her face.

The arrival of the police sent Petra into motion. She jerked against Cole's grip and cried out in German. "Help! Officers! Help me!"

In an instant, both police officers drew their weapons.

"Hands up!" one demanded, his gun aimed in their general direction.

The other aimed at Cole. "Drop it!"

"Here we go again," Cole muttered. He released Petra and held his hands out, the gun pointed in the air, his finger off the trigger.

"Throw your weapon down," the taller of the two officers demanded.

"I'll give it to you, but I'm not putting it down until she's in custody." Cole tilted his head toward Petra. "She tried to kill us."

"I did no such thing. They're trying to rob me." She pointed at Gunnar. "They killed my husband."

The policeman cautiously approached Cole.

Cole relinquished the pistol and said calmly, "It was self-defense."

"That's right," Beckett said. "Her husband shot me."

"This is nonsense. This is my home." She waved toward Beckett and Anna. "These two have been trying to steal from me for weeks. My husband and I didn't do anything wrong."

"I beg to differ." Isabelle stepped forward and retrieved a file from her purse. "I have proof that Gunnar Sauermann hired three separate assassins to eliminate the heirs of Falcon Point."

"What?" Petra's eyes widened. "I didn't know anything about that."

Bram held up his hands. Even in the fading light, his rope burns were impossible to miss."That's not what you said when you had your husband tie us up."

Indignation filled the older woman's voice. "I did no such thing."

"Then why are all of our cell phones in pieces all over the floor in the parlor?" Tess asked. "We didn't destroy them ourselves."

A man in his forties hurried toward them from the road. "I came as fast as I could."

"Thanks, Doc. There's one victim over there." The shorter policeman pointed at Gunnar. He then nodded toward Beckett. "He said he was shot too."

The doctor checked Gunnar and confirmed what they already knew. "He's dead. I'll call the mortician and have them send someone up to get the body." He looked at Beckett. "What about you?"

"I'll be fine," Beckett said. "It's just a flesh wound."

"Doctor, I'll need you to stay here until the mortician arrives." The younger officer pulled his cell phone from his pocket and began photographing the crime scene.

"The mortician won't be here for at least thirty minutes," the doctor protested.

"Sorry, Doc, but we need someone to protect the body." The older officer took Petra by the arm. "As for the rest of you, let's take this conversation inside and sort this mess out."

Cole allowed himself to be escorted into the parlor, where he had been tied up an hour before. Had it really only been an hour since the Sauermanns had shown up and threatened him and his family?

Family. His father's family. He still couldn't quite believe he had found them, nor could he believe they'd uncovered the hiding place of the treasure his ancestors had buried during the war. Generations of history. They were so close.

Anna and Beckett entered the parlor, followed by Tess and Bram.

Tess gasped. "You had to break the chairs to get free?"

"We're in trouble now," Beckett whispered to Cole.

Anna took in the wreckage, her face filled with horror. "Those chairs are antiques. They're worth thousands of euros apiece."

Beckett pointed at Cole. "It was his idea."

"Thanks a lot," Cole said.

Tess's expression reflected Anna's dismay.

Bram took Tess's hand. "Your life is worth more than a few broken chairs," he said.

The police officer took in the ropes and broken chairs scattered on the floor. Then his gaze landed on the remnants of their cell phones. He drew out his handcuffs and pulled Petra's hands behind her back.

"What are you doing?" Petra asked.

"Petra Sauermann, you are being detained for suspicion of attempted murder."

"They're lying!"

The officer ignored her. "Everyone else, please sit down. We need to take your statements before we take Frau Sauermann in for questioning."

The officers gave each of them paper and a pen to write out their statements. As soon as Cole completed his, he crossed to where Isabelle stood alone beside the fireplace.

"What are you doing here?" Cole asked.

"I had a meeting in Linz," Isabelle said, her voice low. "While I was there, I made inquiries about the Sauermanns' finances and stumbled on some suspicious activity."

Cole understood enough about international banking to know Isabelle had left out a lot of details. He leaned closer and whispered in her ear. "You're the one Gwendolyn sent."

Isabelle pulled back, but her eyes remained on his. "What?"

"I suspected you might have followed in your grandfather's footsteps in career choice," Cole said. "I checked you out."

She stilled. "This isn't the kind of conversation I expected to have with you today."

"Me neither, but I'm glad we have that out of the way. It will make getting to know you so much easier."

Isabelle's eyebrows rose. "We only have one date planned."

Cole's grin flashed. "You can't blame me if I'm hoping for more."

The policeman tugged on Petra's arm. "I think we have everything we need for now." He escorted her out the door, his partner following behind him.

"Thank you, officer," Cole said. He led the way to where his cousins were seated with Beckett and Bram and introduced Isabelle.

As soon as the police left, Isabelle retrieved another file from her purse. "You're all going to want to see this."

"What is it?"

"The original trust documentation and the bank accounts for the Lang Family Trust." Isabelle glanced at Cole. "I hope you don't mind that I ran a search for it when I was in Linz."

"Of course not, but how does that help us?" Cole asked.

"The trust clearly states that it was established for the support of the Lang family and the upkeep of Falcon Point," Isabelle said. "With Sauermann dead, your family doesn't have to remove him as trustee. You can simply decide who you want to serve as trustees and how you want to divide responsibilities among you."

Anna, Tess, and Cole exchanged looks.

"I assume my father and Cole's grandfather will want to have a say in that decision," Anna said. "Lars too."

"Yes." Isabelle's gaze swept over the three cousins. "But given the expertise in this room, I'm sure they'll want all of you involved."

Tess nodded. "That's true, especially if we move forward with the resort."

"I can help facilitate your claim with the land authority," Isabelle offered. "It shouldn't take more than a few days to sort out the paperwork, particularly if Anna is on site."

"That would be lovely. Thank you," Anna said. She waved toward Tess. "And we can utilize Tess's expertise with artwork and antiques."

"I'm happy to help in any way I can." Tess frowned at the shattered phones on the floor. "I wish there were a way I could contact Lars right now. I know he'll want to be involved too, and he'd be a great help if the estate's assets include jewelry. We can work together."

"Anna takes care of the house. Tess and Lars oversee the contents," Cole said. "Sounds great to me." The last thing he wanted was to handle mundane details about the renovation or the appraisal of old paintings and furniture.

"All that's left is choosing a trustee," Isabelle said.

Tess and Anna looked at Cole. He held up both hands. "Don't look at me. We'll leave that job to an earlier generation. My grandpa can do it. And Anna's father."

"Cole, you should be involved as well," Tess said.

"I'll be in charge of security." Eager to get back to the bunker, Cole asked Anna, "Any chance you have some flashlights or lanterns around here?"

"There are some in the maintenance shed on the side of the house."

Anna cast a worried glance at Beckett.

Cole followed her gaze. "I'll go get them after we take care of Beckett. Are you sure you don't want to go to the hospital?"

"I'm not going anywhere, at least not until we see what's inside that bunker," Beckett said.

"Maybe the doctor can come treat you in here," Tess suggested.

"He'll be required to wait outside with the body until the coroner arrives," Bram said.

"Then, Bram, you do it," Cole said. "You know Anna and Beckett won't want us to explore the bunker without them."

"I'll see if the doctor will lend me his medical bag."

"Let me take care of that." Cole took a step toward the door. "As soon as Beckett's all bandaged, we'll go together to see what's in that bunker."

"No offense, Cole, but I doubt he'll lend it to you. You aren't a medical professional."

"I know." A sense of mischief rose within him. "But I wasn't going to ask."

Anna's stomach curdled as Bram stitched Beckett's wound closed. If the bullet had been a few inches to the left . . . She shuddered and averted her eyes.

How could Beckett just sit there, unmoving, the only show of pain a darkening of his eyes. He might be stoic, but she certainly wasn't. She fisted her hands to stop their trembling.

What had turned out to be a flesh wound could have ended his life. *And their future.* The words repeated themselves inside her mind, and her last doubts fell away. She didn't know what the upcoming days and months held for them, but she refused to deny her feelings for Beckett any longer.

Bram tied off the last stitch. "All done." He riffled through the medical bag and dug out a roll of gauze. "I don't see any medical tape in here. Any chance you have a first aid kit somewhere?"

"I'll get it." Anna stood, happy to flee the room for a few minutes to collect herself.

Her knees knocked as she went to retrieve the kit from the top shelf of the butler's pantry. Blood always made her queasy. And when it was Beckett's, that made it doubly bad. She dashed some water onto her face from the small sink below the cabinet to calm herself before she went back upstairs.

When she returned, every light in the turquoise salon burned brightly. Beckett sat reading the latest architectural digest in the only undamaged chair, a furrow between his brows. If his blood-stained, button-down shirt hadn't told a different story, Anna would almost have believed this was just another evening at Falcon Point.

Beckett looked up from his magazine, his face pale, his eyes dark.

"Where's Bram? I thought he was going to finish patching you up?" She dropped the first aid kit onto the occasional table beside his large, overstuffed chair.

"Bram went with the others to hunt for flashlights," Beckett said. "I told him you were capable of applying a bandage."

Her insides did a triple flip, and the blood drained from the crown of her head straight to her toes. She peeked at the drying blood on Beckett's arm and looked away again. Her entire repertoire of first aid know-how was next to nil.

"This should be entertaining. I seem to remember you don't care for the sight of blood." Beckett put down the magazine beside his chair and cocked a brow at her.

Anna swallowed and lifted her chin. "Times have changed." What a bunch of crock.

Blood still seeped around his stitches and made her stomach lurch. Opening the kit, she pawed through the medical supplies, looking for the tape.

"Why don't they have a supersize sticking plaster in here?" she muttered.

Even she could handle applying that. But no, Beckett's wound was too long and oozey. Surely she should clean it before applying the bandage. She glanced at the water carafe on top of the liquor cabinet. Empty. Unwilling to leave him a second time, she determined that anything in Sauermann's alcohol collection would do in a pinch. It was liquid after all.

Crossing to the cabinet, she grabbed the nearest bottle and brought it back and set it beside the first aid kit. Picking up the scissors, she cut a large piece of gauze and folded it into a pad.

"I think Petra Sauermann got off light, don't you?"

"She lost her husband, Anna," Beckett reminded her.

"I'm well aware of that, but when I saw my family, people I care about, and the man I love being shot at"—she brought the scissor blades together for emphasis—"something snapped inside me."

"Say that again." Beckett's eyes gleamed.

"Something snapped—"

"Not that. The part about the man you love." His hazel eyes appeared green today and matched his tattered shirt.

Drat.

Anna closed her eyes and berated herself. She hadn't meant to tell Beckett this way, with him wounded and bleeding. That was most definitely not her idea of a romantic interlude. But her emotions were still high. For a few minutes in the woods, she had thought he was dead.

"I don't want to talk about that right now," she said. Tears blurred her eyes, and she turned away to hide them in the guise of cutting more gauze and folding it into another compress. She wet the pad with whiskey and dabbed at the coagulating blood beside the stitches. Her actions didn't fool Beckett. He took her chin with his good hand and lifted her face to his.

"What's this?" Beckett wiped her traitorous tears with the pad of his thumb.

"I thought you were dead when we were in the woods. It was the most horrible moment of my life." Anna sniffed. "Please don't make me say it right now, not before I bandage your arm."

"Say what, my love?" Beckett grinned, exposing perfectly even, white teeth. His eyes dropped to her mouth.

Anna's heart fluttered, and tingles rippled across her skin. The man knew entirely too well what his smiles did to her. She swallowed convulsively and reached for Sauermann's whiskey bottle and sloshed a liberal amount onto the pad. The excess dripped down Beckett's arm.

He shot up in his chair, the smile wiped from his face as a string of Scottish swear words erupted from his mouth. "Are you trying to kill me, lass? Sauermann's bullet didn't hurt like this."

"Sorry, I didn't mean to get it in the wound. The water carafe was empty, and I needed something to help clean off the dried blood."

Beckett twisted in his chair and picked up the bottle off the occasional table. "You poured a single malt Macallan on a cut?"

"It was an accident."

Rendered speechless, he shook his head and closed his eyes while she bound his arm and used enough tape to keep it in place until the new year. When she finished, his eyes had dilated, and his face matched the white bandage.

"After seeing you and your cousins take out Herr Sauermann and company"—Beckett raised his wounded arm—"I'd say bloodthirsty tendencies seem to run in your family. Anna, using that whiskey was positively barbaric."

"You're just jealous because I found the shovel first." Anna sat on the footstool beside his chair and patted his leg.

"You're too far away," he grumbled.

Careful of his arm, Anna climbed onto the chair beside him. It was a tight squeeze. "When I saw Cole and Bram and realized you were missing, I was never so frightened in my life."

"You, frightened? I'd hate to see what terrified looks like on you."

"Very funny."

"Anna, lass. What am I to do with you?"

"I've had some time to think about that lately."

"You have?" Beckett ran his hand through her tousled hair.

"Aye," she said, mimicking his Scots. "I couldn't bear it if you weren't here," she whispered. "I love you, Beckett. I want you back in my life."

His hand stilled in her hair. "You're sure, lass?"

"I'm sure."

"I'll be holding you to that."

He leaned forward. Her stomach fluttered with anticipation. His good hand cupped her face, and he lowered his mouth to hers. Their lips touched, and her heart melted, and tingles swarmed her senses.

Something new had entered Beckett's kisses, an underlying tenderness almost bordering on worship. His gentleness almost made her weep. This is what she had longed for, what had been absent in years past, the culmination of her dreams over the last four barren years.

Beckett pulled back but kept his arm around her. "Would you like to stay on with Genskal after we wrap this project?"

"I suppose I could," she said, "but I wouldn't want to."

"Why? I thought Genskal was your endgame?" His dark brows rose.

"It was, but my plans have changed."

"What do you mean?"

"You hired with Genskal to get back in my good graces."

"I did, but the company's been verra good to me. I'd be happy to stay."

"Beckett, all your life you've wanted to start your own architectural firm. For years, you've put your plans on hold. I won't be the reason to keep you from your dreams. Besides, we've almost eighteen months left on this contract; that's plenty of time to work for Genskal." She touched his jaw, then kissed him briefly. "I happen to know your new firm will need a designer. I have it on good authority that my boss will give you an excellent reference."

"As tempting as that sounds, Anna, I'll not be the reason you give up your goals."

"Beckett, I'm only going to say this once, so pay attention. I admire your designs. They're innovative, challenging, and bold. They would push me as a designer in ways Genskal never could. Got it?"

"More than." He smirked. "And Falcon Point?" he asked, sobering.

"I imagine, in time, that, too, will settle itself."

CHAPTER 47

The clearing was eerily quiet. A slight breeze caught the branches of the pine tree, the needles hissing slightly as they quivered. Somewhere to the right, an owl hooted and a branch snapped. Tess shivered. She took a step closer to Bram, grateful when he slipped his arm around her waist. Across from them, Cole stood with a lantern raised high enough to see each person standing around the bunker's entrance.

"Okay. This is it." Cole glanced around the circle. "The moment of truth."

Anticipation rippled through her. If Oma's earrings were any indication, Liselotte Lang's jewelry could be priceless. And then there were the paintings mentioned in Karl Lang's letters. Unless the Sauermanns had sold them all, it was possible there were some long-lost masterpieces hidden in the bunker.

She studied the shadowed faces around her, marveling that she could feel such a strong connection to people who were strangers to her days ago. Beckett, his arm wrapped in a white bandage, stood next to Anna. Their hands were tightly clasped, and Anna's gaze was on the trapdoor at their feet. Isabelle, whose unexpected appearance less than an hour before had been as timely as the police's, was at Cole's left. Her flashlight was illuminating a brass handle glinting among the fallen pine needles.

"Tess." Excitement fairly shimmered off Cole. "You have the key. If Bram will give you his flashlight and help me with the trapdoor, I think you should be the first one down."

Tess nodded. Bram gave her an encouraging squeeze before handing her the light and moving to stand on the other side of the trapdoor from Cole. On the count of three, the men raised the door. The hinge creaked loudly, and Tess stepped forward. Slipping her hand into her pocket, she wrapped her fingers around the old key. Had Oma known it was hidden in her jewelry box? Had she ever held it as Tess did now, wondering what it had the power to reveal?

Anna moved closer. "Don't forget about that broken stair."

Tess nodded. "Third one down."

"Yes." Anna looked around. "Did the rest of you hear that?"

"Broken stair. Third one down," Cole repeated. "Go for it, Tess. We'll be right behind you."

Shining the flashlight before her, Tess stepped into the opening. The wood shifted under her weight but held. Slowly, favoring her injured knee, she entered the dark bunker.

When she reached the hard-packed earth floor, she moved to the far wall and ran the flashlight across its surface. It was metal. From top to bottom, left to right. And in the center, there was a wide door. She moved closer to examine the lock. Behind her, the sound of footsteps coming down the stairs echoed through the bunker, and within seconds, Anna and Cole were at her side.

"Whoa." Cole ran his hand across the surface of the door, the light of his lantern glinting off the metal studs. "This was built to last."

"A good thing too," Anna said. "Given that the building above it obviously didn't survive."

There were more footsteps on the stairs. Light flickered across the ceiling.

"This is quite the feat of engineering." Beckett's voice bounced off the walls. "I'm impressed."

"Wait until you see the locks," Tess said, her heart sinking as she studied the padlock attached to the door.

"Locks?" Cole said.

It shouldn't have surprised her that Cole had picked up on her use of the plural. "Unfortunately, yes."

Cole lowered his lantern so he could better see the portion of the door illuminated by Tess's flashlight. "A keyhole for the door and a combination lock for the padlock," he muttered.

"A really old, very solid combination lock," Tess said. "Look at the tumblers. They're like round disks of brass with letters engraved on them instead of numbers."

"Letters instead of numbers," Cole repeated. "Letters instead of numbers." He reached into his pocket and pulled out the scrap of paper Gunnar had stolen from him. "Remember those five letters at the end of the cypher that didn't seem to mean anything?"

"They're the code for the combination lock," Anna said.

"Try the key, Tess."

Tess inserted the key into the hole and turned it. She felt it move—stiffly at first. Then, with a resounding click, the key slid into the unlocked position. She looked at Cole and Anna, her fingers still on the key and her heart pounding. "It worked."

"All right." Cole handed the paper and his lantern to Anna. "Read off those last five letters."

"*S E B A M.*"

One after another, Cole turned the tumblers. When the final one was in place, he glanced at Tess and pulled the shackle. It instantly released.

Tess's breath caught. They'd done it. They'd actually done it. She took a shaky step back, and someone reached out to steady her. Bram. She took his hand, grasping it tightly as Cole unhooked the padlock and yanked back the bolt. The screech of metal on metal filled the bunker. Cole reclaimed his lantern and pushed open the door.

The air was cold and smelled stale. Trunks of various sizes lined the metal vault. Three wooden crates sat on top of the largest trunks.

Tess moved closer. Tamping down her excitement, she eyed the crates critically. They were definitely large enough to contain framed art. She could only pray that if they did, the tightly sealed vault had preserved them well.

Cole set his lantern on a trunk and reached for one end of the largest crate. Bram stepped forward and lifted the other end. They set it down in front of Tess.

"What do you think?" Cole said. "Artwork?"

"I think I want to open it." Tess ran her flashlight across the top of the crate. "But we've got to do it carefully." She gave Cole a warning look. "No smashing anything."

Cole grinned unrepentantly. "Anyone see a crowbar?"

"The poker's still outside," Beckett said. "I saw it not far from the big pine tree."

"That might work," Cole said.

"Only if you're not wielding it," Tess said.

"I'll get it." Beckett was already moving toward the stairs. The light from his flashlight had barely disappeared before Cole lifted the lid on the nearest trunk to reveal a gray woolen blanket. He reached for it, but Anna caught his hand.

"Careful," she said. "We don't know what's underneath." Gently, she pulled back the fabric and gasped. A rainbow of colors danced in the beam of her flashlight. Something bright and shiny lay within the chest. "Oh my word. Tess, tell me I'm seeing what I think I'm seeing."

"What do you think you're seeing?" Cole asked impatiently. "Is it different than what I'm seeing?"

"Probably." Anna gave him a longsuffering look. "A Louis XVI armchair is not just a piece of disposable furniture. And those"—she pointed at the contents of the trunk—"are not just any old flower vases."

"Okay. Enlighten me," Cole said.

Tess squeezed past Cole and shone her flashlight inside the trunk. Her heart began to pound. She did not know much about vases, but she knew plenty about hand-painted porcelain—particularly when the style was decidedly Napoleonic and included extensive gold gilding.

She cleared her throat and hoped her voice would emerge. "I would estimate those vases are each worth at least fifteen thousand euros."

Cole stared at her. "Seriously?"

Bram chuckled. "Take it from me, Cole, Tess knows her art. If I were you, I'd move away from the trunk as carefully as you can and try another one."

Cole did not need to be told twice. He opened the next trunk, and with a quick glance at Anna, he carefully removed the sheet on top. This trunk was filled with flat wooden boxes. Releasing the clasp of the first one, Cole lifted the lid on a full set of tarnished cutlery.

"Silver and ivory," Anna said, touching the smooth cream-colored knife handle.

Cole closed the lid and reached for the box beneath. This one contained silver candlesticks. The next housed a full set of bone china plates, cups, and saucers. Anna lifted out a teacup and glanced at the identifying marks on its base. Tess studied the tiny floral pattern running around the edge of the dinner plates and wondered about the woman who had chosen the service and had likely used them on special occasions. Had Oma ever eaten from one of them? Perhaps for a birthday or at Christmastime?

"Try the small one next to you, Isabelle," Cole said.

Tess pushed past her musings and watched as Cole's friend lifted the lid of the brown trunk at her feet. She looked inside, and then her eyes met Cole's. Something unspoken passed between them.

"What is it?" Anna asked.

"Gold." Isabelle lifted her hand so everyone could see the glistening coins.

Cole reached for one of them. "This is crazy."

Tess couldn't agree more. And they still had one more trunk and the crates to open.

Footsteps sounded on the stairs.

"Beckett?" Anna called.

"I found it," he replied. "And a marble bookend, if anyone wants that."

Tess pressed herself against one of the crates to make room for Beckett in the vault. She reached for the poker. "Bram, help me take off this lid. I can't wait any longer."

Bram took the poker from her. "Shine the light on the corner, and I'll see if I can pry it open."

She did as he asked. He pushed the tip of the poker beneath the boards, torquing it slowly to the left and then the right. The wood creaked and cracked. Tess tensed as the first strip of wood gave way. Cole moved closer, grasping the next board and yanking it upward. It broke with a loud snap. She flinched. He reached for the next one as Bram popped off the board on the opposite corner.

"That should do it." Cole tossed the last board out into the bunker, and Tess peered into the open crate.

It looked like there were four frames stacked against each other with an assortment of sheets and blankets between them. Gently removing the first blanket, she shone the flashlight onto the canvas. Her mouth went dry.

"It's . . . it's . . ." she stammered.

"Tess?" She heard the concern in Bram's voice.

She shook her head. With the way her legs had suddenly started shaking, it would probably be a good idea to sit down, but that was the last thing she wanted to do. She took a deep breath. "The first painting is a Renoir."

There was a moment of stunned silence.

Cole was the first to recover. "How sure are you?"

"It would need to be professionally authenticated, but Renoir's style is pretty distinctive." She swallowed. "And his signature is on the corner of the canvas."

Beckett muttered something incomprehensible. Tess guessed it was best that she didn't understand Scottish.

"What about the other paintings?" Isabelle appeared to be the only one thinking straight. She moved to stand beside Tess. "You pass me the coverings, and I'll hold on to them so you can see inside."

Tess carefully slid the sheet off the next frame and shone the light on the woodcut print within. "I think it's an Albrecht Dürer," she said. She uncovered the next one. "And so is this."

Anna leaned closer to look into the crate. "I can't believe it." There was awe in her voice. "I've never seen one outside the museum in Nuremburg."

With shaking hands, Tess carefully removed the last blanket. She paused, taking a moment to collect herself. "This one is by Hieronymus Bosch."

"Who's that?" Cole asked.

"He's a Dutch artist," Tess said, swallowing the lump in her throat. Oma had known—and maybe even loved—Dutch artwork long before she'd adopted the Netherlands as her home. For some unaccountable reason, in the darkness of the bunker and after the nightmare of the last few hours, that single, sweet thought touched her deeply.

She brushed a tear off her cheek with the back of her hand.

Hidden by the shadows, the telltale moisture should not have been noticeable, but somehow, Bram knew. He walked around the open crate and brushed her temple with his lips. "Lars would be proud of you," he said softly. "And so would your Oma."

She leaned against him, and he wrapped his arms around her.

"Shall I open this trunk now?" Anna pointed to the small black chest at her feet.

"Go ahead," Cole said.

Anna lifted the lid and withdrew an envelope. "There's a letter," she said. She glanced at the writing. "I can't read it."

Cole reached for it. "What else is in there?"

"Jewelry boxes. Lots of them." Anna lifted out a thin white box and opened it. "Pearls."

Beckett withdrew another smaller box. "A diamond-and-ruby brooch," he said.

Necklaces, rings, and bracelets came next—each one more stunning than the last. The gemstones sparkled in the lantern light, and Tess's thoughts turned to Lars. She wished he could be here to experience this moment with her.

"I'd say your great-grandmother had excellent taste in jewelry," Isabelle said.

"Yeah." For the first time since she'd met him, Cole appeared floored. "It looks that way, doesn't it?"

"What does it say on the envelope?" Tess asked.

Cole turned it toward the light. "*Zu meiner Familie*."

"In English, please," Anna said.

"'To my Family.'" Cole looked from Anna to Tess. "I suppose that means it's for us." He pulled a single sheet of paper out of the envelope. It was yellowed. The cursive was written in black ink. "It's in German, but I'll translate it as I go."

My Dearest Children,

I hope I'll be with you when the time comes to reclaim our hidden family heritage, but I've seen war before. I know how long it can last and how much it can take from you. I've also seen how the love of a family can heal even the worst wounds. Our family treasure isn't about jewelry and art and foreign bank accounts. It's about love, a willingness to sacrifice for each other, and a hope for the future. We could lose every last item I've hidden away, but if we still have each other, still have that love, then we would be among the richest, most blessed of families.

Casualties come, even in times of peace. Losing your mother as you did taught you that. They come even more swiftly in times of war. I fear for how much you'll see in the years ahead, fear that fleeing Falcon Point will be but the beginning of your challenges. But if you stay true to what I've taught you, if you keep a clear conscience, you can move forward without regrets, regardless of what happens.

If you're digging up what I've left behind, then I'm grateful. It means Falcon Point and all it meant to your mother and me isn't lost, not completely. I hope each of you will be there, and I hope these family heirlooms will bring joy and security. But remember, it's not about the things we've buried in this old cellar. It's about the love we've buried in our hearts, a love that comes from being part of a family.

Love,
Papa

Tess's tears had begun again. Family. That was what had been most important to Leopold Lang. He had sacrificed everything to keep his children safe. And in their own ways, her oma, Anna's granny, and Cole's great-grandfather had done the same. More than any of the treasures at Falcon Point, that was the real Lang legacy. She glanced at Anna and Cole. Emotion shone in their eyes, and her heart swelled. Karl, Ingrid, and Anna Lang were gone, but the unity, integrity, and courage they'd exemplified lived on. Despite all odds, Leopold Lang's family had finally returned home.

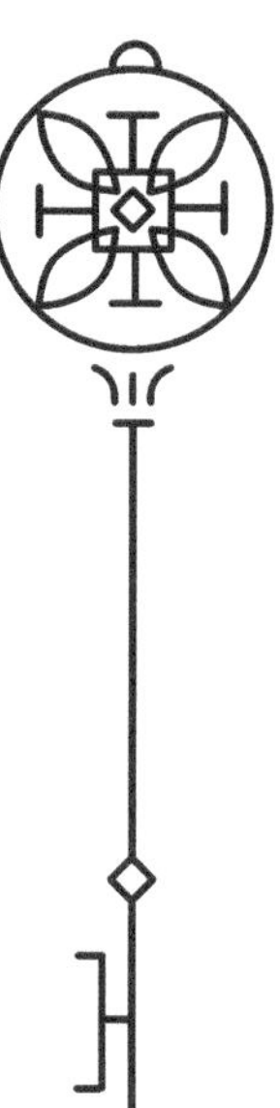

the DANGER *with* DIAMONDS

A Falcon Point Mystery

COMING FALL 2022

TRACI HUNTER ABRAMSON
and SIAN ANN BESSEY

CHAPTER 1

From the driver's seat of the surveillance van, CIA agent Cole Bridger lowered his binoculars. Three armed guards and an unknown number of insurgents hiding inside the cottage. Outnumbered.

Under normal circumstances, Cole would have loved to spend a day or two in this outlying suburb of Budapest. With its rows of quaint houses, the village afforded gorgeous views of the Danube River and easy access to the Pest side of the city. According to the latest intelligence reports, it was also the current location of Trevor Rogers, the CIA agent who had disappeared from Bratislava two nights ago.

The assumption that an arms dealer Rogers had been tracking had orchestrated the kidnapping had caused the CIA to call Cole in from the Vienna office. Cole had crossed paths with Soso Davit multiple times before, but the man had neither demanded a ransom nor changed his daily operations after Rogers had disappeared.

Convinced Davit wasn't the real culprit, Cole had followed one electronic breadcrumb after another in search of other suspects and the location of his missing coworker, a coworker Cole had never met. The trail of surveillance videos and GPS signals had led Cole here, but he had yet to uncover why Trevor Rogers had been kidnapped or who was behind it.

Cole had staked out the house since early this morning, opting to wait for backup before attempting a rescue. As much as he hated waiting to move forward, if his training as a CIA operative hadn't taught him prudence, his upbringing had. He was the fifth generation of Langs and Bridgers to work in intelligence. As a product of his heritage, he had learned to work smart, and part of working smart was making sure someone always had your back.

Of course, when he'd requested backup, he had expected his superiors to send a SEAL team in to help him break his man out. Instead, his support consisted of Jasmine, a fifty-eight-year-old grandmother who hadn't worked in the field in years, and Cas Edgemont, a twenty-five-year-old dead woman.

Known only as Ghost to the intelligence operatives she helped, Cas had faked her death years ago. Had it not been for a breach in her cover last spring, Cole would be as clueless about her identity as the rest of her limited circle of associates.

In the early-morning light, another guard came into view and circled the A-frame structure with its fenced yard. Cole sighed. Make that four armed guards.

Cole slid out of his seat and ducked into the back of the surveillance van. On one side, a long desk held two workstations, complete with computers and monitoring screens. Jasmine and Cas were currently taking advantage of their surveillance technology to give them a clearer understanding of their opposition.

"Just saw a fourth guard checking the perimeter," Cole said.

"We saw that too." Cas motioned to where heat signatures illuminated her screen.

"Maybe we should wait for more backup before we go in," Cole said.

Jasmine swiveled in her seat and glared, her dark skin forming a crease at her brow. Pride and indignation competed with her Southern drawl. "You think we can't handle this?"

"Jazz, when was the last time you fired a weapon?"

"It's like riding a bicycle." To prove her point, she pulled the gun from the holster at her ample waist, released the magazine, checked her ammo, and reloaded. "Besides, we have Ghost here. She does this kind of thing for a living."

"Ghost helps agents sneak out of hostile countries," Cole said. "We're talking about taking on who knows how many armed men."

"And we're just a couple of women?" Jasmine asked.

A couple of overconfident, sassy Southern women. Cole didn't care who he was working with. It could be his seventy-nine-year-old grandfather, as far as he was concerned, but the sass unsettled him. It could translate into arrogance too easily and get someone killed.

Cas motioned to her screen again. "I'm only showing three heat spots inside the house."

"Assuming one of those is Rogers, that's still six against three," Cole said.

"We have the element of surprise," Cas countered. "That evens the odds."

Cas had a point. If they could each eliminate one of the guards and breach the house before the people inside knew they were there, they might have a chance of recovering their agent and all surviving the day.

Resigned to moving forward with the personnel he'd been given, Cole said, "You win, but if we're going to do this, we need a plan to neutralize everyone in there."

"We'll get our man out alive," Cas promised.

"That's our first objective, but that's not all I want. We need to know who these men are and what they're up to."

Jasmine swiveled her laptop toward Cole. "Here's what I have in mind."

Lars Hendriks drew his phone out of his pocket and glanced at the screen. No new texts. And still no sign of Marit. He scanned the crowded plaza again. It was the first week of the Stephansplatz Christmas Market, and despite the chilly November temperatures, the tourists were out in droves. The smell of roasted almonds and gingerbread wafted in the air, making Lars wish he'd arrived early enough to sample them before his appointment at the bank. Perhaps he could do that with Marit afterward. If she ever arrived.

Above his head, the cathedral clock chimed the eleven o'clock hour. Lars frowned. When he'd spoken to Marit on the phone last night, she'd just wrapped up a photo shoot at Schonbrunn Palace and had seemed excited to join him this afternoon. It had been weeks since they'd seen each other, and he'd purposely timed his visit to Vienna to coincide with her modeling job here.

Shifting the strap of his large camera bag more securely onto his shoulder, he stepped to the left as someone exited the building behind him. He didn't want to go in without Marit, but he was pretty sure Cole's grandfather had pulled some strings to schedule him a secure room at the bank for the entire afternoon. That level of service was not easily come by, and he guessed he'd need every hour he'd been given to complete the job ahead.

Reluctantly, he turned to climb the shallow steps leading to the bank's heavy doors.

"Lars! Wait!"

He swung around, immediately spotting Marit's tall, willowy figure and bright-red beanie. She broke free of the Chinese tourists standing in front of the nearby entrance to the U-bahn train station and ran toward him.

"I'm so sorry." She was out of breath. "The train was full, so I had to wait for the next one, and then all the tourists at this stop were blocking the exit . . ." She came to a halt before him, a smile lighting her face. "It's good to see you, Lars."

"It's even better to see you." Lars grinned and drew her in for a hug. "I'm glad you made it."

They exchanged three soft kisses on each other's cheeks. The simple Dutch greeting meant nothing, Lars knew, but the touch of her lips lingered on his skin when she pulled away.

He took another step toward the bank doors and raised an eyebrow. "Want to see some long-lost jewelry?"

"Of course." Her brown eyes sparkled, and he caught the hint of humor dancing there. "Why else would I be here?"

"I asked for that, didn't I?"

She laughed, moving to stand beside him. "One hundred percent."

Isabelle waited near the bank entrance, her eyes scanning the various customers coming and going. Her training as an undercover CIA operative had taught her to look beyond the basics to allow her to recognize both threats and opportunities. That same training also afforded her the ability to shelve her emotions to protect her from unwanted distractions. Too bad she couldn't bury her current emotions permanently. The familiar pain sliced through her, a heartache born of embarrassment, hurt, loss, and disappointment.

A woman walked through the door, a toddler on her hip. A little wave of envy surfaced within Isabelle. Despite a top-notch education and an enviable career, going home to an empty apartment every night left a lot to be desired.

The woman continued past her, and Isabelle turned her attention to the others in the lobby. A man in his twenties with an ill-fitting suit jacket and worn dress shoes stood beside the information desk. Probably applying for the open teller position. By the main counter, a woman waited her turn, a tan line visible on her finger where a wedding ring would typically be worn. Newly divorced? Or dating someone who wasn't her husband? Isabelle studied the woman's expression of determination mixed with a don't-mess-with-me glare. Definitely divorced.

Gerhart Wimmer, one of the senior vice presidents, passed through security and walked toward her. "*Guten morgen*, Isabelle. What are you doing down here?"

"I'm waiting for a client."

"Very good." He took a step toward the elevator before he turned back. "How soon are you going to have your quarterly reports ready?"

"I should have my portion done by this afternoon." She would analyze those quarterly reports for corporate while also ensuring no funds were filtered through this bank that could be used against the United States.

"Good." He gave a nod of approval and continued toward the elevators. Like the others she worked with, Gerhart didn't have a clue that Isabelle was more interested in moving up the ranks to increase her access to information than she was about padding her paycheck.

Though she loved the world of finance, her grandfather's work in the intelligence community had planted the seed of patriotism in her that had bloomed into a desire to do her part to keep her country safe. It was one of her grandfather's dear friends who had put her in her current situation. When Glenn Bridger had contacted her to ask a favor, she had agreed as much to have an opportunity to see Cole again as to help out her longtime family friend.

Her jaw clenched. Three months ago, she would have been excited to spend time with Cole in the hope of continuing their brief relationship. Now she looked forward to giving him a piece of her mind.

She had been present when Cole had joined forces with two of his cousins and found a treasure that had been hidden since the early days of World War II. She had thought her association with the family would continue through her budding romance with Cole. Little had she known Cole would jump at the first field assignment that came his way. Three dates and one kiss good night had been the extent of what she had hoped would lead to something more.

Would Cole even accompany his cousin today? Or would he continue to ignore her the way he had for the past six months?

A tall, blond man walked in with a stunning woman who had long, blonde hair and warm, brown eyes. The man's gaze swept the room. Though he was taller than Cole and his face more angular, the blue eyes were unmistakable. No doubt this man was Lars Hendricks, Cole's cousin. And though Lars wasn't alone, once again, Cole wasn't anywhere to be found.

Lars acknowledged the security guard standing near the bank doors with a polite nod and guided Marit into the vast lobby. Muted voices filled the cavernous room, echoing off the stone pillars and vaulted ceiling above. Across from the main doors, a row of tellers worked behind a high marble-topped counter, their attention alternating between their customers and their computer screens.

"What do we do now?" Marit asked softly.

"Mr. Hendriks?" An attractive young woman approached them wearing a navy-colored business suit. "Welcome to Bankhaus Steiner."

"Thank you." Lars's polite response was instinctive—as was replying in German—but how did this woman know him?

His perplexity must have shown because the woman smiled. "It's eleven o'clock, you are carrying a camera bag, and your resemblance to your sister, Tess, is unmistakable." She extended her hand. "Isabelle Roberts. Mr. Bridger told me to expect you."

Isabelle Roberts. It was the name Cole's grandfather had sent him. His contact at the Viennese bank. Lars had been mildly surprised that someone with so un-German a name would be in a position of such authority. He was twice as surprised now that he'd met her. She couldn't be any older than he was.

"Nice to meet you," he said, shaking her hand before turning to introduce Marit. "This is my friend, Marit Jansen."

The two women exchanged a handshake and smiles.

"How do you know Tess?" Marit asked.

"We met at Falcon Point."

"You were the banker who helped locate the Lang family money," Lars said, the pieces of the puzzle coming together in rapid succession. No wonder Cole and his grandfather had chosen to move the valuables from the estate to this particular bank.

"Yes." She gestured toward the door of a lift at their left, and they started toward it. "Have you visited Falcon Point yet?"

Lars noted the swift change of subject. Maybe she didn't want to speak of tracing funds in the middle of the lobby.

"I was there yesterday," Lars said, the memory of finally meeting his English cousin, Anna, and of touring the remarkable house with her still fresh on his mind. "It's amazing."

"I agree." Isabelle swiped her ID in front of the lift and waited for the door to open. "I saw it in early summer, so I can only imagine how beautiful it looks now that there's snow on the ground. Did you go too, Marit?"

"No. I've heard a lot about Falcon Point, but I haven't been there."

"Yet," Lars added. Marit had spent weeks recovering from injuries sustained during the deadly battle over his family's legacy. Not only did she deserve to see Falcon Point, but she was also the one person he most wished to share it with. "I'm going to take her there as soon as her work schedule allows."

Marit's eyes widened with surprise, and Lars winced inwardly. He'd hoped Marit's recent modeling job would finish early enough for her to go to Falcon Point with him this week, but when she'd told him that she wouldn't be free to meet him until today, he'd held off on issuing the invitation. Now it sounded more like a summons.

"Something to look forward to, then," Isabelle said, filling the momentary silence as they stepped into the lift together.

"Yes. Definitely." Marit had recovered her poise. "And I'm excited to see the jewelry today."

Isabelle smiled. "You'll be the envy of jewelers around the world."

With a ping, the door opened, and she led them down a narrow hall. They passed several closed doors. Most of them had name plaques posted on the wall beside them. Lars assumed they were offices. When they reached the last door on the left, Isabelle stopped and swiped her ID again.

"This is our small conference room," she said. "It's yours for the rest of the day." She pushed open the door and stepped aside so they could enter. "Security delivered the safe deposit boxes half an hour ago."

Lars looked around the small windowless room. A large painting of the Vienna Opera House hung on one wall. In the corner, a computer monitor sat on a rolling cart, an assortment of cables bundled tidily on the shelf beneath. Dominating the room, however, was a highly polished wooden table surrounded by eight chairs. And currently lying on the table were three solid metal boxes.

"I have the bank keys," Isabelle said, holding up a sturdy key ring with several keys of differing sizes hanging from it. "Do you have yours?"

"Yes." Lars withdrew the keys from his pocket.

Cole had sent the safe deposit box keys to his apartment in Amsterdam by special courier when he'd learned that the American Embassy was sending him out of town this weekend. The cousins had kept in fairly regular contact since their first meeting almost six months ago, so Lars knew Cole's work often took him away from Vienna. He'd been disappointed to learn he wouldn't see Cole on this trip.

Isabelle crossed the short distance to the table and waited for Lars and Marit to join her. "Whenever you're ready," she said.

Lars stepped forward. As Coster Diamonds' lead photographer, he worked with precious gems almost every day. But he'd been in the hospital when Tess, Anna, and Cole had uncovered the treasure at Falcon Point, so this would be his first time seeing the jewelry that had once belonged to his great-grandmother. He took a deep breath, attempting to shake off the unexpected emotions coursing through him. No matter that he was in an unfamiliar bank, faced with three sterile metal boxes; this moment suddenly felt intensely personal.

As though she understood his hesitancy, Marit moved closer. "It's okay, Lars." She spoke in Dutch, her voice low. "You've waited months to feel this connection with your past."

He reached for her hand, squeezing it tightly before releasing it and inserting a key into the closest box. Beside him, Isabelle slid her key into place.

"On the count of three," she said.

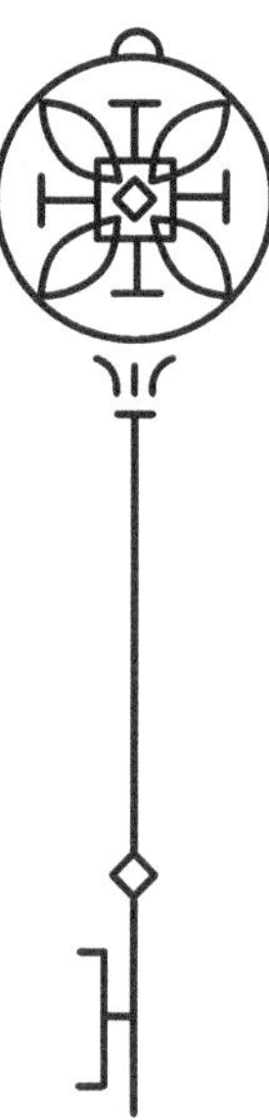

ABOUT THE AUTHORS

TRACI HUNTER ABRAMSON

Traci Hunter Abramson was born in Arizona, where she lived until moving to Venezuela for a study abroad program. After graduating from Brigham Young University, she worked for the Central Intelligence Agency, eventually resigning in order to raise her family. She credits the CIA with giving her a wealth of ideas as well as the skills needed to survive her children's teenage years. She loves to travel and enjoys coaching her local high school swim team. She has written more than thirty best-selling novels and is a seven-time Whitney Award winner, including 2017 and 2019 Best Novel of the Year.

She also loves hearing from her readers. If you would like to contact her, she can be reached through the following:

www.traciabramson.com
Facebook group: Traci's Friends
bookbub.com/authors/traci-hunter-abramson
@traciabramson
facebook.com/tracihabramson
instagram.com/traciabramson.com

OTHER BOOKS AND AUDIOBOOKS
BY TRACI HUNTER ABRAMSON

UNDERCURRENTS SERIES

Undercurrents

Ripple Effect

The Deep End

SAINT SQUAD SERIES

Freefall

Lockdown

Crossfire

Backlash

Smoke Screen

Code Word

Lock and Key

Drop Zone

Spotlight

Tripwire

Redemption

ROYAL SERIES

Royal Target

Royal Secrets

Royal Brides

Royal Heir

GUARDIAN SERIES

Failsafe

Safe House

Sanctuary

On the Run

In Harm's Way

DREAM'S EDGE SERIES

*Dancing to Freedom**

An Unlikely Pair

*Broken Dreams**
(coming Nov. 2021)

Dreams of Gold
(coming Feb. 2022)

FALCON POINT SERIES

Heirs of Falcon Point

The Danger with Diamonds
(coming Fall 2022)

STAND-ALONES

Obsession

Deep Cover

Chances Are

Chance for Home

Kept Secrets

*Twisted Fate**

Proximity

*Entangled**

Mistaken Reality

A Change of Fortune

* Novella

SIAN ANN BESSEY

Sian Ann Bessey was born in Cambridge, England, and grew up on the island of Anglesey, off the coast of North Wales. She left her homeland to attend Brigham Young University, where she earned a bachelor's degree in communications, with a minor in English.

She began her writing career as a college student, publishing several articles in the *New Era*, *Ensign*, and *Liahona* magazines. Since then, she has published historical romance and romantic suspense novels, along with a variety of children's books. She is a *USA Today* best-selling author, a Foreword Reviews Book of the Year finalist, and a Whitney Award finalist.

Sian and her husband, Kent, are the parents of five children and the grandparents of three beautiful girls and two handsome boys. They currently live in Idaho, and although Sian doesn't have the opportunity to speak Welsh very often anymore, *Llanfairpwllgwyngyllgogerychwyrndrobwllllantysiliogogogoch* still rolls off her tongue.

Traveling, reading, cooking, and being with her grandchildren are some of her favorite activities. She also loves hearing from her readers. If you would like to contact her, she can be reached through her website at www.sianannbessey.com, on Facebook at Author Sian Ann Bessey's Corner, and on Instagram @sian_bessey.

OTHER BOOKS AND AUDIOBOOKS BY SIAN ANN BESSEY

GEORGIAN GENTLEMAN SERIES

The Noble Smuggler

An Uncommon Earl

An Alleged Rogue
(coming November 2021)

FALCON POINT SERIES

Heirs of Falcon Point

The Danger with Diamonds
(coming Fall 2022)

HISTORICAL

Within the Dark Hills

One Last Spring

To Win a Lady's Heart

For Castle and Crown

The Heart of the Rebellion

CONTEMPORARY

Forgotten Notes

Cover of Darkness

Deception

You Came for Me

The Insider

The Gem Thief

KIDS ON A MISSION SERIES

Escape from Germany

Uprising in Samoa

Ambushed in Africa

CHILDREN'S

A Family is Forever

Teddy Bear, Blankie, and a Prayer

ANTHOLOGIES AND BOOKLETS

The Perfect Gift

A Hopeful Christmas

No Strangers at Christmas

PAIGE EDWARDS

Paige Edwards is an award-winning author of contemporary Regency romances with a side-order of suspense. Her stories have debuted in the number-one Amazon spot for Christian fiction and have received national five-star reviews by Reader's Favorite and *InD'Tale Magazine.* Her novels appeal to a wide range of readers from Historical Romance to Mystery/Suspense. She holds a degree in interior design and has worked professionally in that field. Due to her strong British roots, Paige's books are often set in the UK, and she hops the pond whenever she gets the chance. She is the Lady Paige Edwards when in Scotland, but her favorite title is Grandma. When she needs a break from writing, she serves as president of her area's Interfaith Community Council, she is fond of digging in the dirt (what some might call gardening), she bikes the battlefields, and she kayaks on the lake. You can follow her on BookBub, Amazon, Goodreads, or Facebook at Paige's Page Pals and other social media sites. Or you can learn more about her and her books by visiting her website: authorpaigeedwards.com.

OTHER BOOKS AND AUDIOBOOKS
BY PAIGE EDWARDS

Pressley-Coombes Series

Catherine's Intrigue

Deadly by Design

Danger on the Loch

Roxbury Heirs Series

Facing the Enemy

(coming April 2022)

Falcon Point Series

Heirs of Falcon Point

A. L. SOWARDS

A. L. Sowards has always been fascinated by the 1940s, but she's grateful she didn't live back then. She doesn't think she could have written a novel on a typewriter, and no one would be able to read her handwriting if she wrote her books out longhand. She does, however, think they had the right idea when they rationed nylon and women went barelegged.

Sowards is the author of multiple historical fiction novels, with settings spanning the globe from the fourteenth to twentieth centuries. Her stories have become Whitney finalists and have won a Whitney Award, reached the number-one spot across multiple Amazon categories, received praise from the Historical Novel Society, and been loved by readers from a variety of backgrounds.

She lives with her husband and three children and has called Washington State, Utah, and Alaska home. She enjoys hiking and swimming, usually manages to keep up with the laundry, and loves it when someone else cooks dinner. She doesn't own a typewriter, but she does own a pair or two of nylons.

Sowards loves connecting with readers and can be found online at her website, alsowards.com, as well as on Instagram, Facebook, and Goodreads.

OTHER BOOKS AND AUDIOBOOKS
BY A. L. SOWARDS

ESPIONAGE SERIES
Espionage
Sworn Enemy
Deadly Alliance

THE LEY BROTHERS SERIES
The Rules in Rome
Defiance

DUCHY OF ATHENS SERIES
Of Sword and Shadow
Of Daggers and Deception
(coming December 2021)

STAND-ALONES
The Spider and the Sparrow
The Redgrave Murders
Heirs of Falcon Point
Before the Fortress Falls
(coming March 2022)

SHORT STORIES
The Perfect Gift